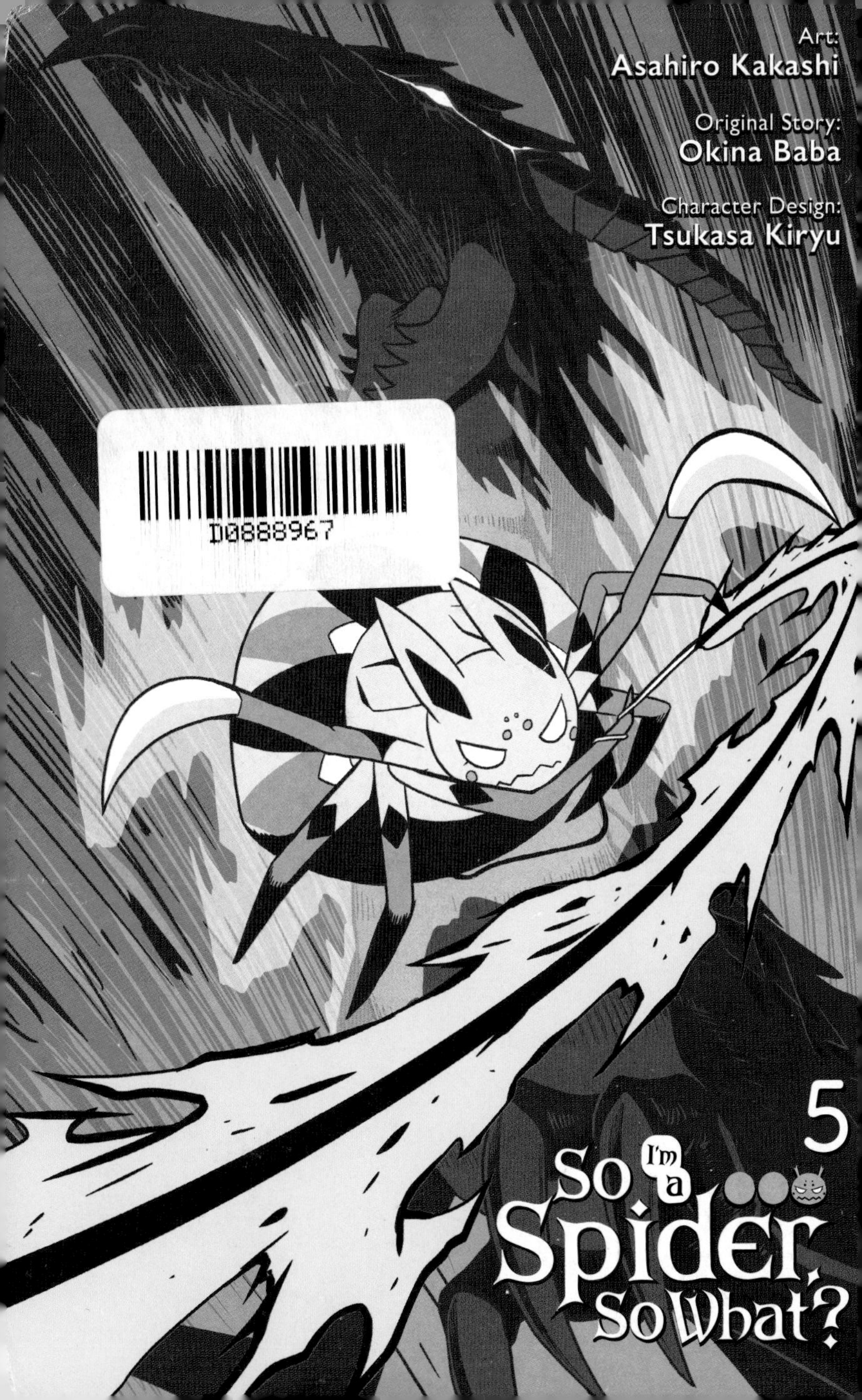
Art:
Asahiro Kakashi
Original Story:
Okina Baba
Character Design:
Tsukasa Kiryu
5
So I'm a Spider, So What?

So I'm a Spider, So What?

CONTENTS

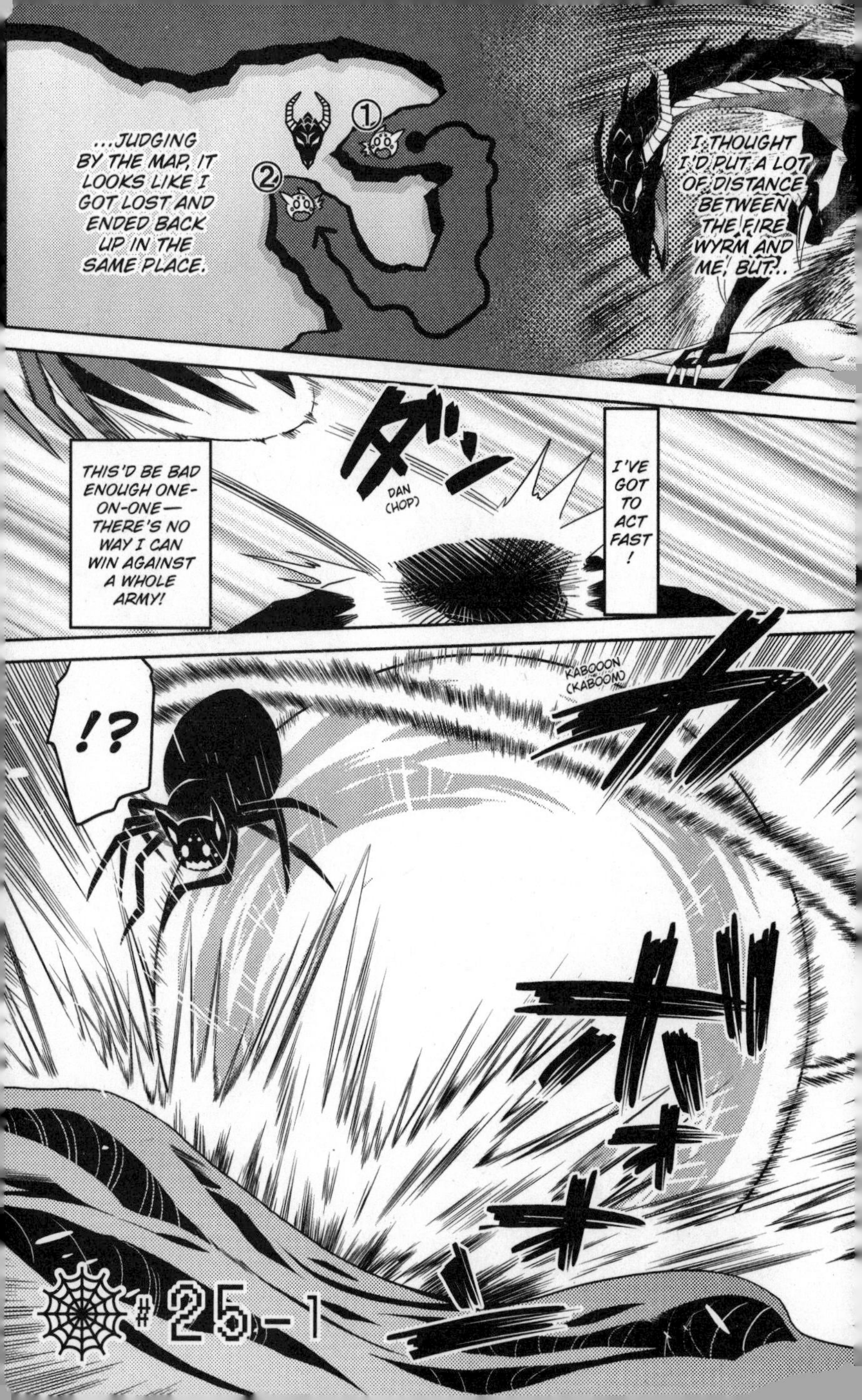
I THOUGHT I'D PUT A LOT OF DISTANCE BETWEEN THE FIRE WYRM AND ME, BUT...
...JUDGING BY THE MAP, IT LOOKS LIKE I GOT LOST AND ENDED BACK UP IN THE SAME PLACE.
I'VE GOT TO ACT FAST!
DAN (HOP)
THIS'D BE BAD ENOUGH ONE-ON-ONE—THERE'S NO WAY I CAN WIN AGAINST A WHOLE ARMY!
KABOOON (KABOOM)
!?
#25-1

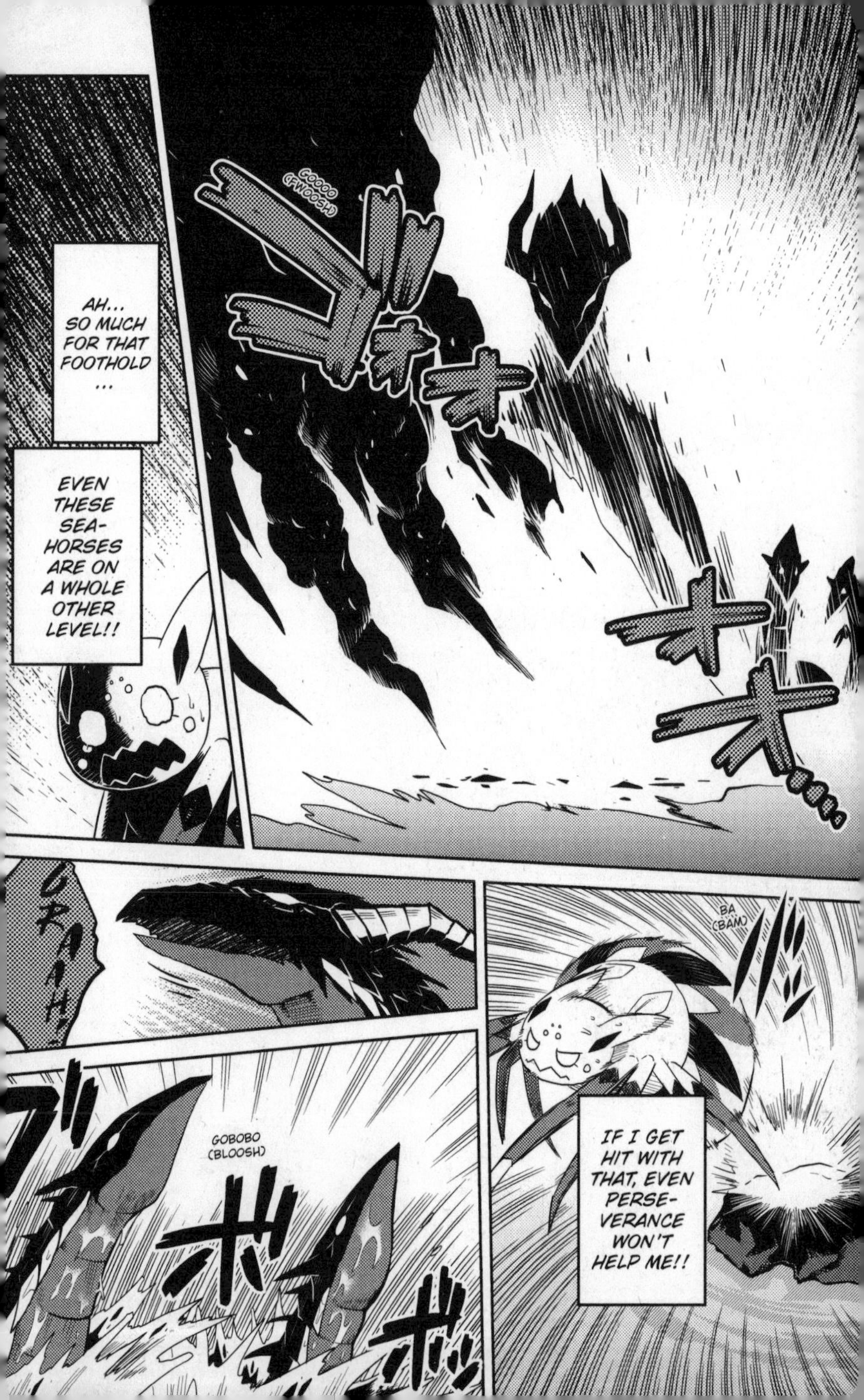
GOOOO
(FWOOSH)
AH... SO MUCH FOR THAT FOOTHOLD...
EVEN THESE SEA-HORSES ARE ON A WHOLE OTHER LEVEL!!
BA
(BAM)
IF I GET HIT WITH THAT, EVEN PERSE-VERANCE WON'T HELP ME!!
GOBOBO
(BLOOSH)

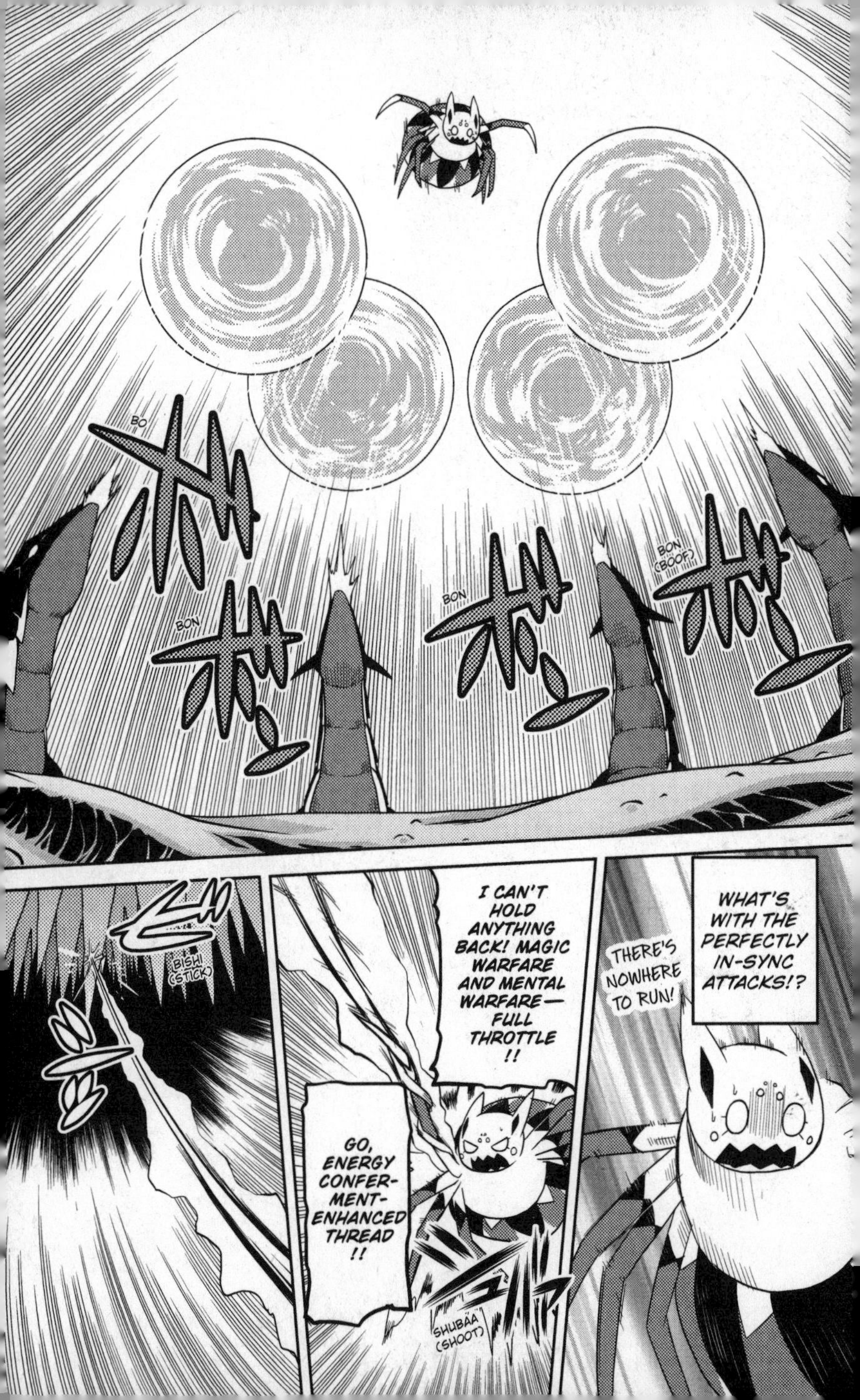
BON (BOOF)
BON
BON
BO
WHAT'S WITH THE PERFECTLY IN-SYNC ATTACKS!?
THERE'S NOWHERE TO RUN!
I CAN'T HOLD ANYTHING BACK! MAGIC WARFARE AND MENTAL WARFARE—FULL THROTTLE!!
GO, ENERGY CONFERMENT-ENHANCED THREAD!!
SHUBÄA (SHOOT)
BISHI (STICK)

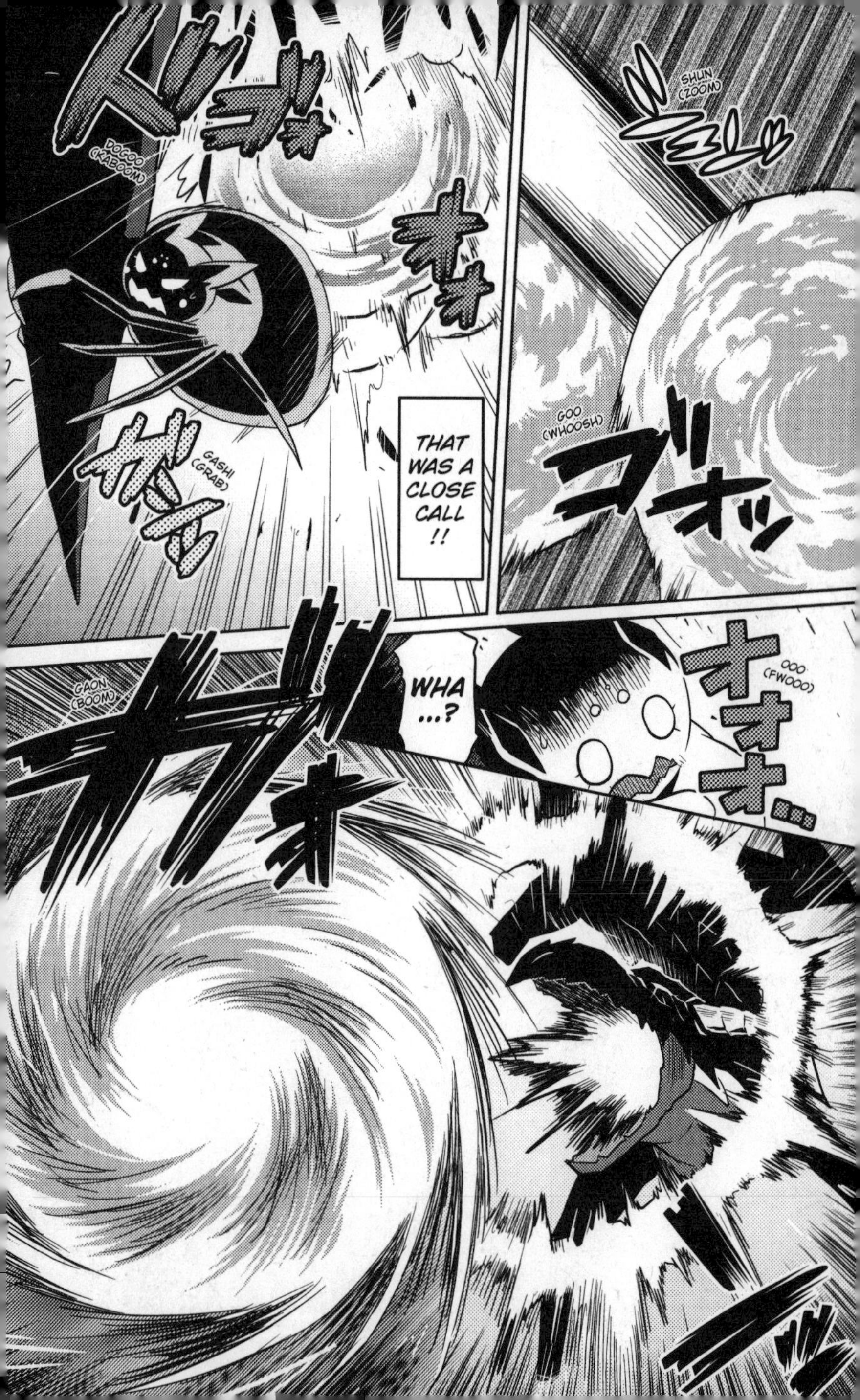
SHUN (ZOOM)
GOO (WHOOSH)
DOGOO (KABOOM)
THAT WAS A CLOSE CALL!!
GASHI (GRAB)
OOO (FWOOO)
WHA ...?
GAON (BOOM)

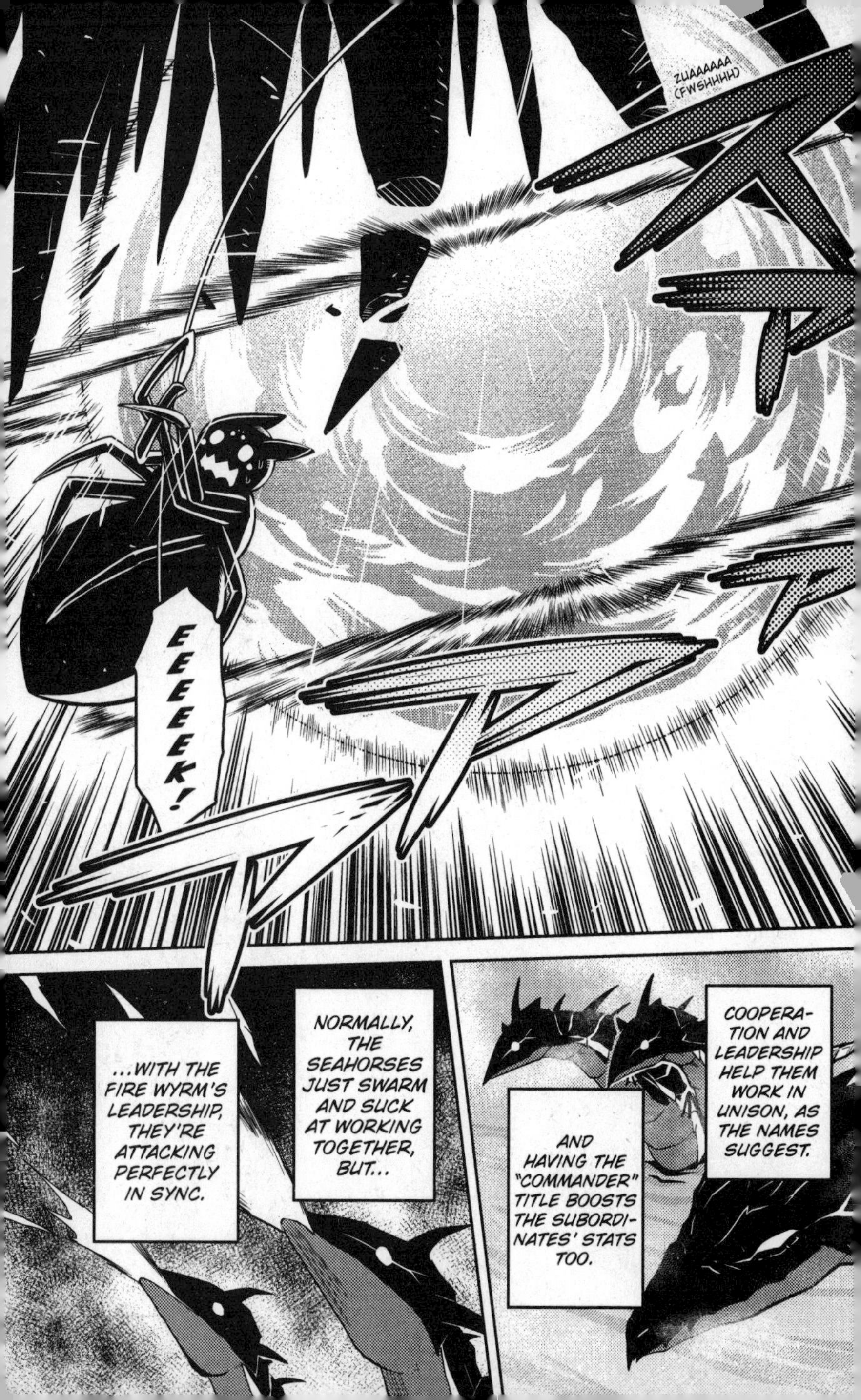
ZUAAAAAA (FWSHHHH)
EEEEEEK!
COOPERATION AND LEADERSHIP HELP THEM WORK IN UNISON, AS THE NAMES SUGGEST.
AND HAVING THE "COMMANDER" TITLE BOOSTS THE SUBORDINATES' STATS TOO.
NORMALLY, THE SEAHORSES JUST SWARM AND SUCK AT WORKING TOGETHER, BUT...
...WITH THE FIRE WYRM'S LEADERSHIP, THEY'RE ATTACKING PERFECTLY IN SYNC.

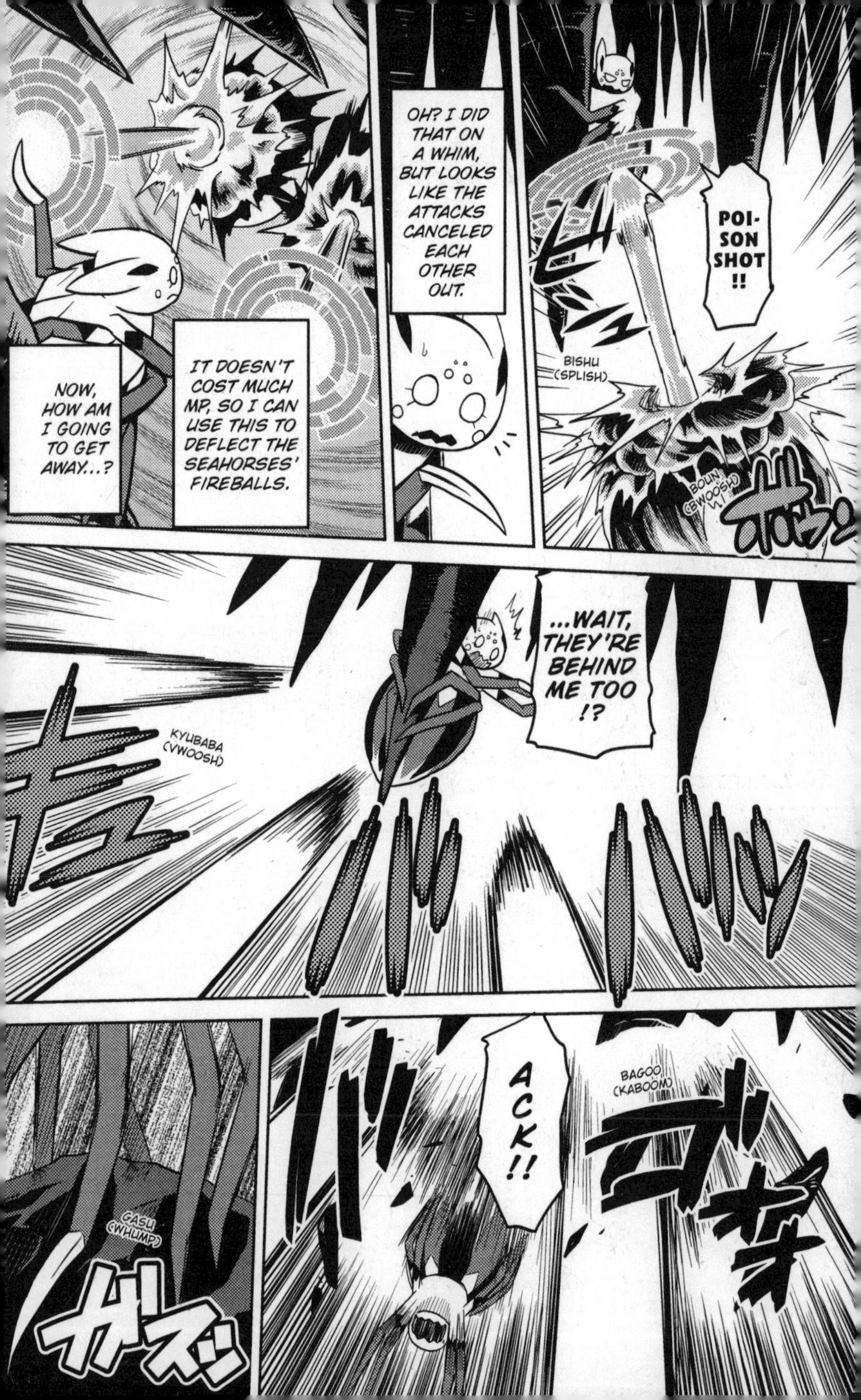
POI-SON SHOT!!
BISHU (SPLISH)
BOUN (BWOOSH)
OH? I DID THAT ON A WHIM, BUT LOOKS LIKE THE ATTACKS CANCELED EACH OTHER OUT.
IT DOESN'T COST MUCH MP, SO I CAN USE THIS TO DEFLECT THE SEAHORSES' FIREBALLS.
NOW, HOW AM I GOING TO GET AWAY...?
...WAIT, THEY'RE BEHIND ME TOO!?
KYUBABA (VWOOSH)
ACK!!
BAGOO (KABOOM)
GASU (WHUMP)

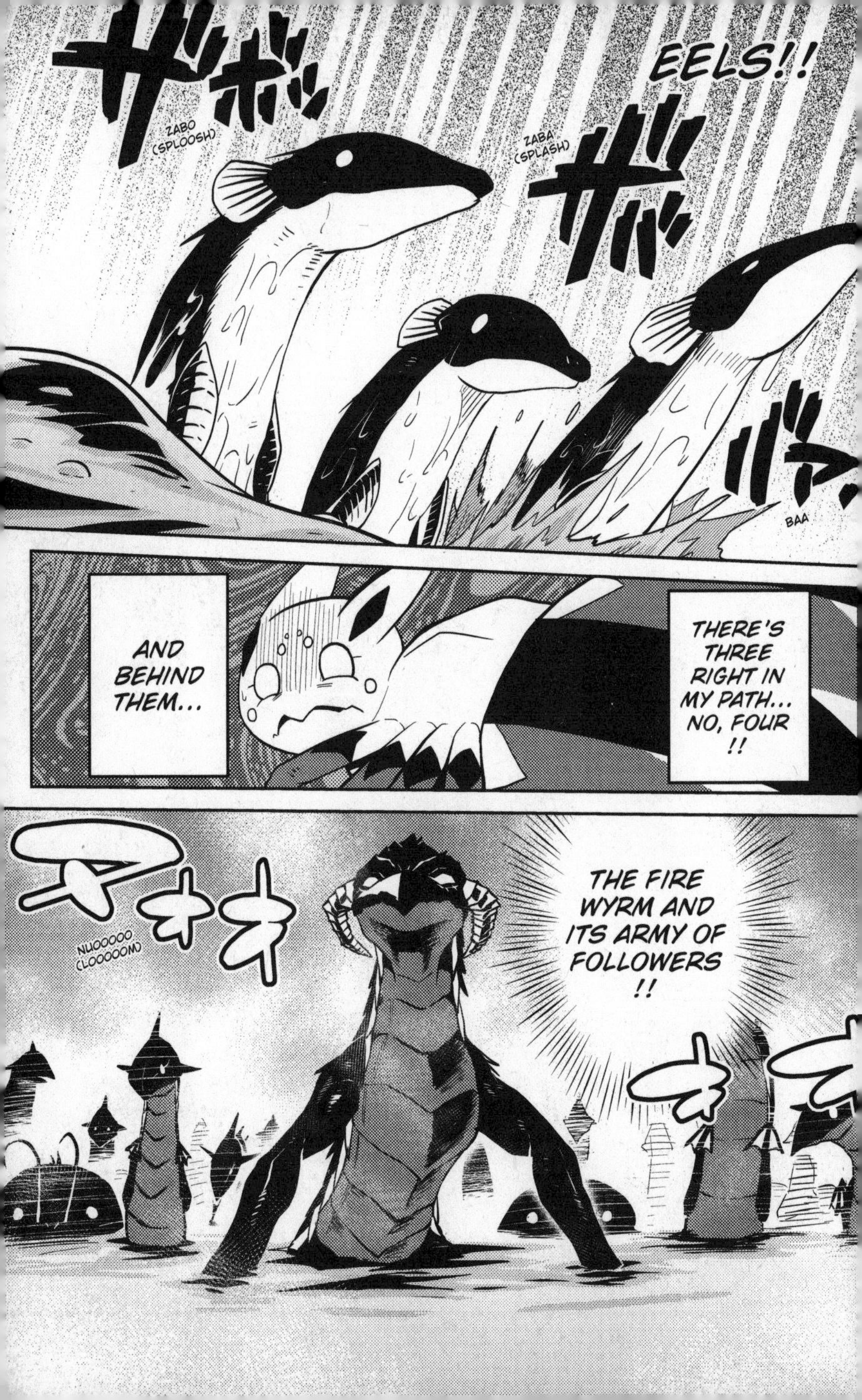
EELS!!
ZABA (SPLASH)
ZABO (SPLOOSH)
BAA
THERE'S THREE RIGHT IN MY PATH... NO, FOUR !!
AND BEHIND THEM...
THE FIRE WYRM AND ITS ARMY OF FOLLOWERS !!
NUOOOOO (LOOOOOM)

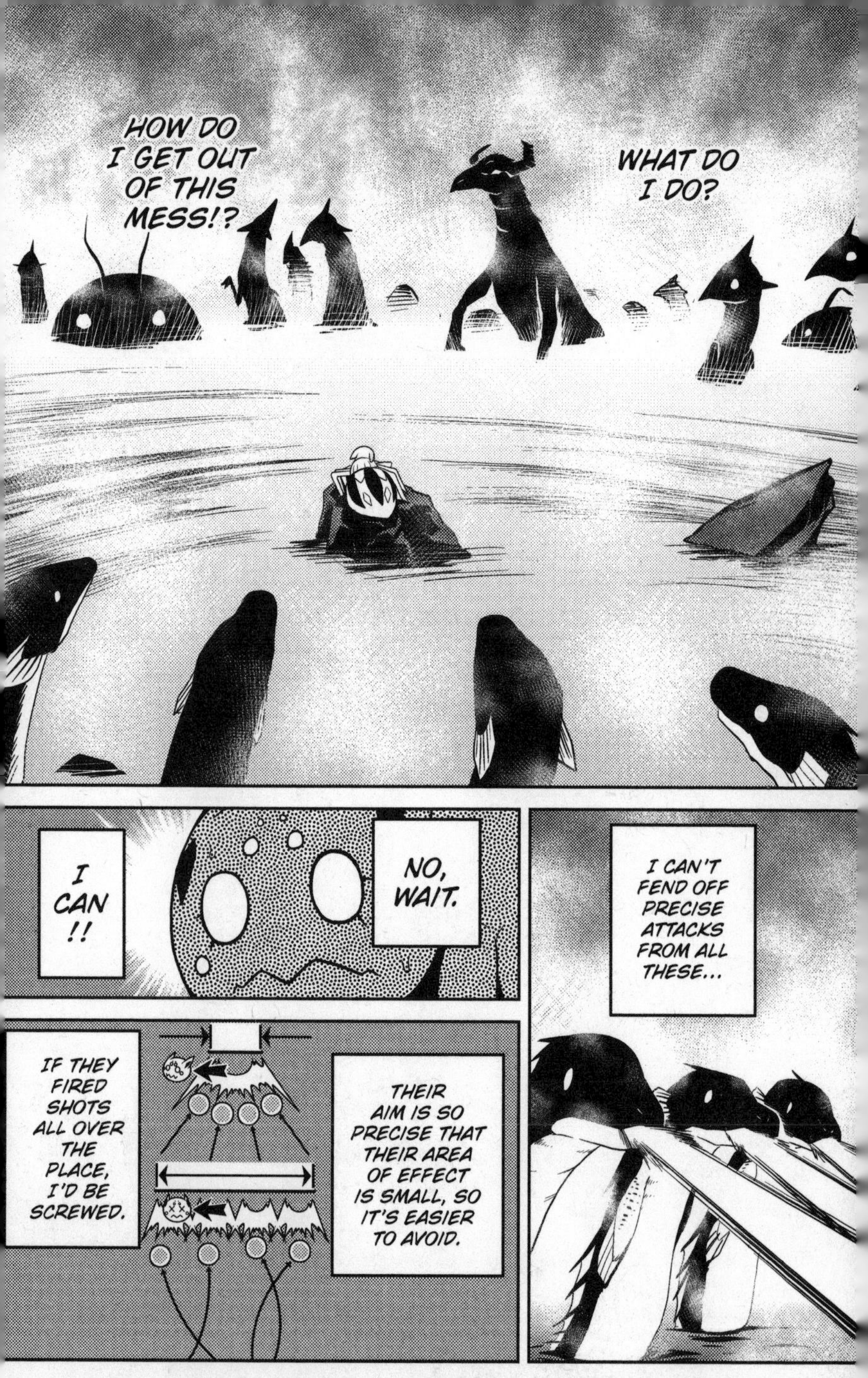
WHAT DO I DO?
HOW DO I GET OUT OF THIS MESS!?
I CAN'T FEND OFF PRECISE ATTACKS FROM ALL THESE...
NO, WAIT.
I CAN!!
THEIR AIM IS SO PRECISE THAT THEIR AREA OF EFFECT IS SMALL, SO IT'S EASIER TO AVOID.
IF THEY FIRED SHOTS ALL OVER THE PLACE, I'D BE SCREWED.

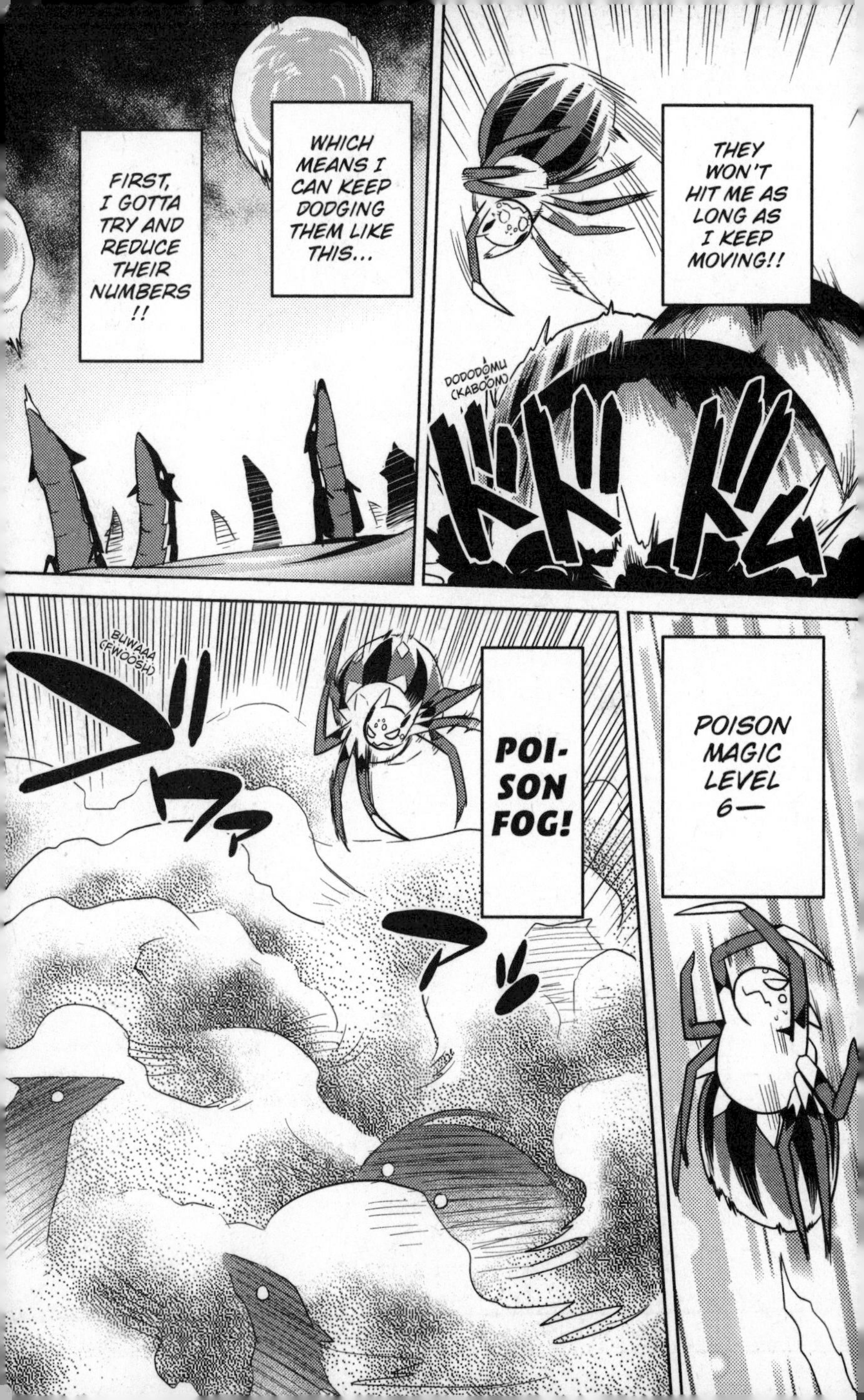
THEY WON'T HIT ME AS LONG AS I KEEP MOVING!!
DODODOMU (KABOOM)
WHICH MEANS I CAN KEEP DODGING THEM LIKE THIS...
FIRST, I GOTTA TRY AND REDUCE THEIR NUMBERS !!
POISON MAGIC LEVEL 6—
POI-SON FOG!
BUWAAA (FWOOSH)

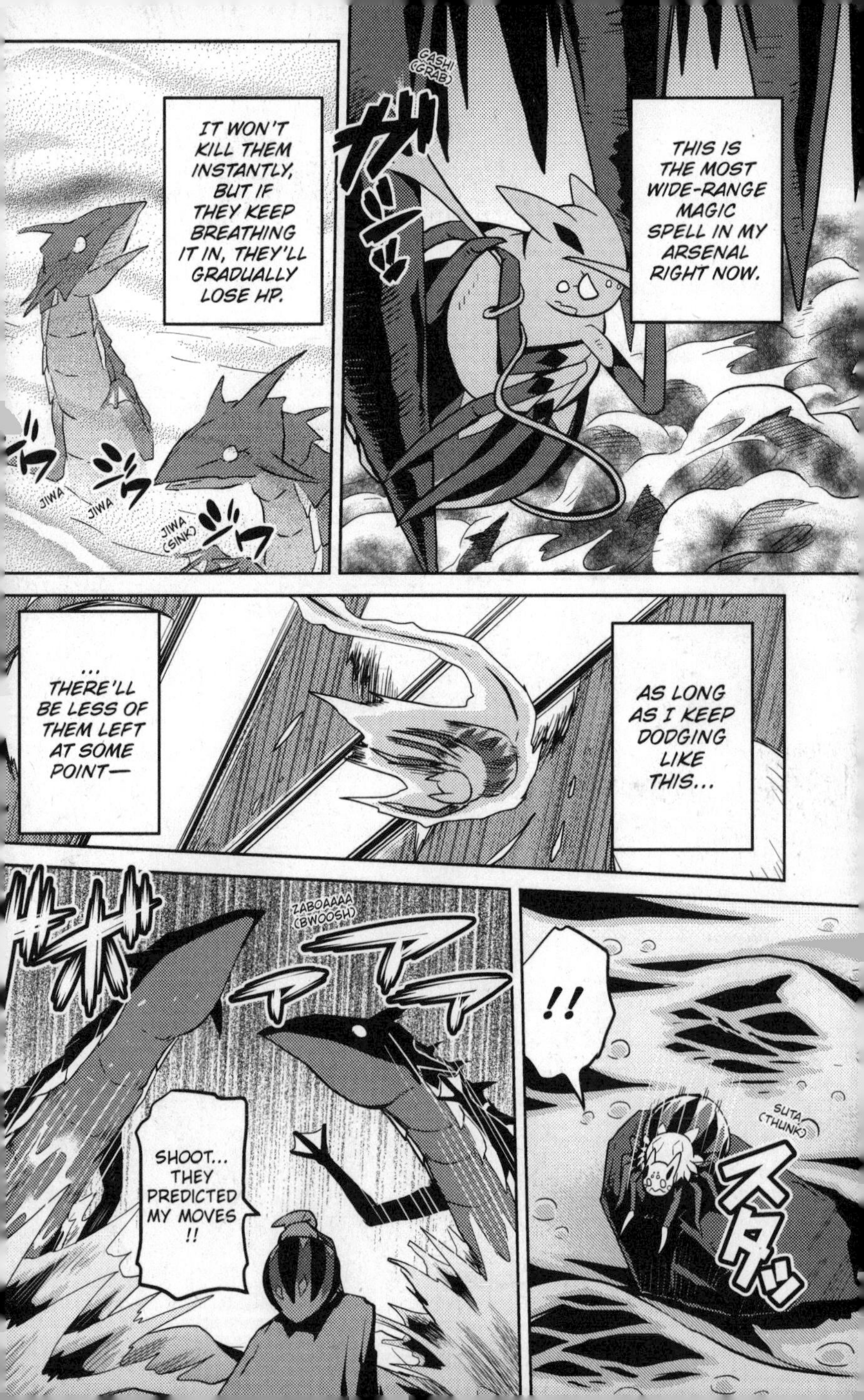
GASHI (GRAB)
THIS IS THE MOST WIDE-RANGE MAGIC SPELL IN MY ARSENAL RIGHT NOW.
IT WON'T KILL THEM INSTANTLY, BUT IF THEY KEEP BREATHING IT IN, THEY'LL GRADUALLY LOSE HP.
JIWA
JIWA
JIWA (SINK)
AS LONG AS I KEEP DODGING LIKE THIS...
... THERE'LL BE LESS OF THEM LEFT AT SOME POINT—
!!
SUTA (THUNK)
ZABOAAAA (BWOOSH)
SHOOT... THEY PREDICTED MY MOVES !!

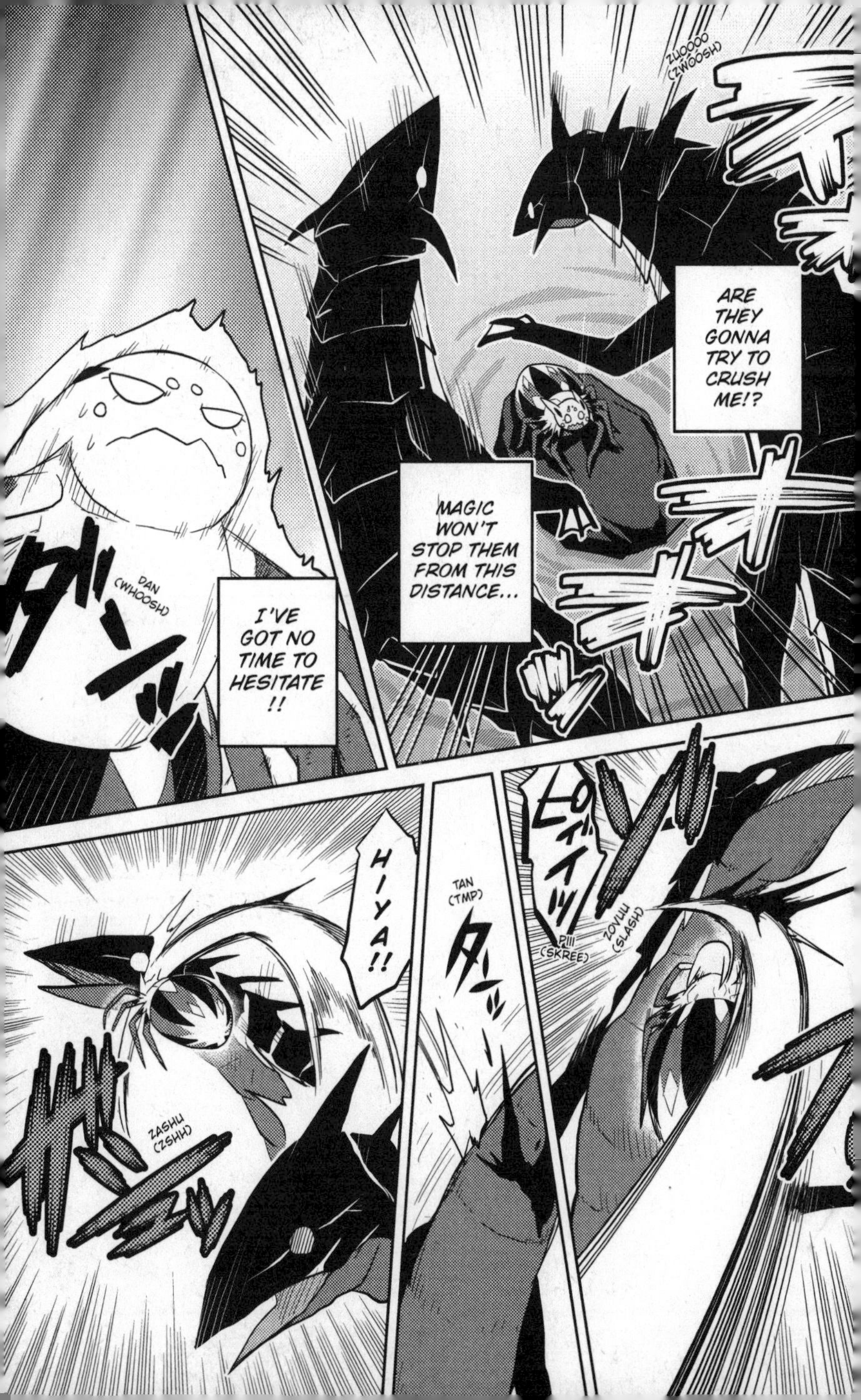
ZUOOOO (ZWOOSH)
ARE THEY GONNA TRY TO CRUSH ME!?
MAGIC WON'T STOP THEM FROM THIS DISTANCE...
DAN (WHOOSH)
I'VE GOT NO TIME TO HESITATE!!
PIII (SKREE)
ZOVUU (SLASH)
TAN (TMP)
HIYA!!
ZASHU (ZSHH)

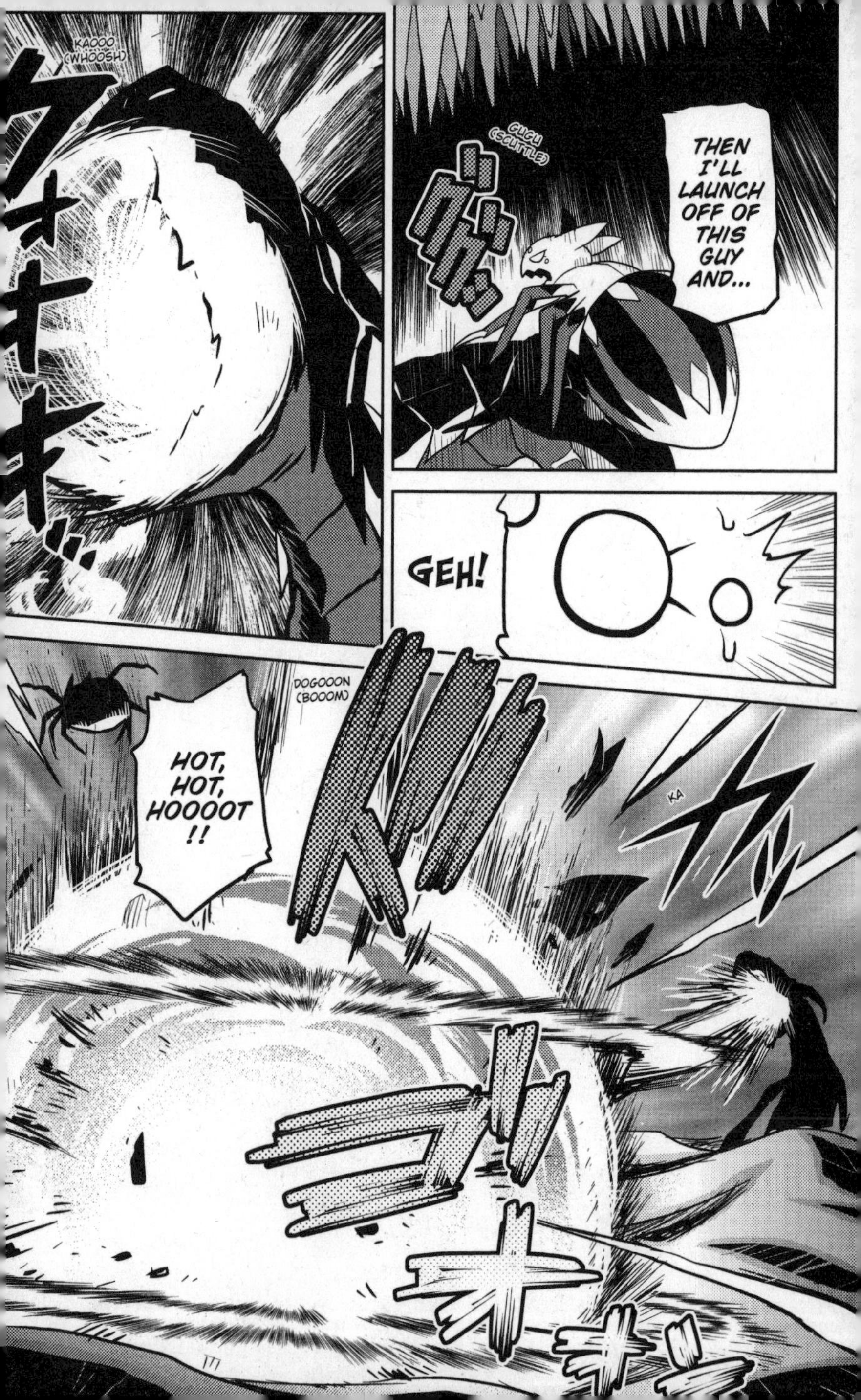
GUGU (SCUTTLE)
THEN I'LL LAUNCH OFF OF THIS GUY AND...
GEH!
KAOOO (WHOOSH)
DOGOOON (BOOOM)
KA
HOT, HOT, HOOOOT!!

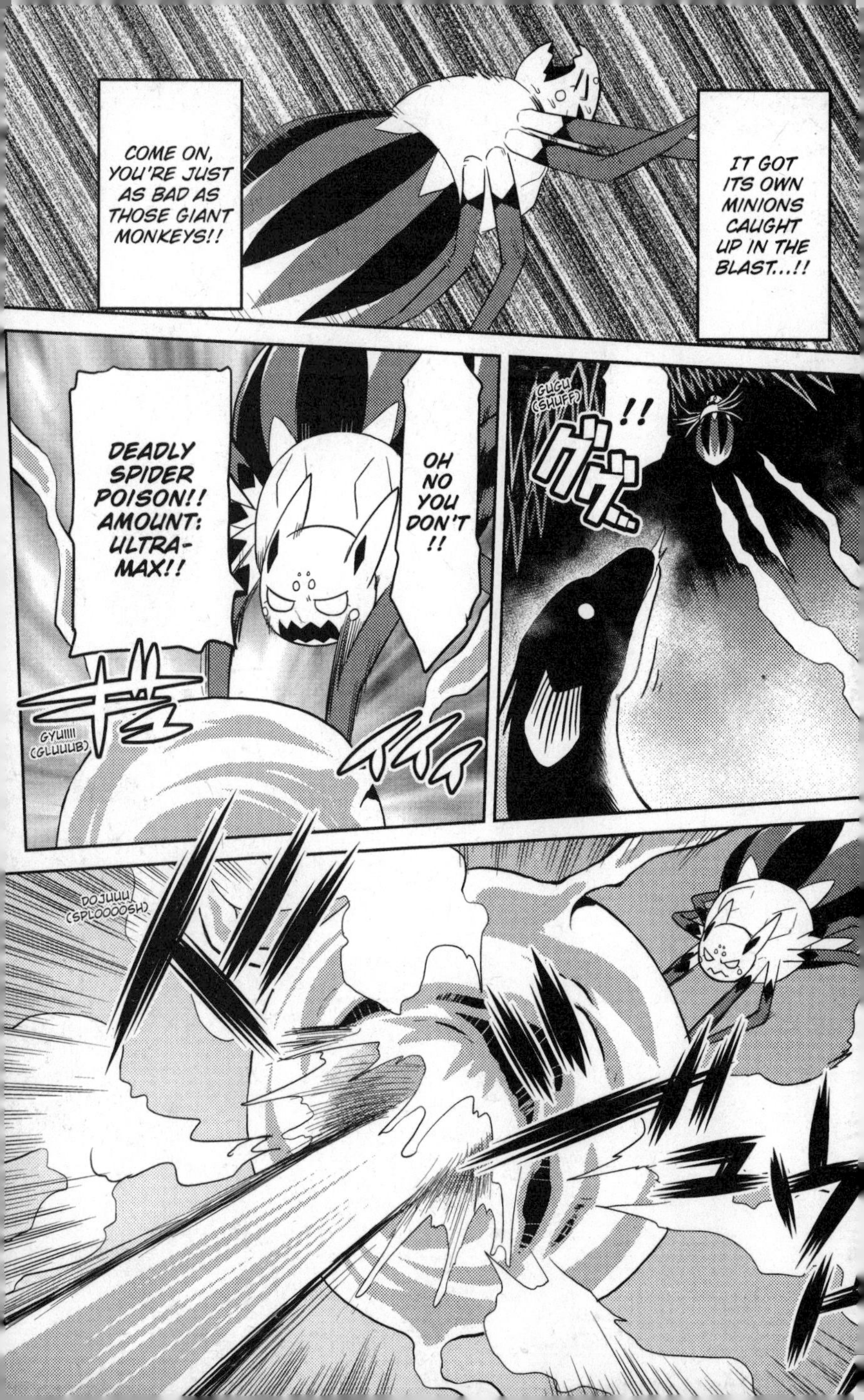
IT GOT ITS OWN MINIONS CAUGHT UP IN THE BLAST...!!
COME ON, YOU'RE JUST AS BAD AS THOSE GIANT MONKEYS!!
GUGU (SHUFF)
!!
OH NO YOU DON'T!!
DEADLY SPIDER POISON!! AMOUNT: ULTRA-MAX!!
GYUIIII (GLUUUB)
DOJUUU (SPLOOOOSH)

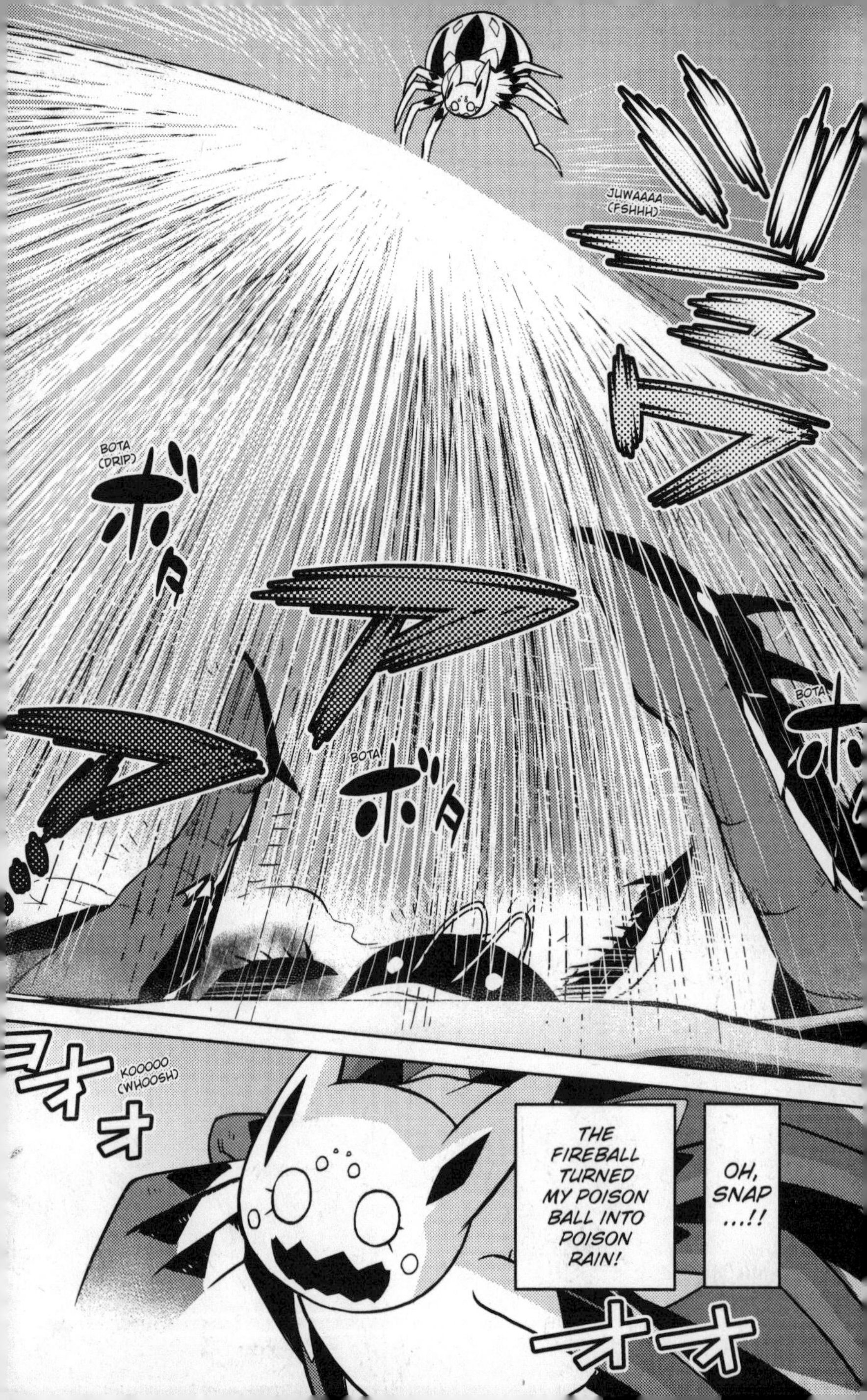
JUWAAAA
(FSHHH)
BOTA
(DRIP)
BOTA
BOTA
OH, SNAP ...!!
THE FIREBALL TURNED MY POISON BALL INTO POISON RAIN!
KOOOOO
(WHOOSH)

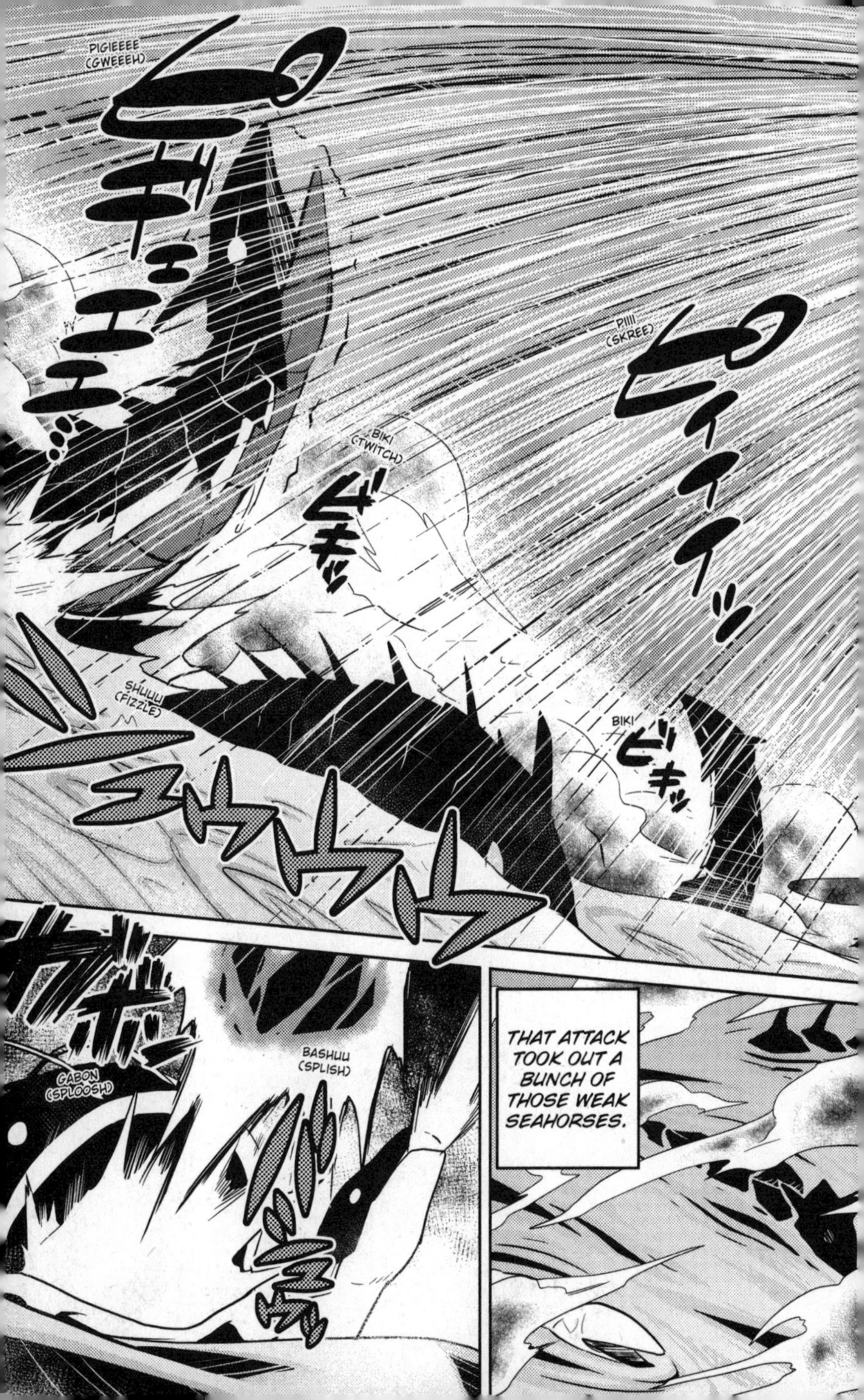
PIGIEEEE (GWEEEH)
PIIII (SKREE)
BIKI (TWITCH)
BIKI
SHUUU (FIZZLE)
THAT ATTACK TOOK OUT A BUNCH OF THOSE WEAK SEAHORSES.
BASHUU (SPLISH)
GABON (SPLOOSH)

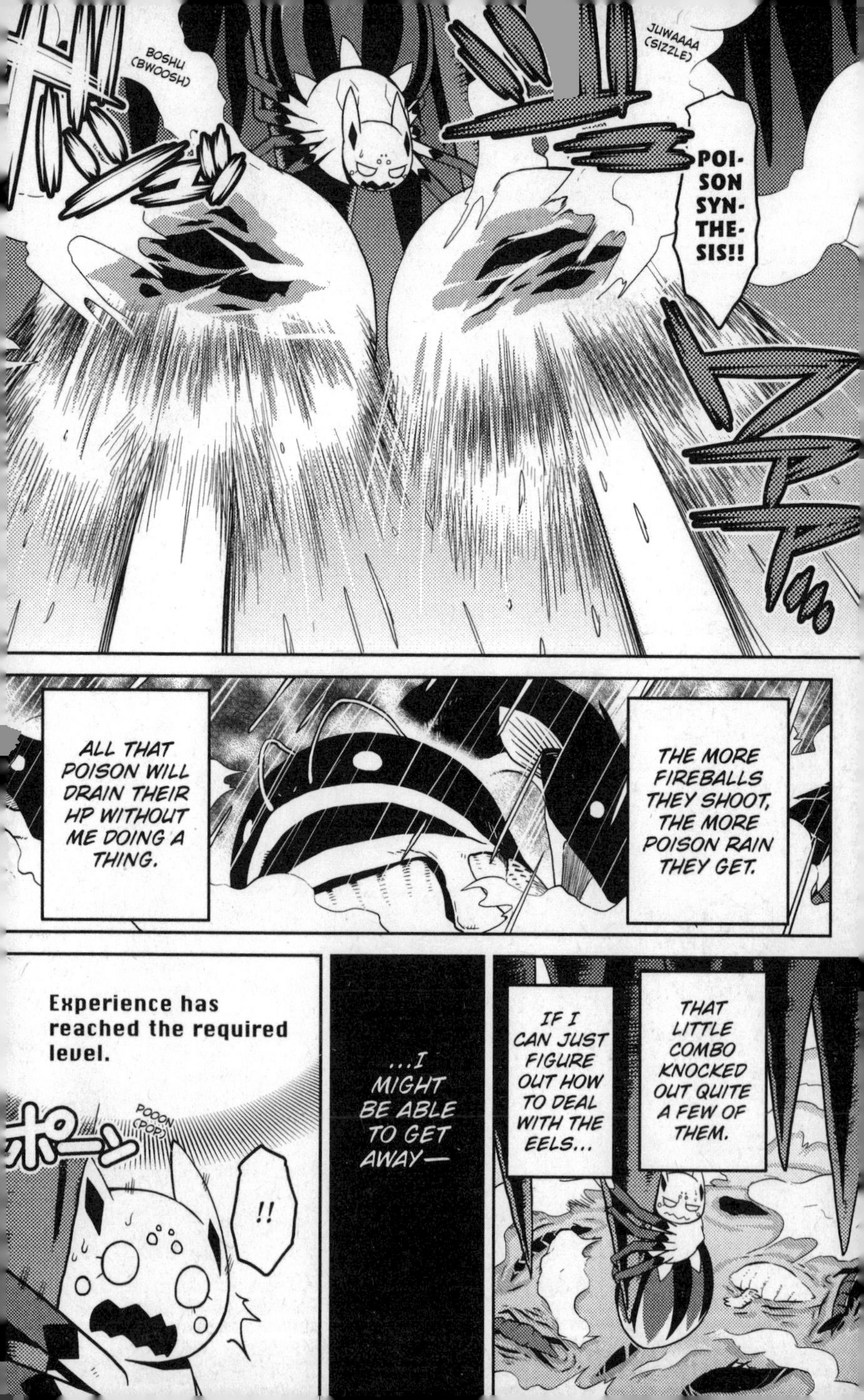
JUWAAAA (SIZZLE)
POI-SON SYN-THE-SIS!!
BOSHU (BWOOSH)
THE MORE FIREBALLS THEY SHOOT, THE MORE POISON RAIN THEY GET.
ALL THAT POISON WILL DRAIN THEIR HP WITHOUT ME DOING A THING.
THAT LITTLE COMBO KNOCKED OUT QUITE A FEW OF THEM.
IF I CAN JUST FIGURE OUT HOW TO DEAL WITH THE EELS...
...I MIGHT BE ABLE TO GET AWAY—
Experience has reached the required level.
POOON (POP)
!!

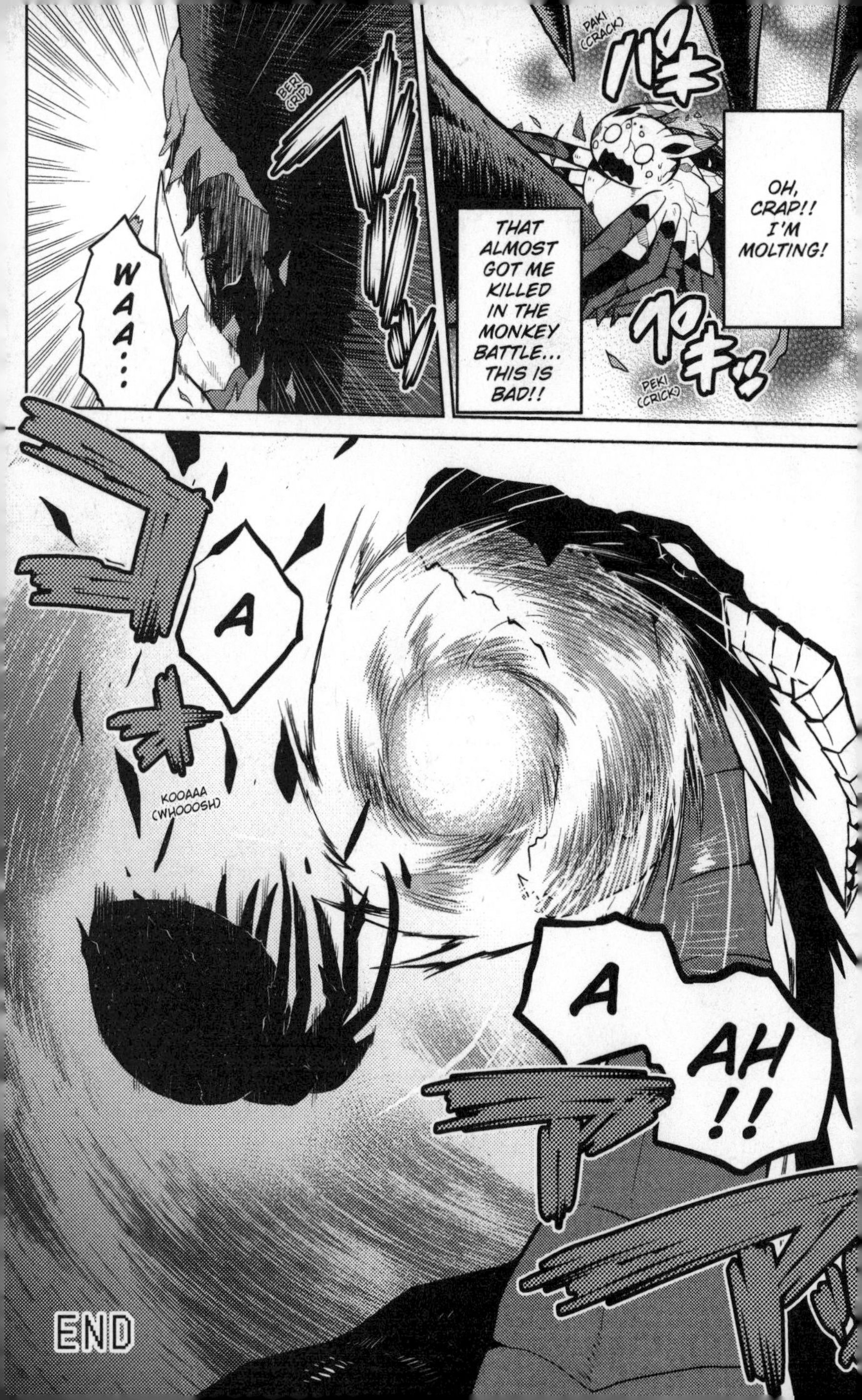
PAKI (CRACK)
OH, CRAP!! I'M MOLTING!
THAT ALMOST GOT ME KILLED IN THE MONKEY BATTLE... THIS IS BAD!!
PEKI (CRICK)
BERI (RIP)
WAAA...
A
KOOAAA (WHOOOSH)
A AH!!
END

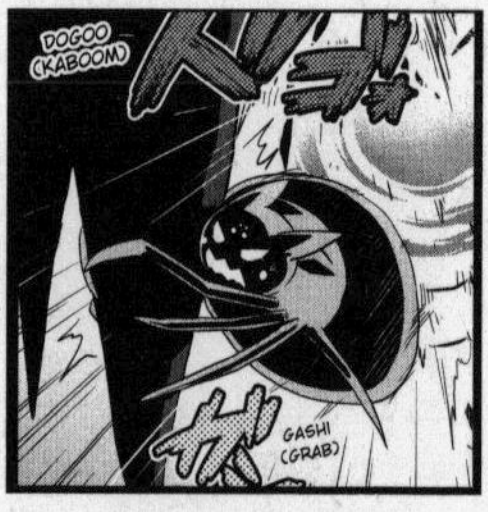
DOGOO
(KABOOM)
GASHI
(GRAB)

#25-2

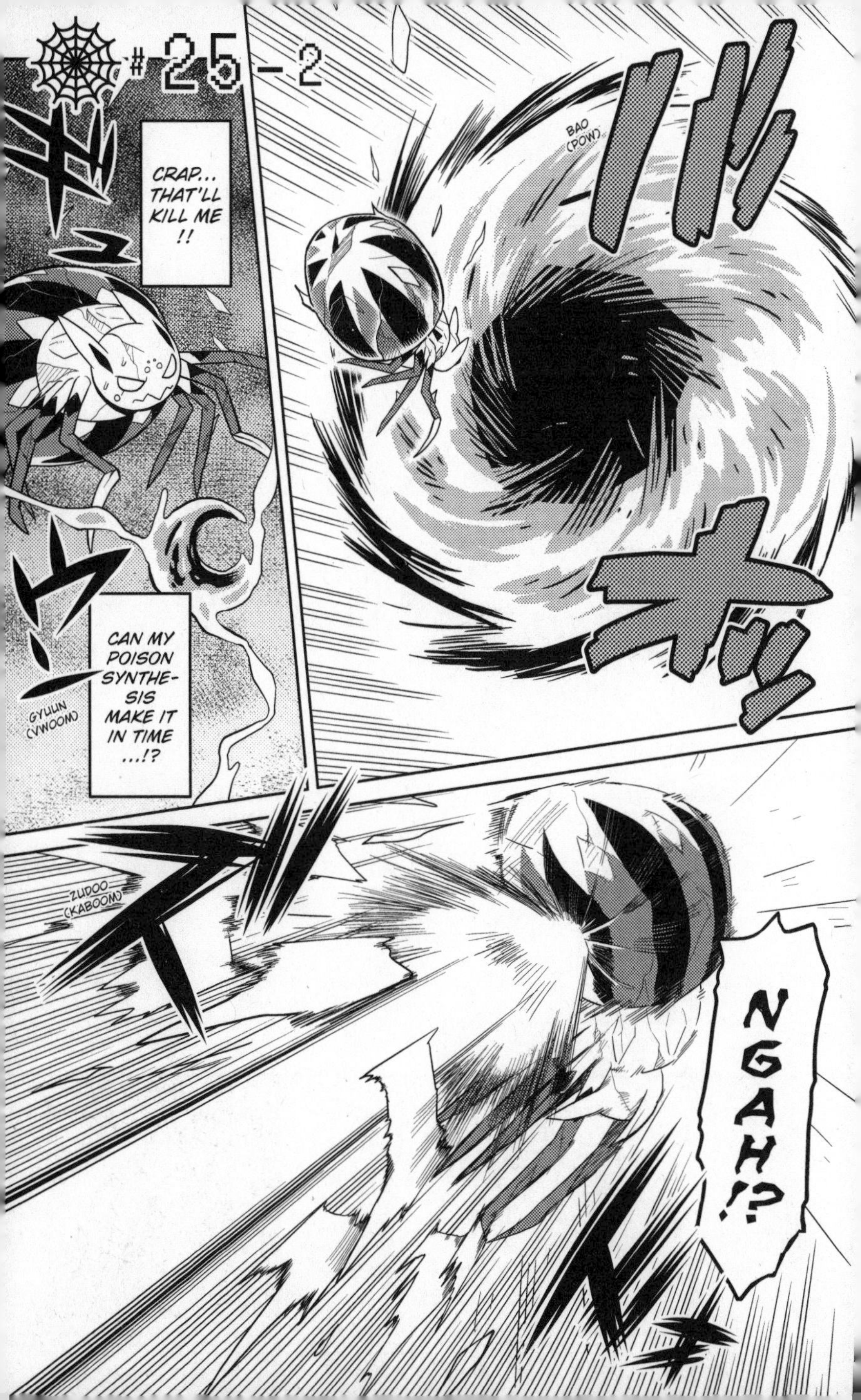
BAO (POW)
CRAP... THAT'LL KILL ME !!
CAN MY POISON SYNTHESIS MAKE IT IN TIME ...!?
GYUUN (VWOOM)
NGAH!?
ZUDOO (KABOOM)

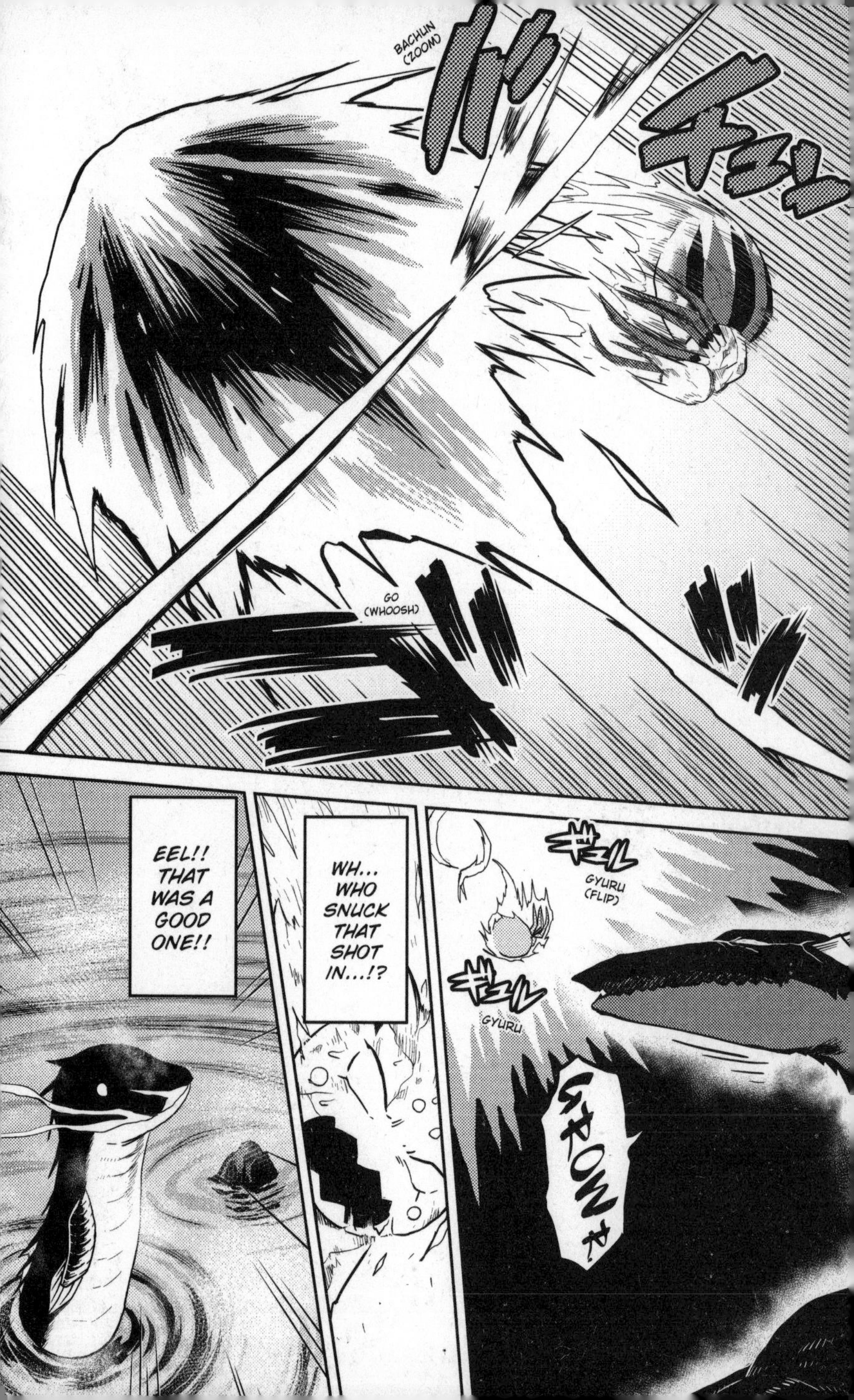
BACHUN (ZOOM)
GO (WHOOSH)
GYURU (FLIP)
GYURU
GROWR
WH... WHO SNUCK THAT SHOT IN...!?
EEL!! THAT WAS A GOOD ONE!!

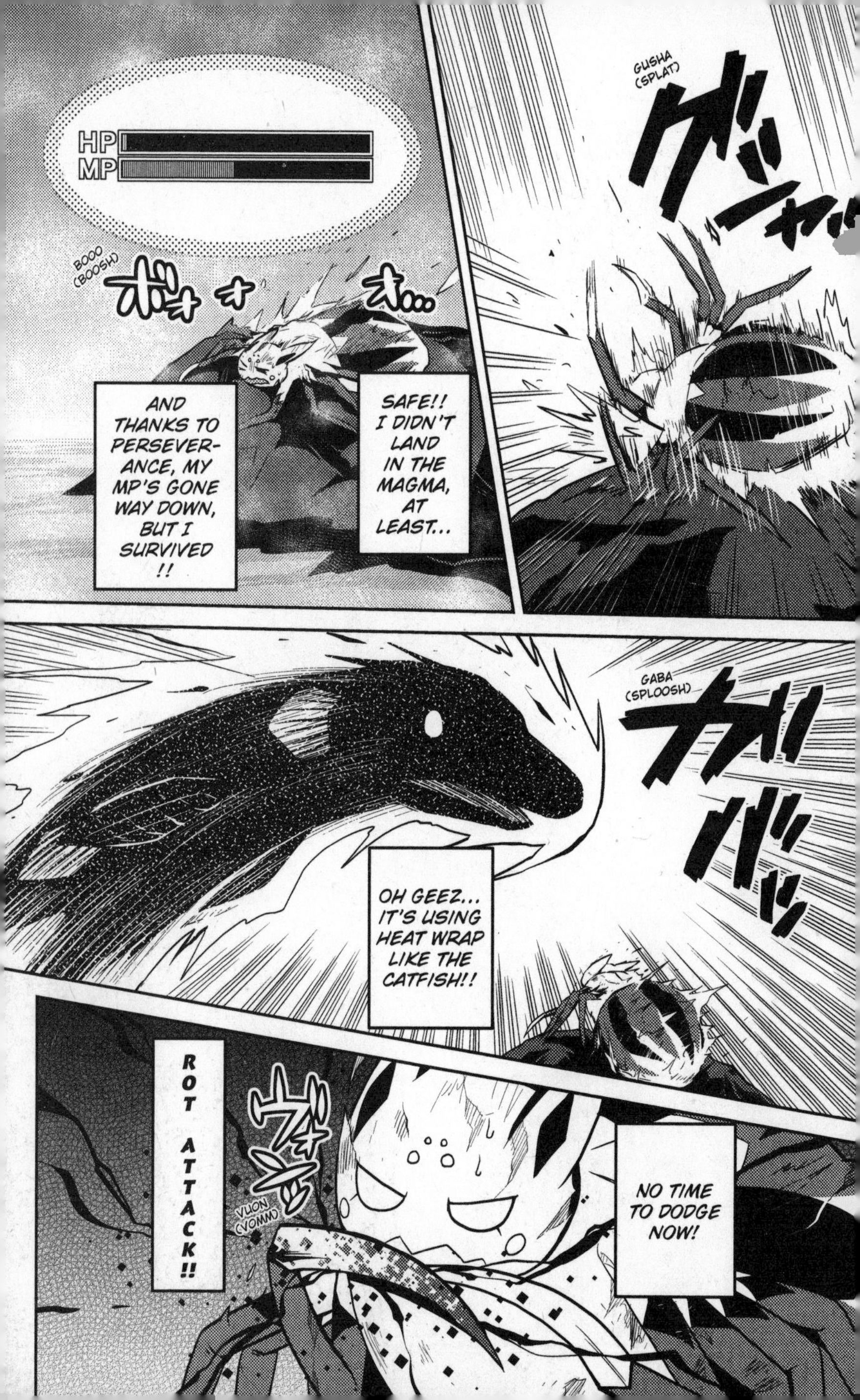
GUSHA (SPLAT)
HP
MP
BOOO (BOOSH)
SAFE!! I DIDN'T LAND IN THE MAGMA, AT LEAST...
AND THANKS TO PERSEVER-ANCE, MY MP'S GONE WAY DOWN, BUT I SURVIVED !!
GABA (SPLOOSH)
OH GEEZ... IT'S USING HEAT WRAP LIKE THE CATFISH!!
NO TIME TO DODGE NOW!
VUON (VOMM)
ROT ATTACK!!

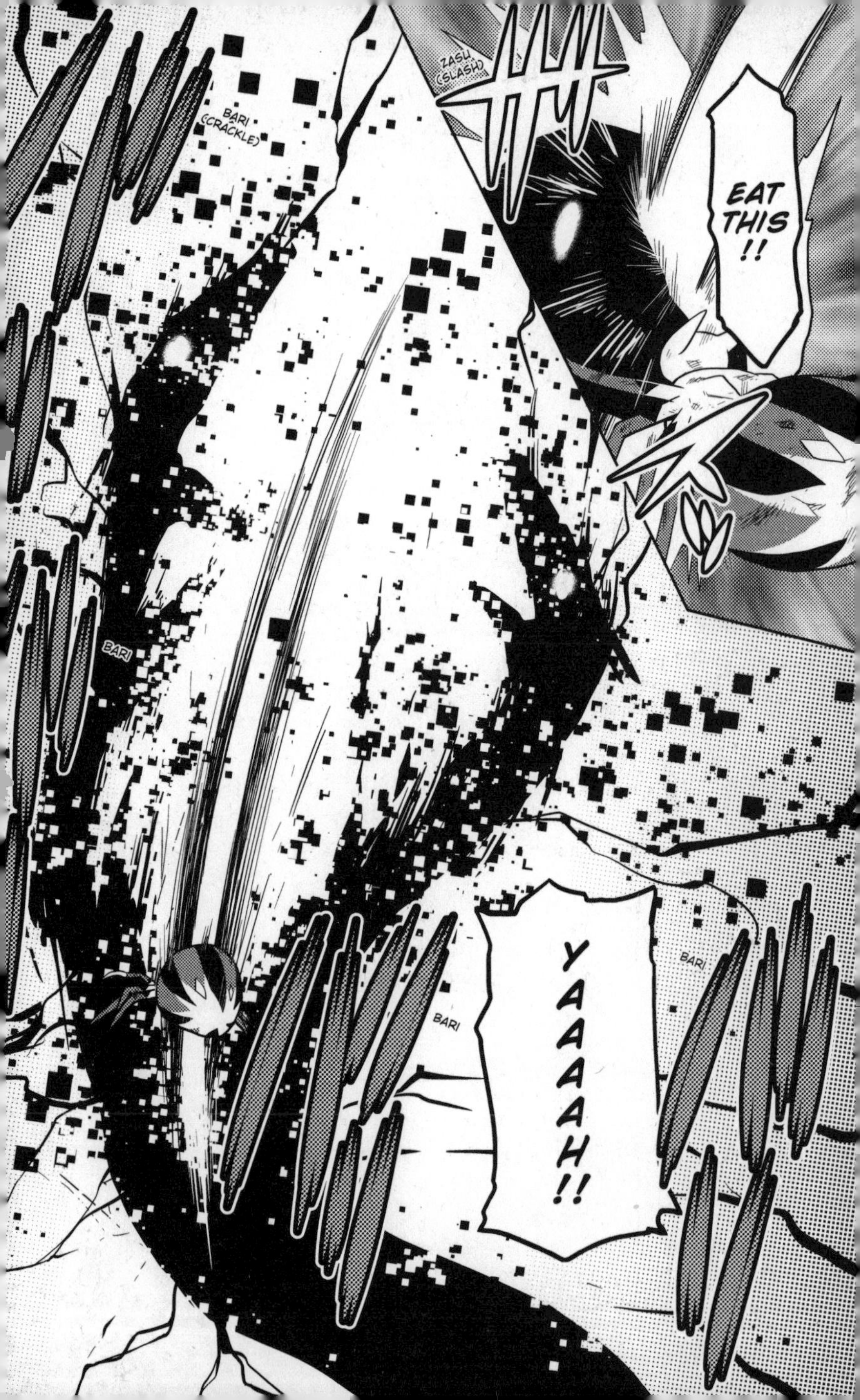
ZASU (SLASH)
EAT THIS!!
BARI (CRACKLE)
BARI
YAAAAAH!!
BARI
BARI

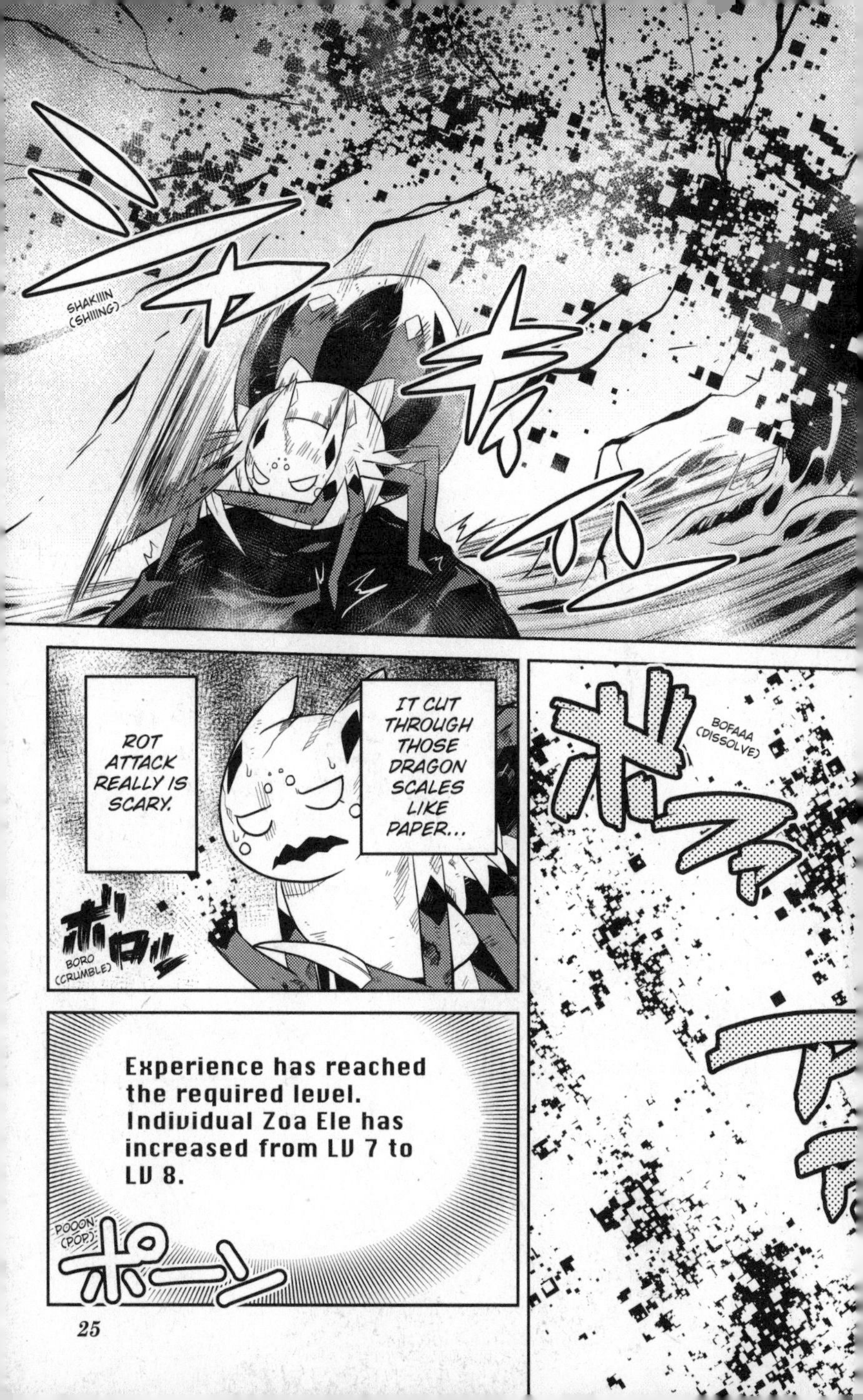
SHAKIIIN (SHIIING)
BOFAAA (DISSOLVE)
IT CUT THROUGH THOSE DRAGON SCALES LIKE PAPER...
ROT ATTACK REALLY IS SCARY.
BORO (CRUMBLE)
Experience has reached the required level. Individual Zoa Ele has increased from LV 7 to LV 8.
POOON (POP)

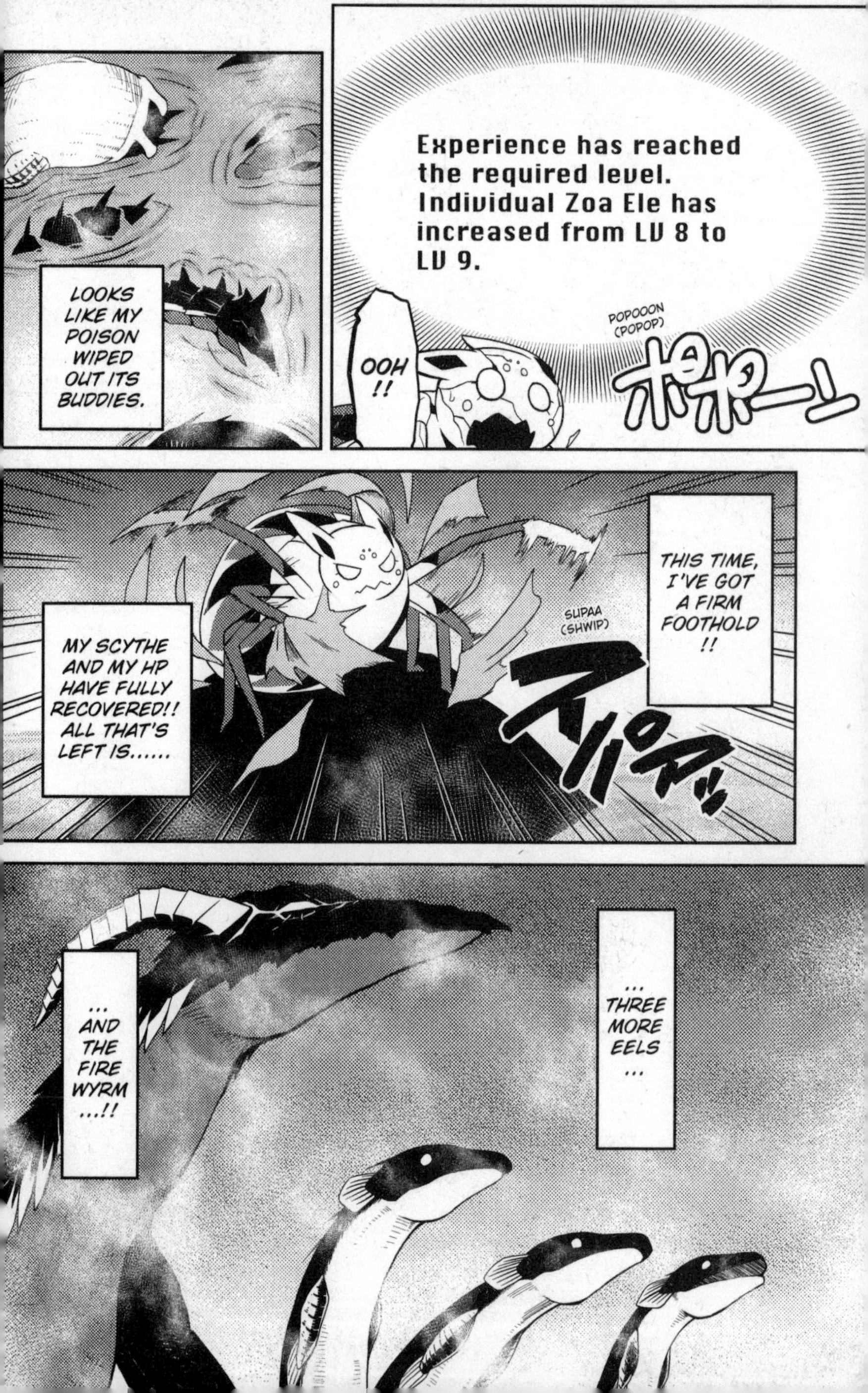

Experience has reached the required level. Individual Zoa Ele has increased from LV 8 to LV 9.
POPOOON (POPOP)
OOH!!
LOOKS LIKE MY POISON WIPED OUT ITS BUDDIES.
THIS TIME, I'VE GOT A FIRM FOOTHOLD!!
SUPAA (SHWIP)
MY SCYTHE AND MY HP HAVE FULLY RECOVERED!! ALL THAT'S LEFT IS......
...THREE MORE EELS...
...AND THE FIRE WYRM...!!

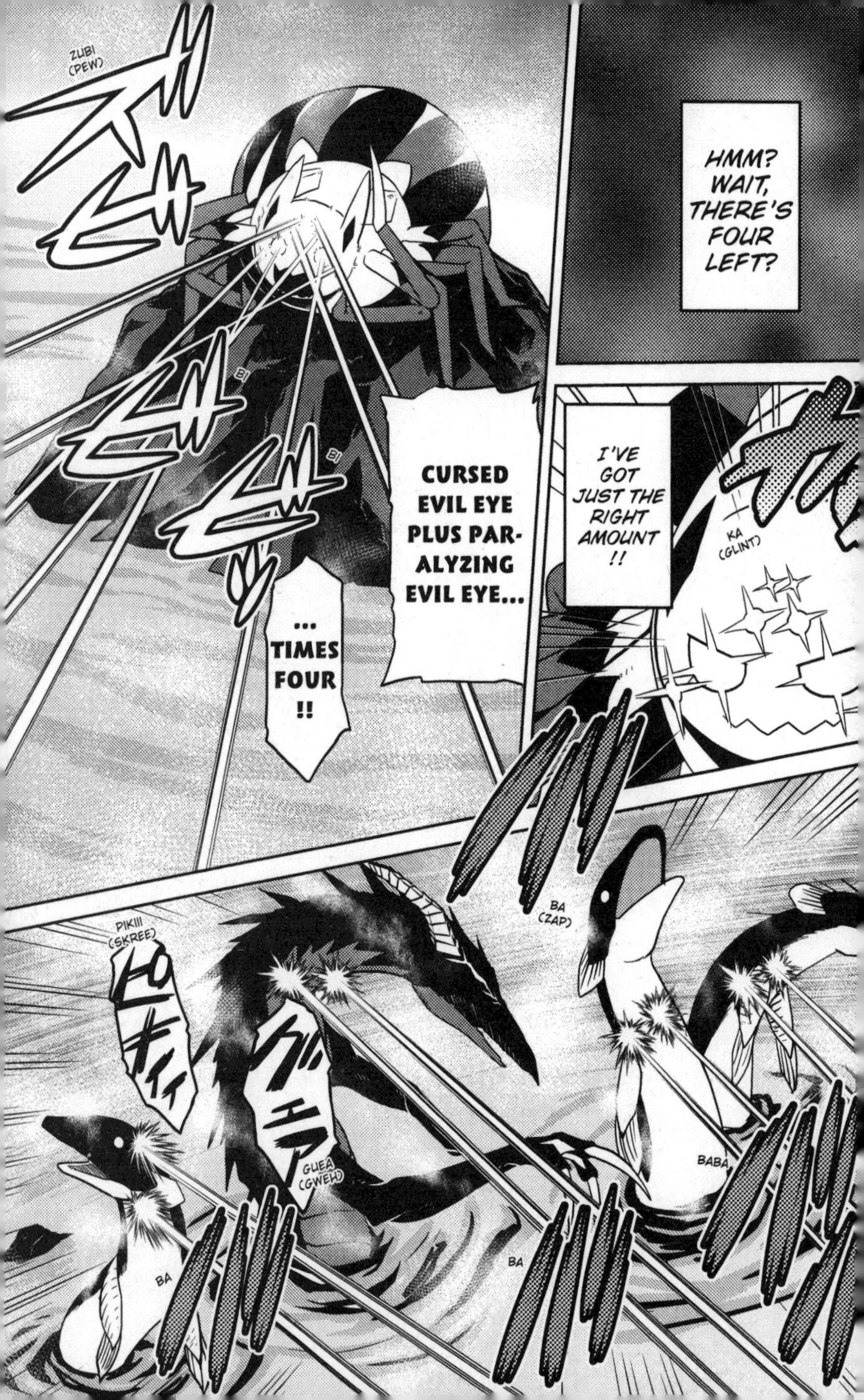
HMM? WAIT, THERE'S FOUR LEFT?
I'VE GOT JUST THE RIGHT AMOUNT !!
KA (GLINT)
ZUBI (PEW)
BI
BI
CURSED EVIL EYE PLUS PAR-ALYZING EVIL EYE...
... TIMES FOUR !!
BA (ZAP)
PIKIII (SKREE)
GUEA (GWEH)
BABA
BA
BA

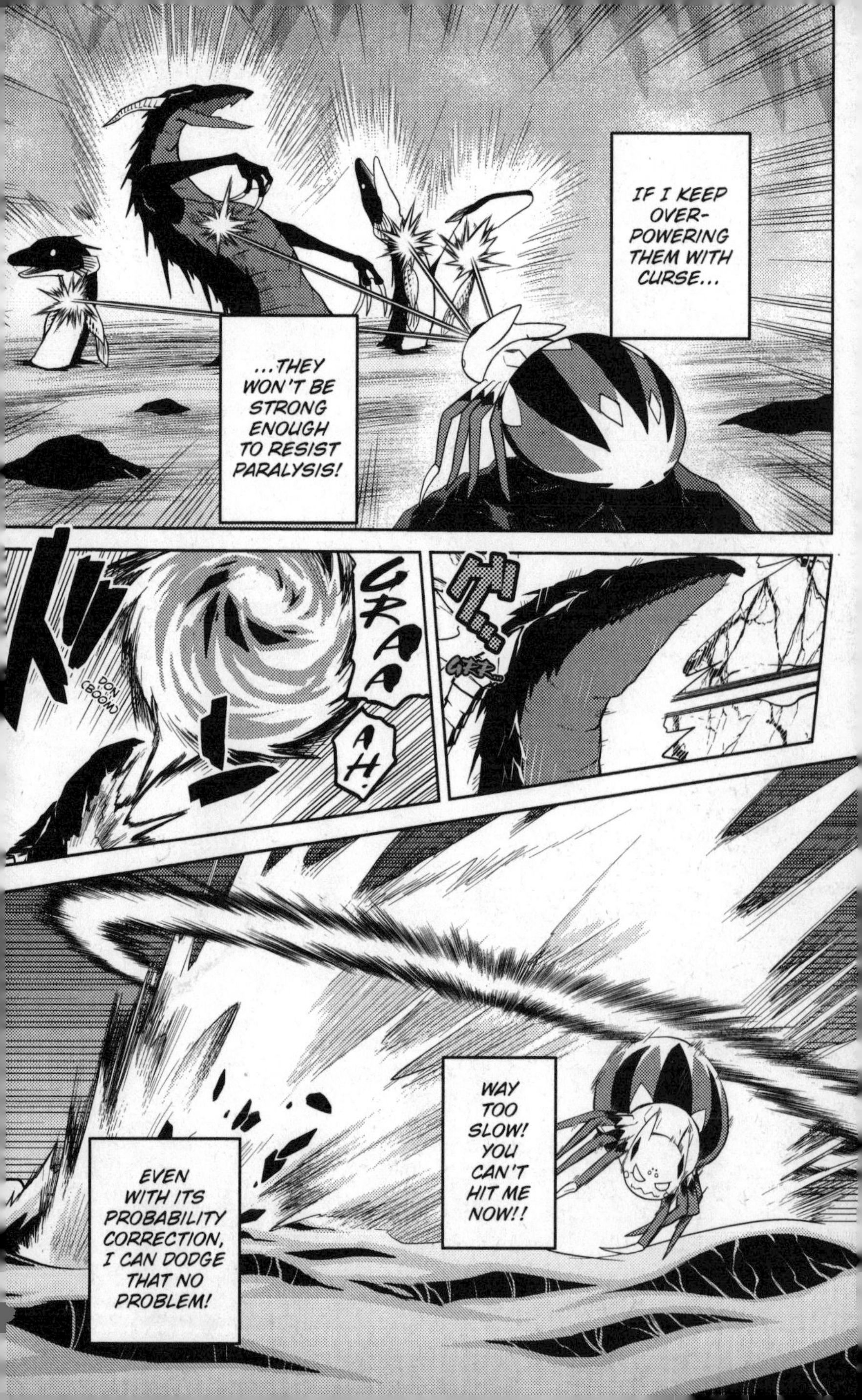
IF I KEEP OVER-POWERING THEM WITH CURSE...
...THEY WON'T BE STRONG ENOUGH TO RESIST PARALYSIS!
GRR...
GRAAAH!
DON (BOOM)
WAY TOO SLOW! YOU CAN'T HIT ME NOW!!
EVEN WITH ITS PROBABILITY CORRECTION, I CAN DODGE THAT NO PROBLEM!

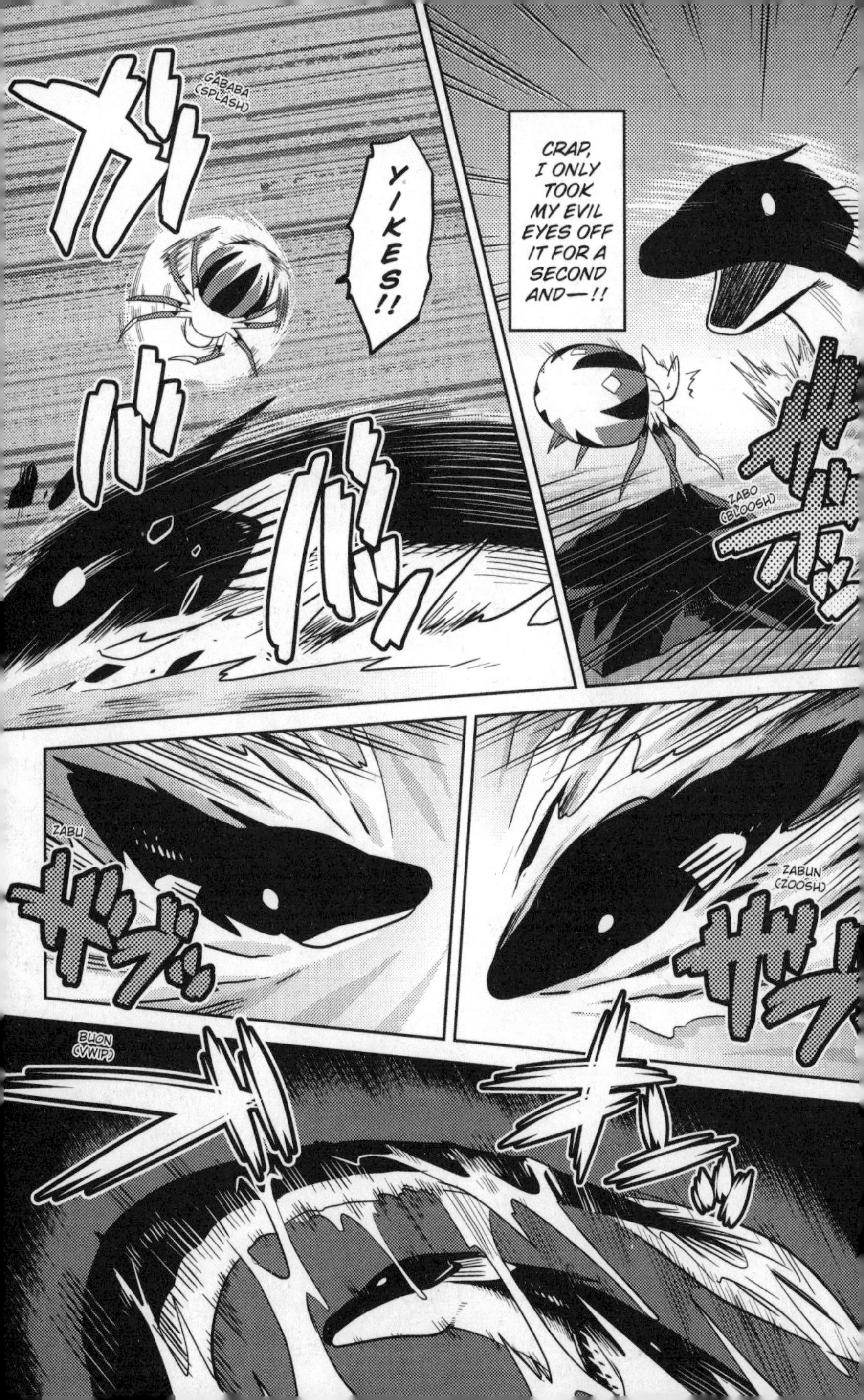
CRAP, I ONLY TOOK MY EVIL EYES OFF IT FOR A SECOND AND—!!
ZABO (BLOOSH)
GABABA (SPLASH)
YIKES!!
ZABUN (ZOOSH)
ZABU
BUON (VWIP)

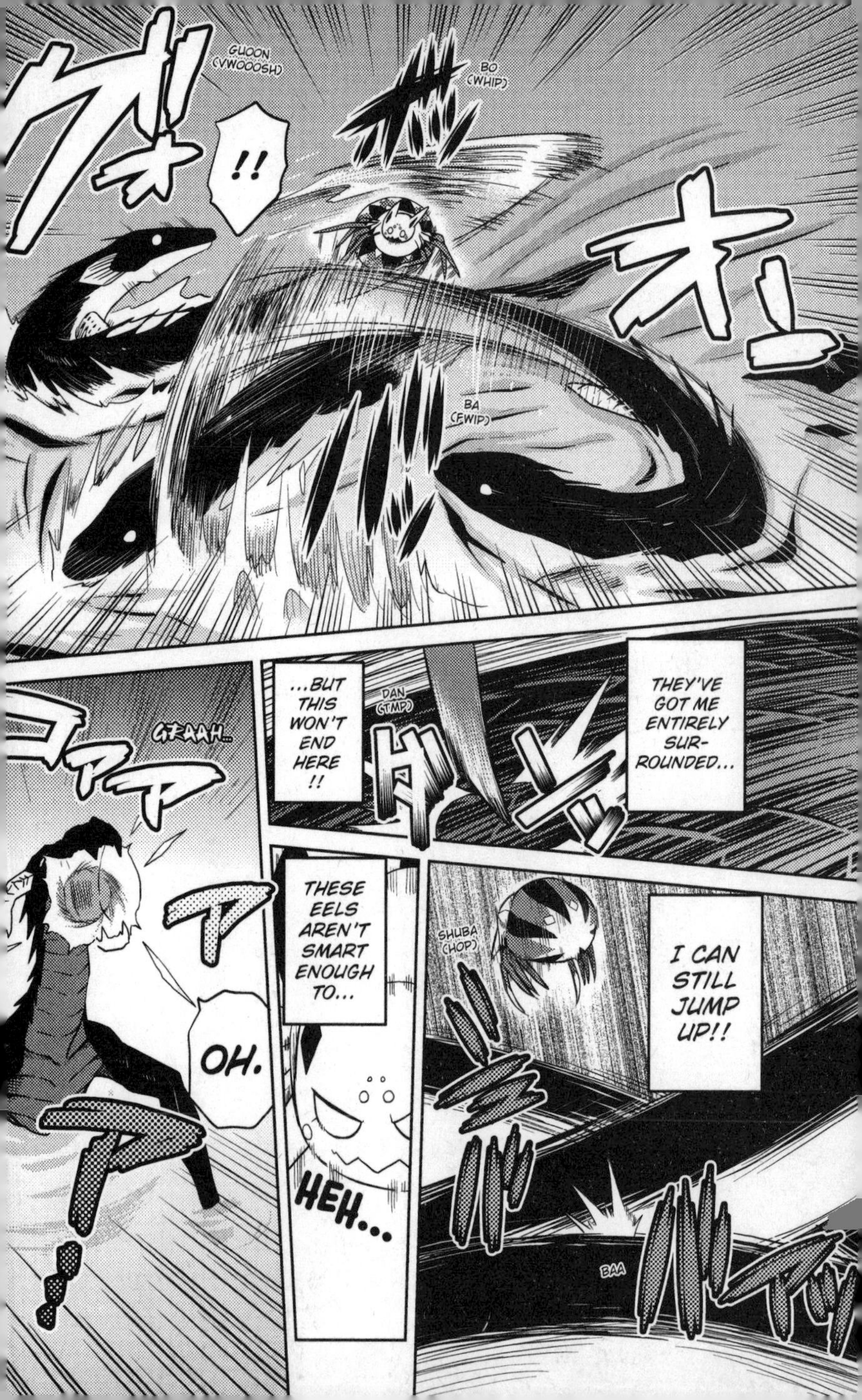
BO (WHIP)
GUOON (VWOOOSH)
!!
BA (FWIP)
THEY'VE GOT ME ENTIRELY SUR-ROUNDED...
DAN (TMP)
...BUT THIS WON'T END HERE!!
I CAN STILL JUMP UP!!
SHUBA (HOP)
BAA
THESE EELS AREN'T SMART ENOUGH TO...
HEH...
GRAAH...
OH.

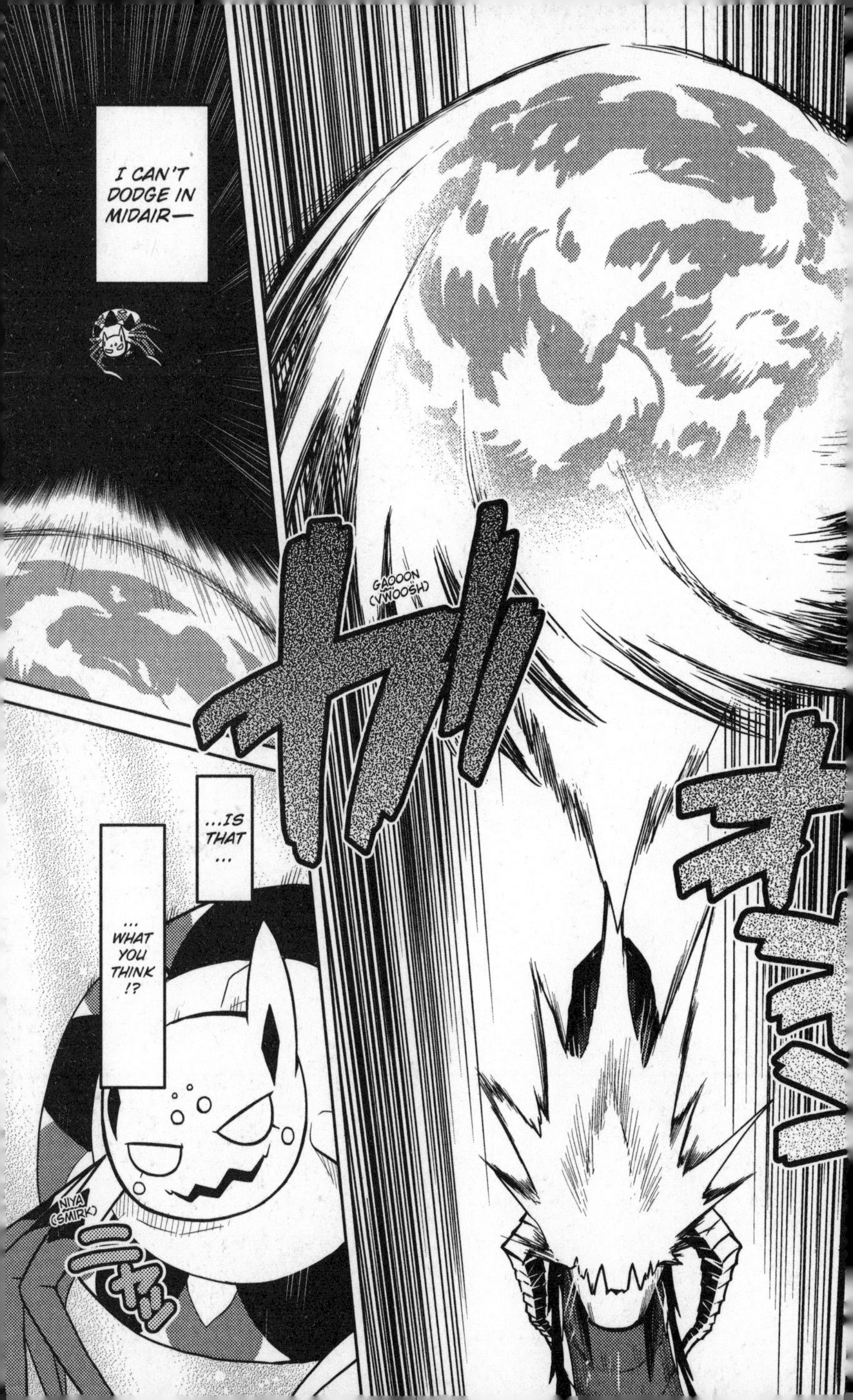
GAOOON (VWOOSH)
I CAN'T DODGE IN MIDAIR—
...IS THAT ...
... WHAT YOU THINK !?
NIYA (SMIRK)

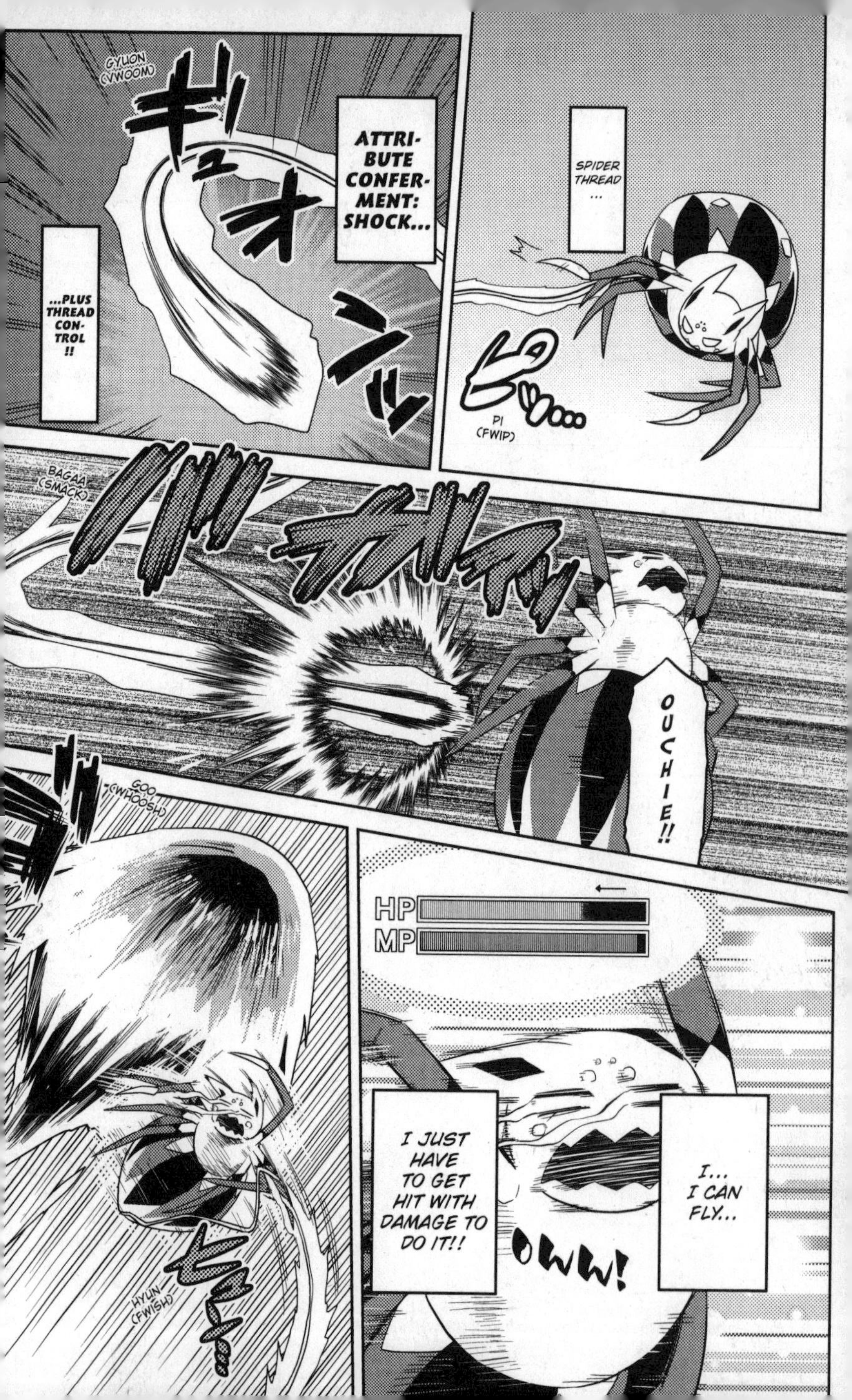
SPIDER THREAD ...
PI (FWIP)
ATTRIBUTE CONFERMENT: SHOCK...
GYUON (VWOOM)
...PLUS THREAD CONTROL!!
BAGAA (SMACK)
OUCHIE!!
HP
MP
I... I CAN FLY...
I JUST HAVE TO GET HIT WITH DAMAGE TO DO IT!!
OWW!
GOO (WHOOSH)
HYUN (FWISH)

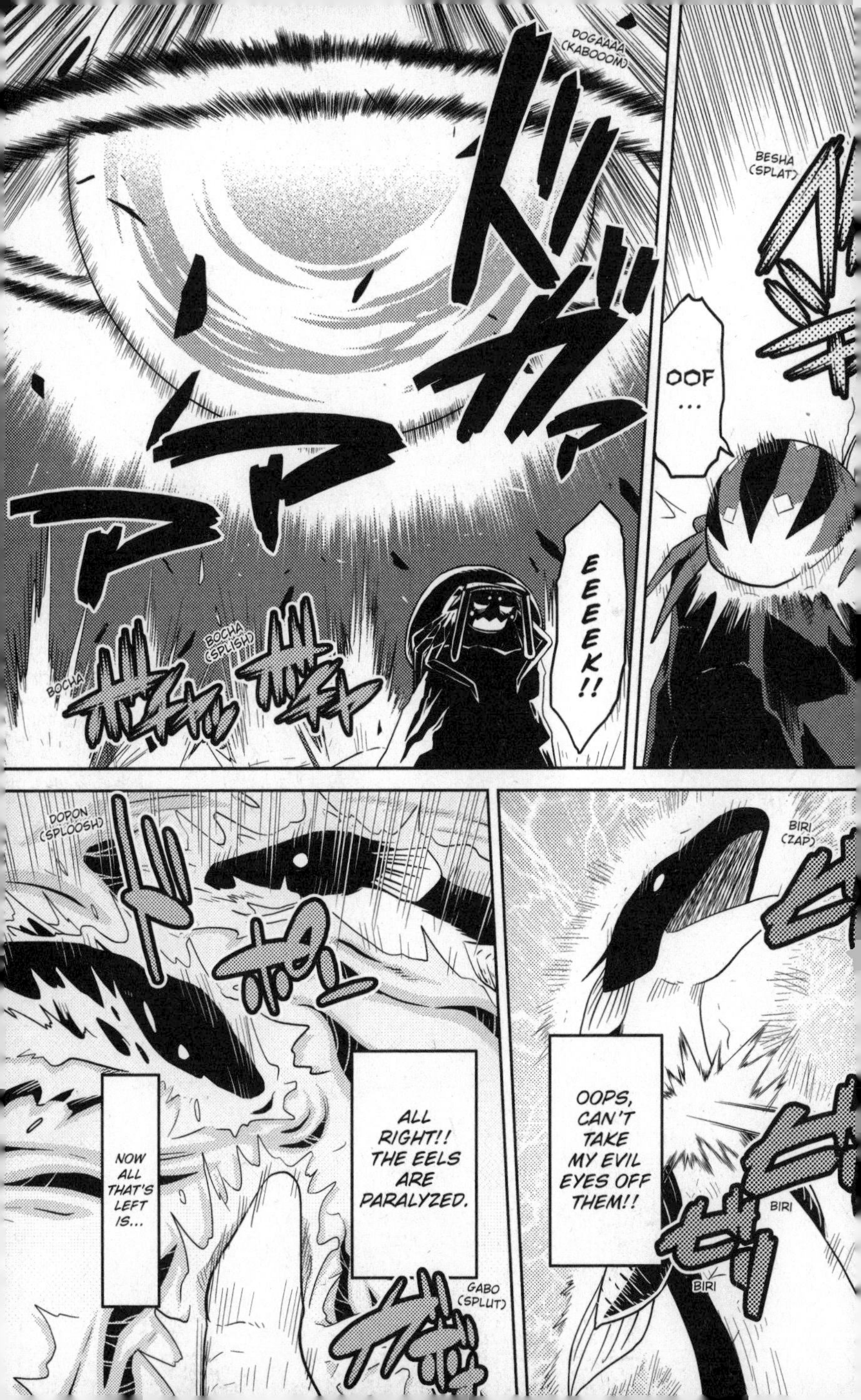
BESHA (SPLAT)
OOF...
DOGAAAA (KABOOOM)
EEEEEK!!
BOCHA (SPLISH)
BOCHA
BIRI (ZAP)
OOPS, CAN'T TAKE MY EVIL EYES OFF THEM!!
BIRI
BIRI
DOPON (SPLOOSH)
ALL RIGHT!! THE EELS ARE PARALYZED.
GABO (SPLUT)
NOW ALL THAT'S LEFT IS...

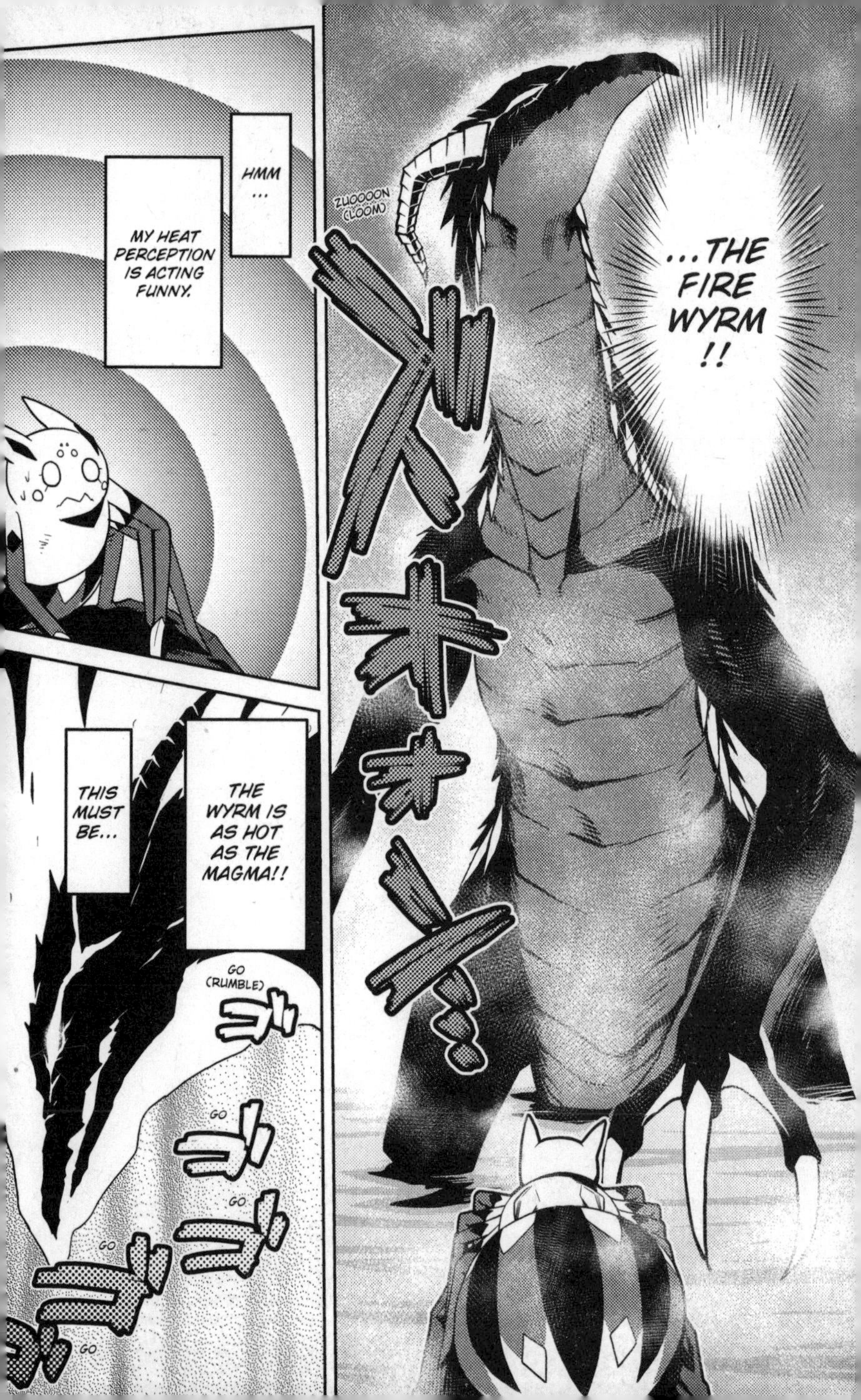
HMM...
MY HEAT PERCEPTION IS ACTING FUNNY.
THE WYRM IS AS HOT AS THE MAGMA!!
THIS MUST BE...
GO (RUMBLE)
GO
GO
GO
GO
...THE FIRE WYRM!!
ZUOOOON (LOOM)

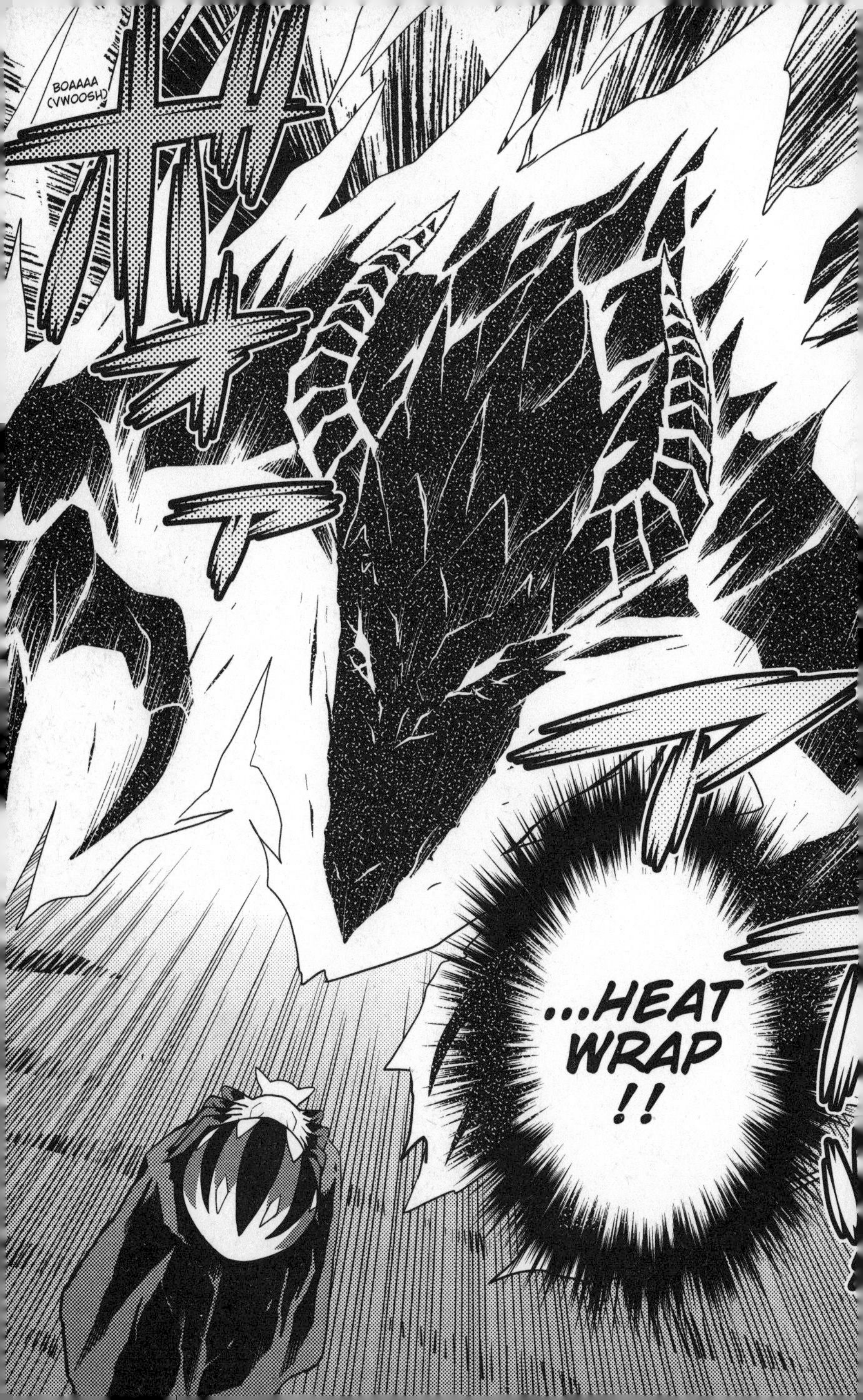
BOAAAA
(VWOOSH)
...HEAT
WRAP
!!

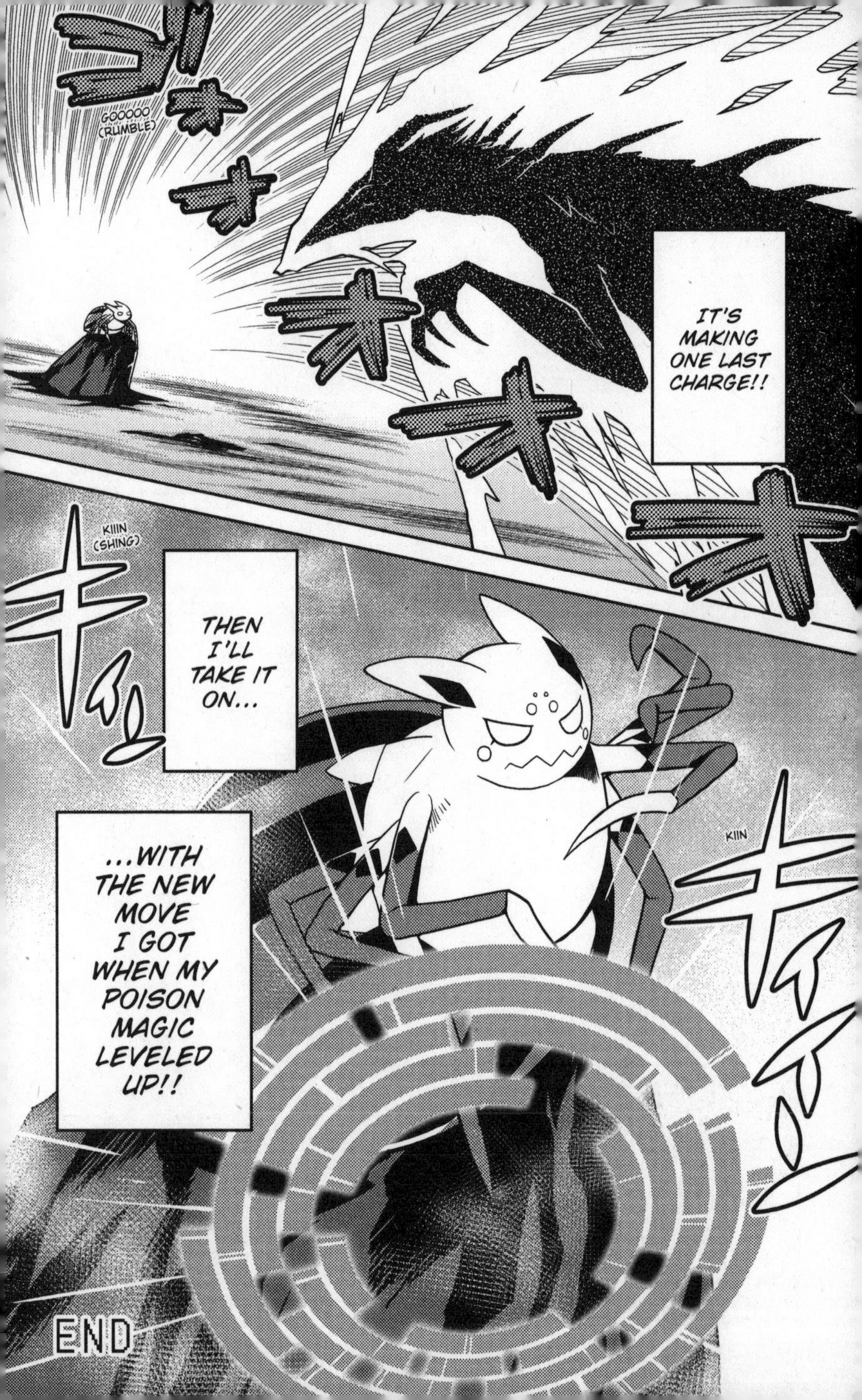
GOOOOO
(RUMBLE)
IT'S MAKING ONE LAST CHARGE!!
KIIN
THEN I'LL TAKE IT ON...
KIIN
(SHING)
...WITH THE NEW MOVE I GOT WHEN MY POISON MAGIC LEVELED UP!!
END

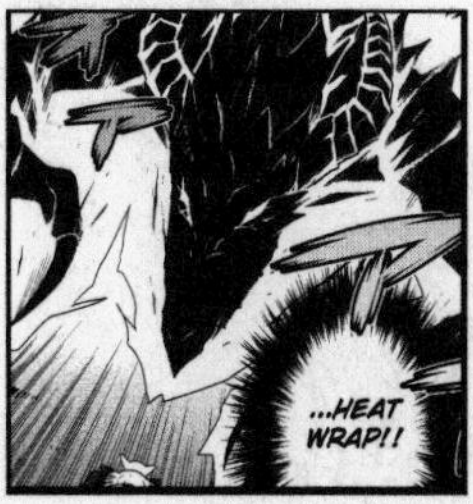
...HEAT
WRAP!!

So I'm a Spider, So What?

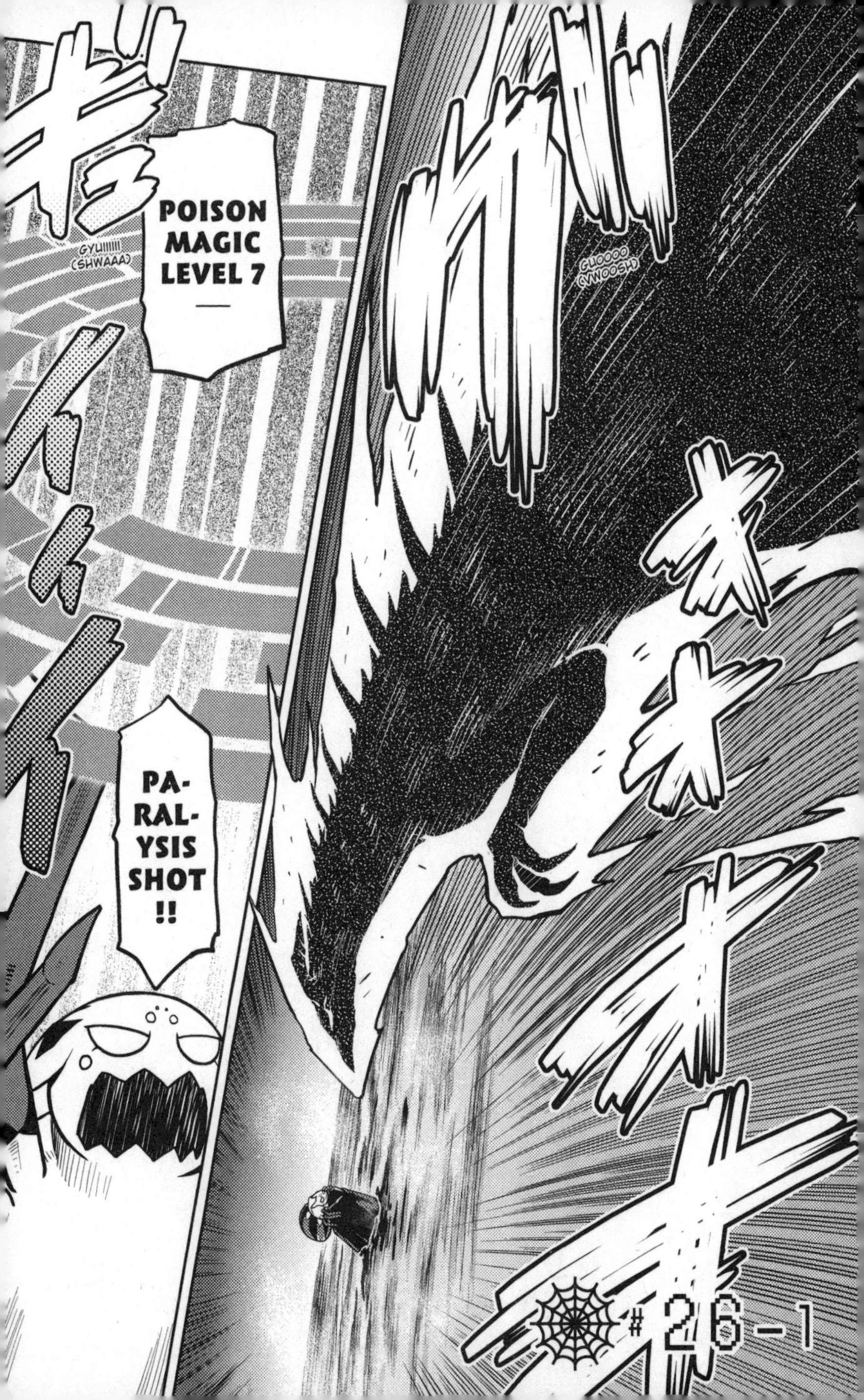
GUOOOO (VWOOSH)
POISON MAGIC LEVEL 7 —
GYUIIIIIII (SHWAAA)
PA-RAL-YSIS SHOT!!
#26-1

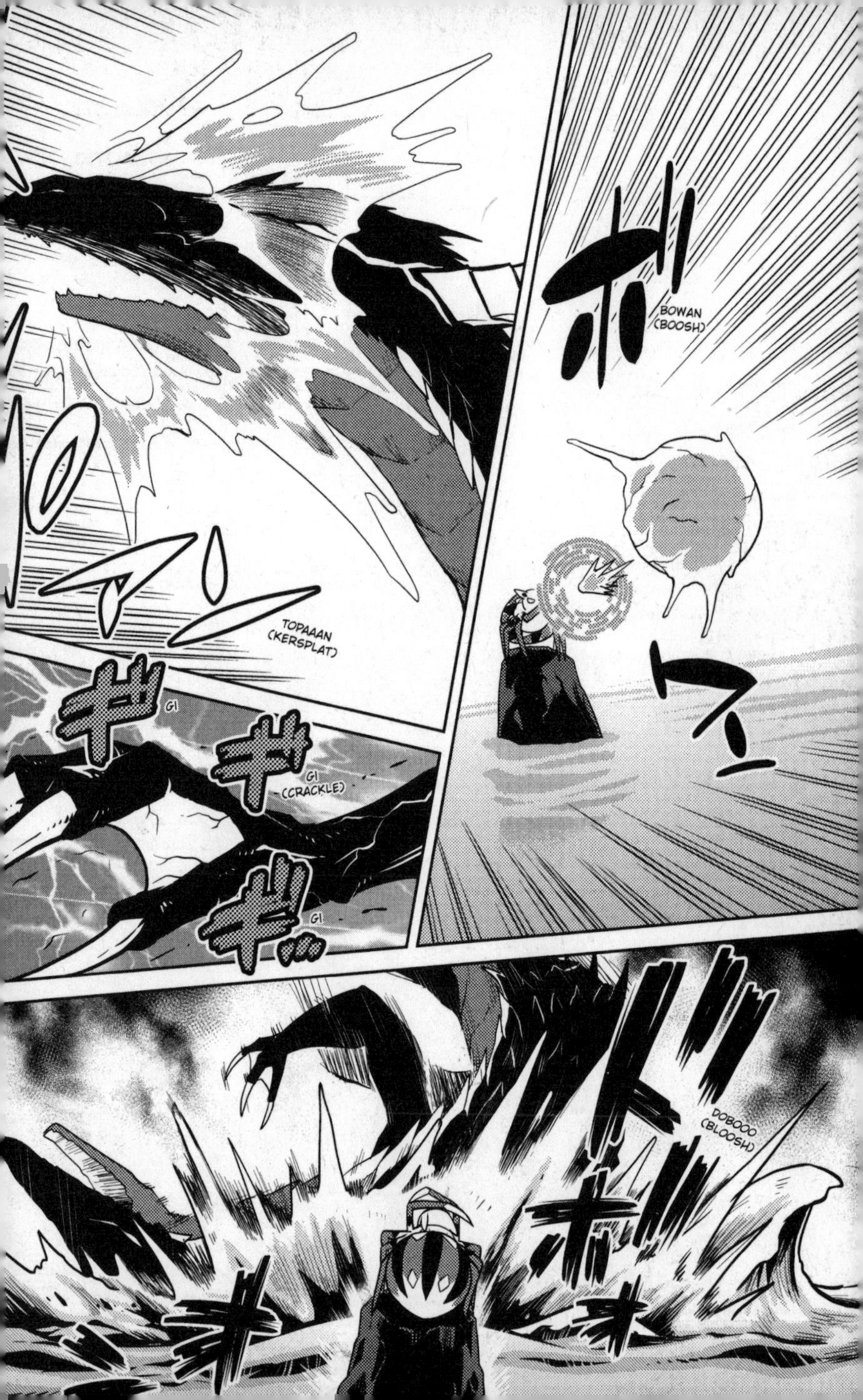
BOWAN
(BOOSH)
TOPAAAN
(KERSPLAT)
GI
GI
(CRACKLE)
GI
DOBOOO
(BLOOSH)

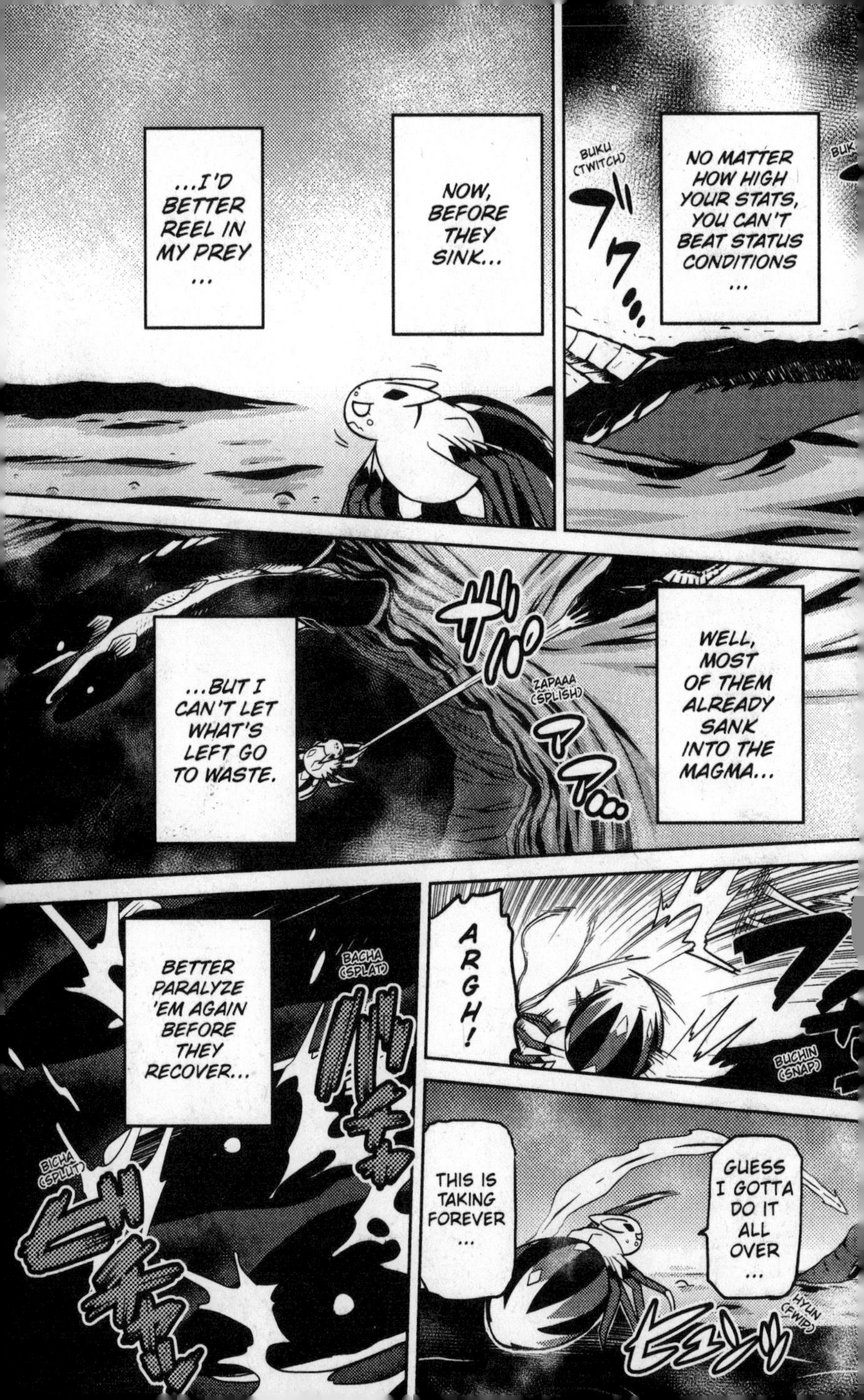
BUK
NO MATTER HOW HIGH YOUR STATS, YOU CAN'T BEAT STATUS CONDITIONS...
BUKU (TWITCH)
NOW, BEFORE THEY SINK...
...I'D BETTER REEL IN MY PREY...
WELL, MOST OF THEM ALREADY SANK INTO THE MAGMA...
ZAPAAA (SPLISH)
...BUT I CAN'T LET WHAT'S LEFT GO TO WASTE.
ARGH!
BUCHIN (SNAP)
GUESS I GOTTA DO IT ALL OVER...
THIS IS TAKING FOREVER...
HYUN (FWIP)
BETTER PARALYZE 'EM AGAIN BEFORE THEY RECOVER...
BACHA (SPLAT)
BICHA (SPLUT)

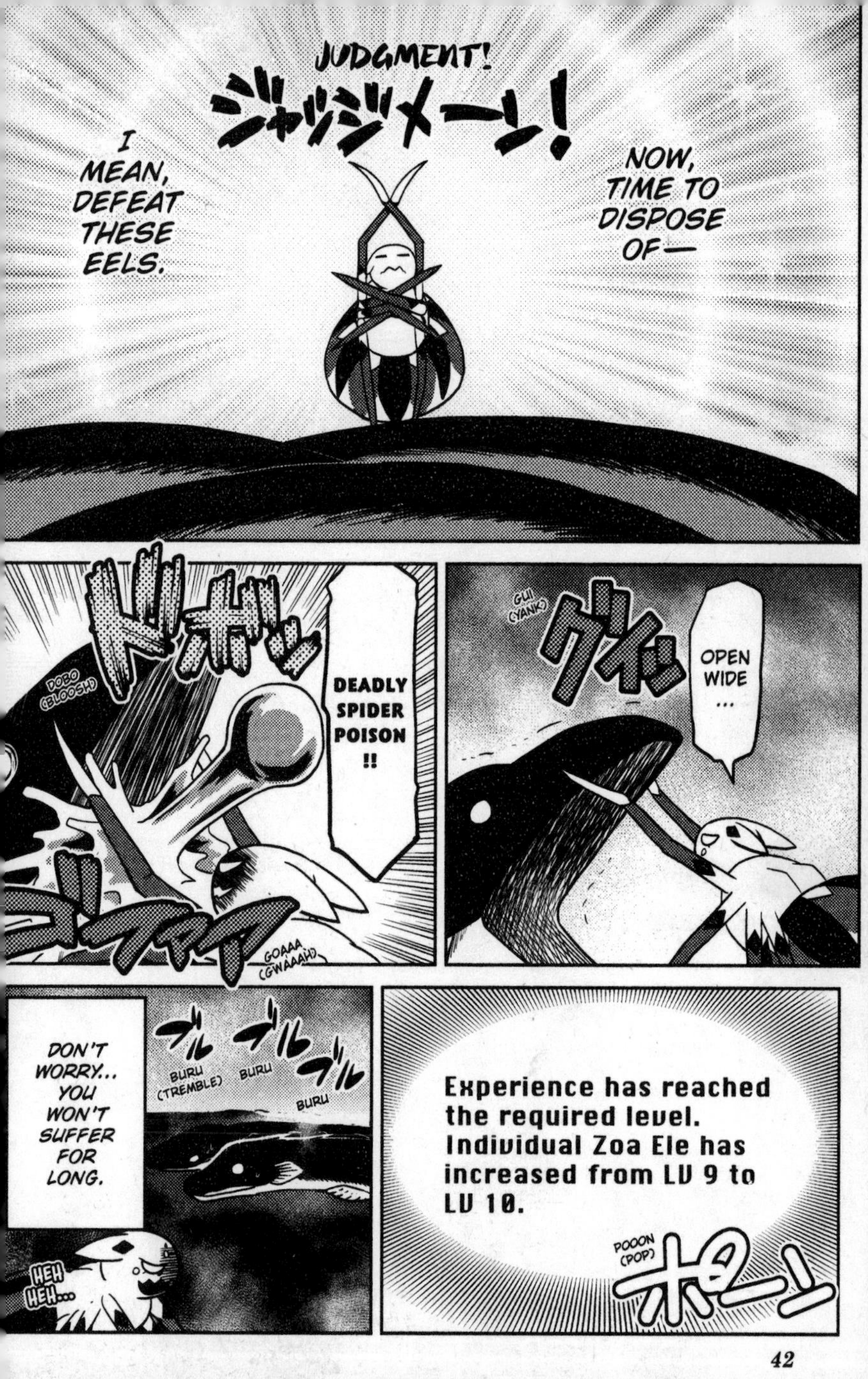
NOW, TIME TO DISPOSE OF—
JUDGMENT!
I MEAN, DEFEAT THESE EELS.
GUI (YANK)
OPEN WIDE ...
DOBO (BLOOSH)
DEADLY SPIDER POISON!!
GOAAA (GWAAAH)
Experience has reached the required level. Individual Zoa Ele has increased from LV 9 to LV 10.
POOON (POP)
BURU (TREMBLE)
BURU
BURU
DON'T WORRY... YOU WON'T SUFFER FOR LONG.
HEH HEH...

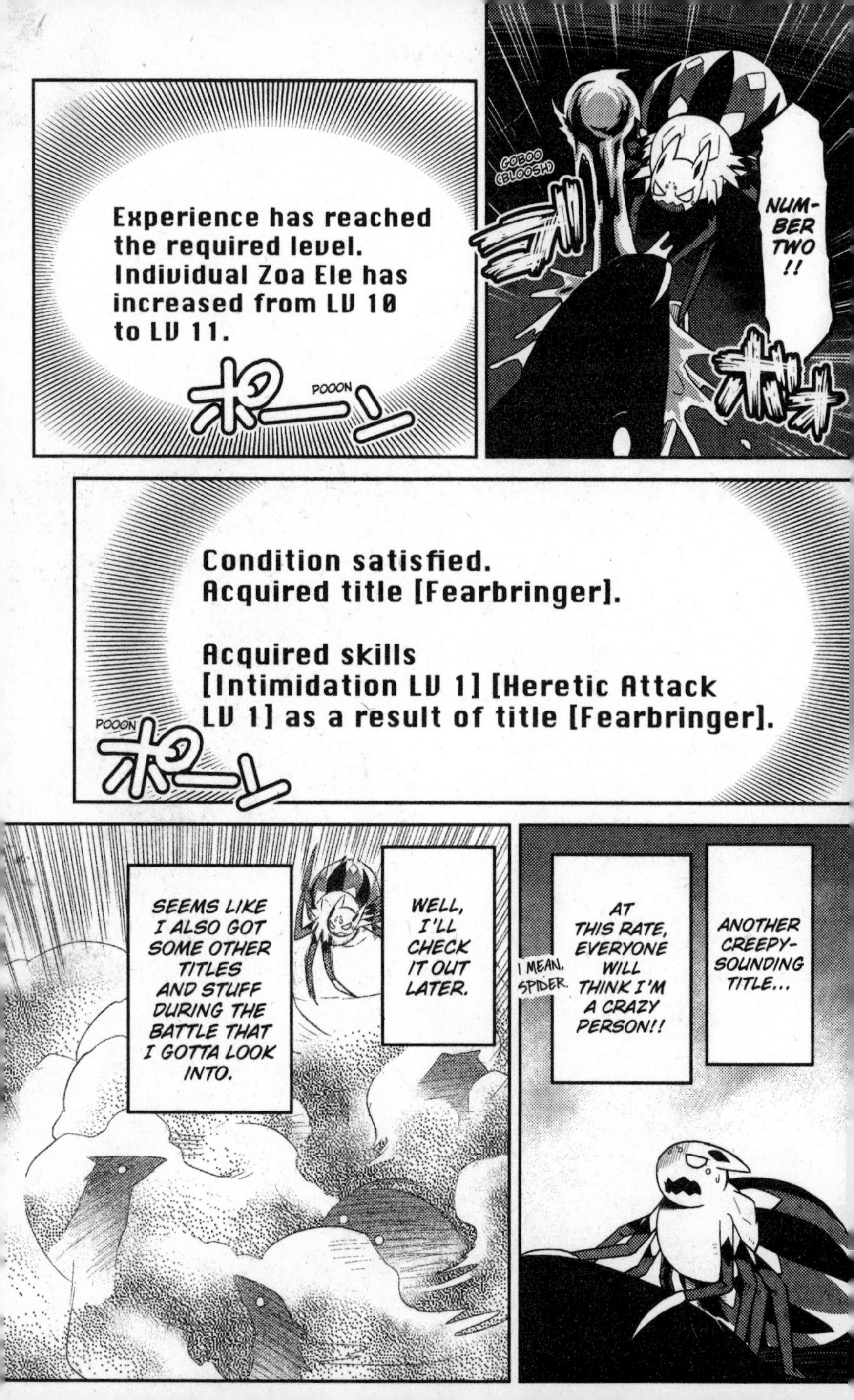
GOBOO (BLOOSH)
NUM-BER TWO!!
Experience has reached the required level. Individual Zoa Ele has increased from LV 10 to LV 11.
POOON
Condition satisfied. Acquired title [Fearbringer].
Acquired skills [Intimidation LV 1] [Heretic Attack LV 1] as a result of title [Fearbringer].
POOON
ANOTHER CREEPY-SOUNDING TITLE...
AT THIS RATE, EVERYONE WILL THINK I'M A CRAZY PERSON!!
I MEAN, SPIDER.
WELL, I'LL CHECK IT OUT LATER.
SEEMS LIKE I ALSO GOT SOME OTHER TITLES AND STUFF DURING THE BATTLE THAT I GOTTA LOOK INTO.

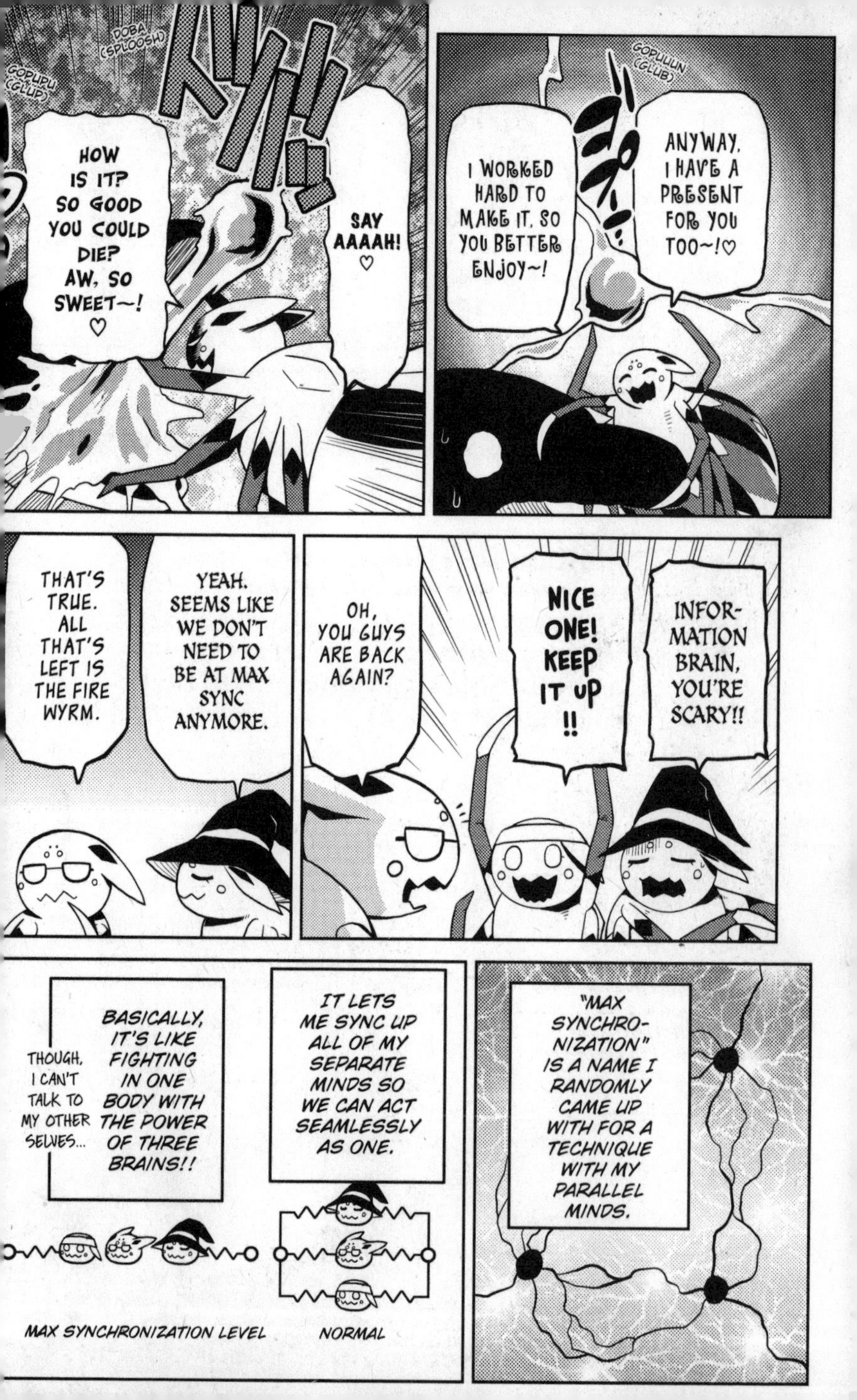
GOPUUUN (GLUB)
ANYWAY, I HAVE A PRESENT FOR YOU TOO~!♡
I WORKED HARD TO MAKE IT, SO YOU BETTER ENJOY~!
DOBA (SPLOOSH)
SAY AAAAH! ♡
GOPUPU (GLUB)
HOW IS IT? SO GOOD YOU COULD DIE? AW, SO SWEET~! ♡
INFORMATION BRAIN, YOU'RE SCARY!!
NICE ONE! KEEP IT UP!!
OH, YOU GUYS ARE BACK AGAIN?
YEAH. SEEMS LIKE WE DON'T NEED TO BE AT MAX SYNC ANYMORE.
THAT'S TRUE. ALL THAT'S LEFT IS THE FIRE WYRM.
"MAX SYNCHRONIZATION" IS A NAME I RANDOMLY CAME UP WITH FOR A TECHNIQUE WITH MY PARALLEL MINDS.
IT LETS ME SYNC UP ALL OF MY SEPARATE MINDS SO WE CAN ACT SEAMLESSLY AS ONE.
NORMAL
BASICALLY, IT'S LIKE FIGHTING IN ONE BODY WITH THE POWER OF THREE BRAINS!!
THOUGH, I CAN'T TALK TO MY OTHER SELVES...
MAX SYNCHRONIZATION LEVEL

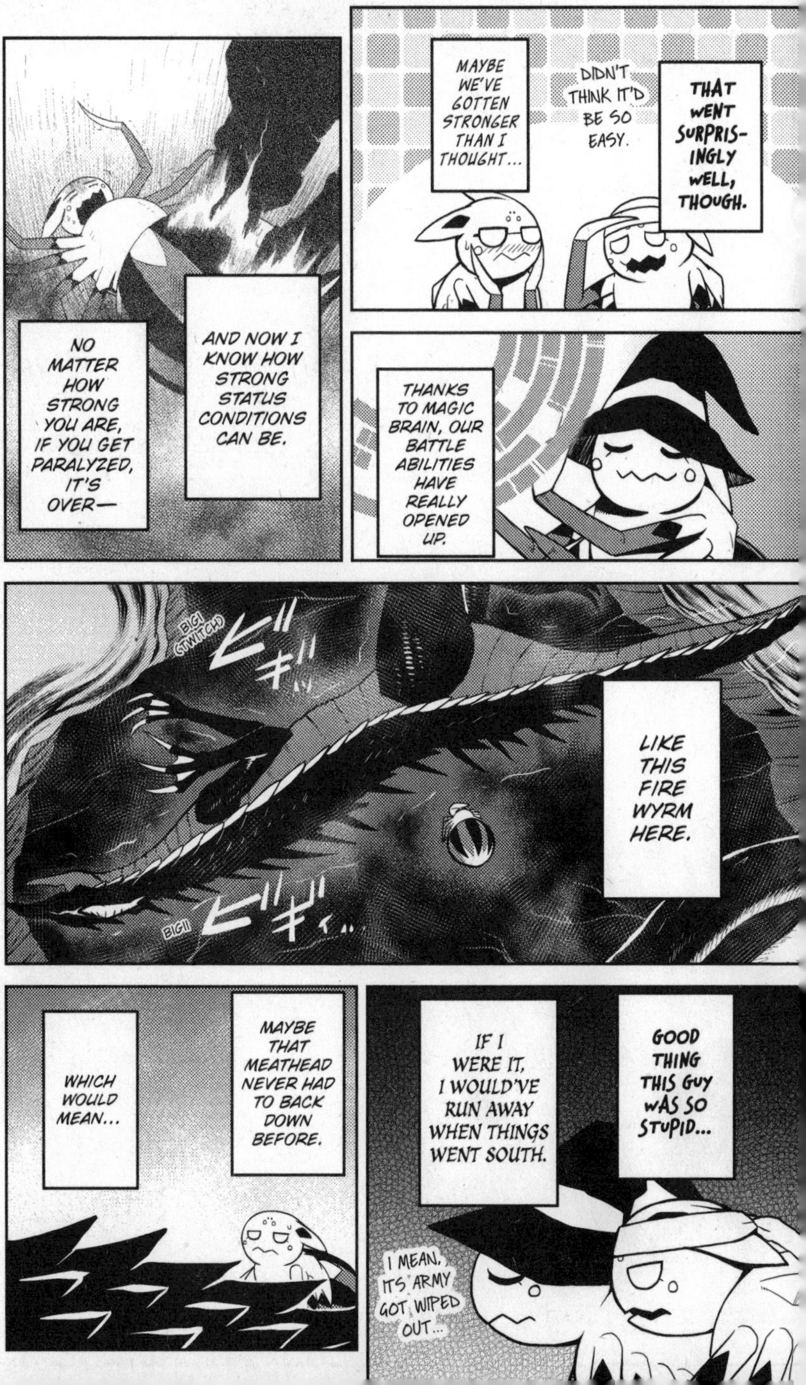
THAT WENT SURPRISINGLY WELL, THOUGH.
DIDN'T THINK IT'D BE SO EASY.
MAYBE WE'VE GOTTEN STRONGER THAN I THOUGHT...
THANKS TO MAGIC BRAIN, OUR BATTLE ABILITIES HAVE REALLY OPENED UP.
AND NOW I KNOW HOW STRONG STATUS CONDITIONS CAN BE.
NO MATTER HOW STRONG YOU ARE, IF YOU GET PARALYZED, IT'S OVER—
LIKE THIS FIRE WYRM HERE.
BIGI (TWITCH)
BIGII
GOOD THING THIS GUY WAS SO STUPID...
IF I WERE IT, I WOULD'VE RUN AWAY WHEN THINGS WENT SOUTH.
I MEAN, ITS ARMY GOT WIPED OUT...
MAYBE THAT MEATHEAD NEVER HAD TO BACK DOWN BEFORE.
WHICH WOULD MEAN...

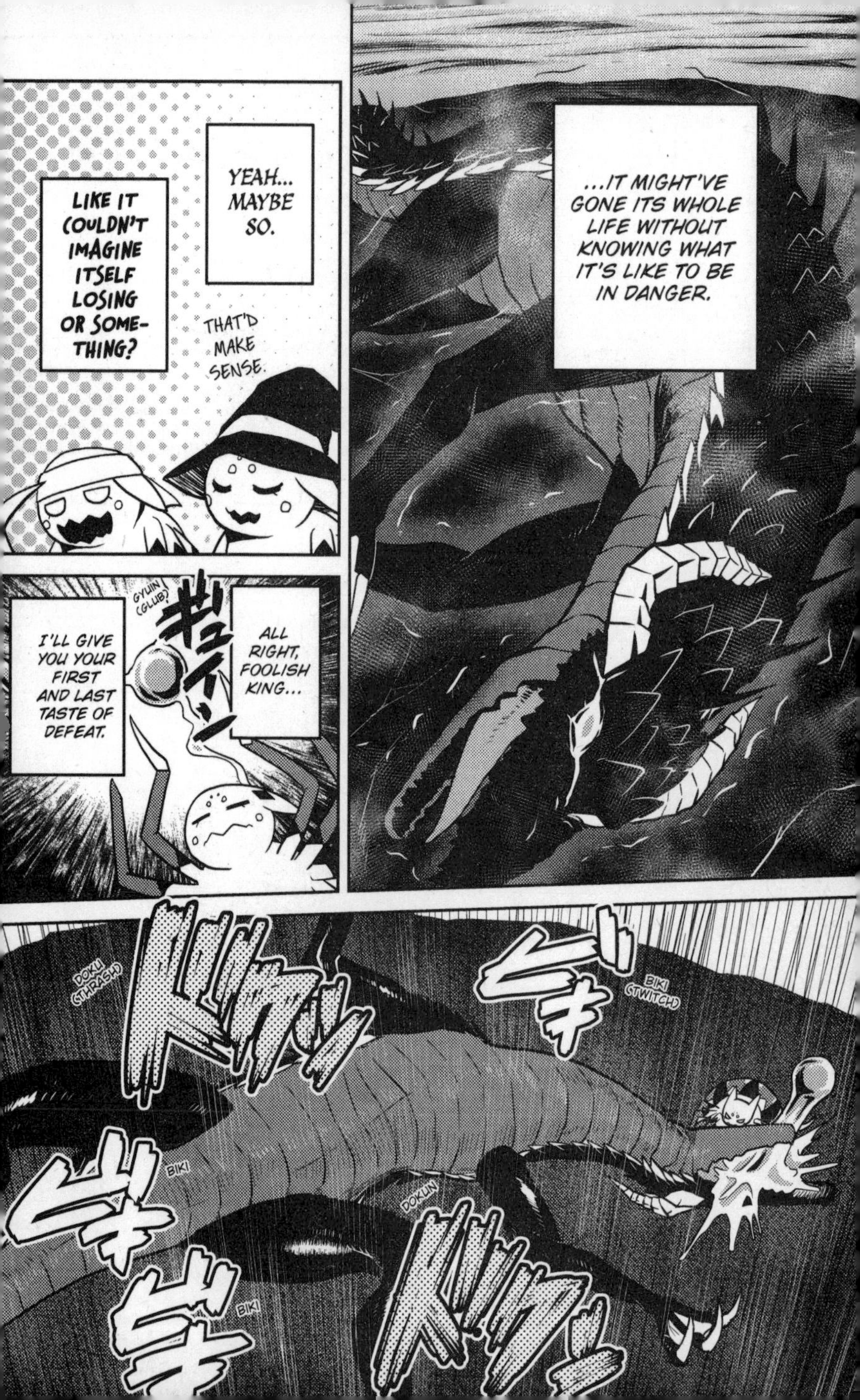
...IT MIGHT'VE GONE ITS WHOLE LIFE WITHOUT KNOWING WHAT IT'S LIKE TO BE IN DANGER.
YEAH... MAYBE SO.
LIKE IT COULDN'T IMAGINE ITSELF LOSING OR SOME-THING?
THAT'D MAKE SENSE.
ALL RIGHT, FOOLISH KING...
GYUIN (GLUB)
I'LL GIVE YOU YOUR FIRST AND LAST TASTE OF DEFEAT.
BIKI (TWITCH)
DOKUN
DOKU (THRASH)
BIKI
BIKI

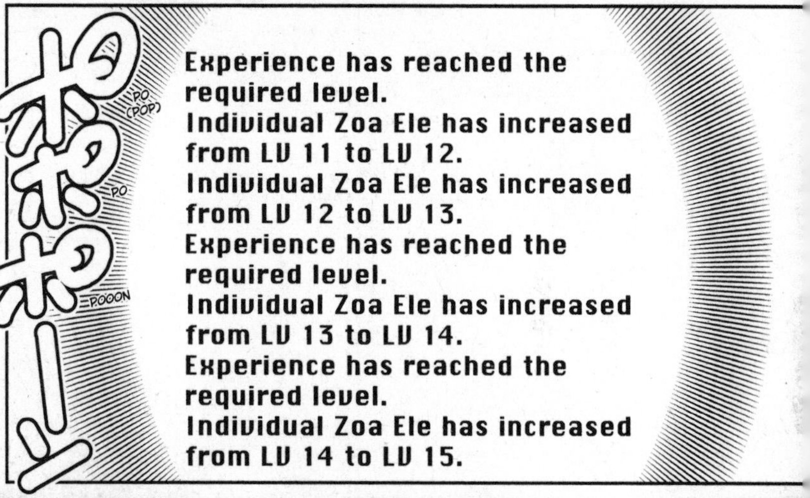
Experience has reached the required level.
Individual Zoa Ele has increased from LV 11 to LV 12.
Individual Zoa Ele has increased from LV 12 to LV 13.
Experience has reached the required level.
Individual Zoa Ele has increased from LV 13 to LV 14.
Experience has reached the required level.
Individual Zoa Ele has increased from LV 14 to LV 15.
ポポポーン
PO (POP)
PO
POOON
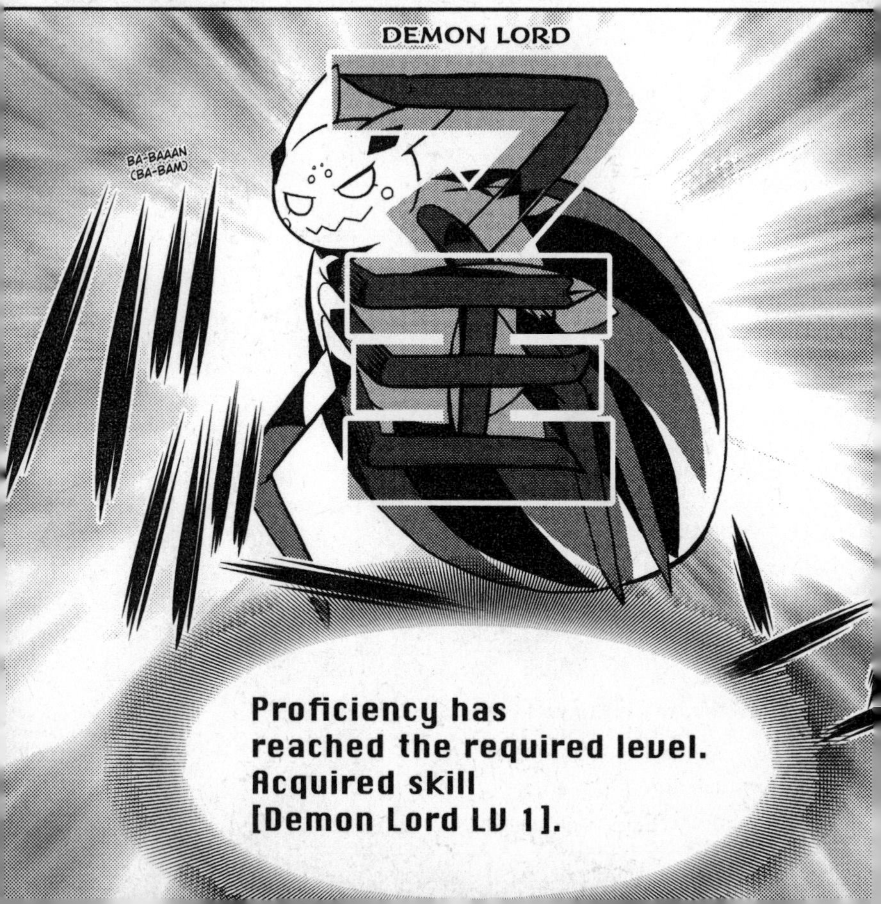
DEMON LORD
魔王
BA-BAAAN (BA-BAM)
Proficiency has reached the required level.
Acquired skill [Demon Lord LV 1].

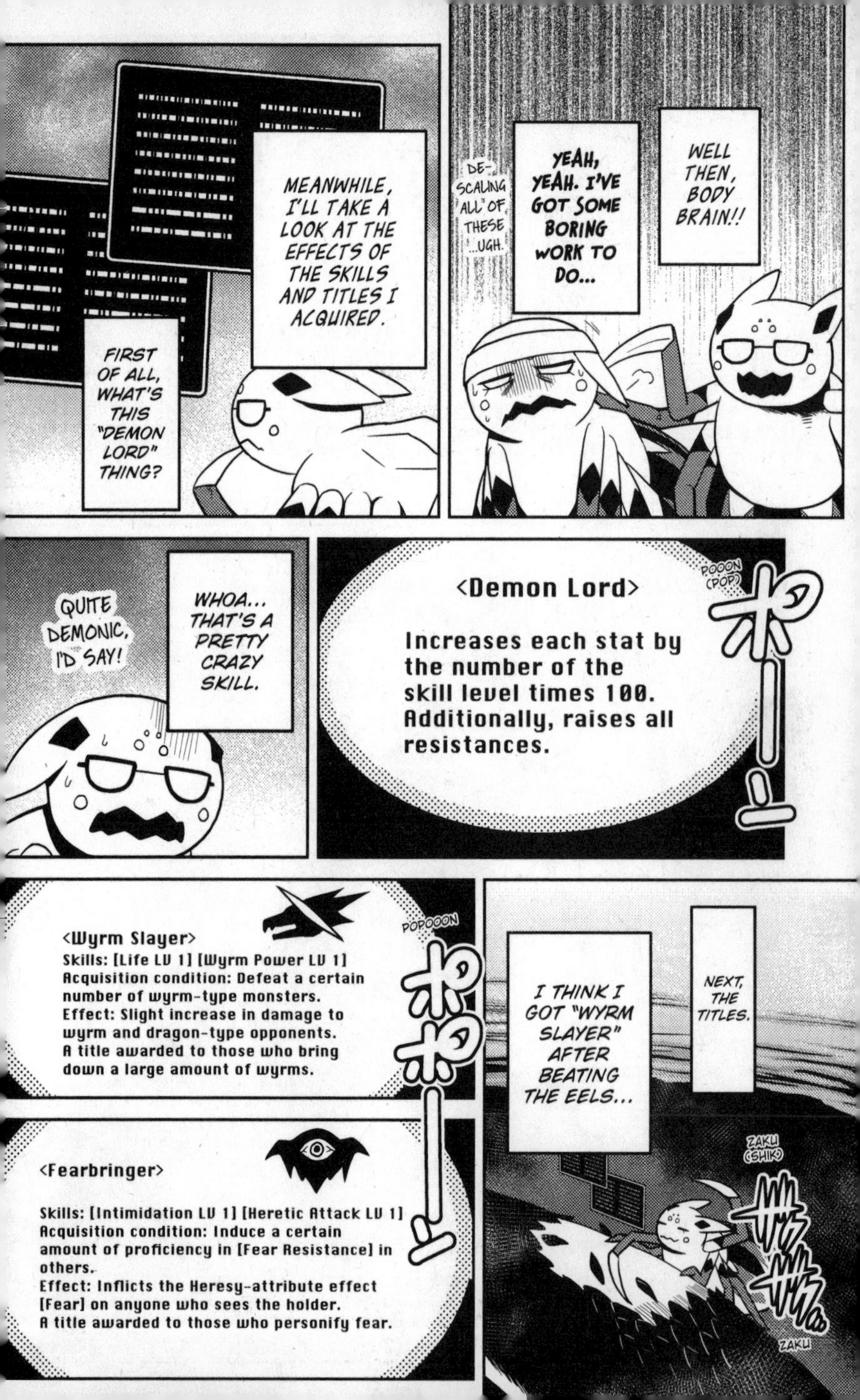
WELL THEN, BODY BRAIN!!
YEAH, YEAH. I'VE GOT SOME BORING WORK TO DO...
DE-SCALING ALL OF THESE ...UGH.
MEANWHILE, I'LL TAKE A LOOK AT THE EFFECTS OF THE SKILLS AND TITLES I ACQUIRED.
FIRST OF ALL, WHAT'S THIS "DEMON LORD" THING?
<Demon Lord>
Increases each stat by the number of the skill level times 100. Additionally, raises all resistances.
POOON (POP)
WHOA... THAT'S A PRETTY CRAZY SKILL.
QUITE DEMONIC, I'D SAY!
NEXT, THE TITLES.
I THINK I GOT "WYRM SLAYER" AFTER BEATING THE EELS...
ZAKU (SHIK)
ZAKU
<Wyrm Slayer>
Skills: [Life LV 1] [Wyrm Power LV 1]
Acquisition condition: Defeat a certain number of wyrm-type monsters.
Effect: Slight increase in damage to wyrm and dragon-type opponents.
A title awarded to those who bring down a large amount of wyrms.
POPOOON
<Fearbringer>
Skills: [Intimidation LV 1] [Heretic Attack LV 1]
Acquisition condition: Induce a certain amount of proficiency in [Fear Resistance] in others.
Effect: Inflicts the Heresy-attribute effect [Fear] on anyone who sees the holder.
A title awarded to those who personify fear.

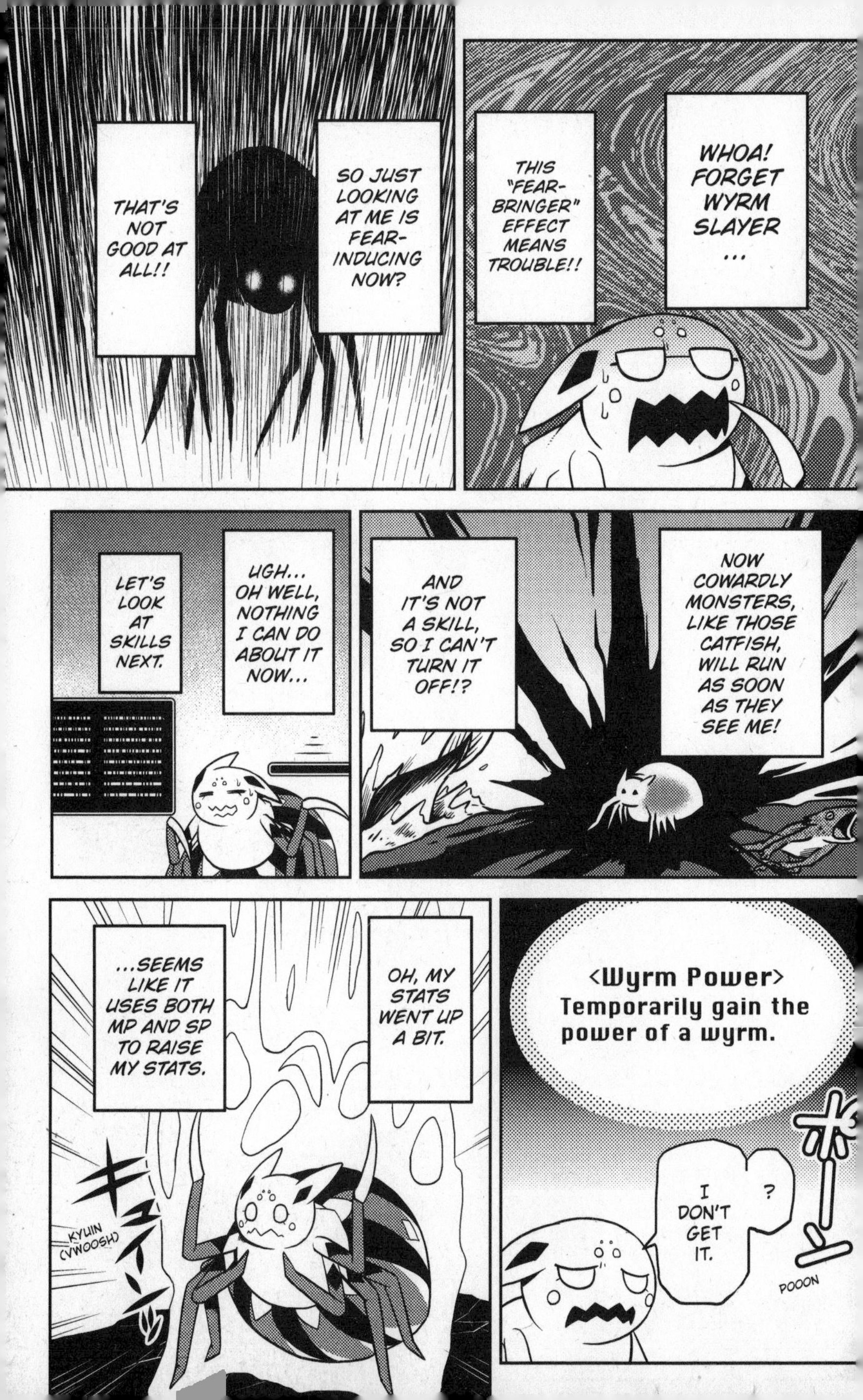
WHOA! FORGET WYRM SLAYER ...
THIS "FEAR-BRINGER" EFFECT MEANS TROUBLE!!
SO JUST LOOKING AT ME IS FEAR-INDUCING NOW?
THAT'S NOT GOOD AT ALL!!
NOW COWARDLY MONSTERS, LIKE THOSE CATFISH, WILL RUN AS SOON AS THEY SEE ME!
AND IT'S NOT A SKILL, SO I CAN'T TURN IT OFF!?
UGH... OH WELL, NOTHING I CAN DO ABOUT IT NOW...
LET'S LOOK AT SKILLS NEXT.
<Wyrm Power> Temporarily gain the power of a wyrm.
I DON'T GET IT. ?
POOON
OH, MY STATS WENT UP A BIT.
...SEEMS LIKE IT USES BOTH MP AND SP TO RAISE MY STATS.
KYUIN (VWOOSH)

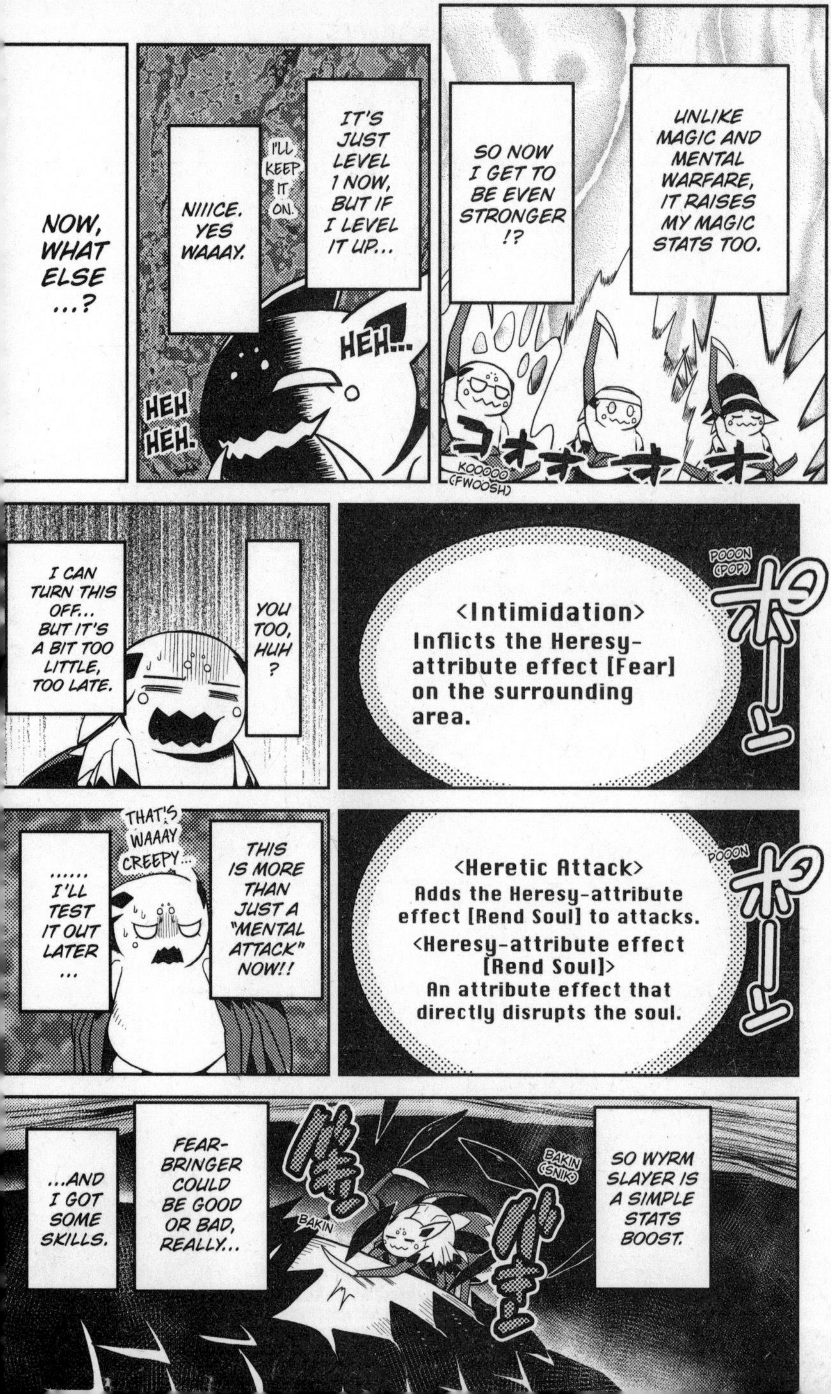
UNLIKE MAGIC AND MENTAL WARFARE, IT RAISES MY MAGIC STATS TOO.
SO NOW I GET TO BE EVEN STRONGER!?
KOOOOO (FWOOSH)
IT'S JUST LEVEL 1 NOW, BUT IF I LEVEL IT UP...
HEH...
I'LL KEEP IT ON.
NIIICE. YES WAAAY.
HEH HEH.
NOW, WHAT ELSE...?
POOON (POP)
<Intimidation>
Inflicts the Heresy-attribute effect [Fear] on the surrounding area.
YOU TOO, HUH?
I CAN TURN THIS OFF... BUT IT'S A BIT TOO LITTLE, TOO LATE.
POOON
<Heretic Attack>
Adds the Heresy-attribute effect [Rend Soul] to attacks.
<Heresy-attribute effect [Rend Soul]>
An attribute effect that directly disrupts the soul.
THIS IS MORE THAN JUST A "MENTAL ATTACK" NOW!!
THAT'S WAAAY CREEPY...
......I'LL TEST IT OUT LATER...
SO WYRM SLAYER IS A SIMPLE STATS BOOST.
BAKIN (SNIK)
BAKIN
FEAR-BRINGER COULD BE GOOD OR BAD, REALLY...
...AND I GOT SOME SKILLS.

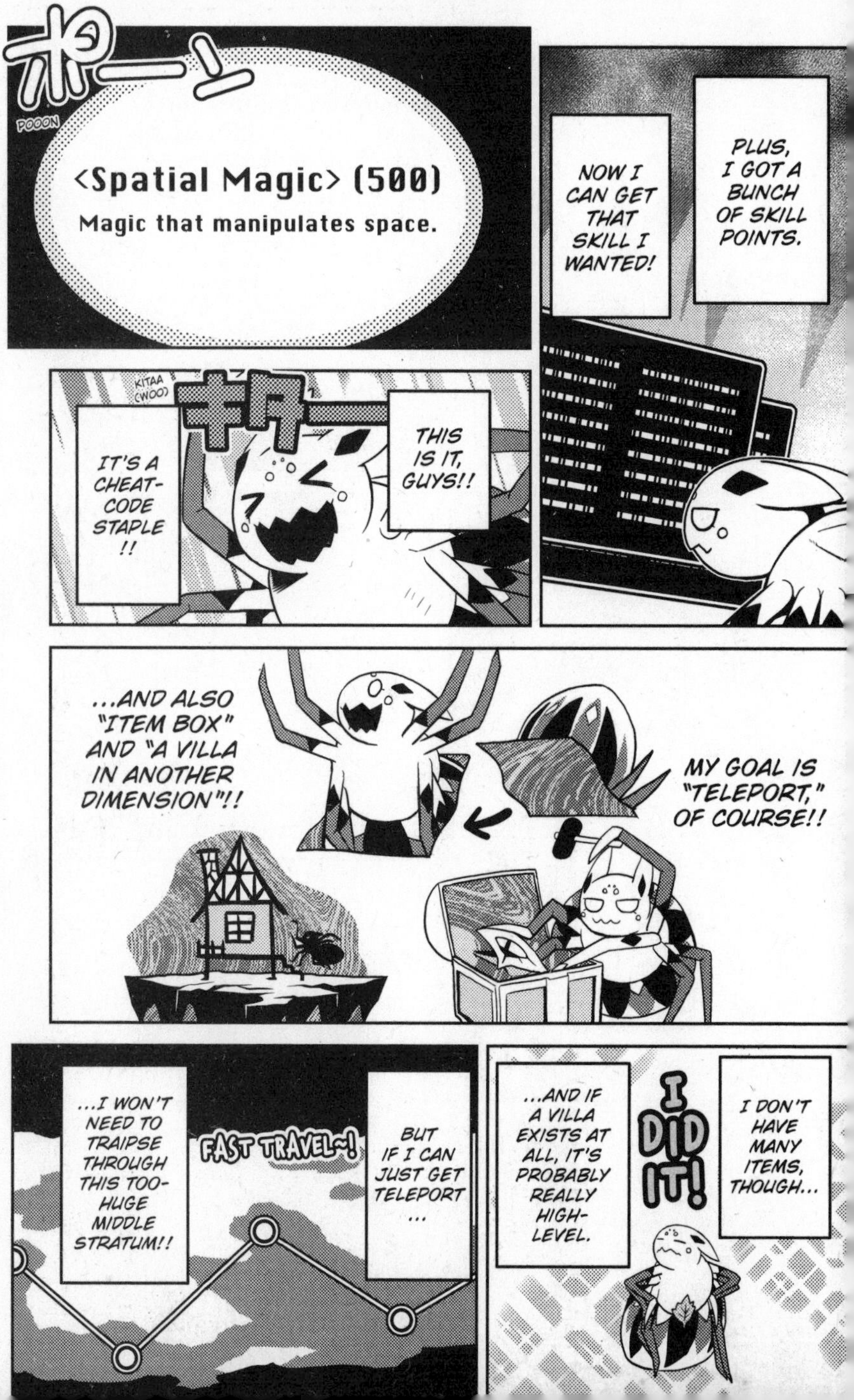
PLUS, I GOT A BUNCH OF SKILL POINTS.
NOW I CAN GET THAT SKILL I WANTED!
POOON
<Spatial Magic> (500)
Magic that manipulates space.
THIS IS IT, GUYS!!
KITAA (WOO)
IT'S A CHEAT-CODE STAPLE!!
MY GOAL IS "TELEPORT," OF COURSE!!
...AND ALSO "ITEM BOX" AND "A VILLA IN ANOTHER DIMENSION"!!
I DON'T HAVE MANY ITEMS, THOUGH...
I DID IT!
...AND IF A VILLA EXISTS AT ALL, IT'S PROBABLY REALLY HIGH-LEVEL.
BUT IF I CAN JUST GET TELEPORT...
FAST TRAVEL~!
...I WON'T NEED TO TRAIPSE THROUGH THIS TOO-HUGE MIDDLE STRATUM!!

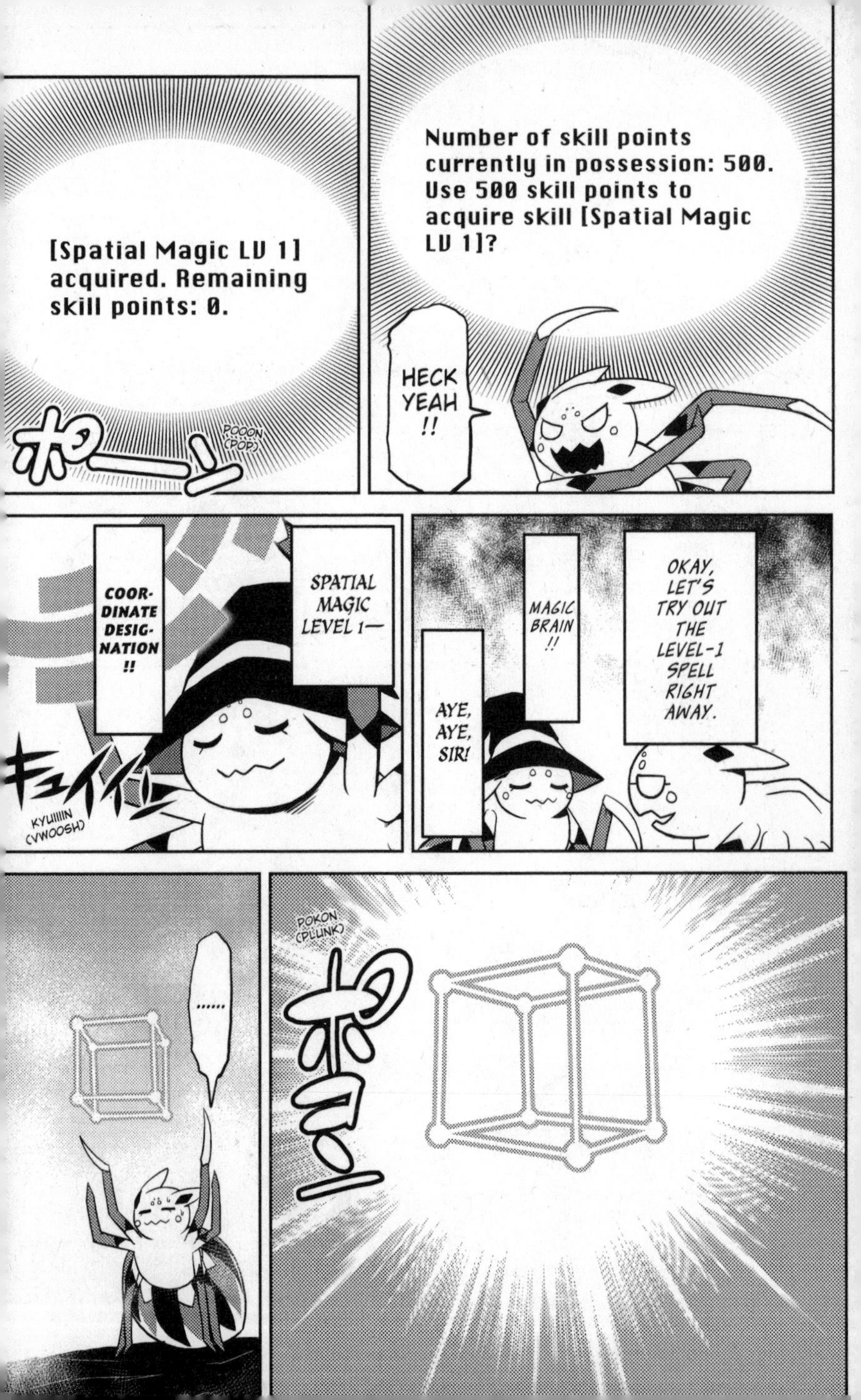
Number of skill points currently in possession: 500. Use 500 skill points to acquire skill [Spatial Magic LV 1]?
HECK YEAH !!
[Spatial Magic LV 1] acquired. Remaining skill points: 0.
POOON (POP)
OKAY, LET'S TRY OUT THE LEVEL-1 SPELL RIGHT AWAY.
MAGIC BRAIN !!
AYE, AYE, SIR!
SPATIAL MAGIC LEVEL 1—
COOR-DINATE DESIG-NATION !!
KYUIIIIN (VWOOSH)
POKON (PLUNK)
......

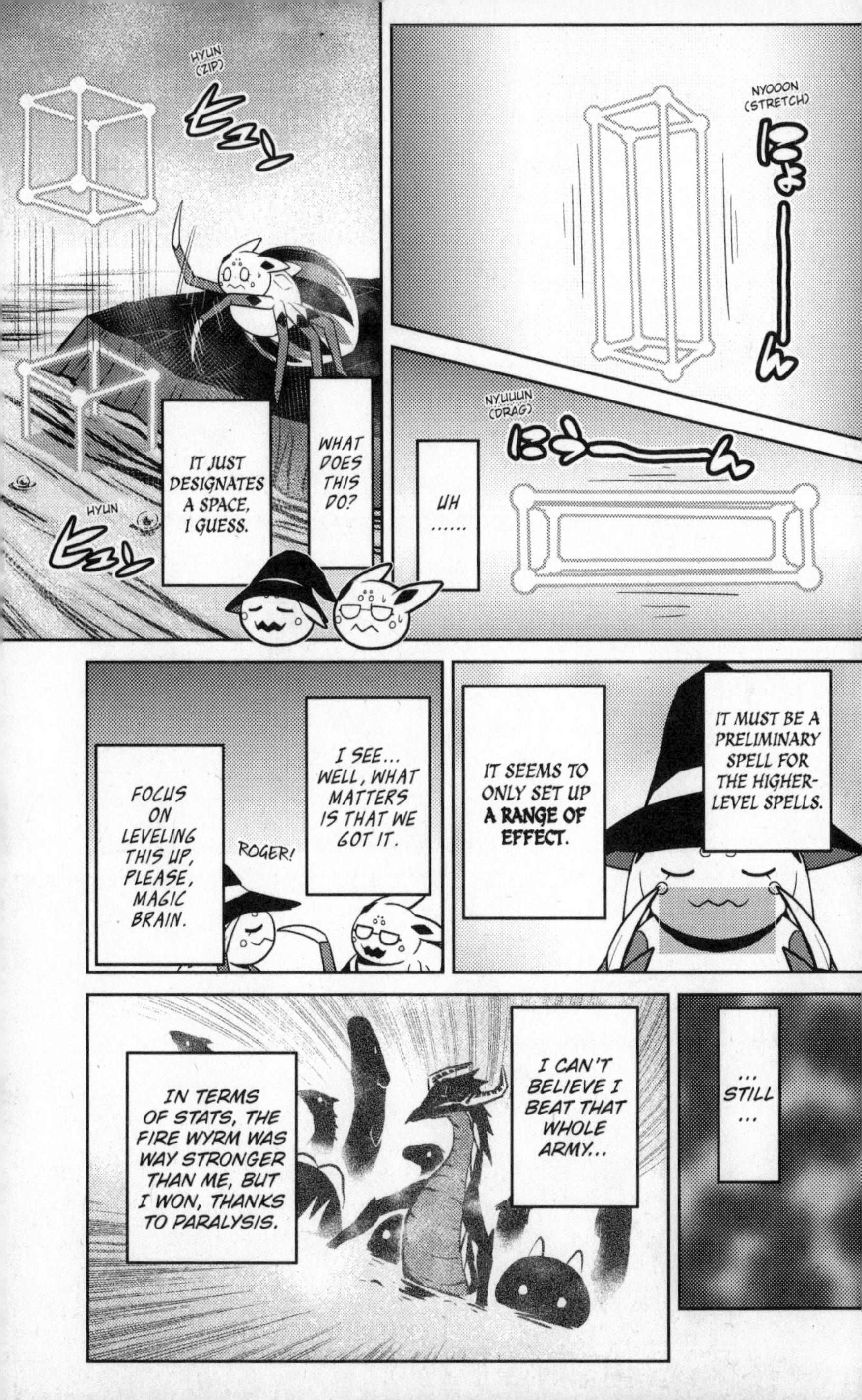
NYOOON (STRETCH)
NYUUUN (DRAG)
UH ......
HYUN (ZIP)
WHAT DOES THIS DO?
IT JUST DESIGNATES A SPACE, I GUESS.
HYUN
IT MUST BE A PRELIMINARY SPELL FOR THE HIGHER-LEVEL SPELLS.
IT SEEMS TO ONLY SET UP A RANGE OF EFFECT.
I SEE... WELL, WHAT MATTERS IS THAT WE GOT IT.
ROGER!
FOCUS ON LEVELING THIS UP, PLEASE, MAGIC BRAIN.
... STILL ...
I CAN'T BELIEVE I BEAT THAT WHOLE ARMY...
IN TERMS OF STATS, THE FIRE WYRM WAS WAY STRONGER THAN ME, BUT I WON, THANKS TO PARALYSIS.

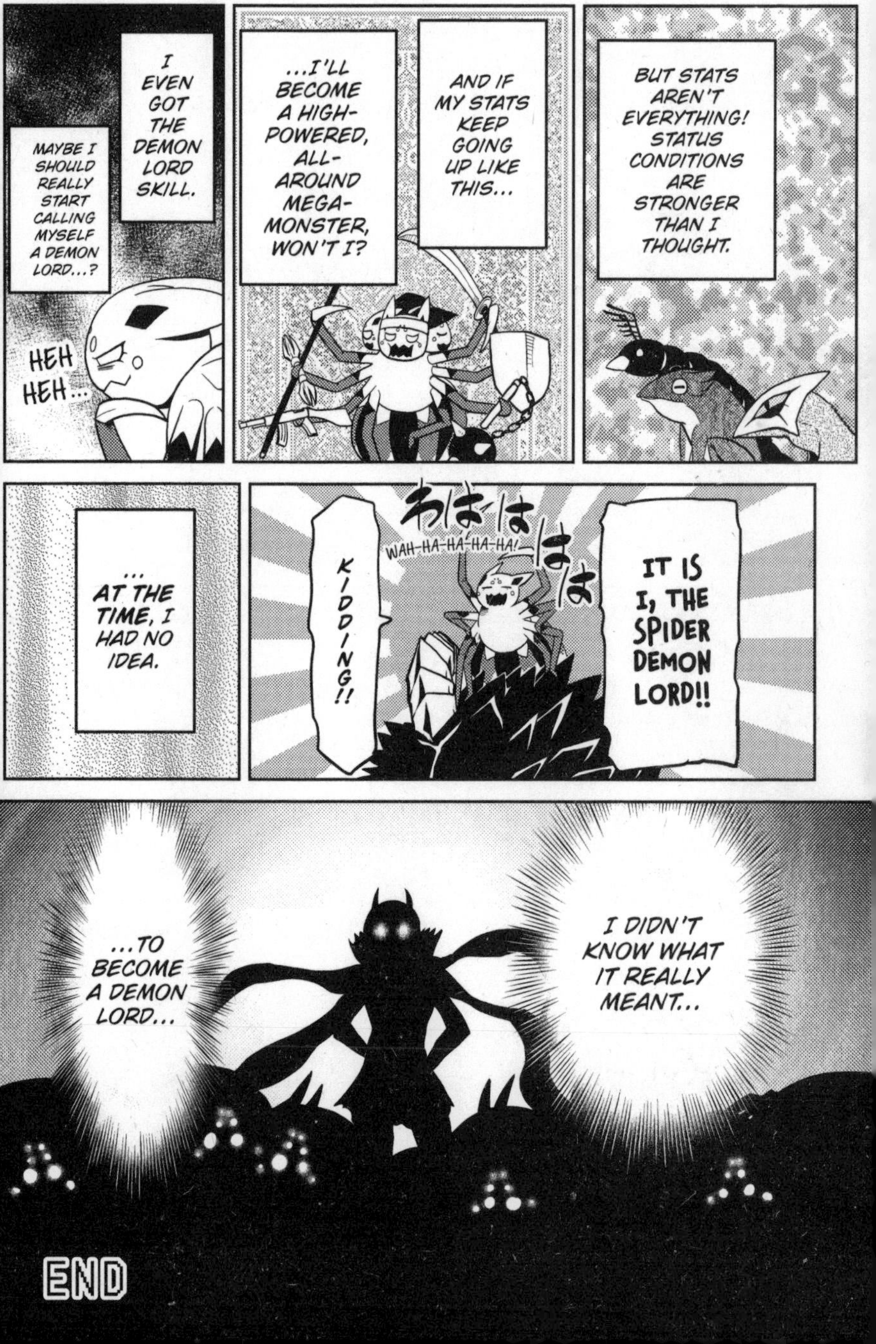
BUT STATS AREN'T EVERYTHING! STATUS CONDITIONS ARE STRONGER THAN I THOUGHT.
AND IF MY STATS KEEP GOING UP LIKE THIS...
...I'LL BECOME A HIGH-POWERED, ALL-AROUND MEGA-MONSTER, WON'T I?
I EVEN GOT THE DEMON LORD SKILL.
MAYBE I SHOULD REALLY START CALLING MYSELF A DEMON LORD...?
HEH HEH...
IT IS I, THE SPIDER DEMON LORD!!
わばははは
WAH-HA-HA-HA-HA!
KIDDING!!
... AT THE TIME, I HAD NO IDEA.
I DIDN'T KNOW WHAT IT REALLY MEANT...
...TO BECOME A DEMON LORD...
END

So I'm a Spider, So What?

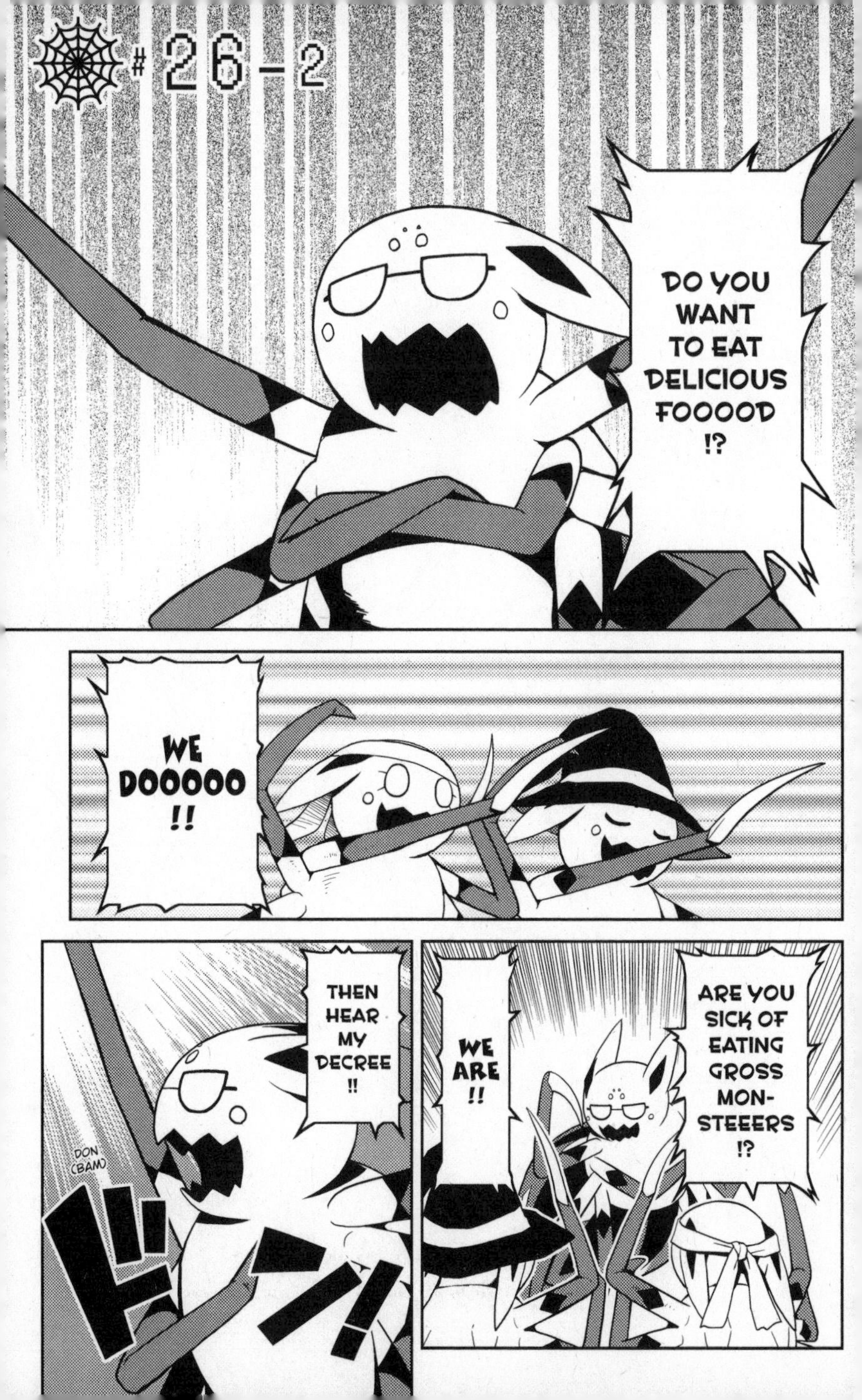
#26-2
DO YOU WANT TO EAT DELICIOUS FOOOOD !?
WE DOOOOO !!
ARE YOU SICK OF EATING GROSS MON-STEEERS !?
WE ARE !!
THEN HEAR MY DECREE !!
DON (BAM)

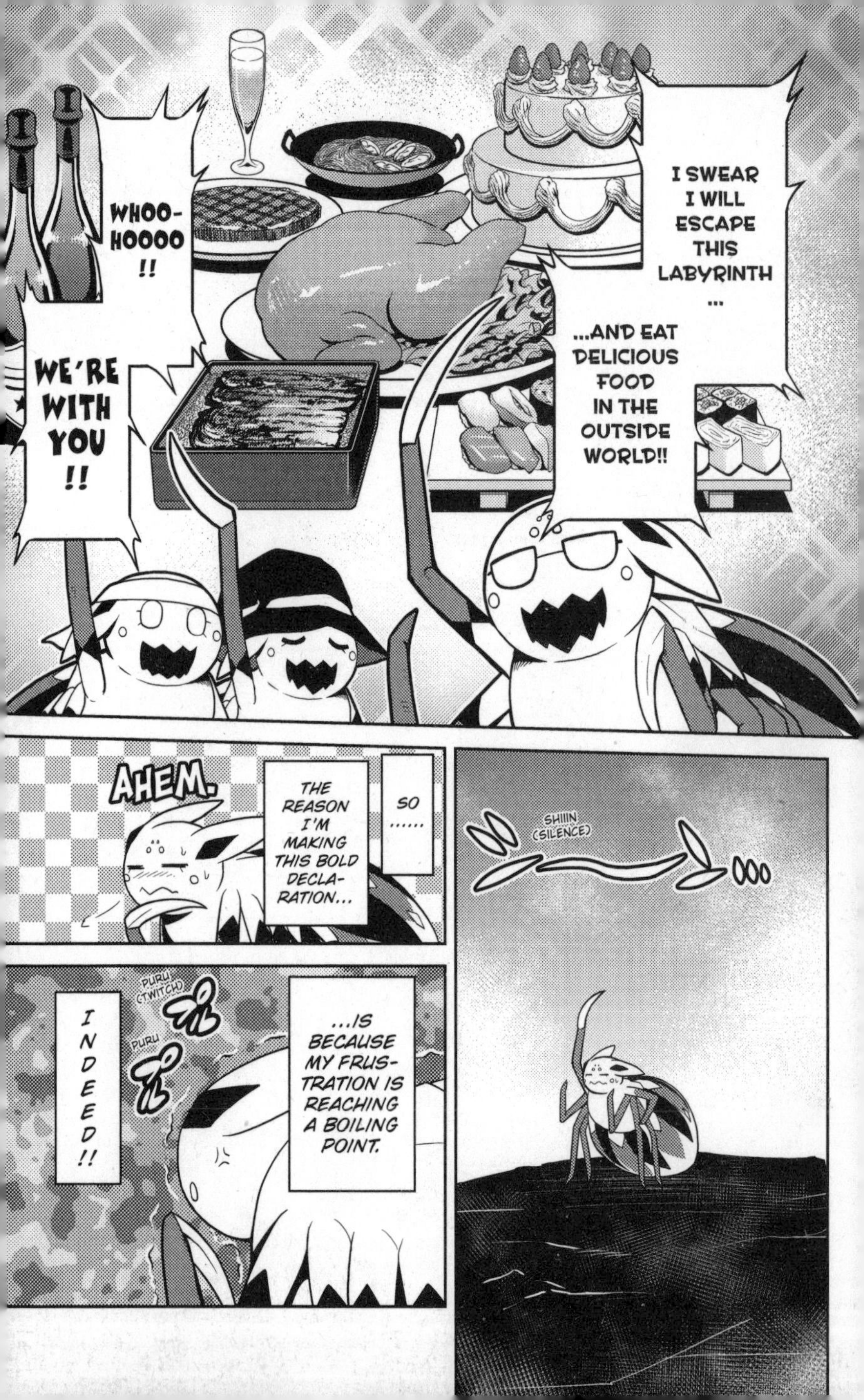
I SWEAR I WILL ESCAPE THIS LABYRINTH ...
...AND EAT DELICIOUS FOOD IN THE OUTSIDE WORLD!!
WHOO-HOOOO!!
WE'RE WITH YOU!!
SHIIIN (SILENCE)
SO......
THE REASON I'M MAKING THIS BOLD DECLA-RATION...
AHEM.
...IS BECAUSE MY FRUS-TRATION IS REACHING A BOILING POINT.
PURU (TWITCH)
PURU
INDEED!!

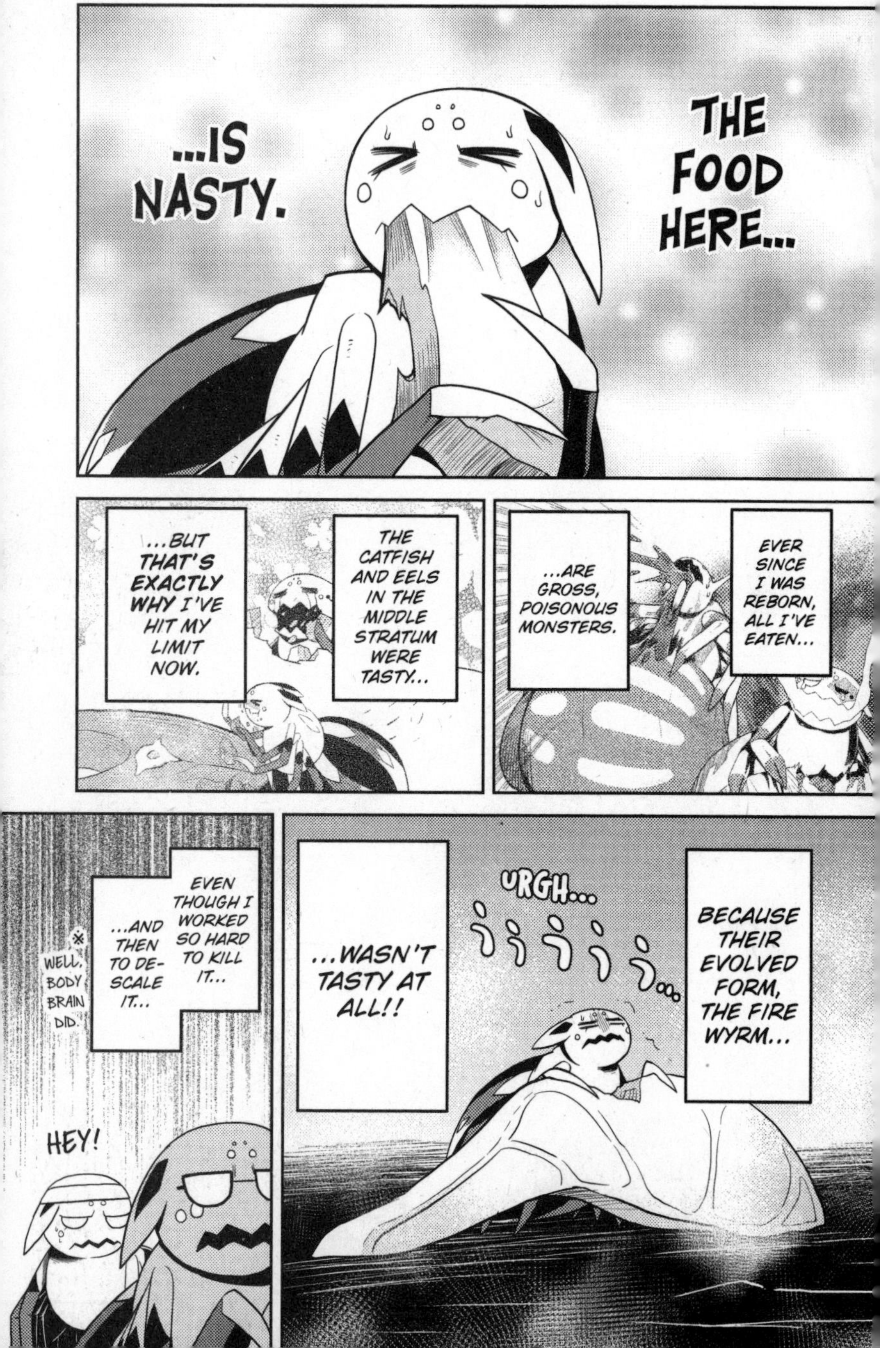
THE FOOD HERE...
...IS NASTY.
EVER SINCE I WAS REBORN, ALL I'VE EATEN...
...ARE GROSS, POISONOUS MONSTERS.
THE CATFISH AND EELS IN THE MIDDLE STRATUM WERE TASTY...
...BUT THAT'S EXACTLY WHY I'VE HIT MY LIMIT NOW.
BECAUSE THEIR EVOLVED FORM, THE FIRE WYRM...
URGH...
...WASN'T TASTY AT ALL!!
EVEN THOUGH I WORKED SO HARD TO KILL IT...
...AND THEN TO DE-SCALE IT...
※WELL, BODY BRAIN DID.
HEY!

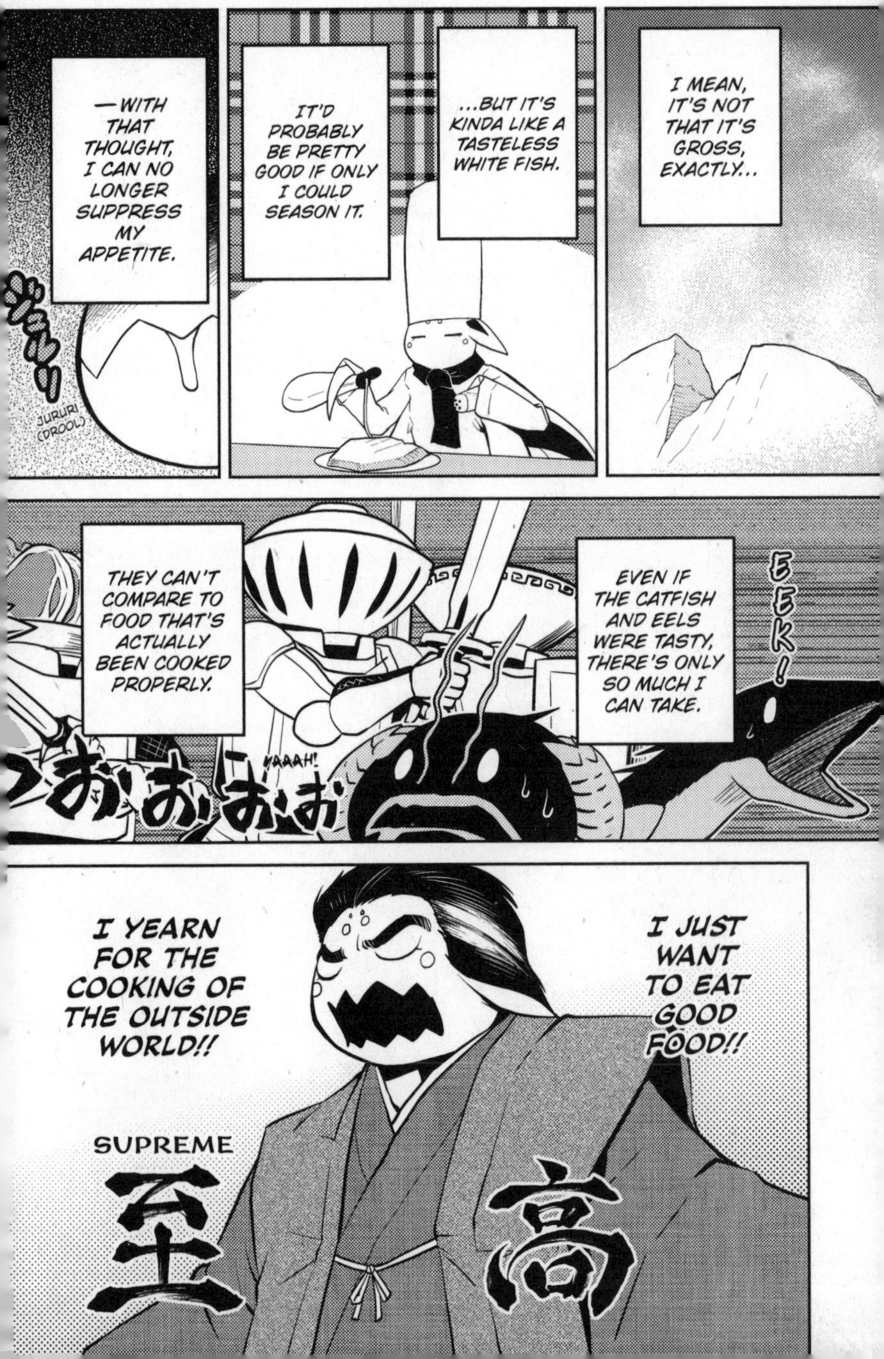
I MEAN, IT'S NOT THAT IT'S GROSS, EXACTLY...
...BUT IT'S KINDA LIKE A TASTELESS WHITE FISH.
IT'D PROBABLY BE PRETTY GOOD IF ONLY I COULD SEASON IT.
—WITH THAT THOUGHT, I CAN NO LONGER SUPPRESS MY APPETITE.
JURURI (DROOL)
EEK!
EVEN IF THE CATFISH AND EELS WERE TASTY, THERE'S ONLY SO MUCH I CAN TAKE.
THEY CAN'T COMPARE TO FOOD THAT'S ACTUALLY BEEN COOKED PROPERLY.
YAAAH!
I JUST WANT TO EAT GOOD FOOD!!
I YEARN FOR THE COOKING OF THE OUTSIDE WORLD!!
至高
SUPREME

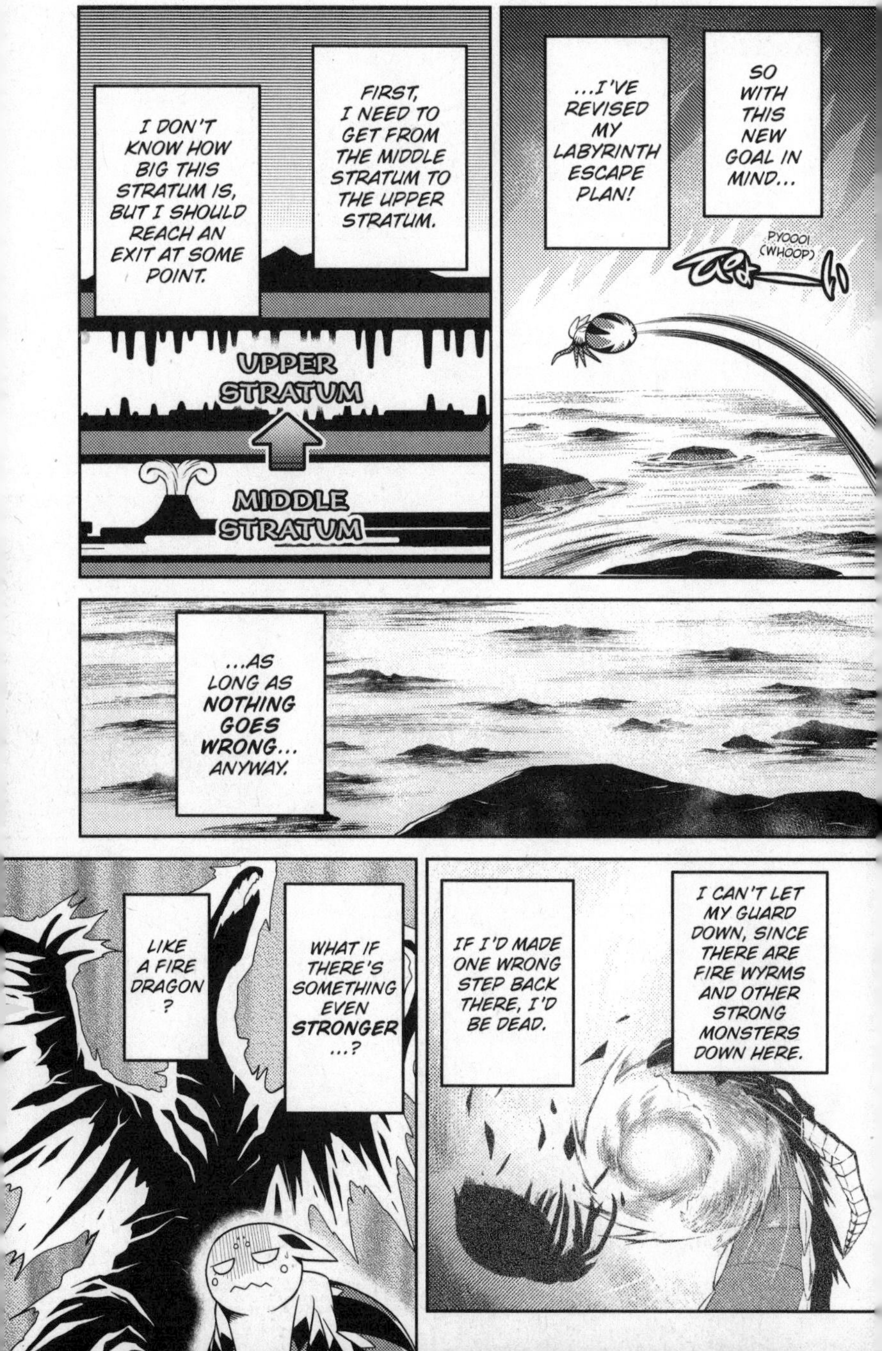
SO WITH THIS NEW GOAL IN MIND...
...I'VE REVISED MY LABYRINTH ESCAPE PLAN!
PYOOO! (WHOOP)
FIRST, I NEED TO GET FROM THE MIDDLE STRATUM TO THE UPPER STRATUM.
I DON'T KNOW HOW BIG THIS STRATUM IS, BUT I SHOULD REACH AN EXIT AT SOME POINT.
UPPER STRATUM
MIDDLE STRATUM
...AS LONG AS NOTHING GOES WRONG... ANYWAY.
I CAN'T LET MY GUARD DOWN, SINCE THERE ARE FIRE WYRMS AND OTHER STRONG MONSTERS DOWN HERE.
IF I'D MADE ONE WRONG STEP BACK THERE, I'D BE DEAD.
WHAT IF THERE'S SOMETHING EVEN STRONGER ...?
LIKE A FIRE DRAGON ?

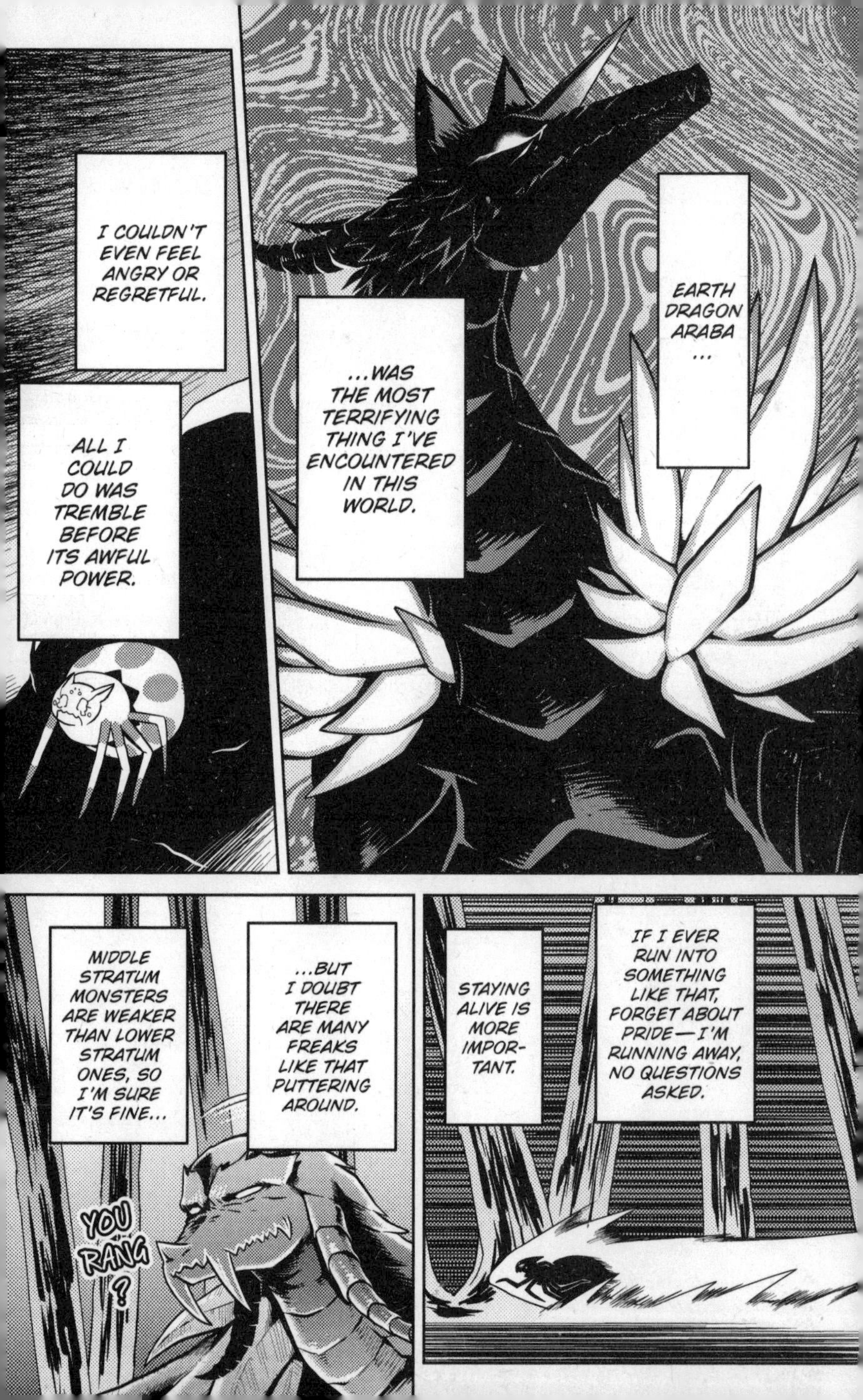
EARTH DRAGON ARABA...
...WAS THE MOST TERRIFYING THING I'VE ENCOUNTERED IN THIS WORLD.
I COULDN'T EVEN FEEL ANGRY OR REGRETFUL.
ALL I COULD DO WAS TREMBLE BEFORE ITS AWFUL POWER.
IF I EVER RUN INTO SOMETHING LIKE THAT, FORGET ABOUT PRIDE—I'M RUNNING AWAY, NO QUESTIONS ASKED.
STAYING ALIVE IS MORE IMPOR-TANT.
MIDDLE STRATUM MONSTERS ARE WEAKER THAN LOWER STRATUM ONES, SO I'M SURE IT'S FINE...
...BUT I DOUBT THERE ARE MANY FREAKS LIKE THAT PUTTERING AROUND.
YOU RANG?

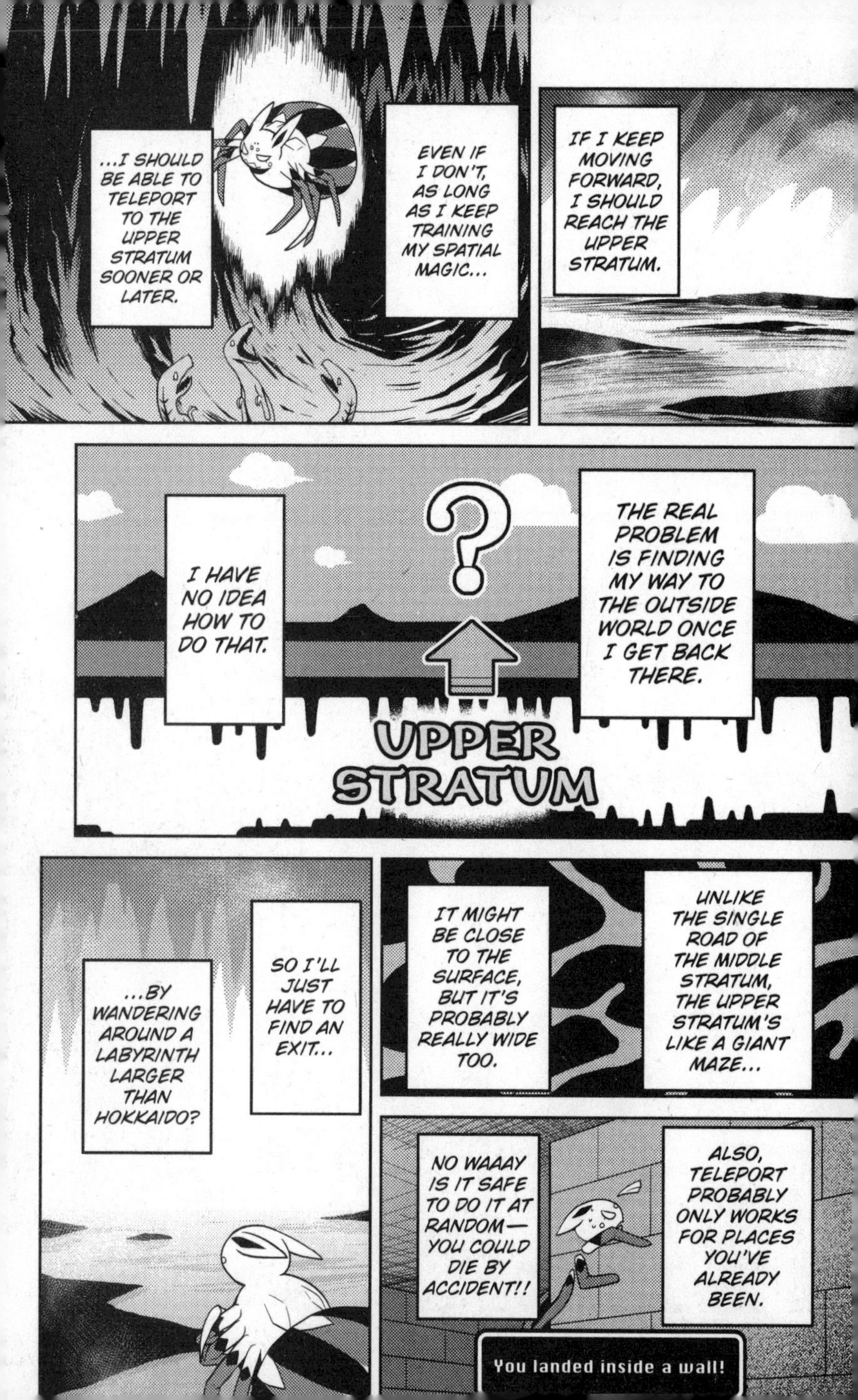
IF I KEEP MOVING FORWARD, I SHOULD REACH THE UPPER STRATUM.
EVEN IF I DON'T, AS LONG AS I KEEP TRAINING MY SPATIAL MAGIC...
...I SHOULD BE ABLE TO TELEPORT TO THE UPPER STRATUM SOONER OR LATER.
THE REAL PROBLEM IS FINDING MY WAY TO THE OUTSIDE WORLD ONCE I GET BACK THERE.
?
UPPER STRATUM
I HAVE NO IDEA HOW TO DO THAT.
UNLIKE THE SINGLE ROAD OF THE MIDDLE STRATUM, THE UPPER STRATUM'S LIKE A GIANT MAZE...
IT MIGHT BE CLOSE TO THE SURFACE, BUT IT'S PROBABLY REALLY WIDE TOO.
ALSO, TELEPORT PROBABLY ONLY WORKS FOR PLACES YOU'VE ALREADY BEEN.
NO WAAAY IS IT SAFE TO DO IT AT RANDOM—YOU COULD DIE BY ACCIDENT!!
You landed inside a wall!
SO I'LL JUST HAVE TO FIND AN EXIT...
...BY WANDERING AROUND A LABYRINTH LARGER THAN HOKKAIDO?

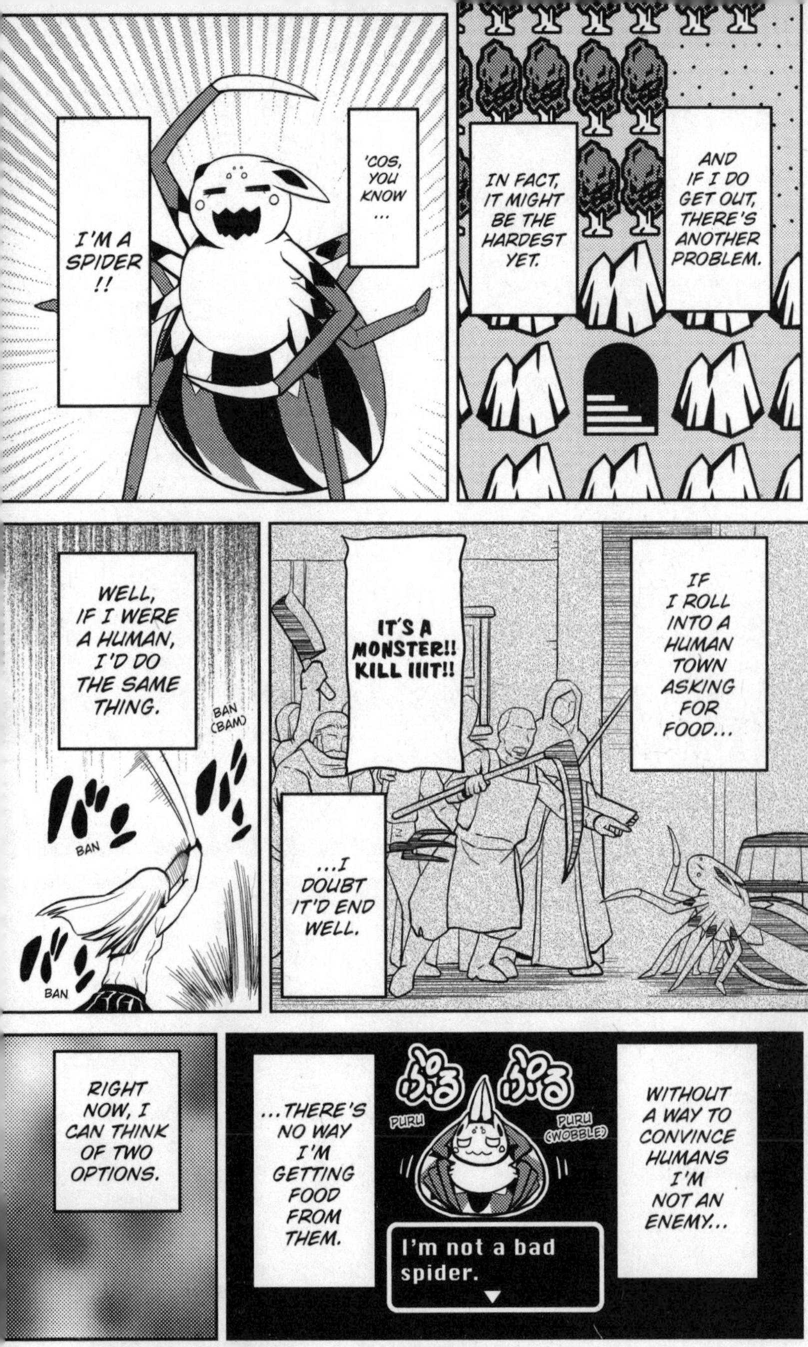
AND IF I DO GET OUT, THERE'S ANOTHER PROBLEM.
IN FACT, IT MIGHT BE THE HARDEST YET.
'COS, YOU KNOW...
I'M A SPIDER!!
IF I ROLL INTO A HUMAN TOWN ASKING FOR FOOD...
IT'S A MONSTER!! KILL IIIT!!
...I DOUBT IT'D END WELL.
WELL, IF I WERE A HUMAN, I'D DO THE SAME THING.
BAN (BAM)
BAN
BAN
WITHOUT A WAY TO CONVINCE HUMANS I'M NOT AN ENEMY...
ぷる ぷる
PURU
PURU (WOBBLE)
I'm not a bad spider.
...THERE'S NO WAY I'M GETTING FOOD FROM THEM.
RIGHT NOW, I CAN THINK OF TWO OPTIONS.

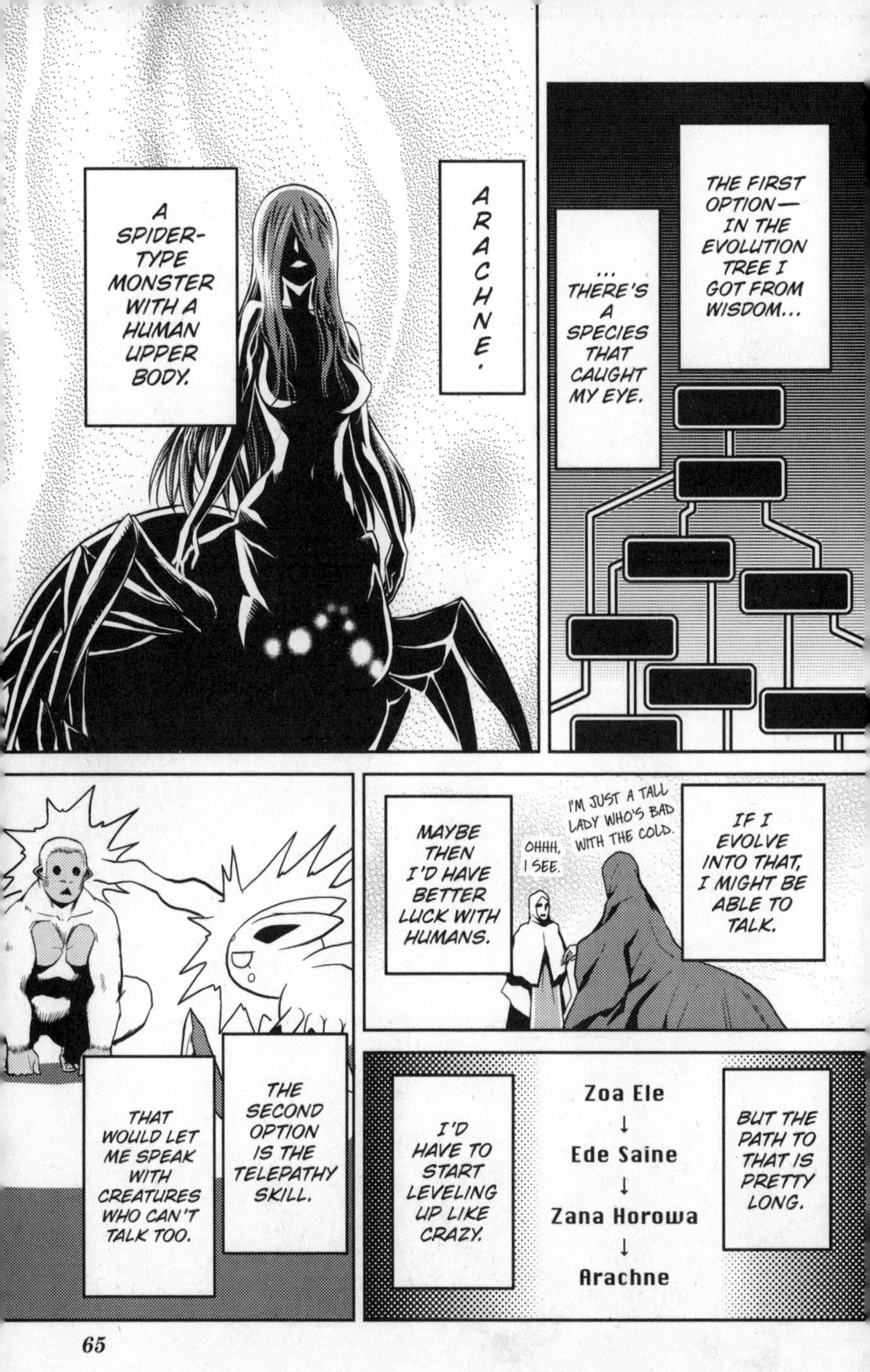
THE FIRST OPTION— IN THE EVOLUTION TREE I GOT FROM WISDOM...
...THERE'S A SPECIES THAT CAUGHT MY EYE.
ARACHNE.
A SPIDER-TYPE MONSTER WITH A HUMAN UPPER BODY.
IF I EVOLVE INTO THAT, I MIGHT BE ABLE TO TALK.
I'M JUST A TALL LADY WHO'S BAD WITH THE COLD.
OHHH, I SEE.
MAYBE THEN I'D HAVE BETTER LUCK WITH HUMANS.
BUT THE PATH TO THAT IS PRETTY LONG.
Zoa Ele
↓
Ede Saine
↓
Zana Horowa
↓
Arachne
I'D HAVE TO START LEVELING UP LIKE CRAZY.
THE SECOND OPTION IS THE TELEPATHY SKILL.
THAT WOULD LET ME SPEAK WITH CREATURES WHO CAN'T TALK TOO.

BE- SIDES...

ZUGYUUN (BANG)

I CAN'T SPARE SKILL POINTS ON TELEPATHIC COMMUNI- CATION.

SURVIVAL IS MY TOP PRIORITY.

WAIT! IF I COULD SPEAK, YOU'D UNDERSTAND.

...BUT I DON'T THINK IT'D BE VERY USEFUL IN COMBAT...

TELEPATHY IS FAIRLY EASY TO GET WITH SKILL POINTS...

...I DON'T SPEAK THIS WORLD'S LANGUAGE !!

JAPAN

...WHETHER I GO FOR BECOMING AN ARACHNE OR GETTING TELEPATHY...

ZAPPAAAN (SPLASH)

I'M REALLY BAD AT TALKING TO PEOPLE.

AND EVEN IF THEY DO—

SAFER TO ASSUME THEY WON'T UNDER- STAND ME.

THE DIVINE VOICE SPEAKS JAPANESE, BUT WHO KNOWS?

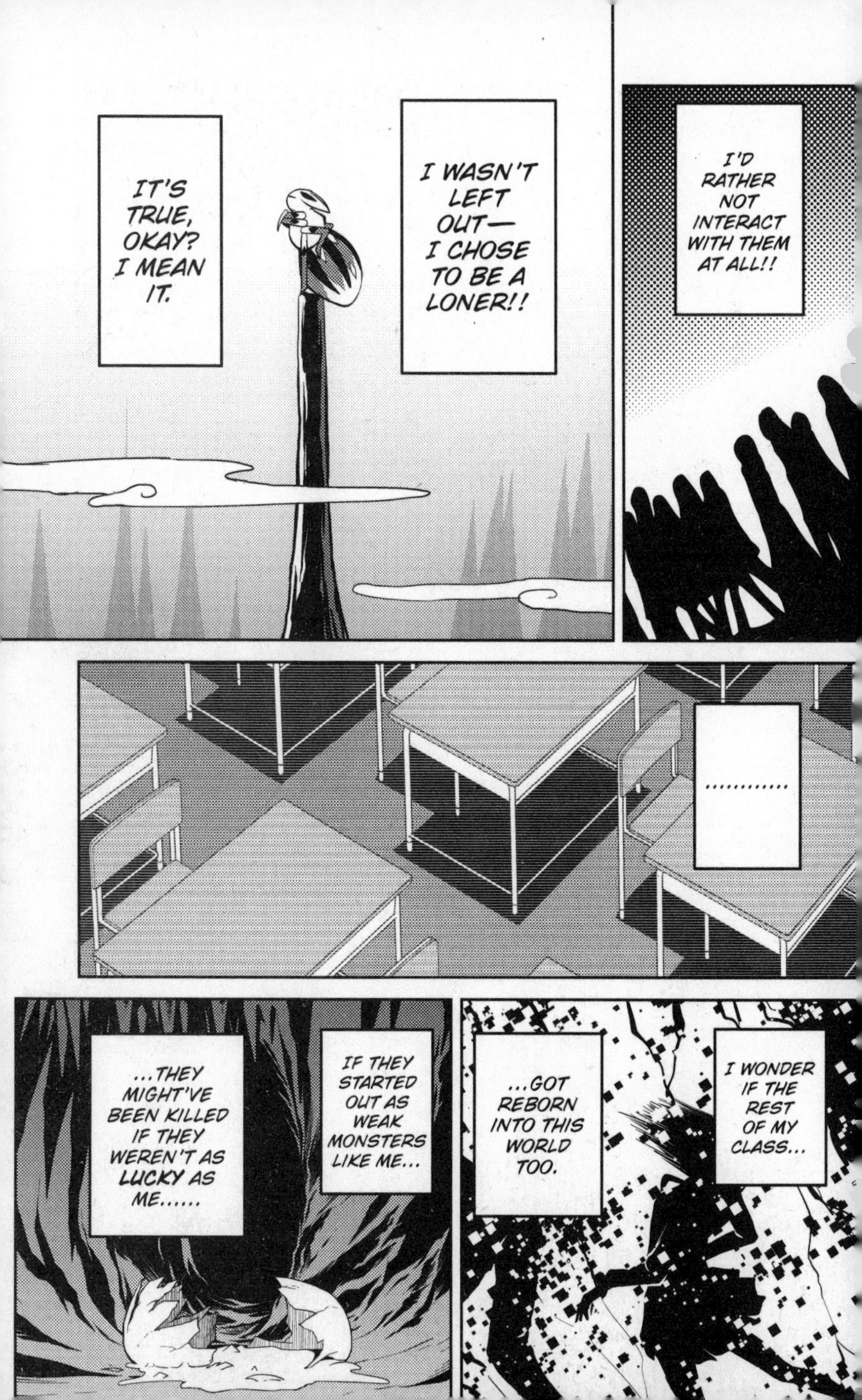
I'D RATHER NOT INTERACT WITH THEM AT ALL!!
I WASN'T LEFT OUT— I CHOSE TO BE A LONER!!
IT'S TRUE, OKAY? I MEAN IT.
....
I WONDER IF THE REST OF MY CLASS...
...GOT REBORN INTO THIS WORLD TOO.
IF THEY STARTED OUT AS WEAK MONSTERS LIKE ME...
...THEY MIGHT'VE BEEN KILLED IF THEY WEREN'T AS **LUCKY** AS ME......

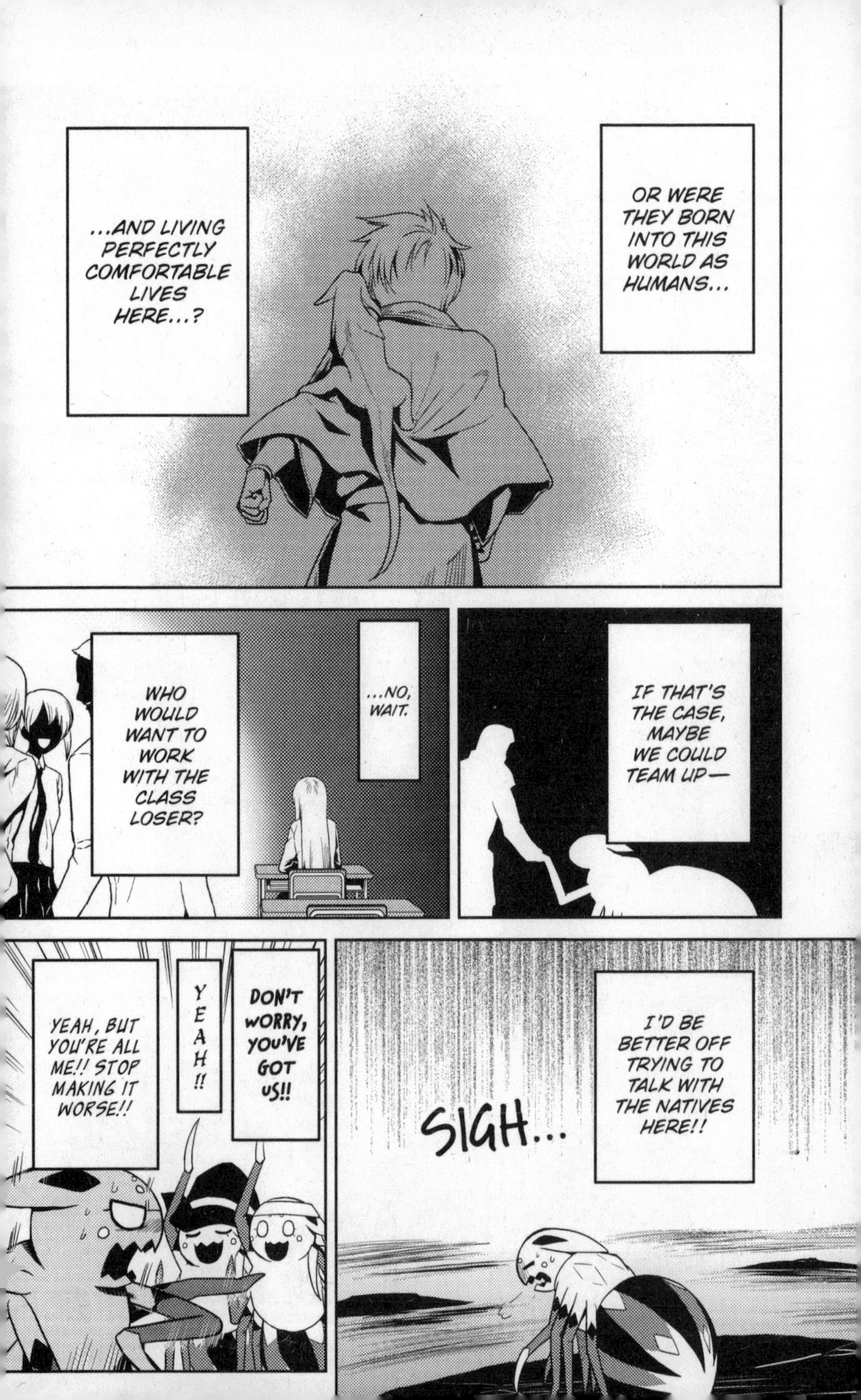
OR WERE THEY BORN INTO THIS WORLD AS HUMANS...
...AND LIVING PERFECTLY COMFORTABLE LIVES HERE...?
IF THAT'S THE CASE, MAYBE WE COULD TEAM UP—
...NO, WAIT.
WHO WOULD WANT TO WORK WITH THE CLASS LOSER?
I'D BE BETTER OFF TRYING TO TALK WITH THE NATIVES HERE!!
SIGH...
DON'T WORRY, YOU'VE GOT US!!
YEAH!!
YEAH, BUT YOU'RE ALL ME!! STOP MAKING IT WORSE!!

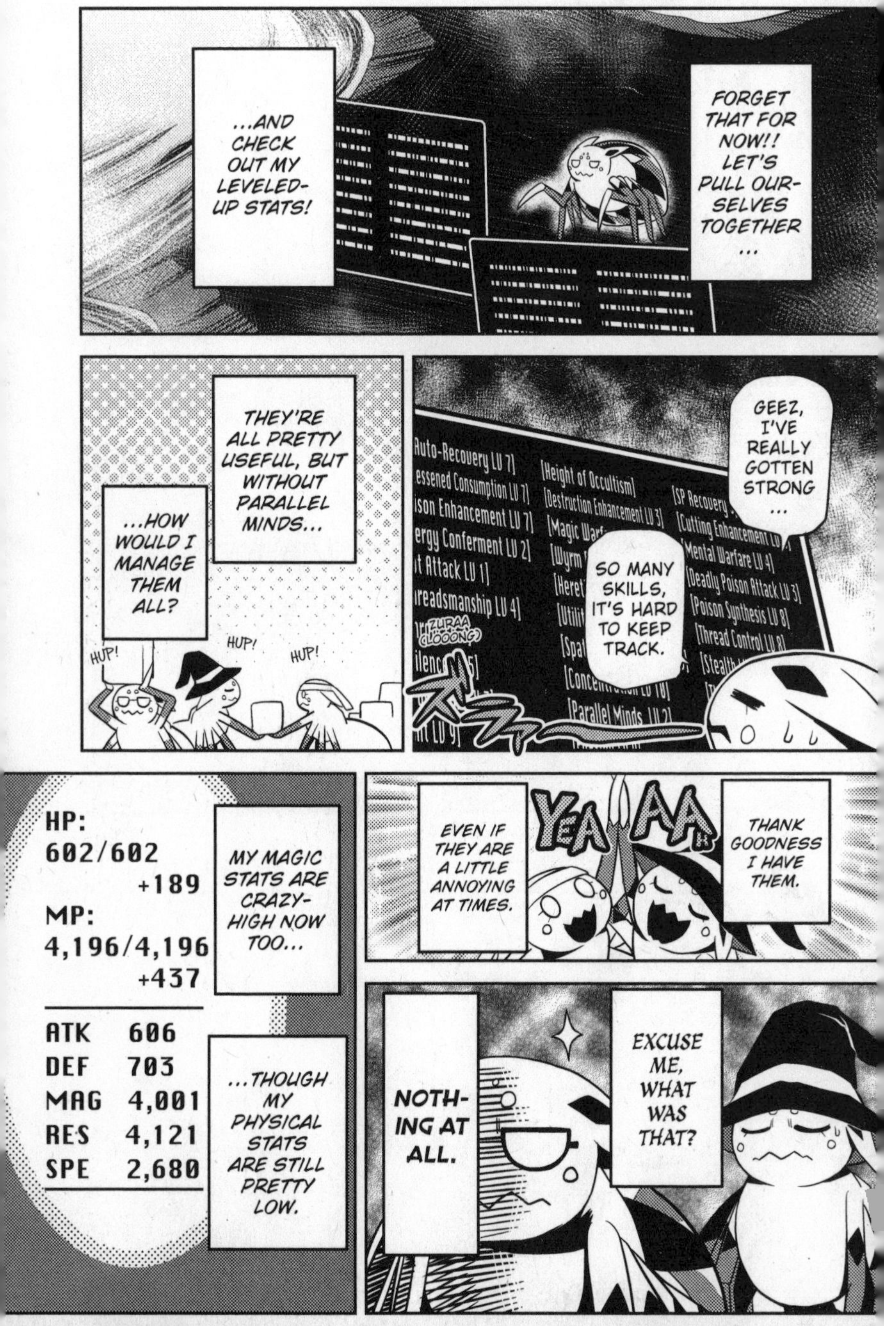
FORGET THAT FOR NOW!! LET'S PULL OURSELVES TOGETHER...
...AND CHECK OUT MY LEVELED-UP STATS!
GEEZ, I'VE REALLY GOTTEN STRONG...
SO MANY SKILLS, IT'S HARD TO KEEP TRACK.
[Height of Occultism]
[Destruction Enhancement LV 3]
[Mental Warfare LV 4]
[Deadly Poison Attack LV 3]
[Poison Synthesis LV 8]
[Thread Control LV 8]
[Parallel Minds LV 2]
ZURAA (LOOONG)
THEY'RE ALL PRETTY USEFUL, BUT WITHOUT PARALLEL MINDS...
...HOW WOULD I MANAGE THEM ALL?
HUP!
HUP!
HUP!
THANK GOODNESS I HAVE THEM.
YEAAA
EVEN IF THEY ARE A LITTLE ANNOYING AT TIMES.
EXCUSE ME, WHAT WAS THAT?
NOTHING AT ALL.
HP: 602/602 +189
MP: 4,196/4,196 +437
ATK 606
DEF 703
MAG 4,001
RES 4,121
SPE 2,680
MY MAGIC STATS ARE CRAZY-HIGH NOW TOO...
...THOUGH MY PHYSICAL STATS ARE STILL PRETTY LOW.

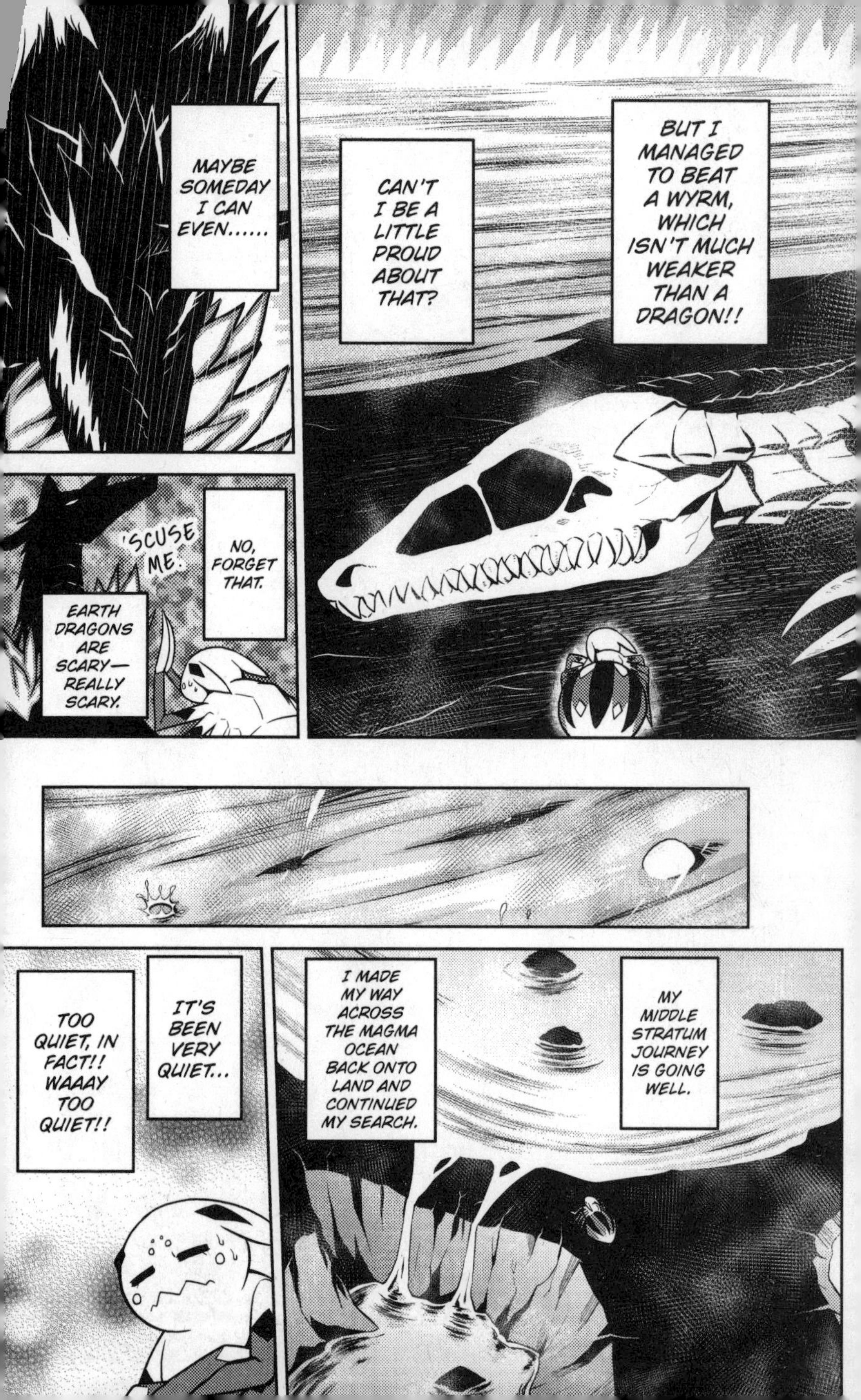
BUT I MANAGED TO BEAT A WYRM, WHICH ISN'T MUCH WEAKER THAN A DRAGON!!
CAN'T I BE A LITTLE PROUD ABOUT THAT?
MAYBE SOMEDAY I CAN EVEN......
NO, FORGET THAT.
'SCUSE ME.
EARTH DRAGONS ARE SCARY— REALLY SCARY.
MY MIDDLE STRATUM JOURNEY IS GOING WELL.
I MADE MY WAY ACROSS THE MAGMA OCEAN BACK ONTO LAND AND CONTINUED MY SEARCH.
IT'S BEEN VERY QUIET...
TOO QUIET, IN FACT!! WAAAY TOO QUIET!!

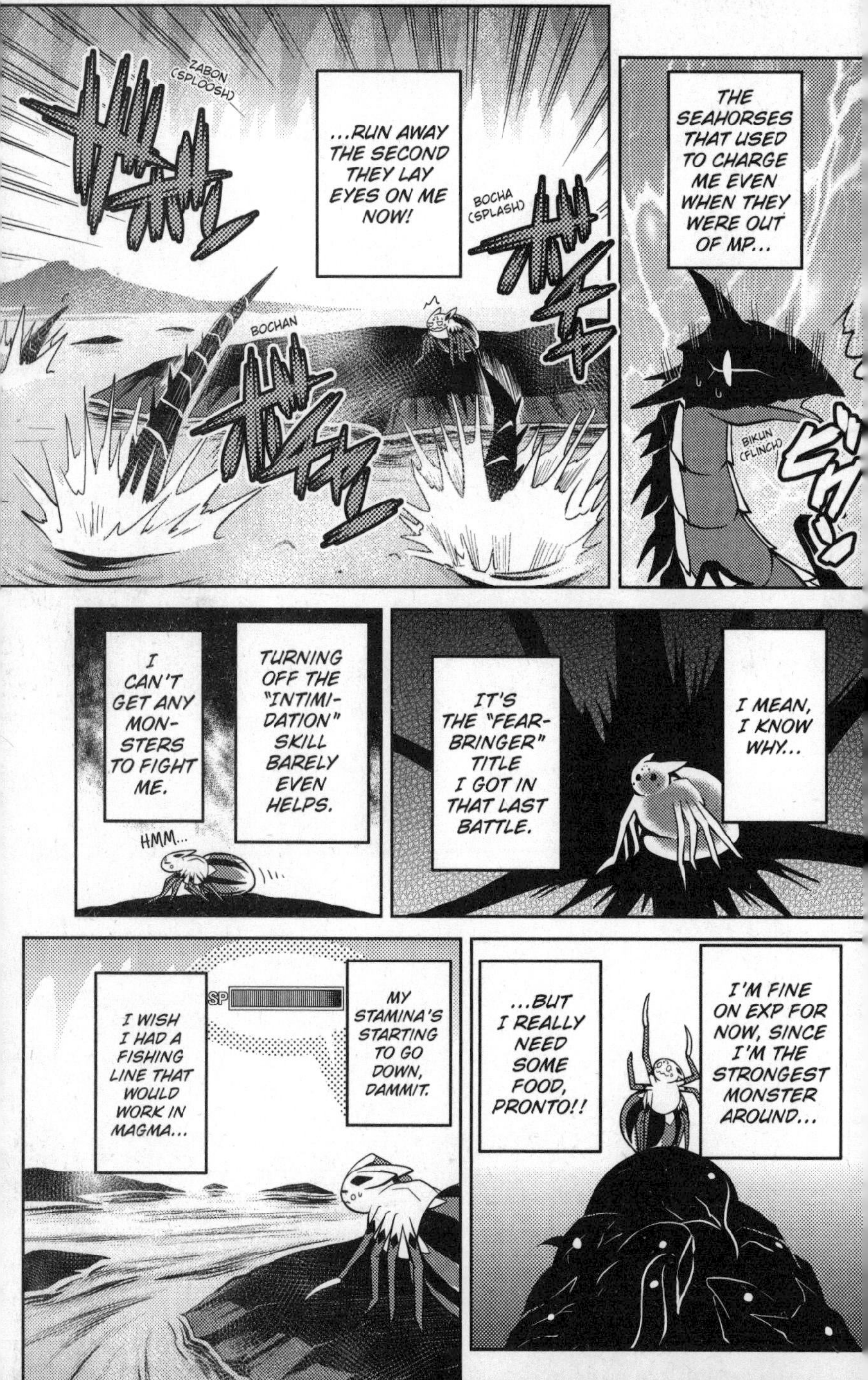
THE SEAHORSES THAT USED TO CHARGE ME EVEN WHEN THEY WERE OUT OF MP...
BIKUN (FLINCH)
...RUN AWAY THE SECOND THEY LAY EYES ON ME NOW!
BOCHA (SPLASH)
ZABON (SPLOOSH)
BOCHAN
I MEAN, I KNOW WHY...
IT'S THE "FEAR-BRINGER" TITLE I GOT IN THAT LAST BATTLE.
TURNING OFF THE "INTIMIDATION" SKILL BARELY EVEN HELPS.
I CAN'T GET ANY MONSTERS TO FIGHT ME.
HMM...
I'M FINE ON EXP FOR NOW, SINCE I'M THE STRONGEST MONSTER AROUND...
...BUT I REALLY NEED SOME FOOD, PRONTO!!
MY STAMINA'S STARTING TO GO DOWN, DAMMIT.
SP
I WISH I HAD A FISHING LINE THAT WOULD WORK IN MAGMA...

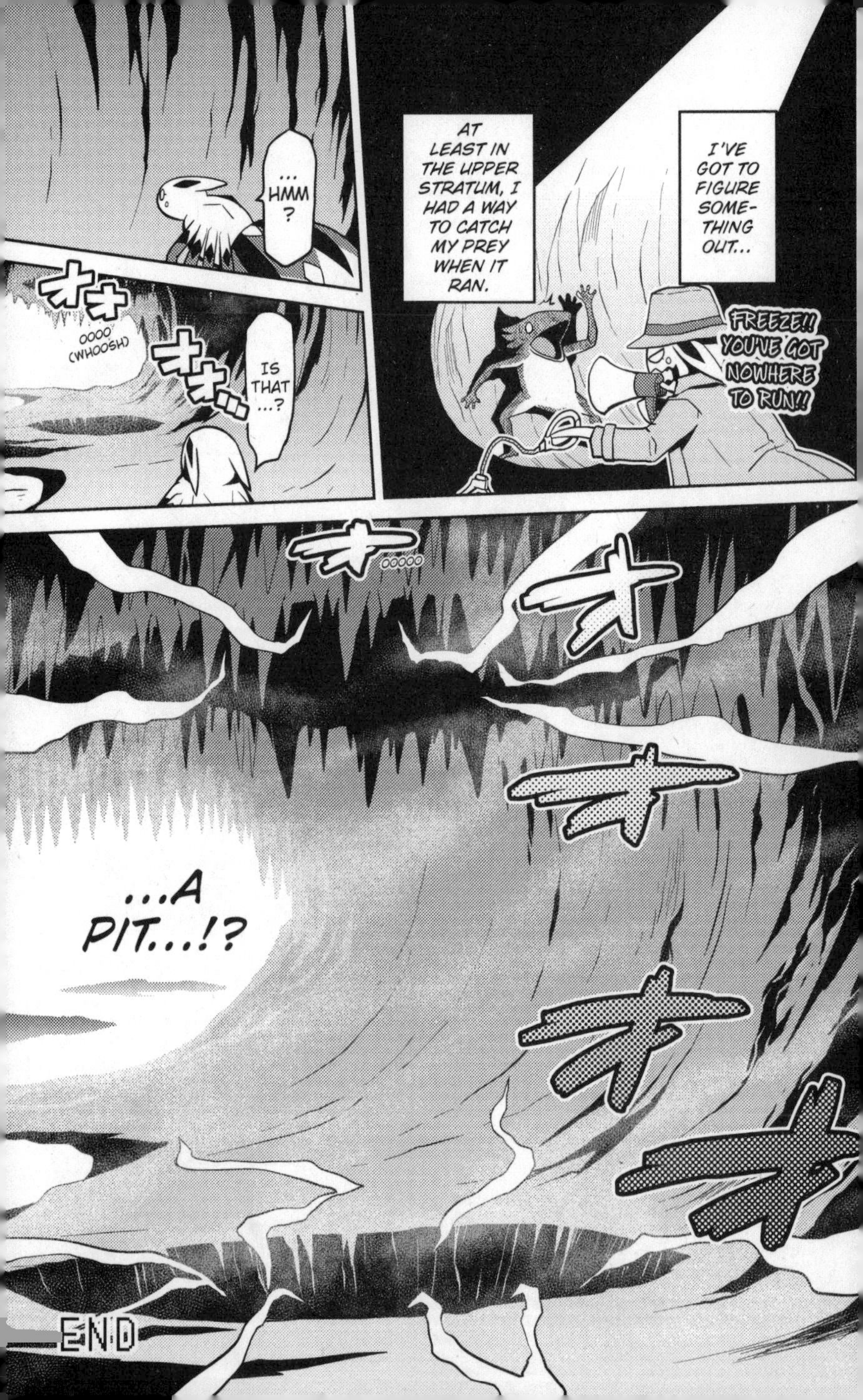

I'VE GOT TO FIGURE SOME-THING OUT...
AT LEAST IN THE UPPER STRATUM, I HAD A WAY TO CATCH MY PREY WHEN IT RAN.
FREEZE!! YOU'VE GOT NOWHERE TO RUN!!
...HMM?
オォ
OOOO (WHOOSH)
オォッ
IS THAT ...?
オ
OOOOO
...A PIT...!?
END

So I'm a Spider, So What?

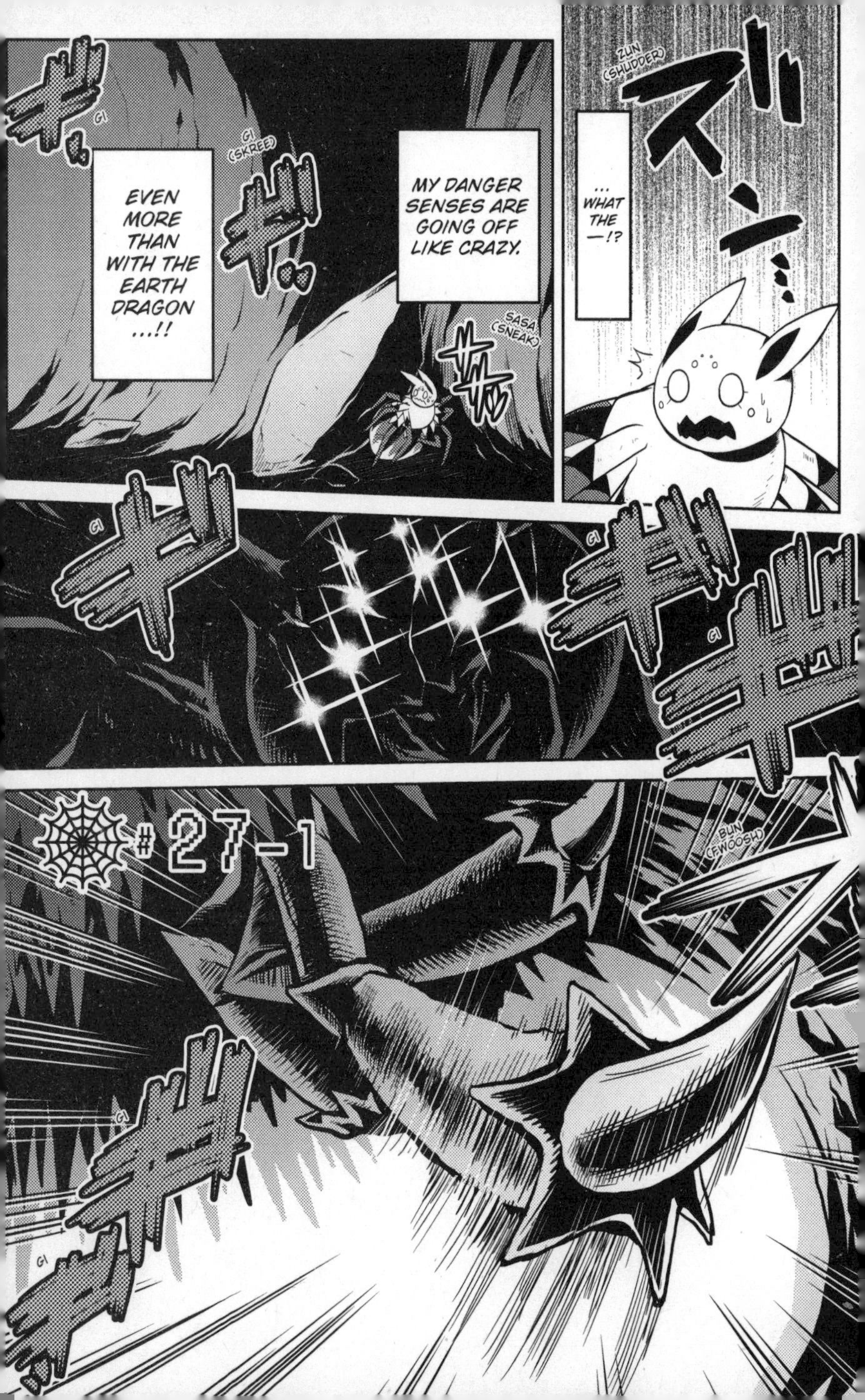
ZUN (SHUDDER)
... WHAT THE—!?
MY DANGER SENSES ARE GOING OFF LIKE CRAZY.
SASA (SNEAK)
GI (SKREE)
EVEN MORE THAN WITH THE EARTH DRAGON ...!!
GI
GI
GI
GI
#27-1
BUN (FWOOSH)
GI
GI

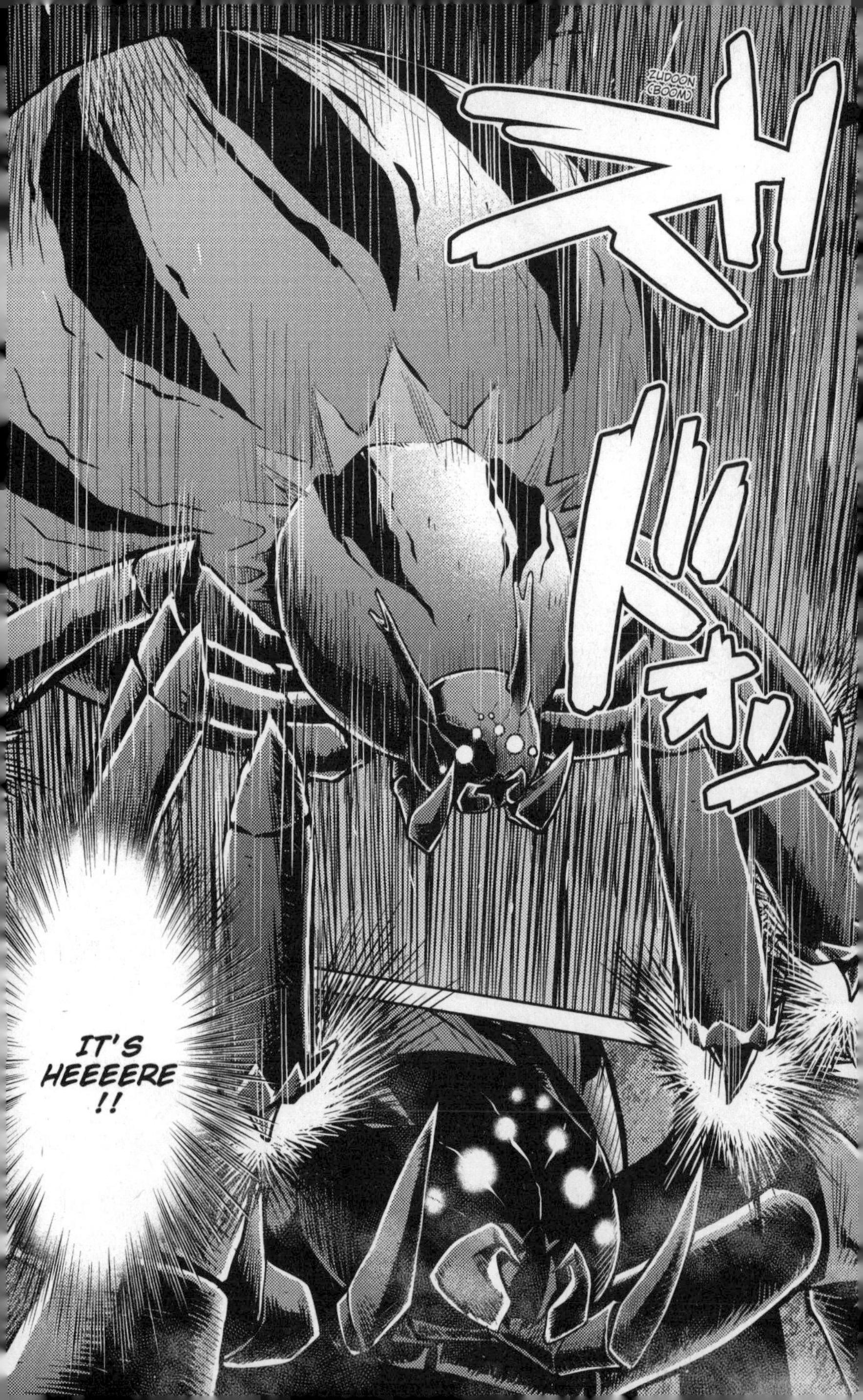
ZUDOON (BOOM)
IT'S HEEEERE !!

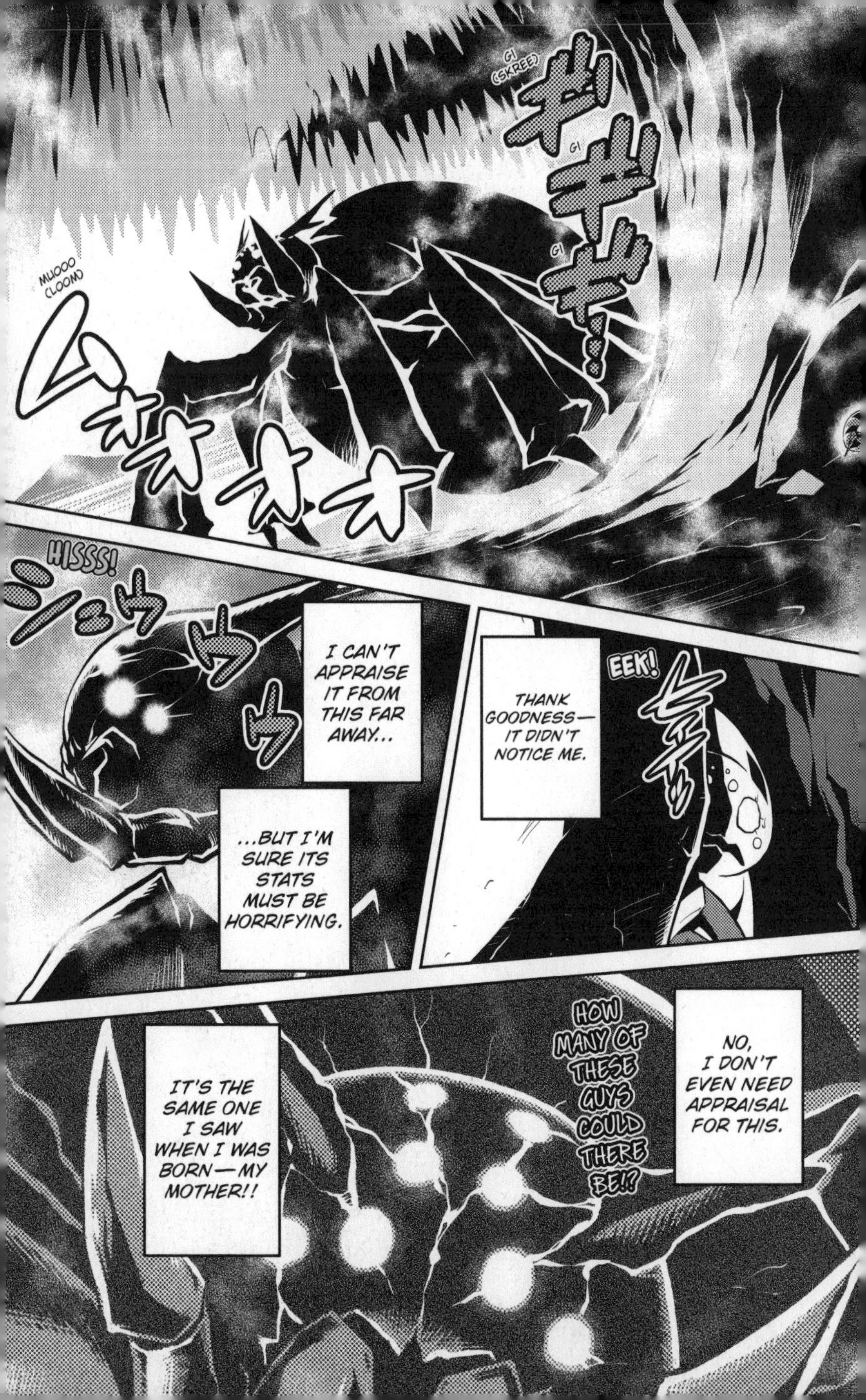
GI (SKREE)
GI
GI
MUOOO (LOOM)
EEK!
THANK GOODNESS—IT DIDN'T NOTICE ME.
HISSS!
I CAN'T APPRAISE IT FROM THIS FAR AWAY...
...BUT I'M SURE ITS STATS MUST BE HORRIFYING.
NO, I DON'T EVEN NEED APPRAISAL FOR THIS.
HOW MANY OF THESE GUYS COULD THERE BE!?
IT'S THE SAME ONE I SAW WHEN I WAS BORN—MY MOTHER!!

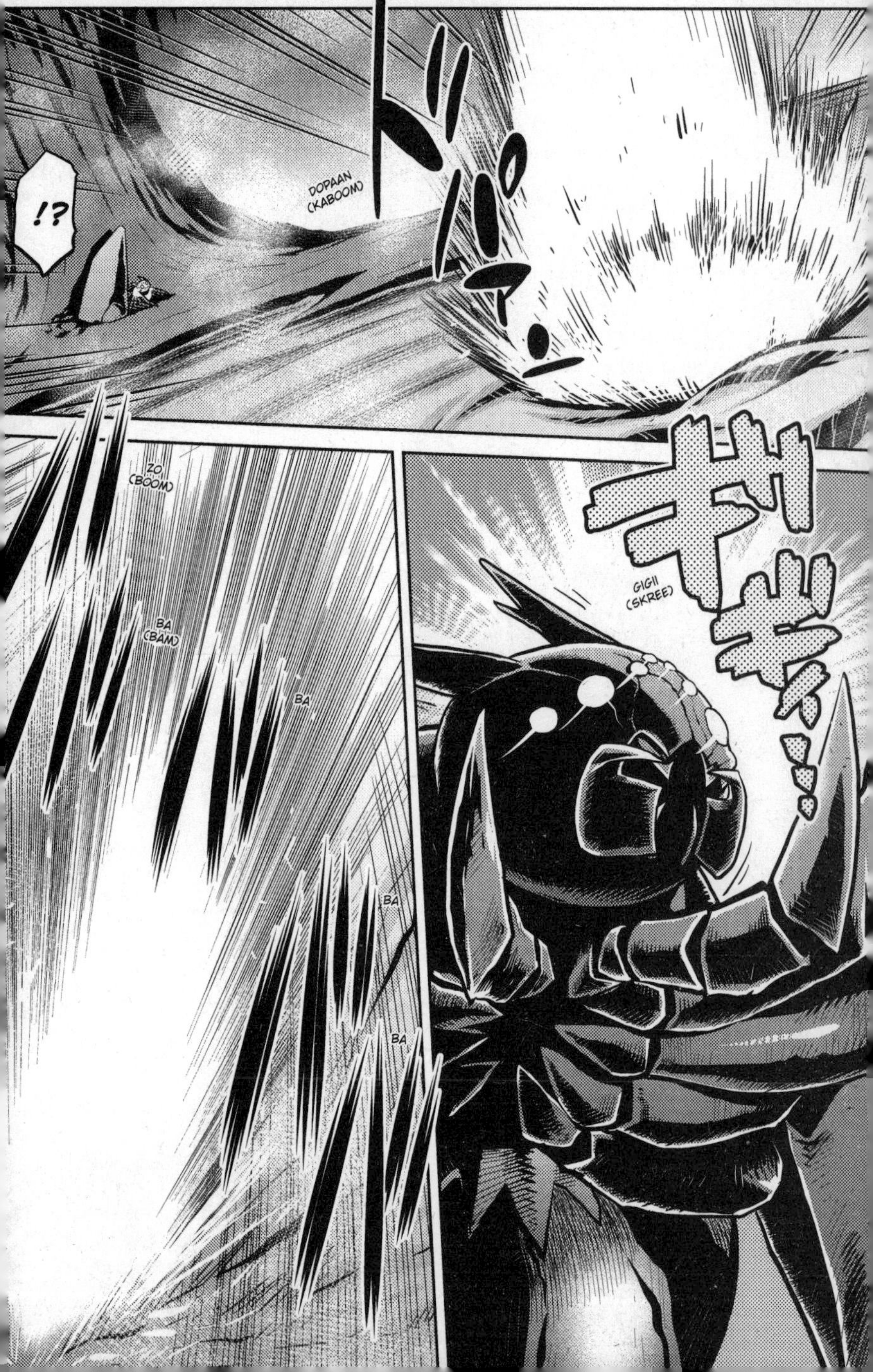
DOPAAN
(KABOOM)
!?
GIGII
(SKREE)
ZO
(BOOM)
BA
(BAM)
BA
BA
BA

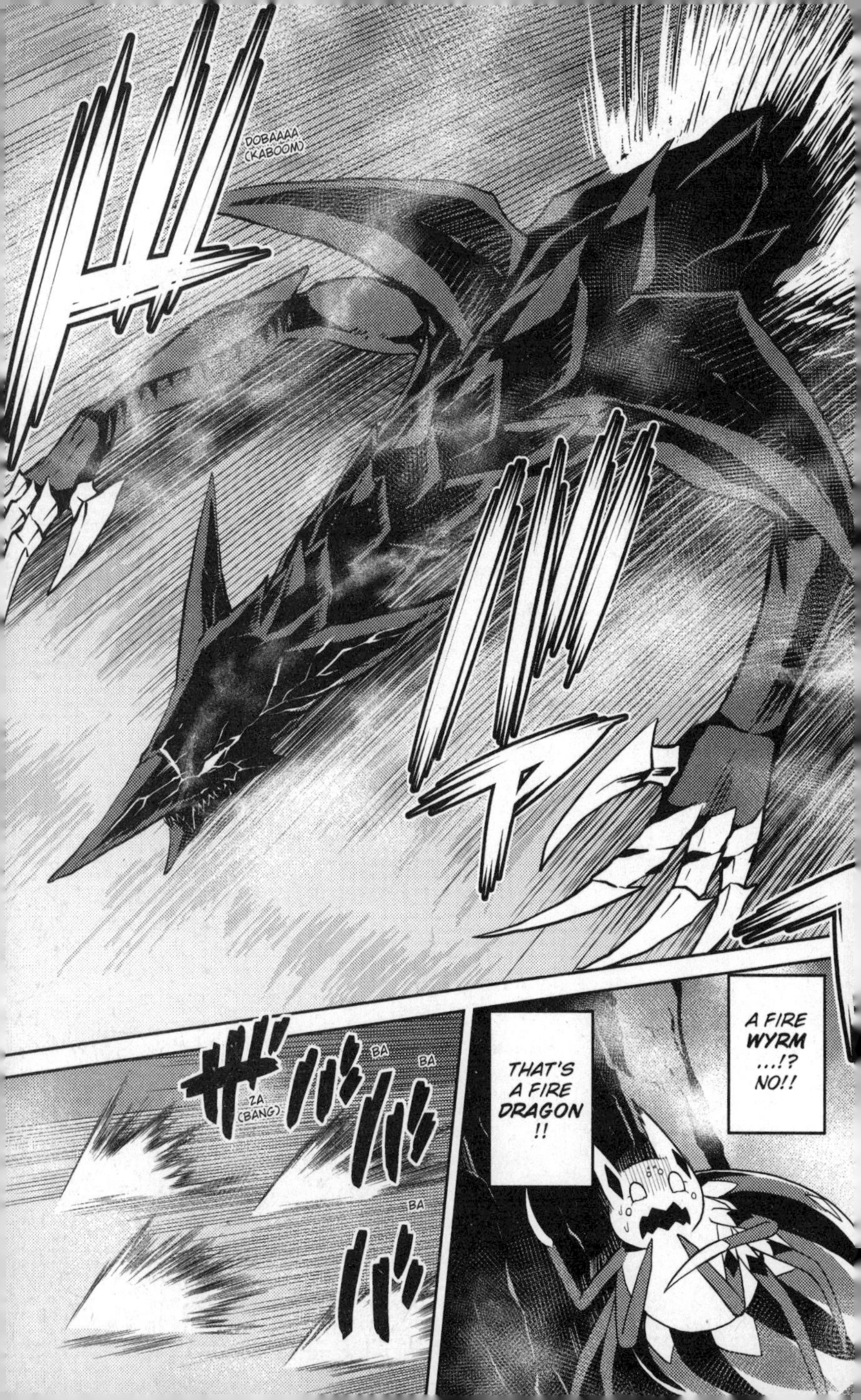
DOBAAAA
(KABOOM)
A FIRE WYRM ...!? NO!!
THAT'S A FIRE DRAGON !!
BA
BA
ZA
(BANG)
BA

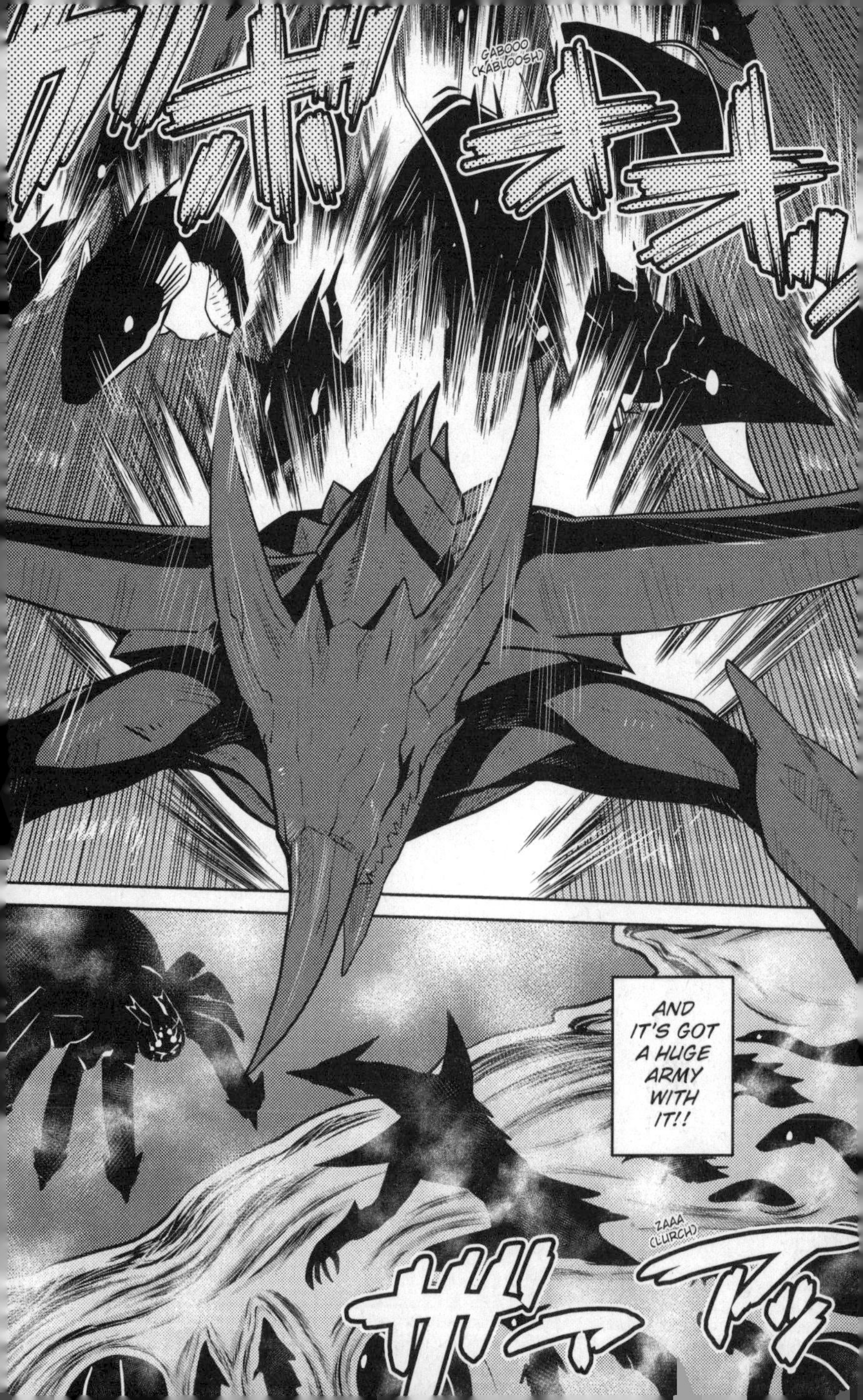
GABOOO
(KABLOOSH)
AND IT'S GOT A HUGE ARMY WITH IT!!
ZAAA
(LURCH)

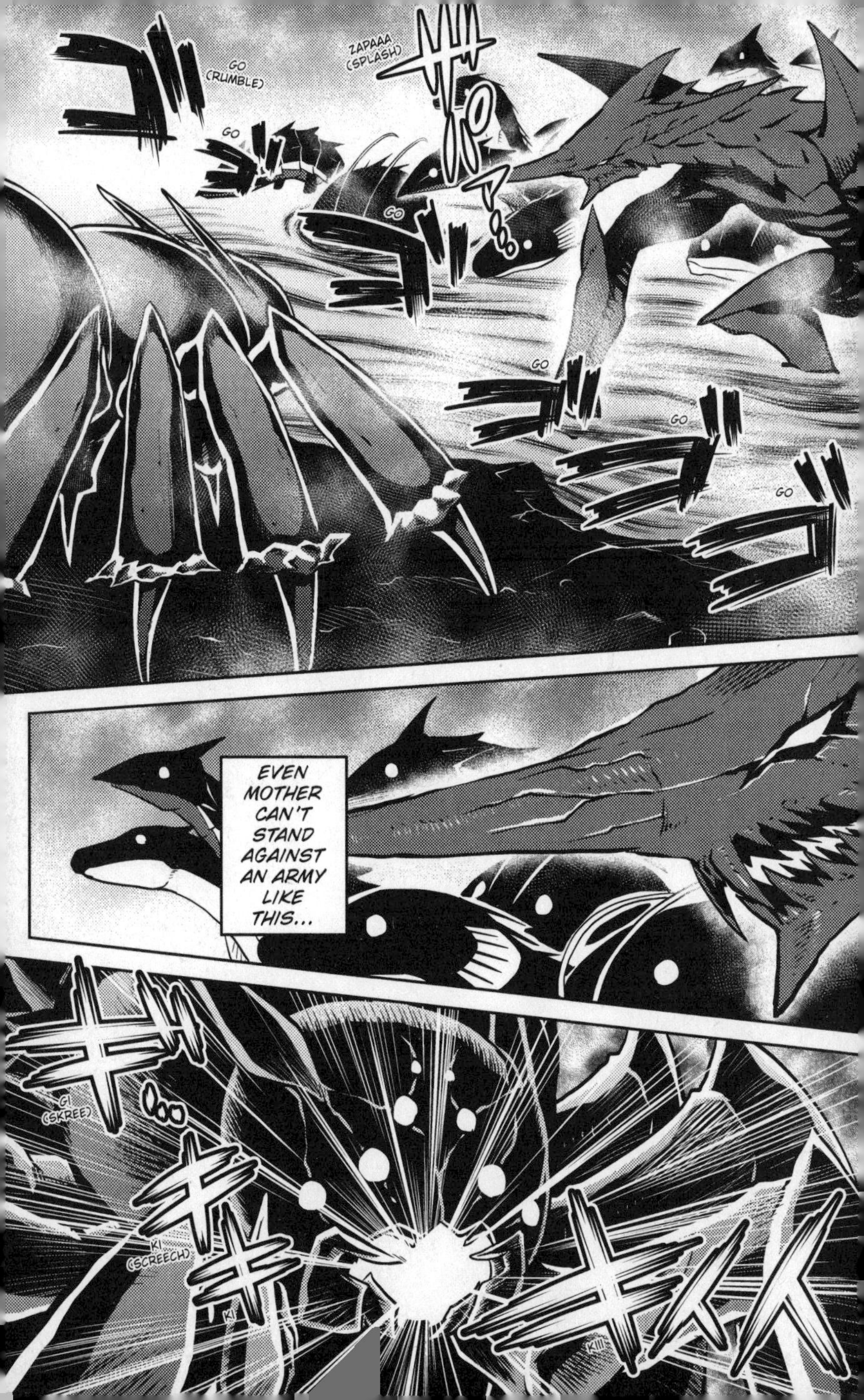
ZAPAAA (SPLASH)
GO (RUMBLE)
GO
GO
GO
GO
GO
EVEN MOTHER CAN'T STAND AGAINST AN ARMY LIKE THIS...
GI (SKREE)
KI (SCREECH)
KI
KIII

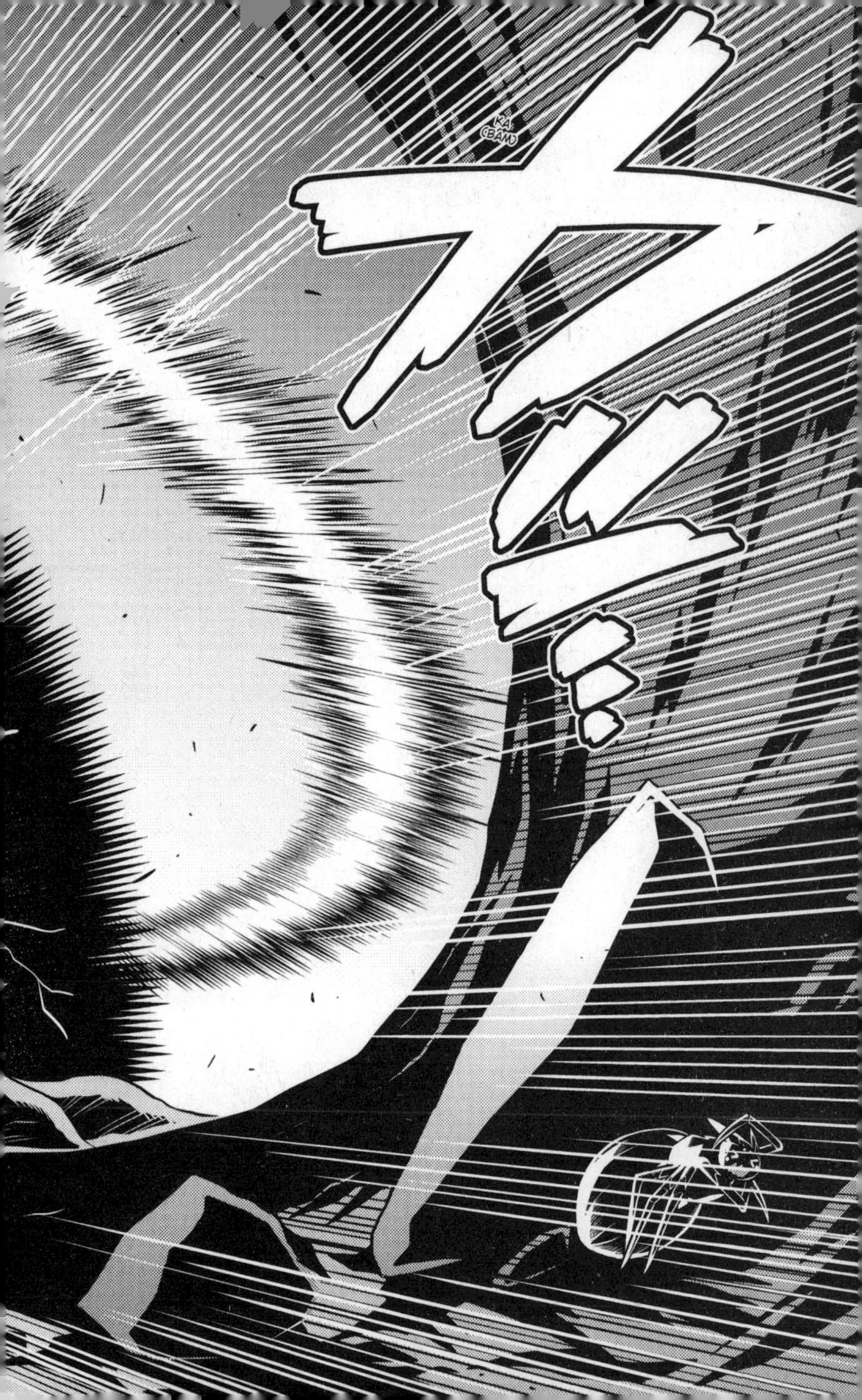
KA
(BAM)

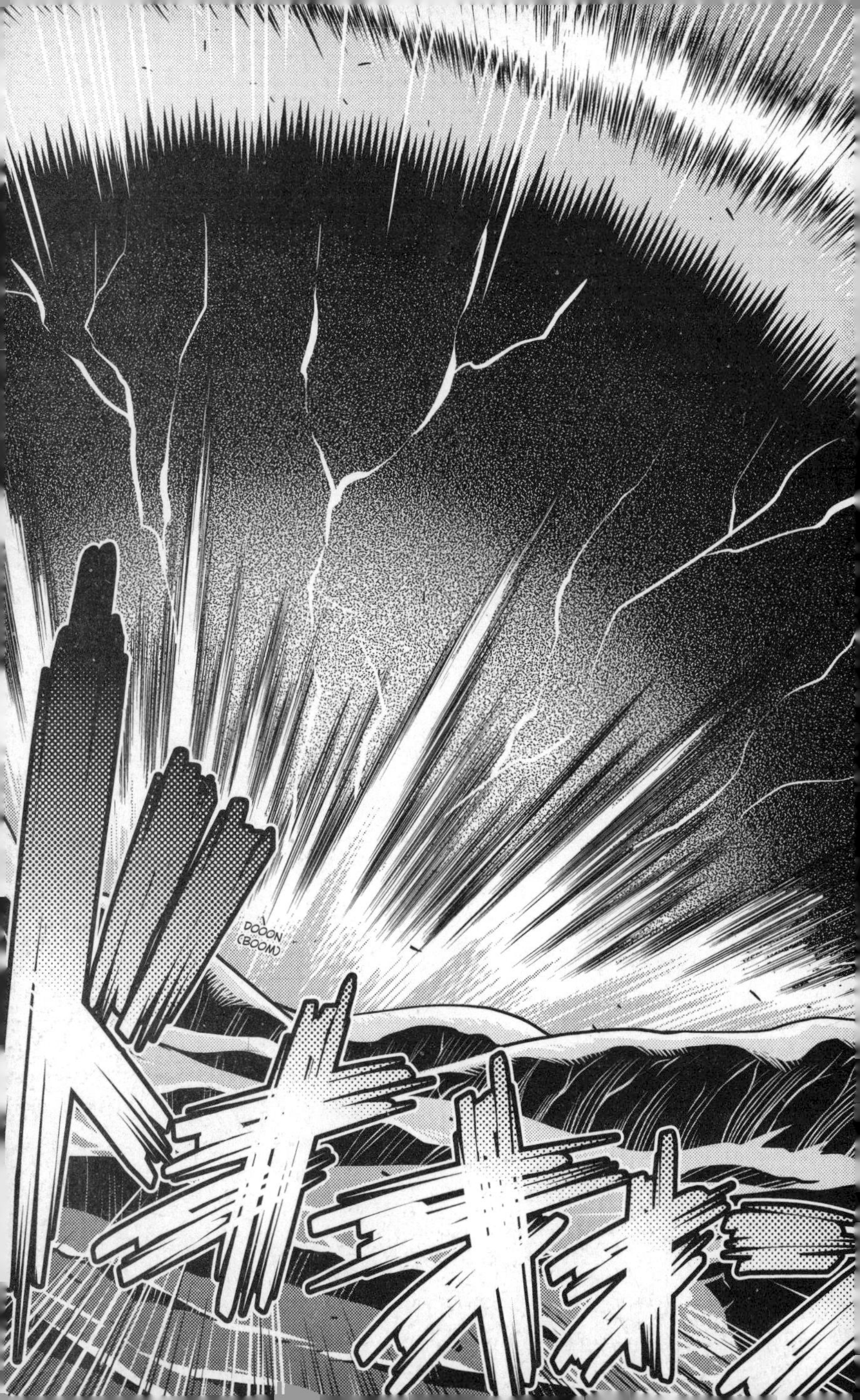
DOOON
(BOOM)

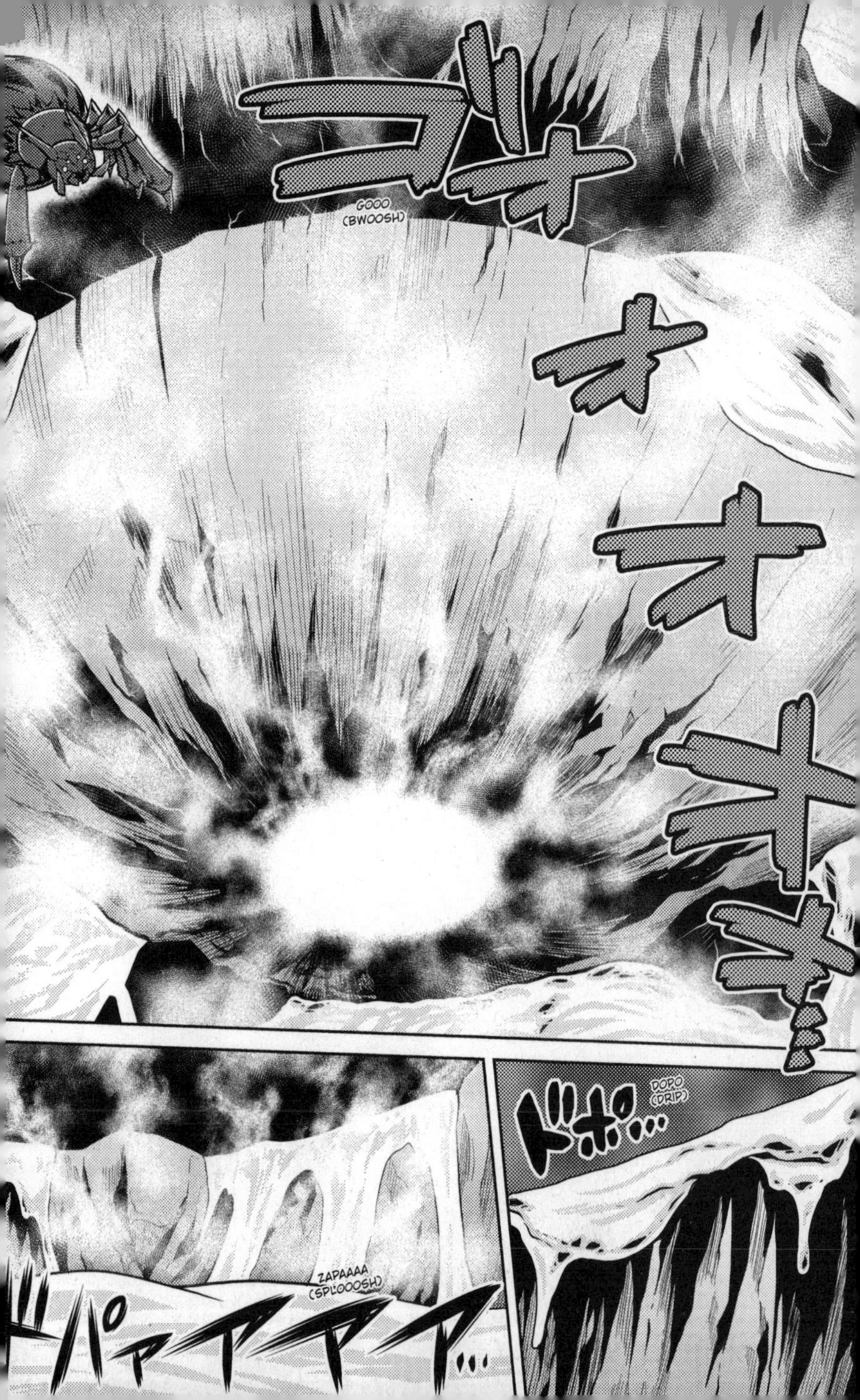
ゴォォォォ
GOOO (BWOOSH)
ドポ...
DOPO (DRIP)
ザパァァァ...
ZAPAAAA (SPLOOOSH)

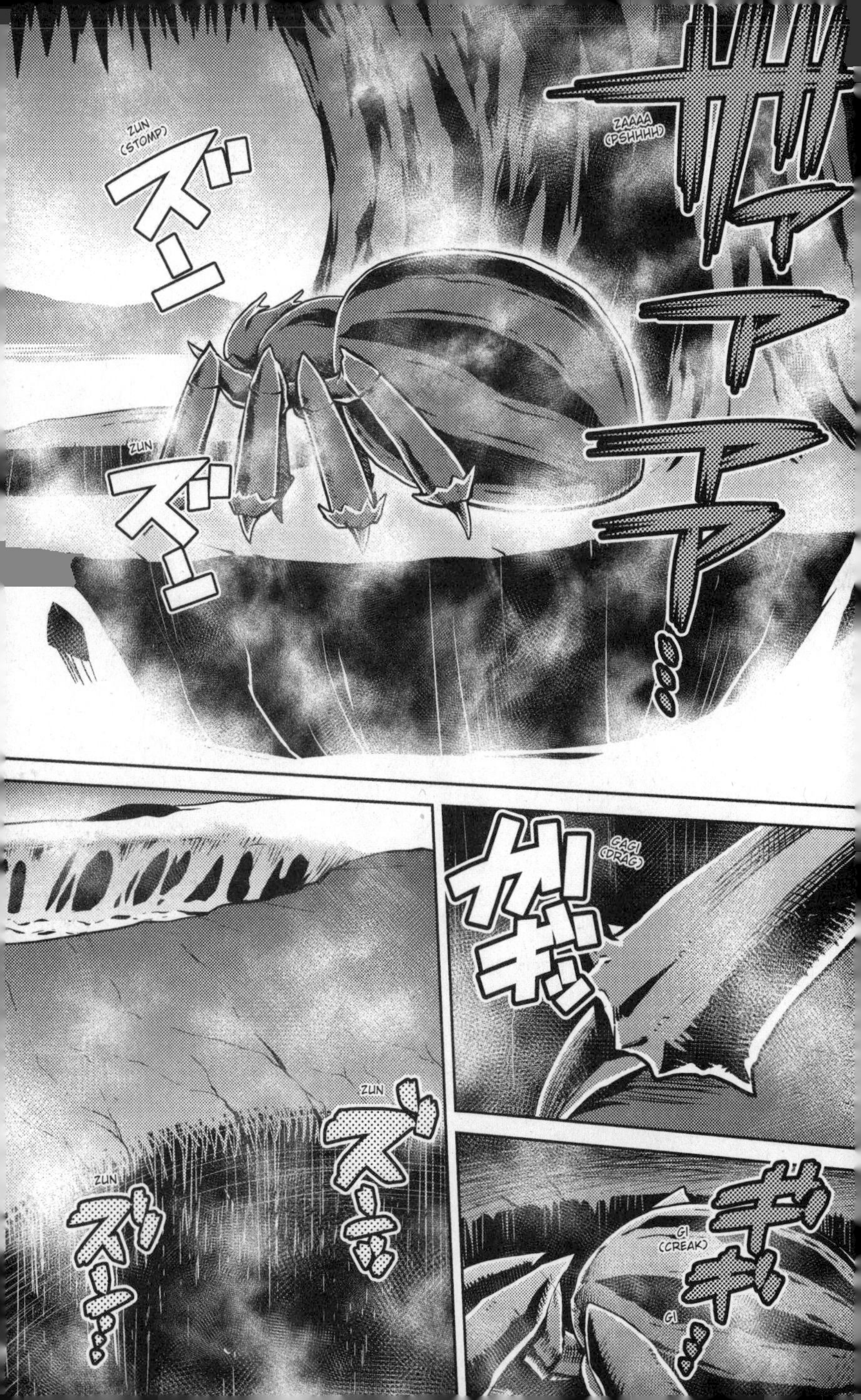
ZAAAA (PSHHHH)
ZUN (STOMP)
ZUN
GAGI (DRAG)
GI (CREAK)
GI
ZUN
ZUN

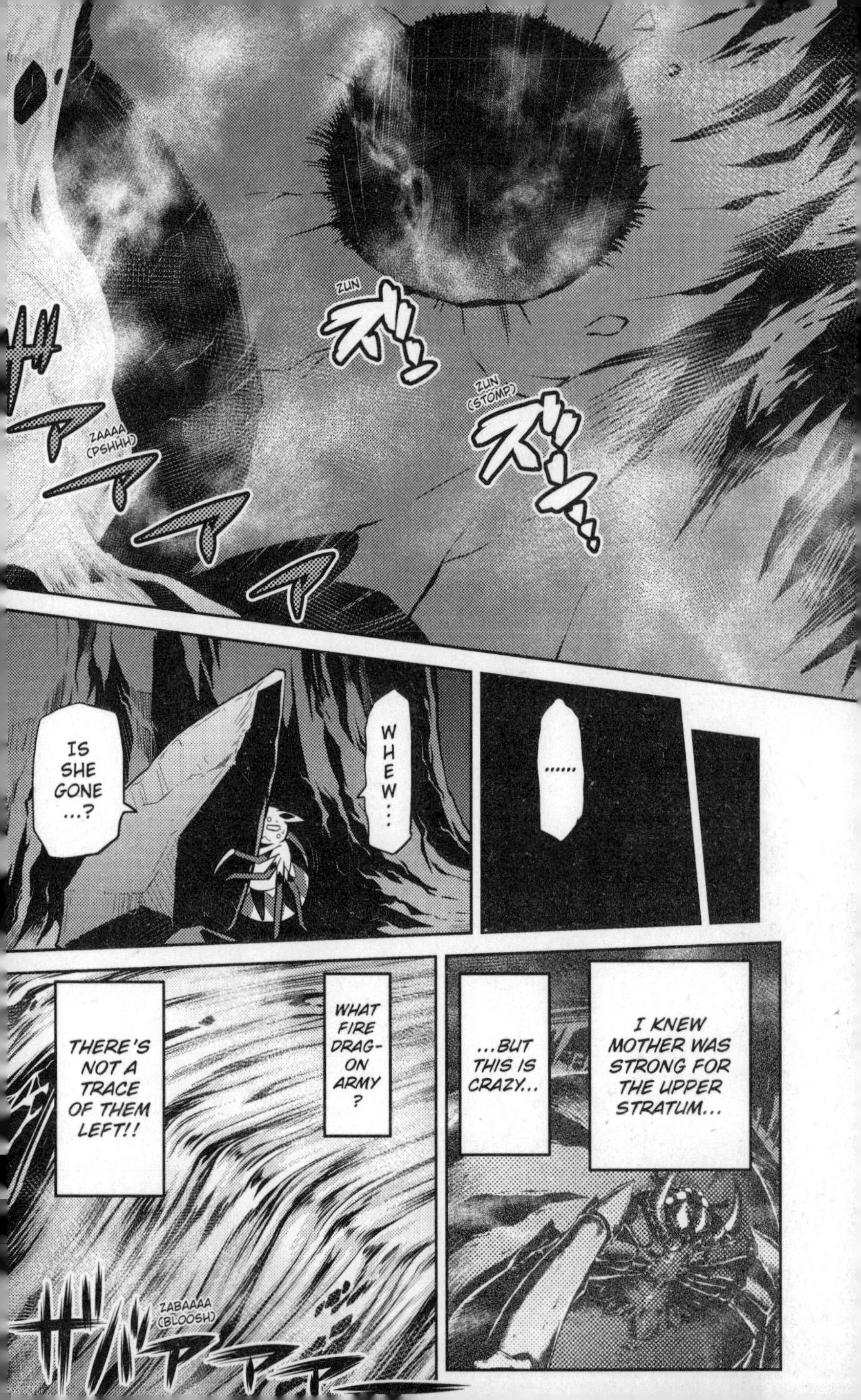
ZUN
ZUN (STOMP)
ZAAAA (PSHHH)
......
WHEW...
IS SHE GONE...?
I KNEW MOTHER WAS STRONG FOR THE UPPER STRATUM...
...BUT THIS IS CRAZY...
WHAT FIRE DRAG-ON ARMY?
THERE'S NOT A TRACE OF THEM LEFT!!
ZABAAAA (BLOOSH)

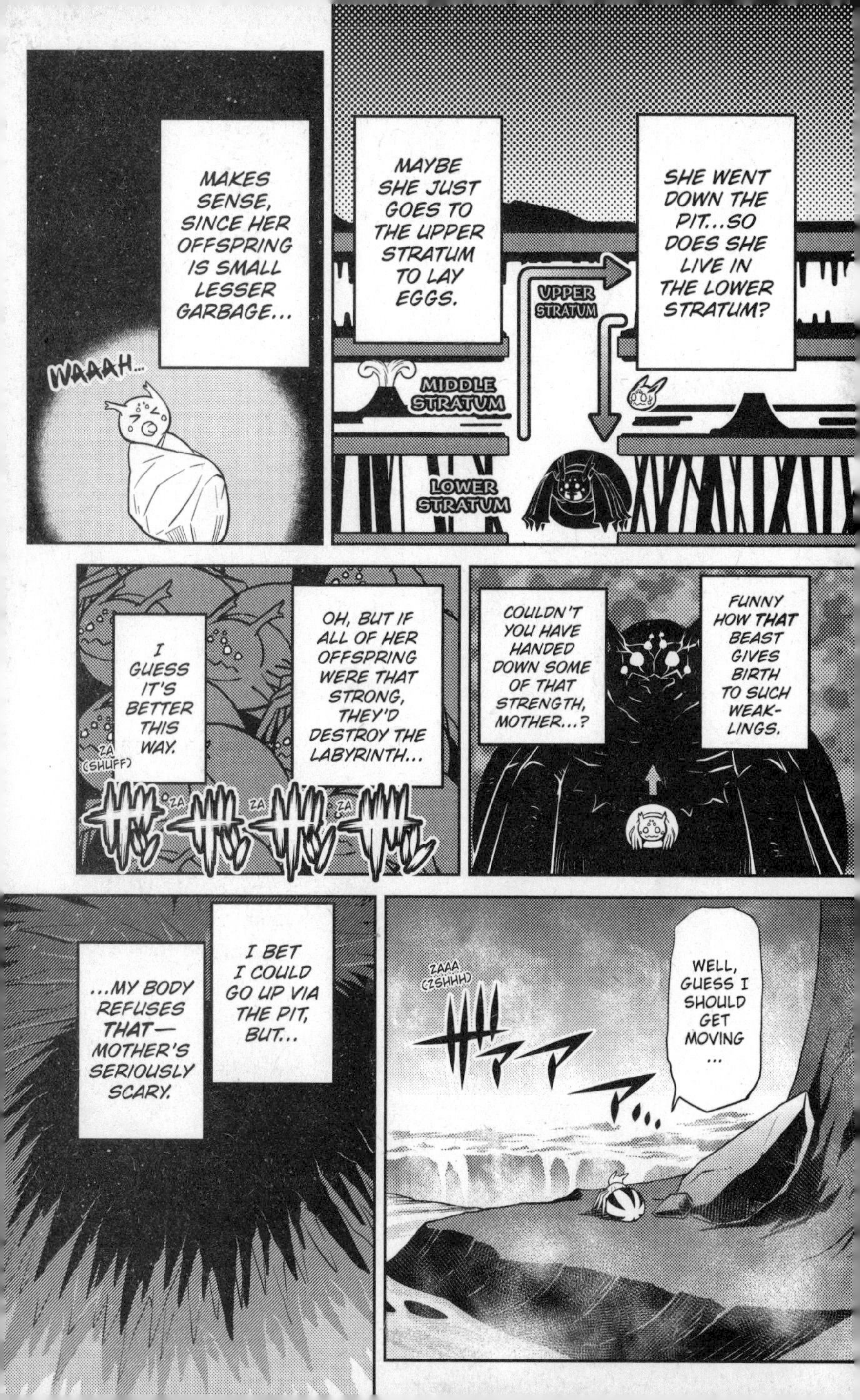
SHE WENT DOWN THE PIT...SO DOES SHE LIVE IN THE LOWER STRATUM?
MAYBE SHE JUST GOES TO THE UPPER STRATUM TO LAY EGGS.
UPPER STRATUM
MIDDLE STRATUM
LOWER STRATUM
MAKES SENSE, SINCE HER OFFSPRING IS SMALL LESSER GARBAGE...
WAAAH...
FUNNY HOW THAT BEAST GIVES BIRTH TO SUCH WEAK-LINGS.
COULDN'T YOU HAVE HANDED DOWN SOME OF THAT STRENGTH, MOTHER...?
OH, BUT IF ALL OF HER OFFSPRING WERE THAT STRONG, THEY'D DESTROY THE LABYRINTH...
I GUESS IT'S BETTER THIS WAY.
ZA (SHUFF)
ZA
ZA
ZA
WELL, GUESS I SHOULD GET MOVING ...
ZAAA (ZSHHH)
I BET I COULD GO UP VIA THE PIT, BUT...
...MY BODY REFUSES THAT—MOTHER'S SERIOUSLY SCARY.

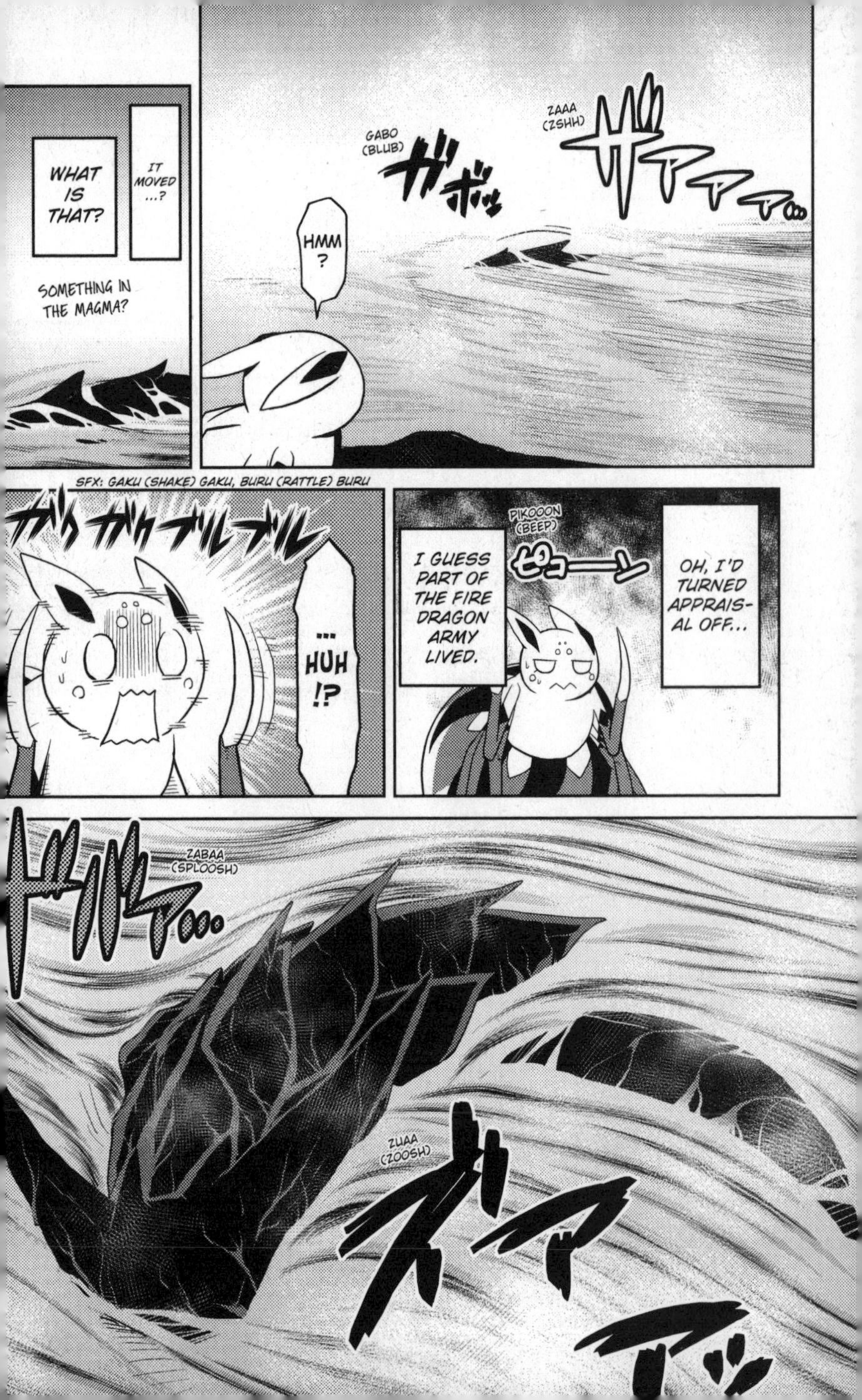
ZAAA (ZSHH)
GABO (BLUB)
HMM?
IT MOVED...?
WHAT IS THAT?
SOMETHING IN THE MAGMA?
OH, I'D TURNED APPRAIS-AL OFF...
PIKOOON (BEEP)
I GUESS PART OF THE FIRE DRAGON ARMY LIVED.
SFX: GAKU (SHAKE) GAKU, BURU (RATTLE) BURU
...HUH!?
ZABAA (SPLOOSH)
ZUAA (ZOOSH)

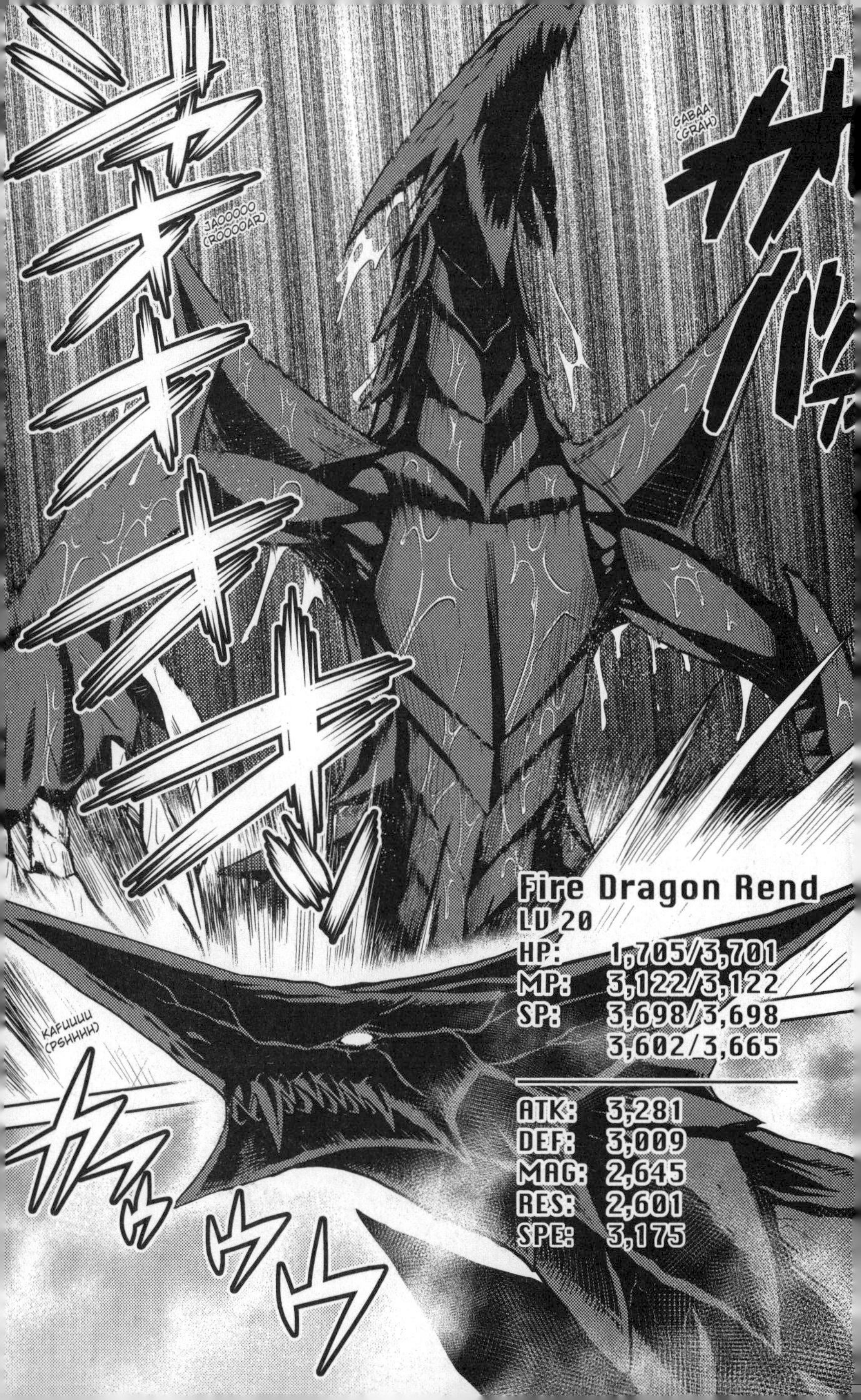
GABAA (GRAH)
JAOOOOO (ROOOOAR)
Fire Dragon Rend
LV 20
HP: 1,705/3,701
MP: 3,122/3,122
SP: 3,698/3,698
3,602/3,665
ATK: 3,281
DEF: 3,009
MAG: 2,645
RES: 2,601
SPE: 3,175
KAFUUUU (PSHHHH)

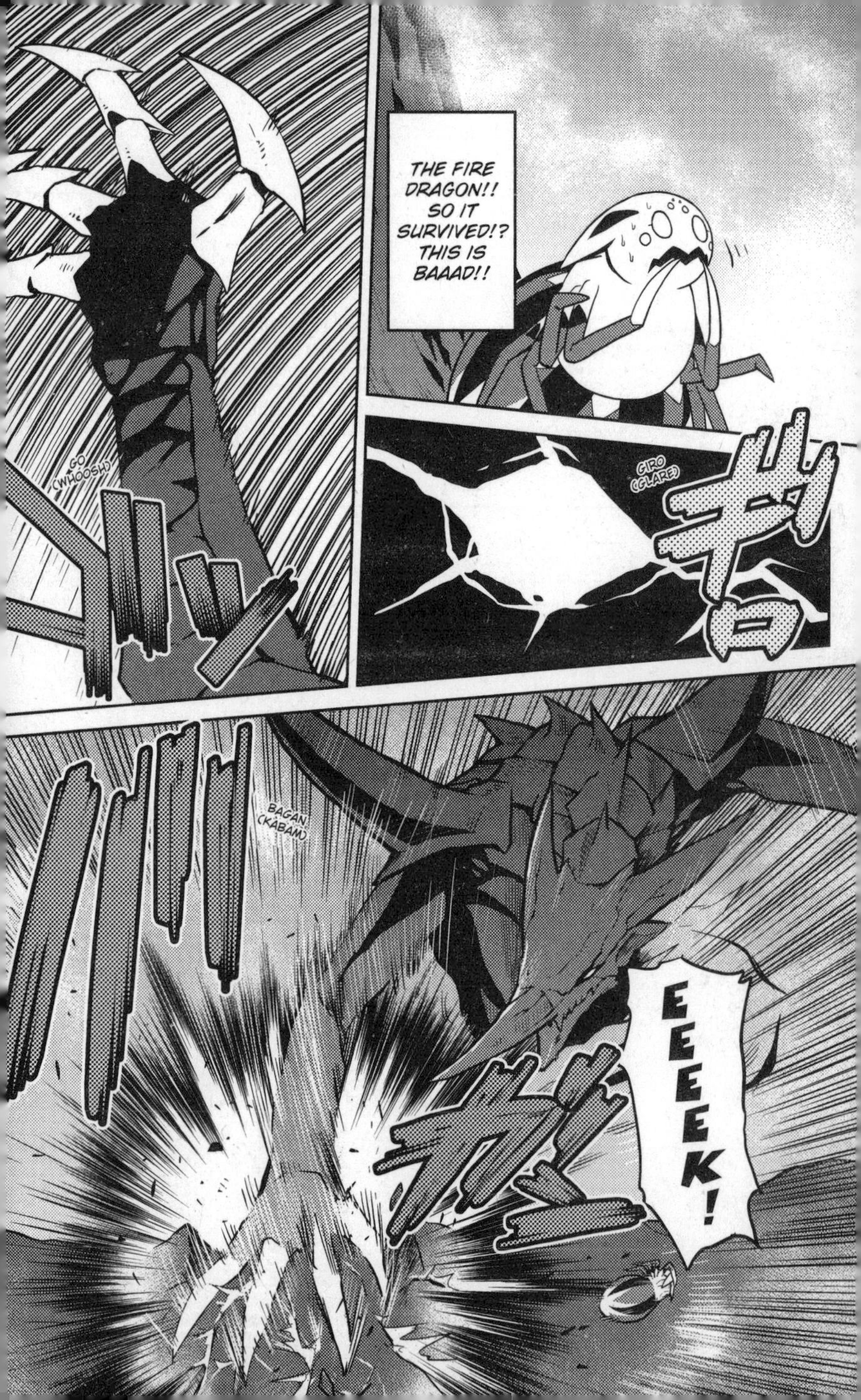
THE FIRE DRAGON!! SO IT SURVIVED!? THIS IS BAAAD!!
GIRO (GLARE)
GO (WHOOSH)
BAGAN (KABAM)
EEEEK!

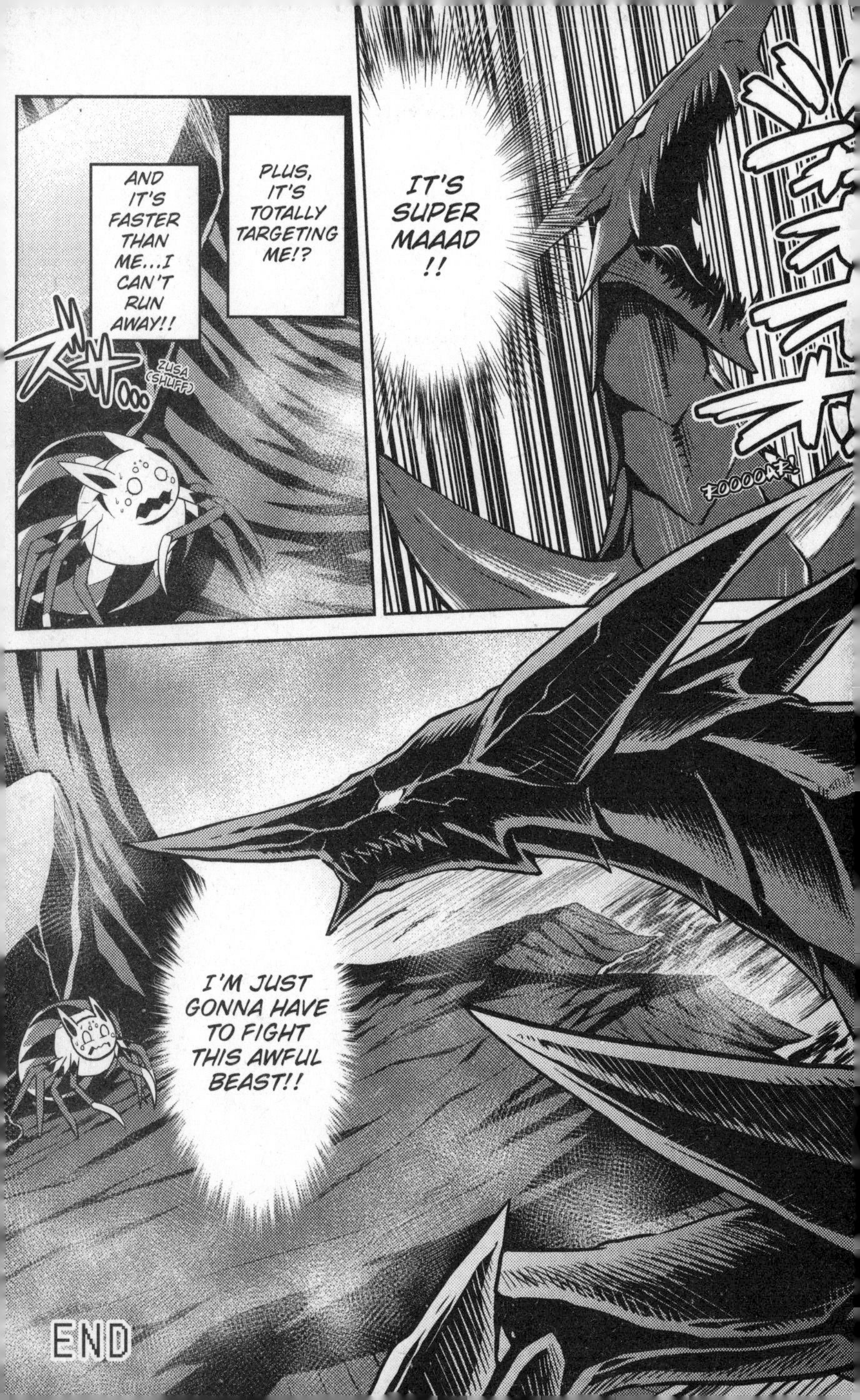
IT'S SUPER MAAAD!!
ROOOOAR!
PLUS, IT'S TOTALLY TARGETING ME!?
AND IT'S FASTER THAN ME...I CAN'T RUN AWAY!!
ZUSA (SHUFF)
I'M JUST GONNA HAVE TO FIGHT THIS AWFUL BEAST!!
END

27-2

HONESTLY, I DON'T SEE HOW I CAN WIN HERE.

NORMALLY, I CAN USE SKILLS TO MAKE UP FOR MY STATS, BUT THE DRAGON'S GOT SKILLS FOR DAYS TOO.

[Fire Dragon LV 1]
[MP Auto-Recovery LV 6]
[Magic Power Operation LV 4]
[Magic Power Attack LV 4]
[Destruction Enhancement LV 6]
[Impact Super-Enhancement LV 2]
[Spatial Maneuvering LV 4]
[Probability Super-Correction LV 5]
[Heat Perception LV 3]
[Fire Magic LV 4]
[Impact Super-Resistance LV 1]
[Longevity LV 5]
[Endurance LV 5]
[Monk LV 4]
[Gluttony LV 2]

[Imperial Scales LV 8]
[MP Lessened Consumpti...
[SP Rapid Recovery LV 1]
[Flame Attack LV 9]
[Cutting Enhancement LV 2]
[Cooperation LV 10]
[Hit LV 10]
[Presence Perception LV 10]
[Flight LV 7]
[Cutting Resistance LV 1]
[Heat Nullification]
[Magic Hoard LV 4]
[Herculean Strength LV 5]
[Talisman LV 3]

...LV 3)
...rception
[SP Minimized Consumption
[Flame Enhancement LV 7]
[Piercing Enhancement LV 2]
[Command LV 2]
[Evasion LV 10]
[Danger Perception LV 10]
[High-Speed Swimming LV 10]
[Piercing Resistance LV 1]
[Status Condition Resistance LV 1]
[Instant Body LV 5]

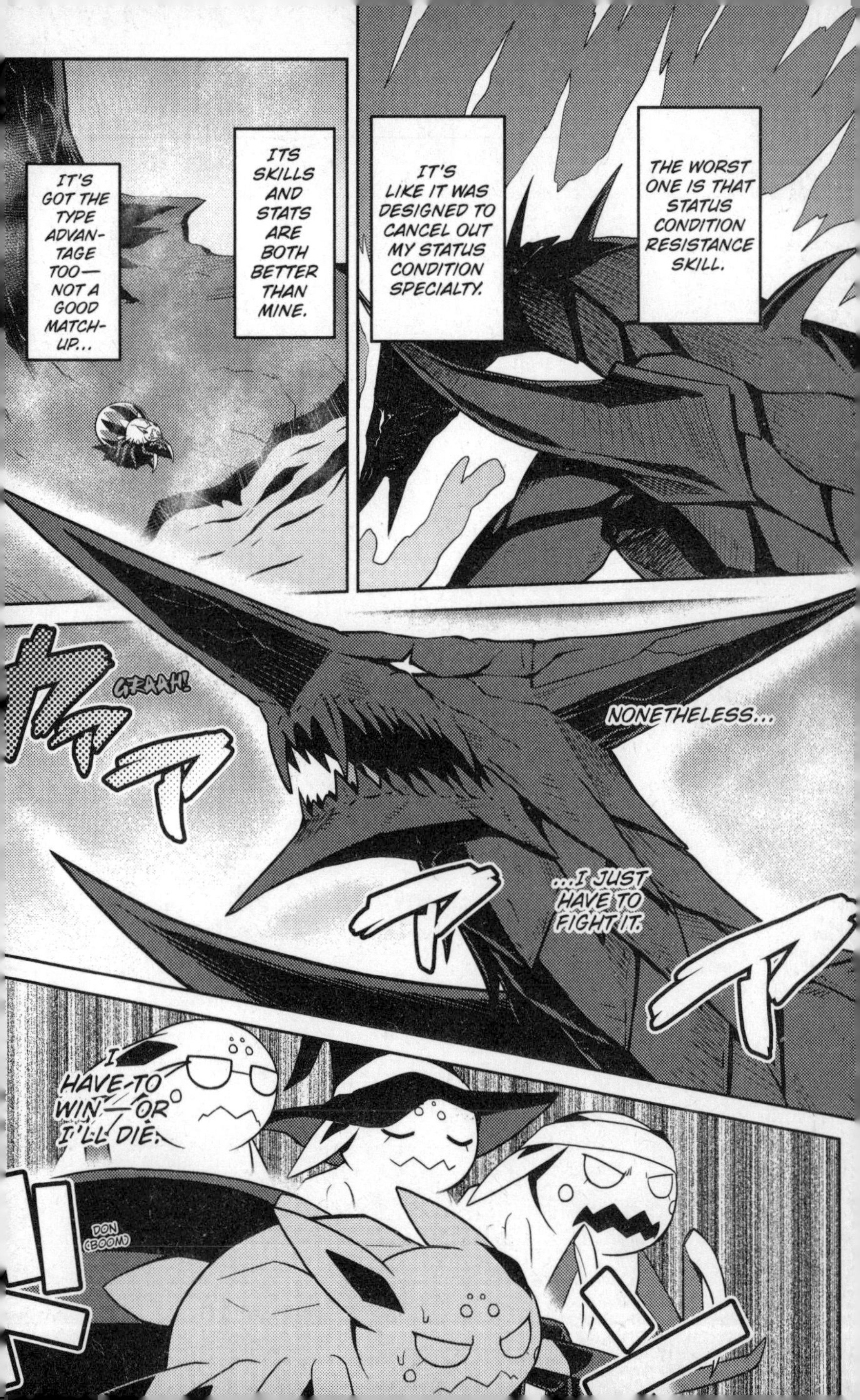
THE WORST ONE IS THAT STATUS CONDITION RESISTANCE SKILL.
IT'S LIKE IT WAS DESIGNED TO CANCEL OUT MY STATUS CONDITION SPECIALTY.
ITS SKILLS AND STATS ARE BOTH BETTER THAN MINE.
IT'S GOT THE TYPE ADVANTAGE TOO—NOT A GOOD MATCH-UP...
NONETHELESS...
...I JUST HAVE TO FIGHT IT.
GRAAH!
I HAVE TO WIN—OR I'LL DIE.
DON (BOOM)

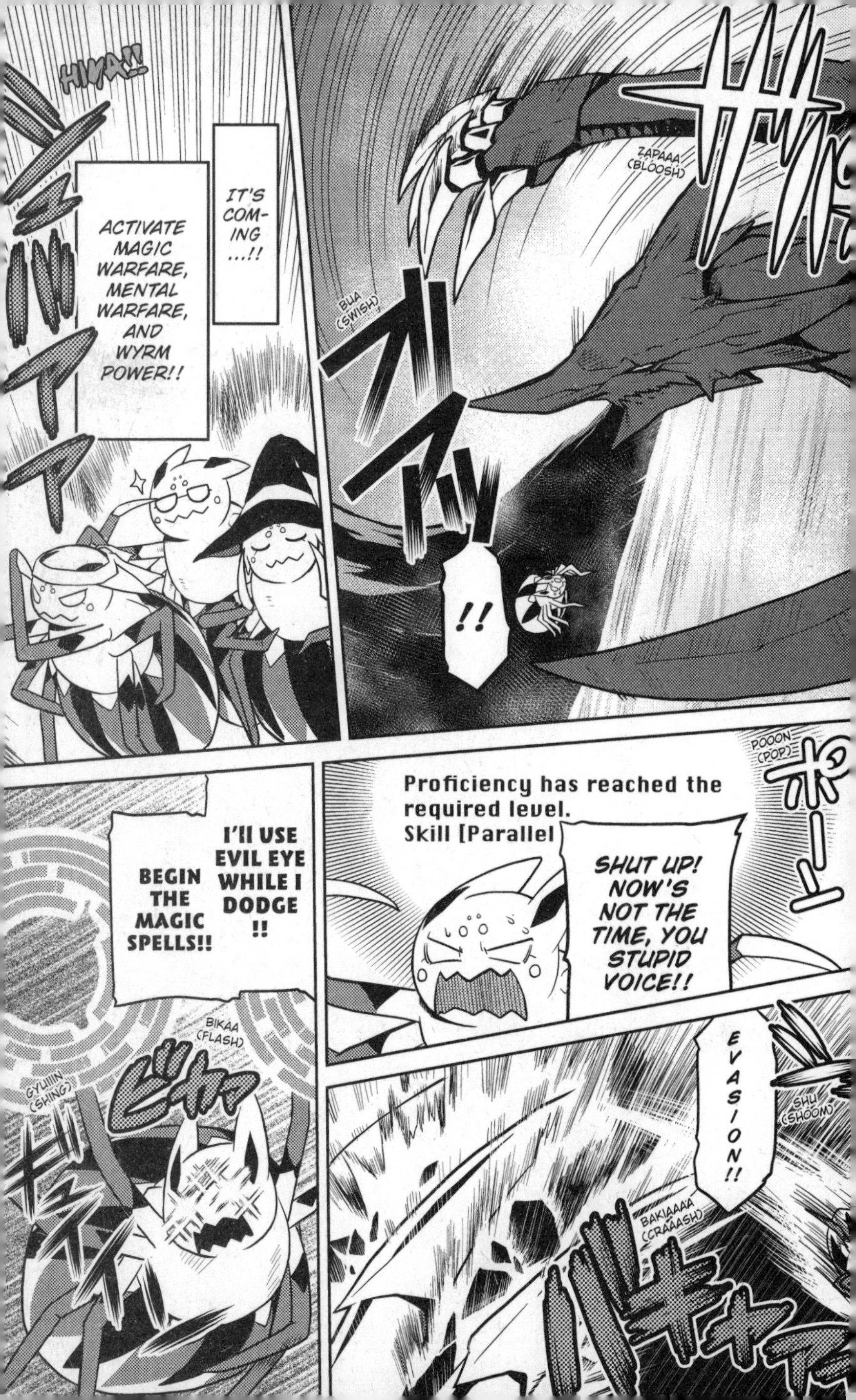

ZAPAAA (BLOOSH)
BUA (SWISH)
!!
IT'S COMING...!!
ACTIVATE MAGIC WARFARE, MENTAL WARFARE, AND WYRM POWER!!
HIYA!!
POOON (POP)
Proficiency has reached the required level. Skill [Parallel
SHUT UP! NOW'S NOT THE TIME, YOU STUPID VOICE!!
SHU (SHOOM)
EVASION!!
BAKIAAAA (CRAAASH)
I'll USE EVIL EYE WHILE I DODGE!!
BEGIN THE MAGIC SPELLS!!
BIKAA (FLASH)
GYUIIIN (SHING)

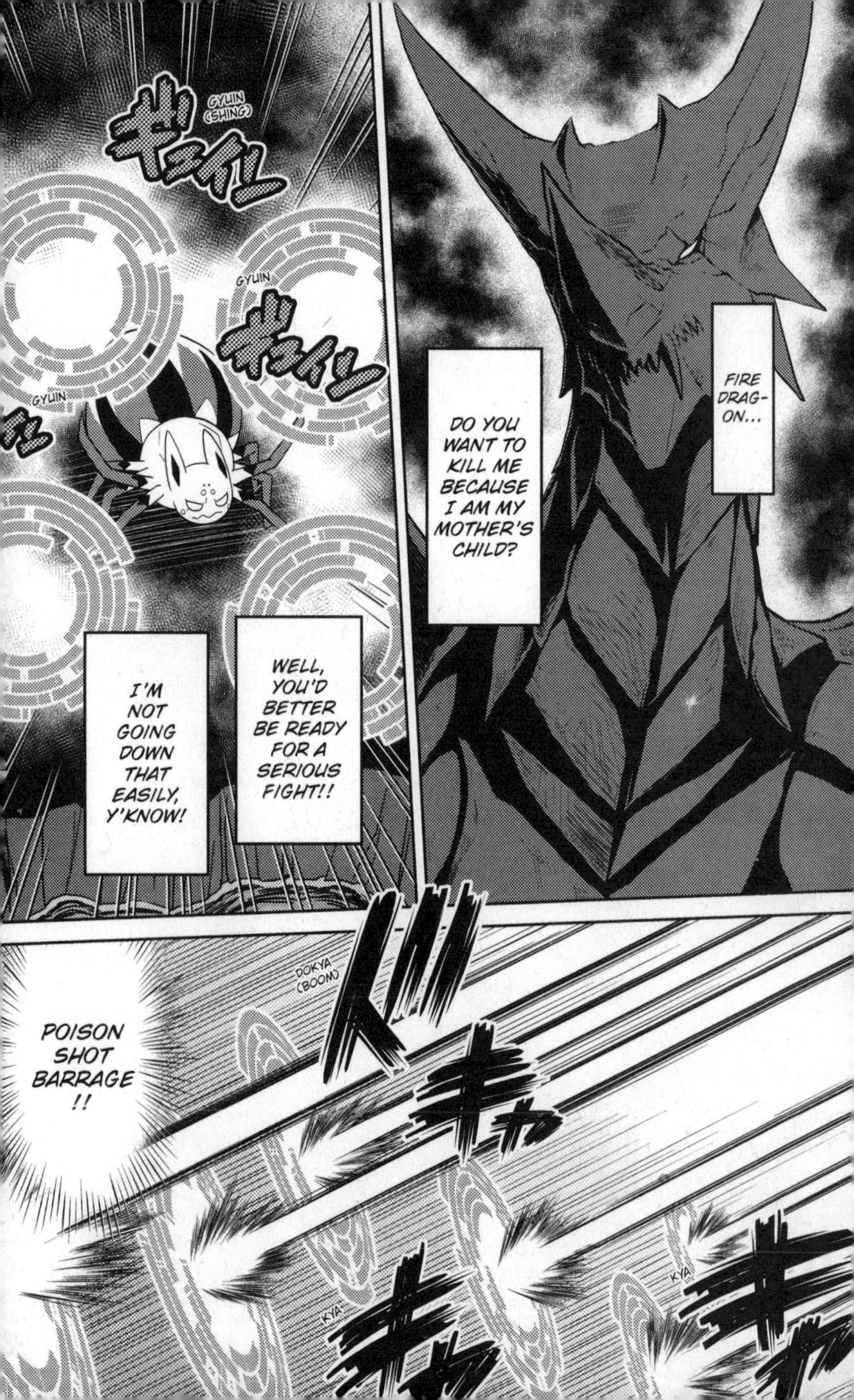
FIRE DRAG-ON...
DO YOU WANT TO KILL ME BECAUSE I AM MY MOTHER'S CHILD?
GYUIN (SHING)
GYUIN
GYUIN
WELL, YOU'D BETTER BE READY FOR A SERIOUS FIGHT!!
I'M NOT GOING DOWN THAT EASILY, Y'KNOW!
DOKYA (BOOM)
POISON SHOT BARRAGE!!
KYA
KYA

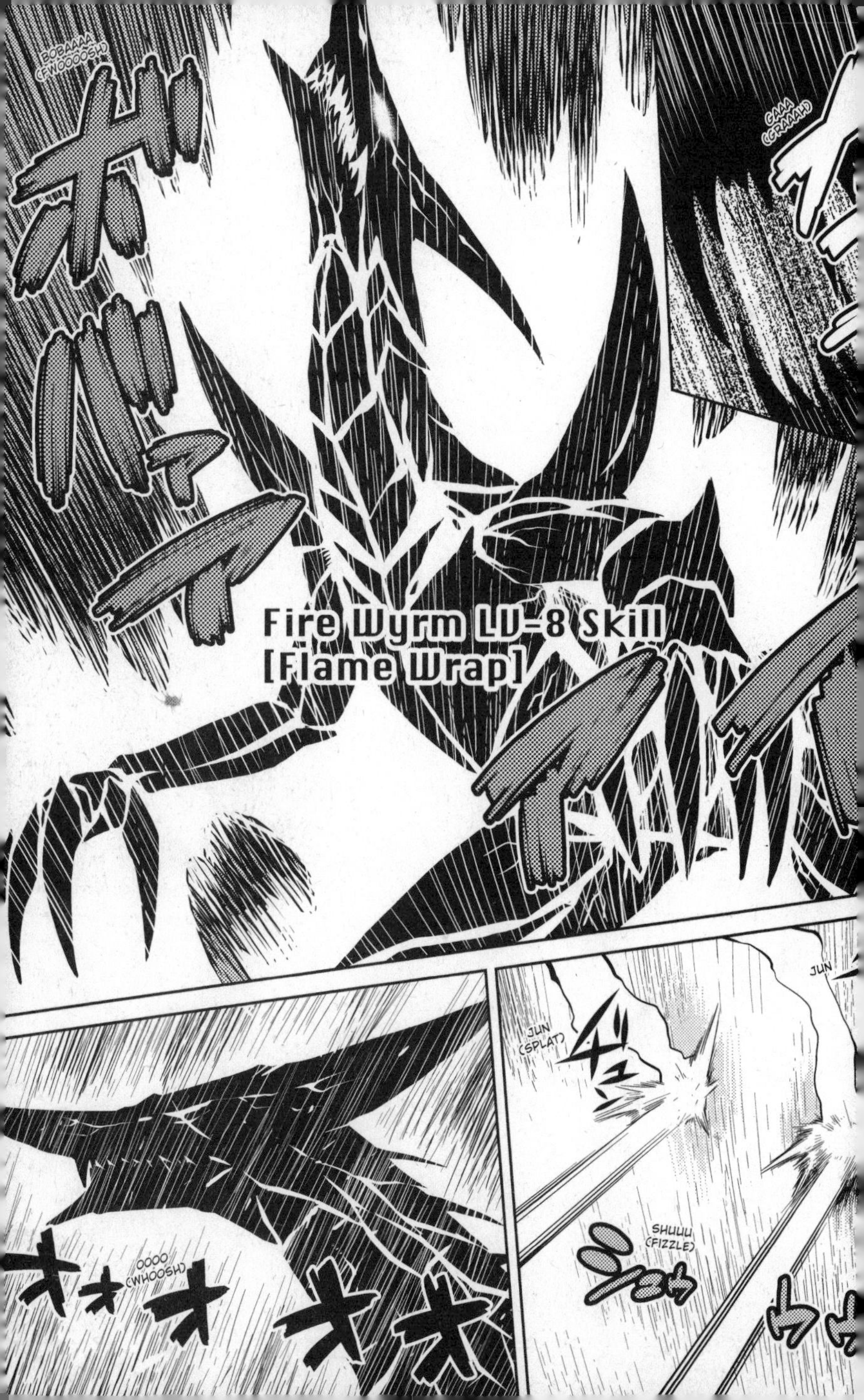
GAAA (GRAAAH)
BOBAAAA (FWOOOSH)
Fire Wyrm LV-8 Skill
[Flame Wrap]
JUN
JUN (SPLAT)
SHUUU (FIZZLE)
OOOO (WHOOSH)

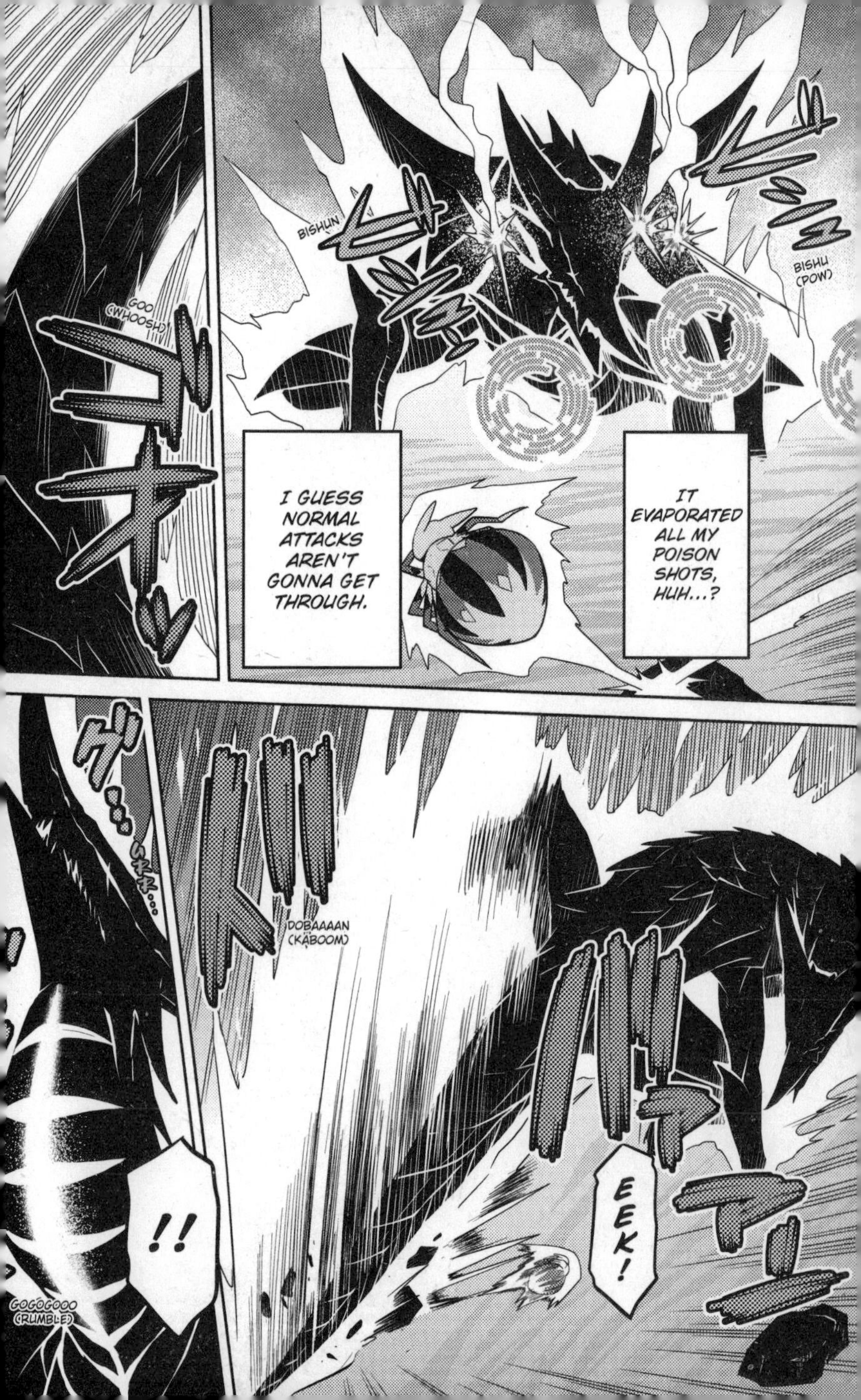
BISHU (POW)
BISHUN
IT EVAPORATED ALL MY POISON SHOTS, HUH...?
I GUESS NORMAL ATTACKS AREN'T GONNA GET THROUGH.
GOO (WHOOSH)
EEK!
DOBAAAAN (KABOOM)
!!
GOGOGOOO (RUMBLE)

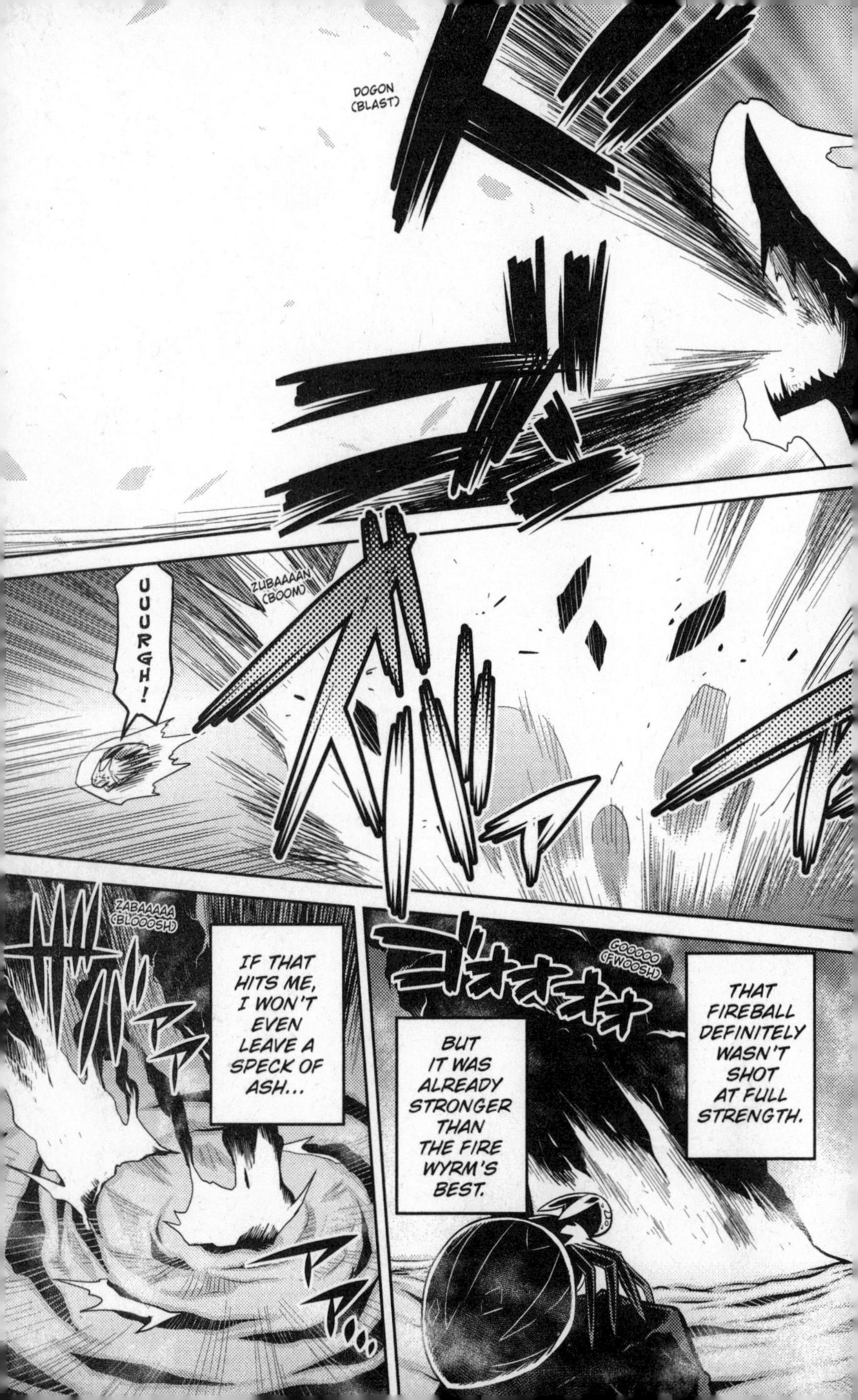
DOGON (BLAST)
ZUBAAAAN (BOOM)
UUURGH!
GOOOOO (FWOOSH)
THAT FIREBALL DEFINITELY WASN'T SHOT AT FULL STRENGTH.
BUT IT WAS ALREADY STRONGER THAN THE FIRE WYRM'S BEST.
ZABAAAAA (BLOOOSH)
IF THAT HITS ME, I WON'T EVEN LEAVE A SPECK OF ASH...

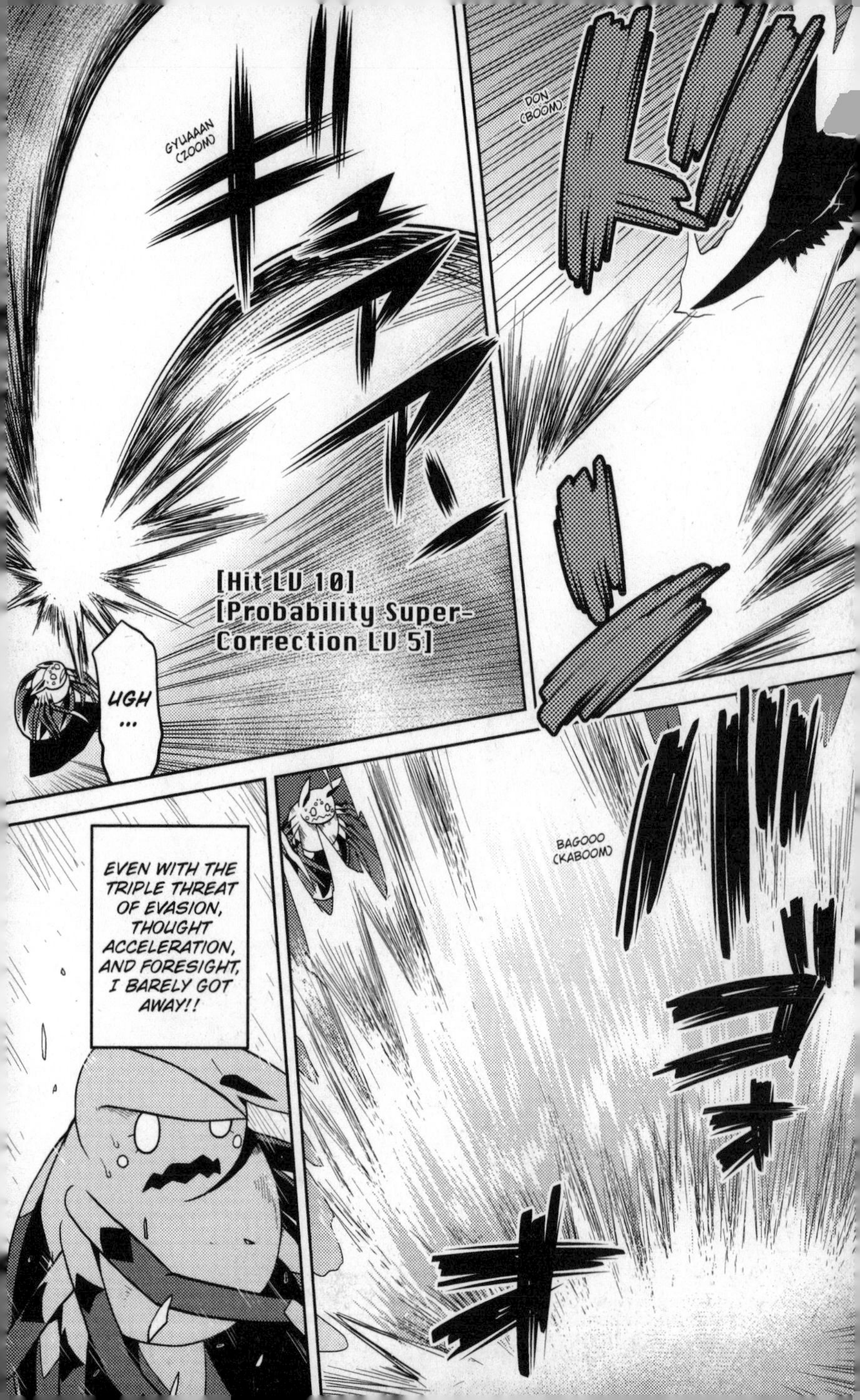
DON (BOOM)
GYUAAAN (ZOOM)
[Hit LV 10]
[Probability Super-Correction LV 5]
UGH ...
BAGOOO (KABOOM)
EVEN WITH THE TRIPLE THREAT OF EVASION, THOUGHT ACCELERATION, AND FORESIGHT, I BARELY GOT AWAY!!

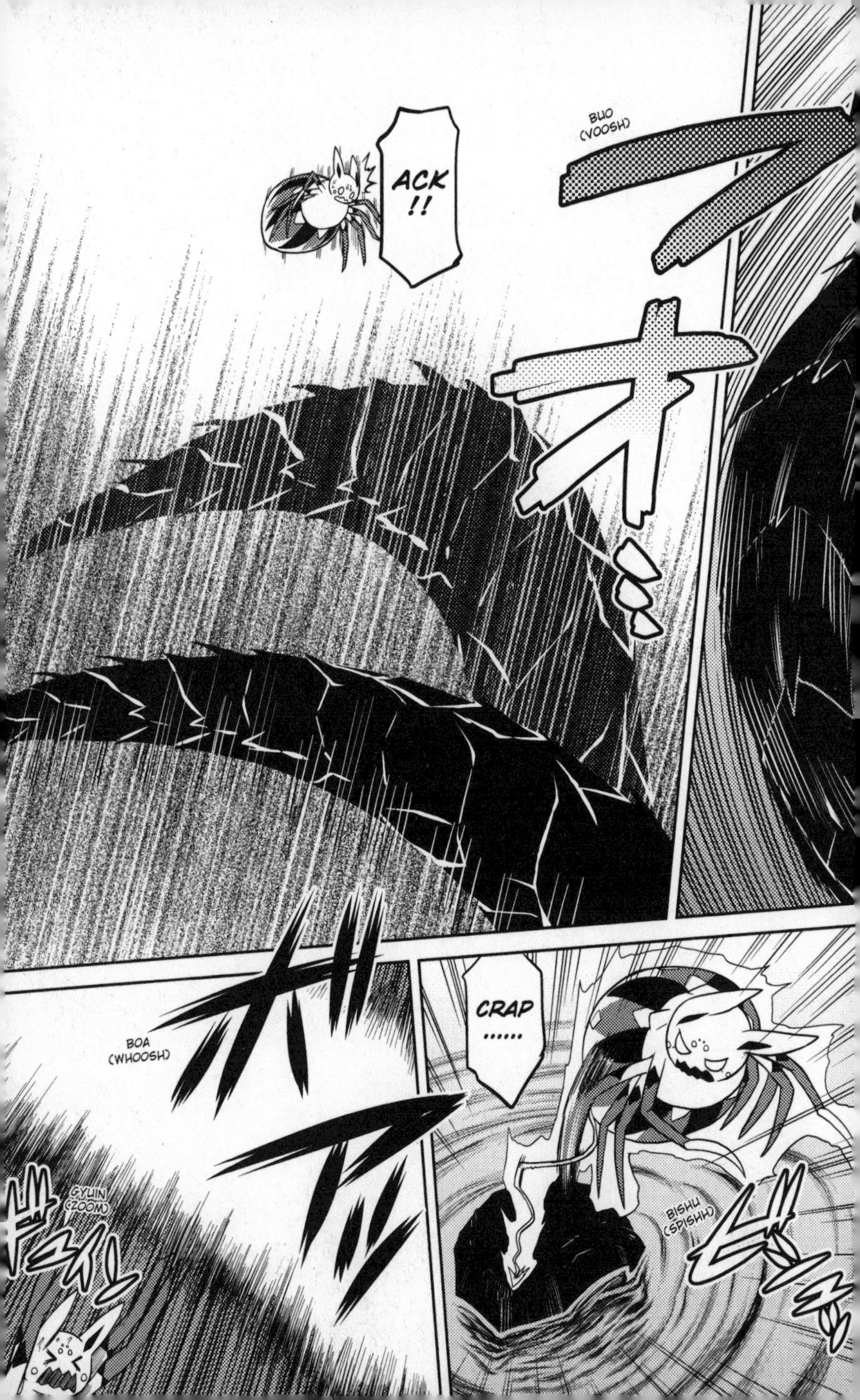
BUO
(VOOSH)
ACK
!!
CRAP
......
BISHU
(SPISHH)
BOA
(WHOOSH)
GYUIN
(ZOOM)

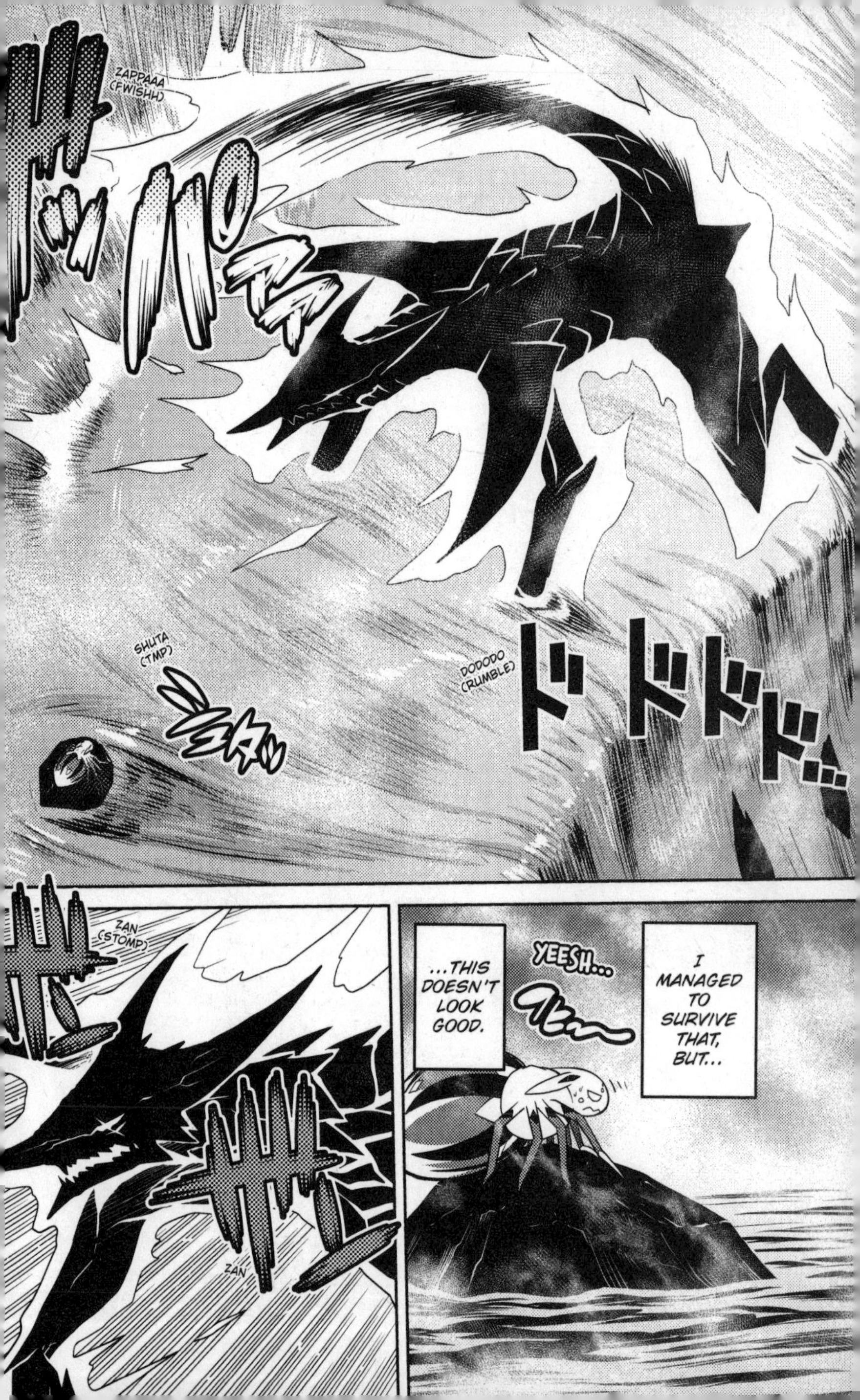
ZAPPAAA (FWISHH)
DODODO (RUMBLE)
ドドドド…
SHUTA (TMP)
I MANAGED TO SURVIVE THAT, BUT...
YEESH...
...THIS DOESN'T LOOK GOOD.
ZAN (STOMP)
ZAN

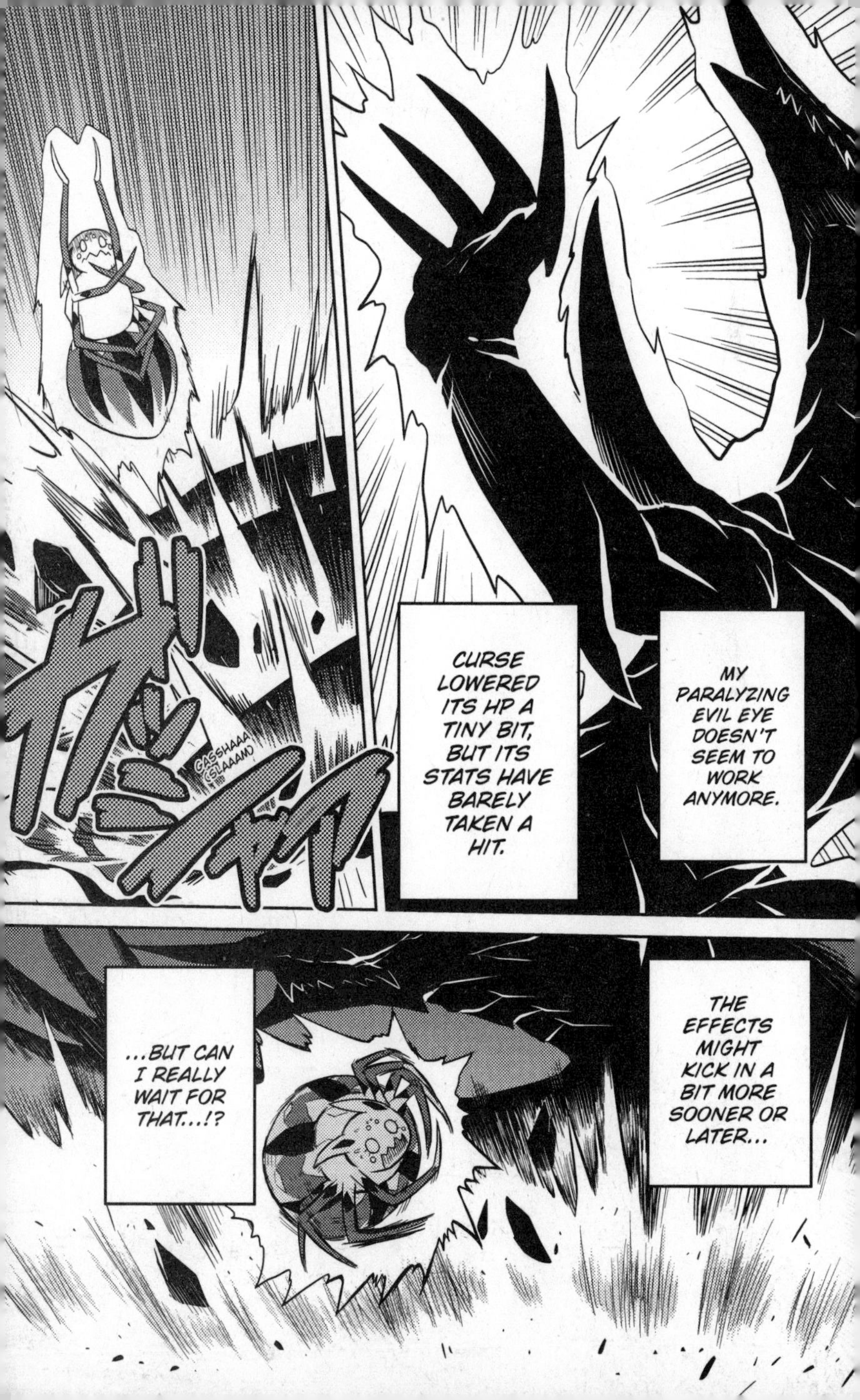
MY PARALYZING EVIL EYE DOESN'T SEEM TO WORK ANYMORE.
CURSE LOWERED ITS HP A TINY BIT, BUT ITS STATS HAVE BARELY TAKEN A HIT.
GASSHAAA (SLAAAM)
THE EFFECTS MIGHT KICK IN A BIT MORE SOONER OR LATER...
...BUT CAN I REALLY WAIT FOR THAT...!?

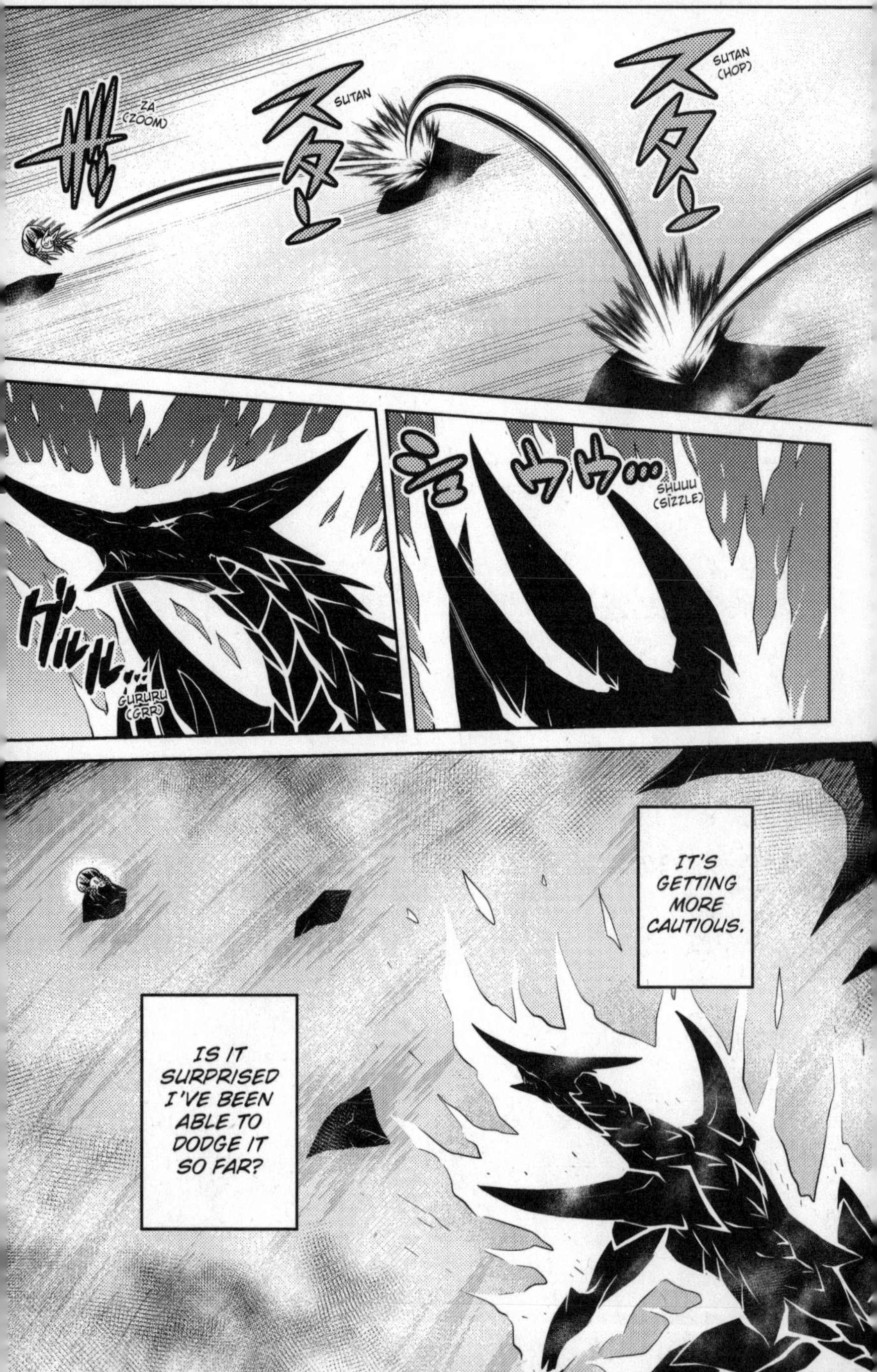
SUTAN (HOP)
SUTAN
ZA (ZOOM)
SHUUU (SIZZLE)
GURURU (GRR)
IT'S GETTING MORE CAUTIOUS.
IS IT SURPRISED I'VE BEEN ABLE TO DODGE IT SO FAR?

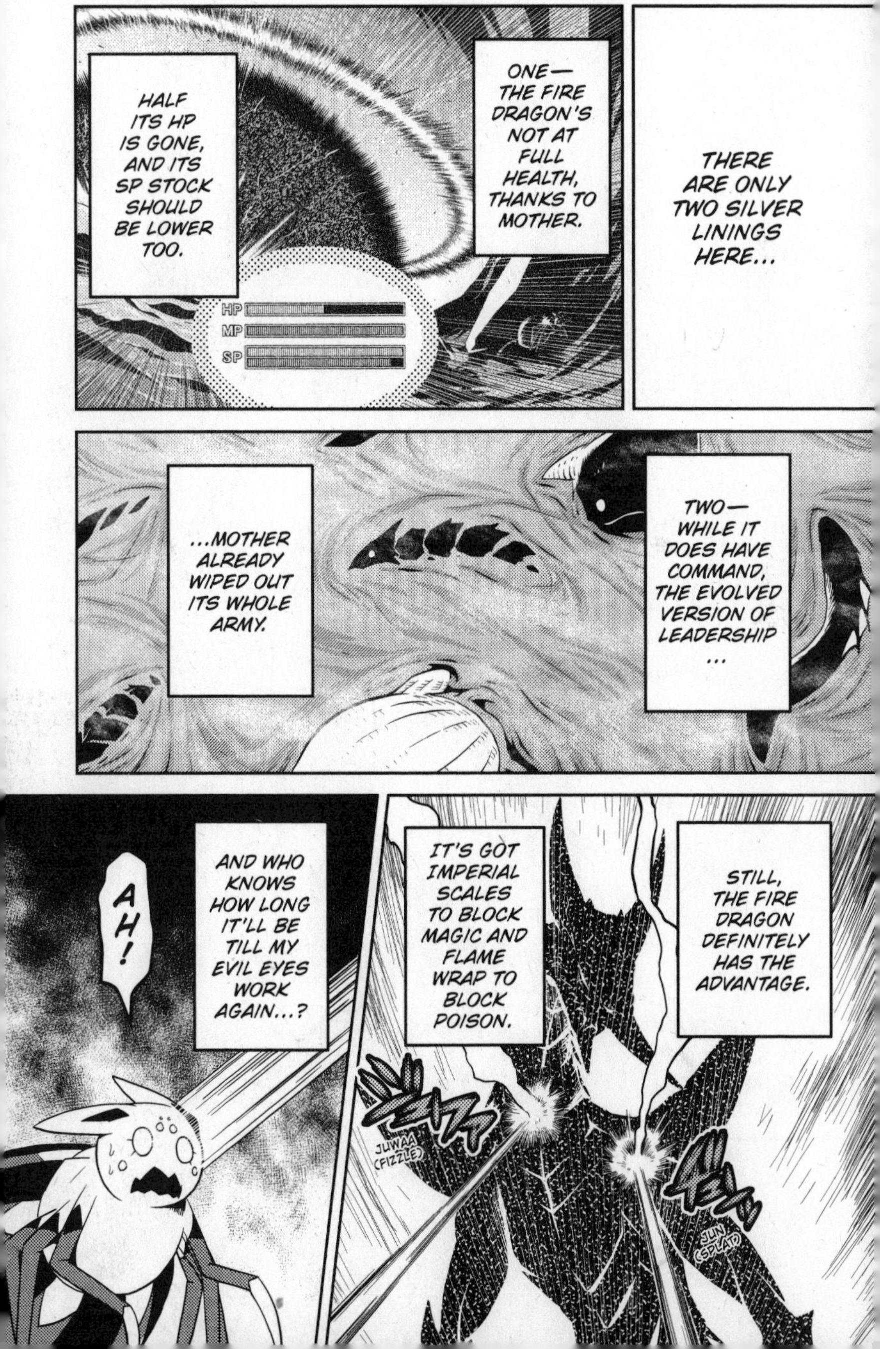
THERE ARE ONLY TWO SILVER LININGS HERE...
ONE— THE FIRE DRAGON'S NOT AT FULL HEALTH, THANKS TO MOTHER.
HALF ITS HP IS GONE, AND ITS SP STOCK SHOULD BE LOWER TOO.
HP
MP
SP
TWO— WHILE IT DOES HAVE COMMAND, THE EVOLVED VERSION OF LEADERSHIP ...
...MOTHER ALREADY WIPED OUT ITS WHOLE ARMY.
STILL, THE FIRE DRAGON DEFINITELY HAS THE ADVANTAGE.
IT'S GOT IMPERIAL SCALES TO BLOCK MAGIC AND FLAME WRAP TO BLOCK POISON.
JUN (SPLAT)
JUWAA (FIZZLE)
AND WHO KNOWS HOW LONG IT'LL BE TILL MY EVIL EYES WORK AGAIN...?
AH!

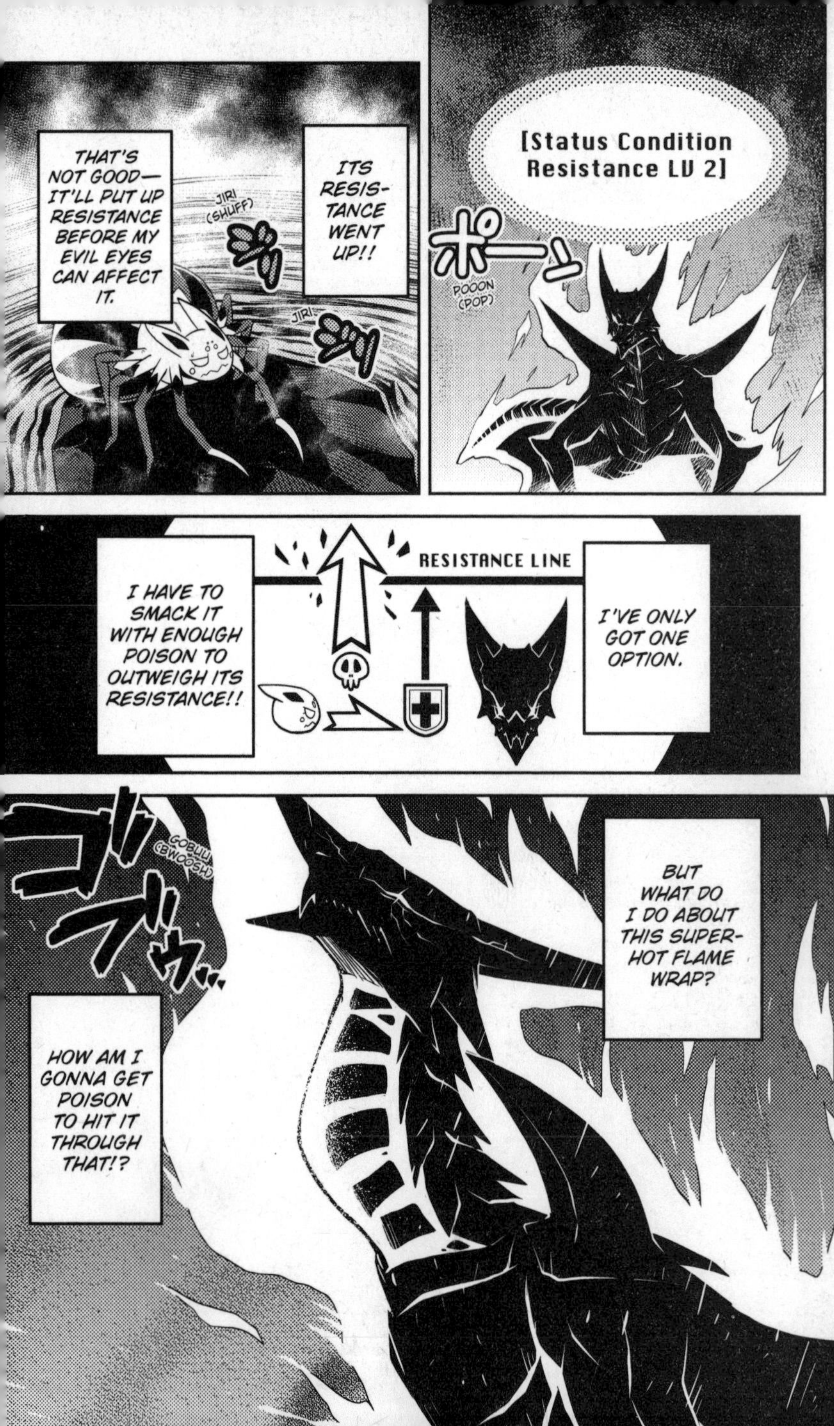
[Status Condition Resistance LV 2]
POOON (POP)
ITS RESIS-TANCE WENT UP!!
JIRI (SHUFF)
THAT'S NOT GOOD—IT'LL PUT UP RESISTANCE BEFORE MY EVIL EYES CAN AFFECT IT.
JIRI
I'VE ONLY GOT ONE OPTION.
RESISTANCE LINE
I HAVE TO SMACK IT WITH ENOUGH POISON TO OUTWEIGH ITS RESISTANCE!!
BUT WHAT DO I DO ABOUT THIS SUPER-HOT FLAME WRAP?
GOBUU (BWOOSH)
HOW AM I GONNA GET POISON TO HIT IT THROUGH THAT!?

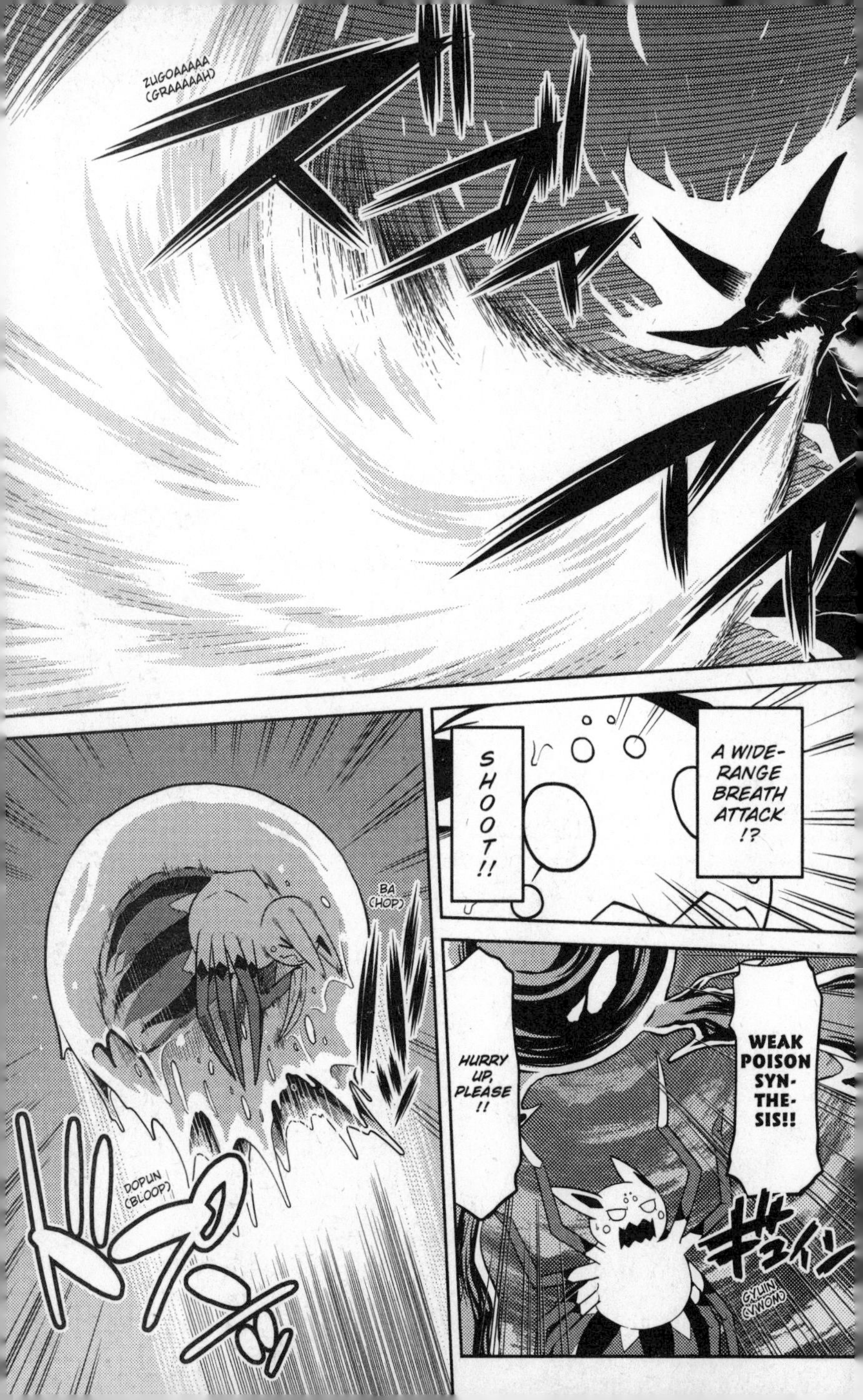
ZUGOAAAAA (GRAAAAAH)
A WIDE-RANGE BREATH ATTACK !?
SHOOOT!!
WEAK POISON SYN-THE-SIS!!
HURRY UP, PLEASE !!
GYUIN (VWOM)
BA (HOP)
DOPUN (BLOOP)

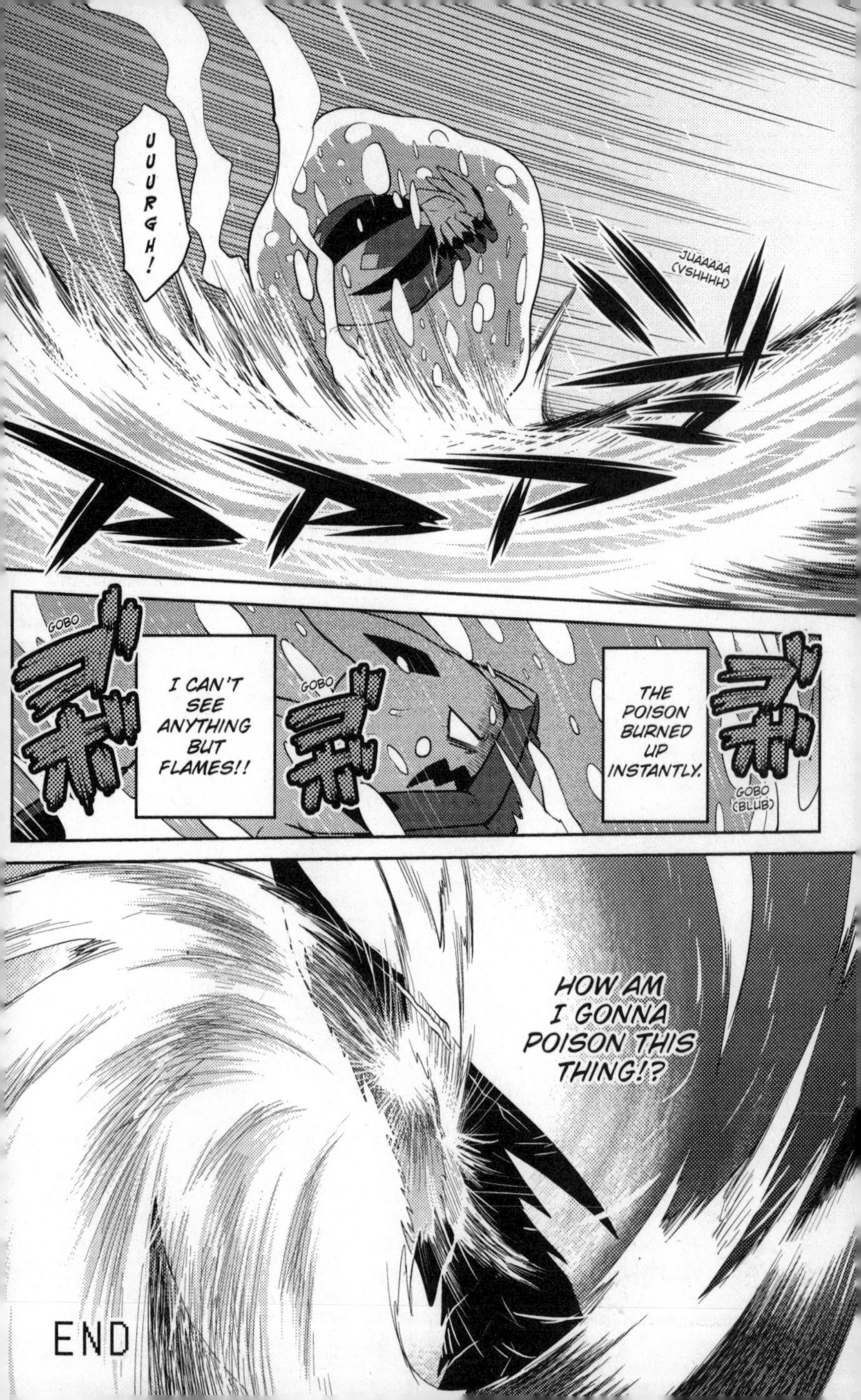
JUAAAAA (VSHHHH)
UUURGH!
GOBO (BLUB)
THE POISON BURNED UP INSTANTLY.
GOBO
I CAN'T SEE ANYTHING BUT FLAMES!!
GOBO
HOW AM I GONNA POISON THIS THING!?
END

So I'm a Spider, So What?

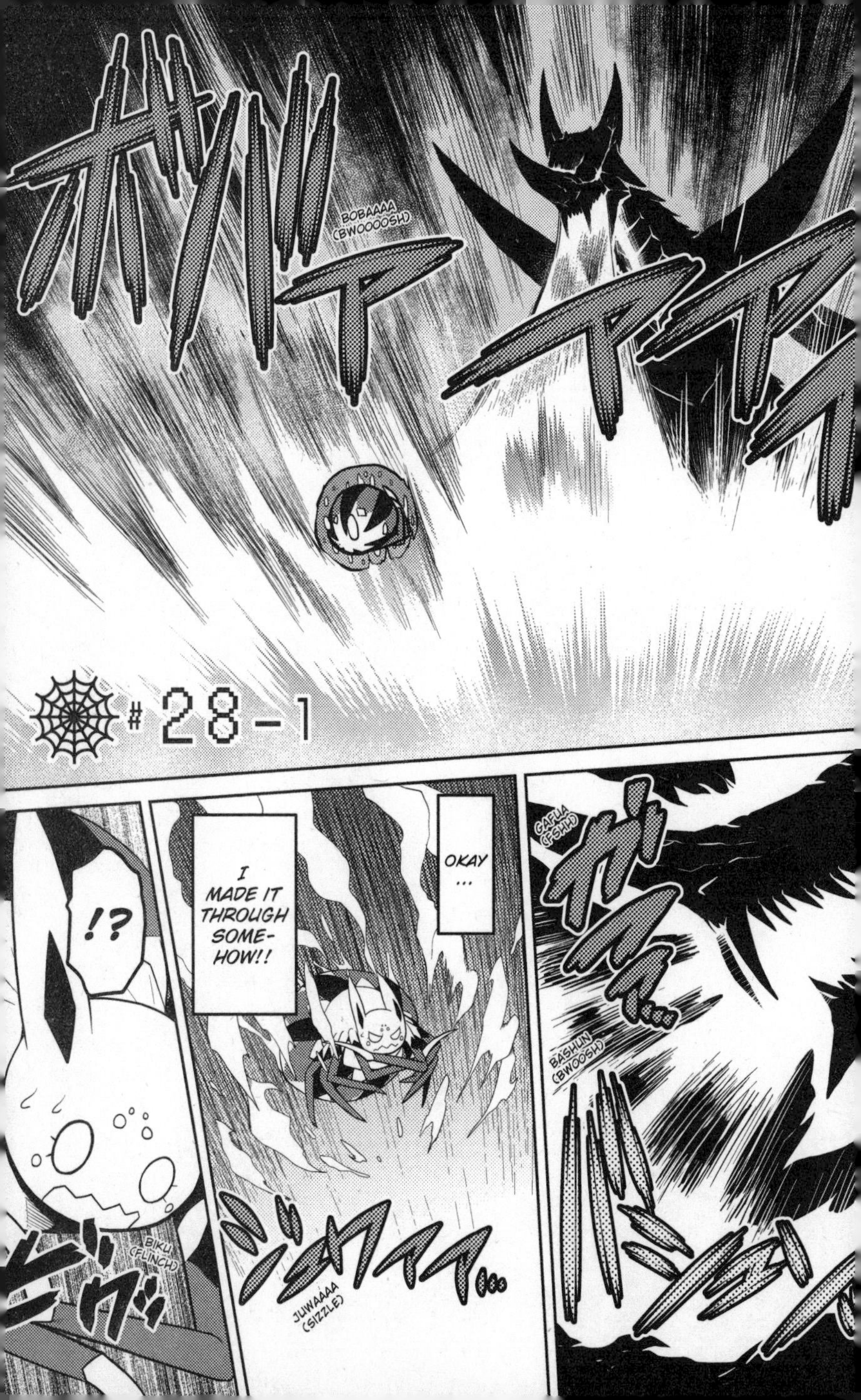
BOBAAAA
(BWOOOOSH)
#28-1
GAFUA
(FSHH)
BASHUN
(BWOOSH)
OKAY ...
I MADE IT THROUGH SOME-HOW!!
JUWAAAA
(SIZZLE)
!?
BIKU
(FLINCH)

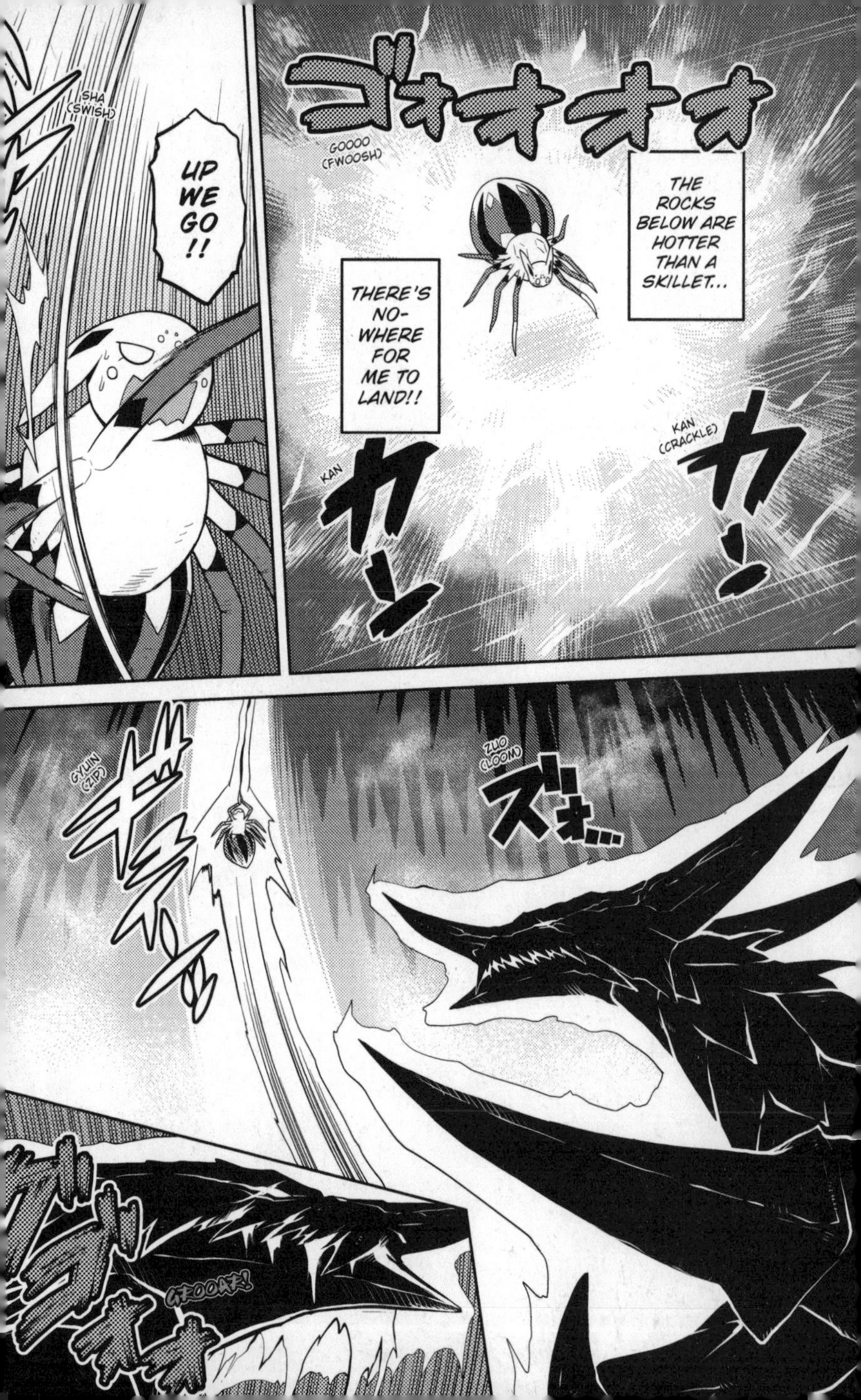
GOOOO (FWOOSH)
THE ROCKS BELOW ARE HOTTER THAN A SKILLET...
THERE'S NO-WHERE FOR ME TO LAND!!
KAN (CRACKLE)
KAN
SHA (SWISH)
UP WE GO!!
ZUO (LOOM)
GYUIN (ZIP)
GROOAR!

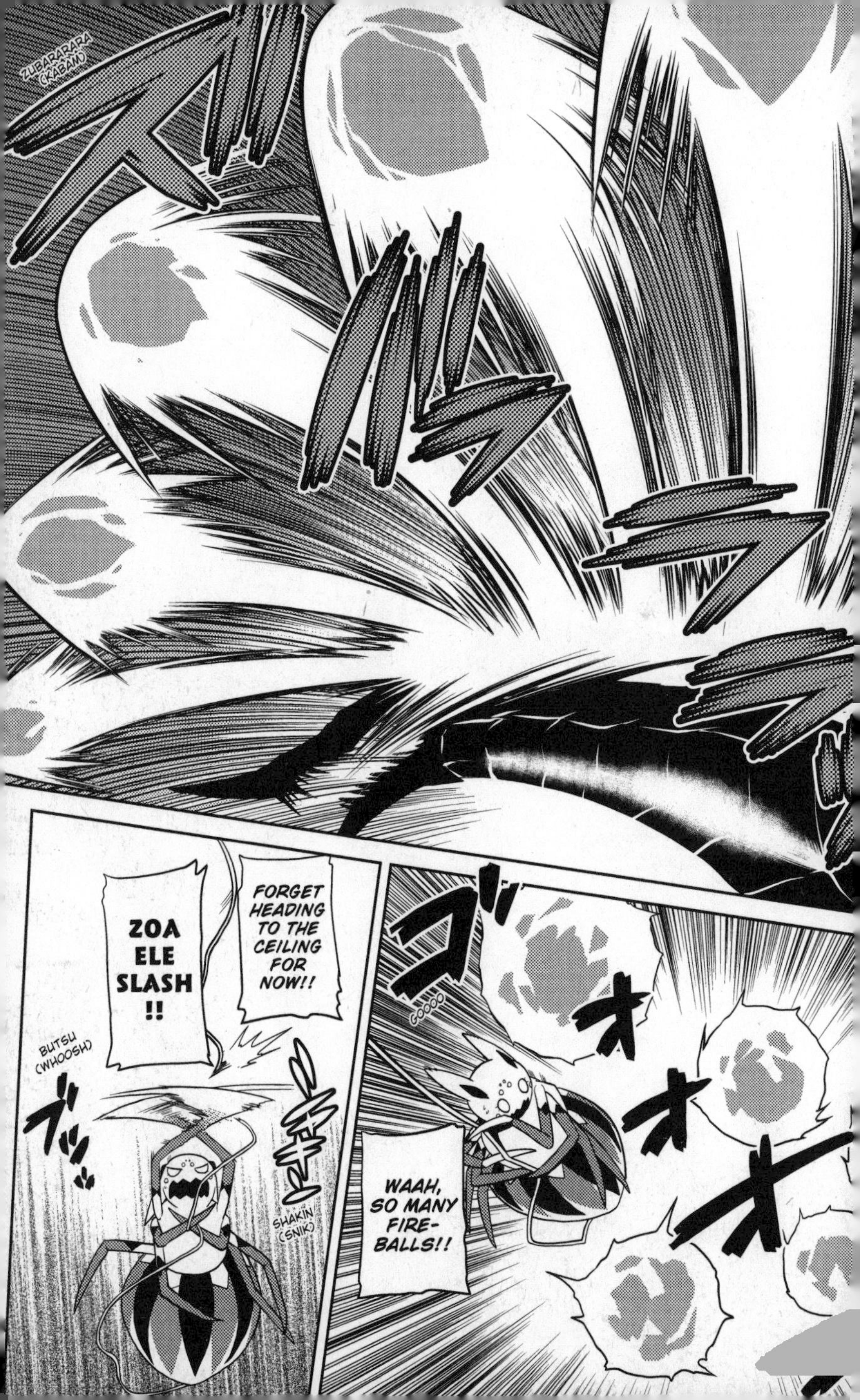
ZUBARARARA (KABAM)
GOOOO
WAAH, SO MANY FIRE-BALLS!!
FORGET HEADING TO THE CEILING FOR NOW!!
ZOA ELE SLASH !!
BUTSU (WHOOSH)
SHAKIN (SNIK)

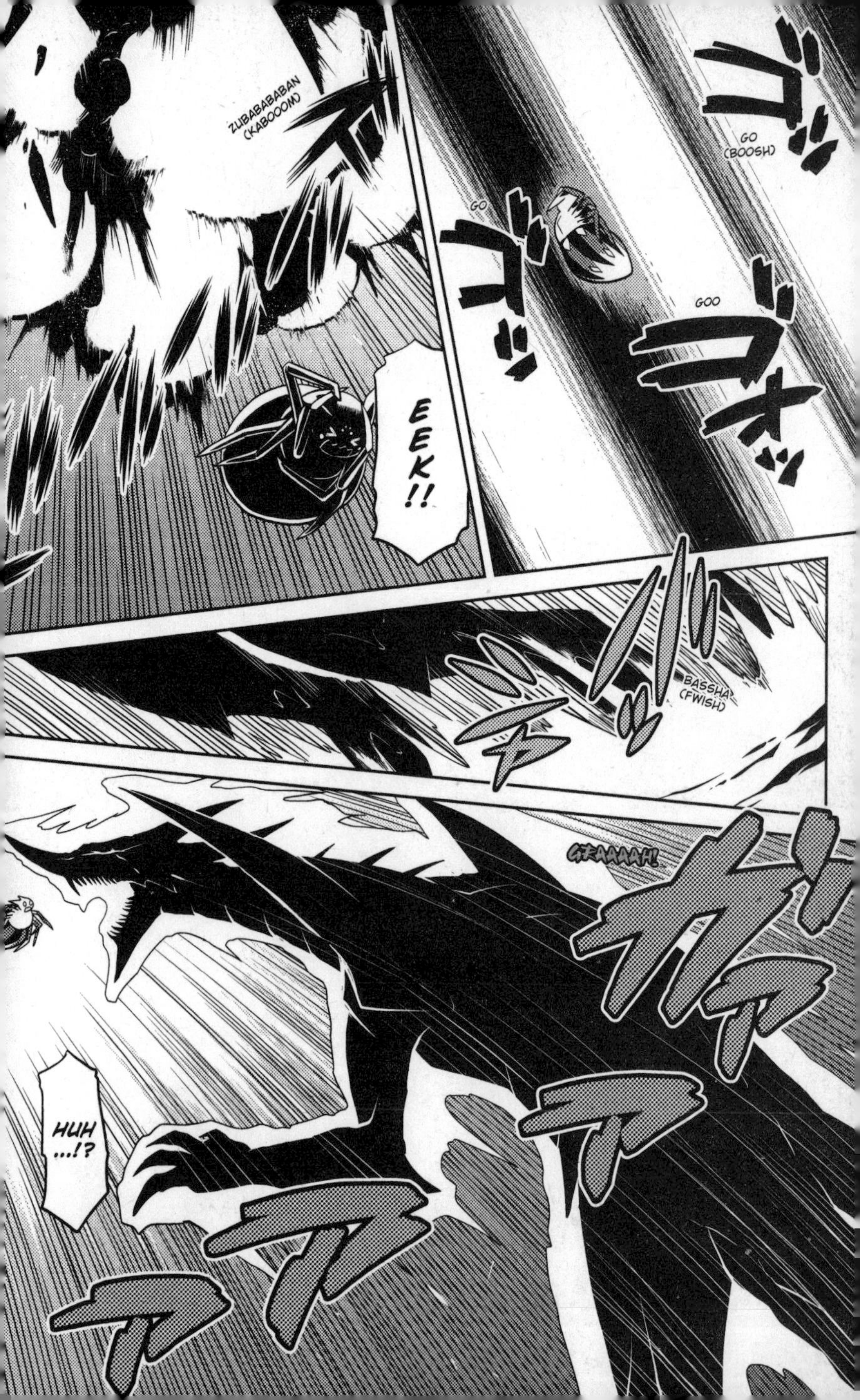
GO
(BOOSH)
GO
GOO
ZUBABABABAN
(KABOOOM)
EEK!!
BASSHA
(FWISH)
GRAAAAH!
HUH
...!?

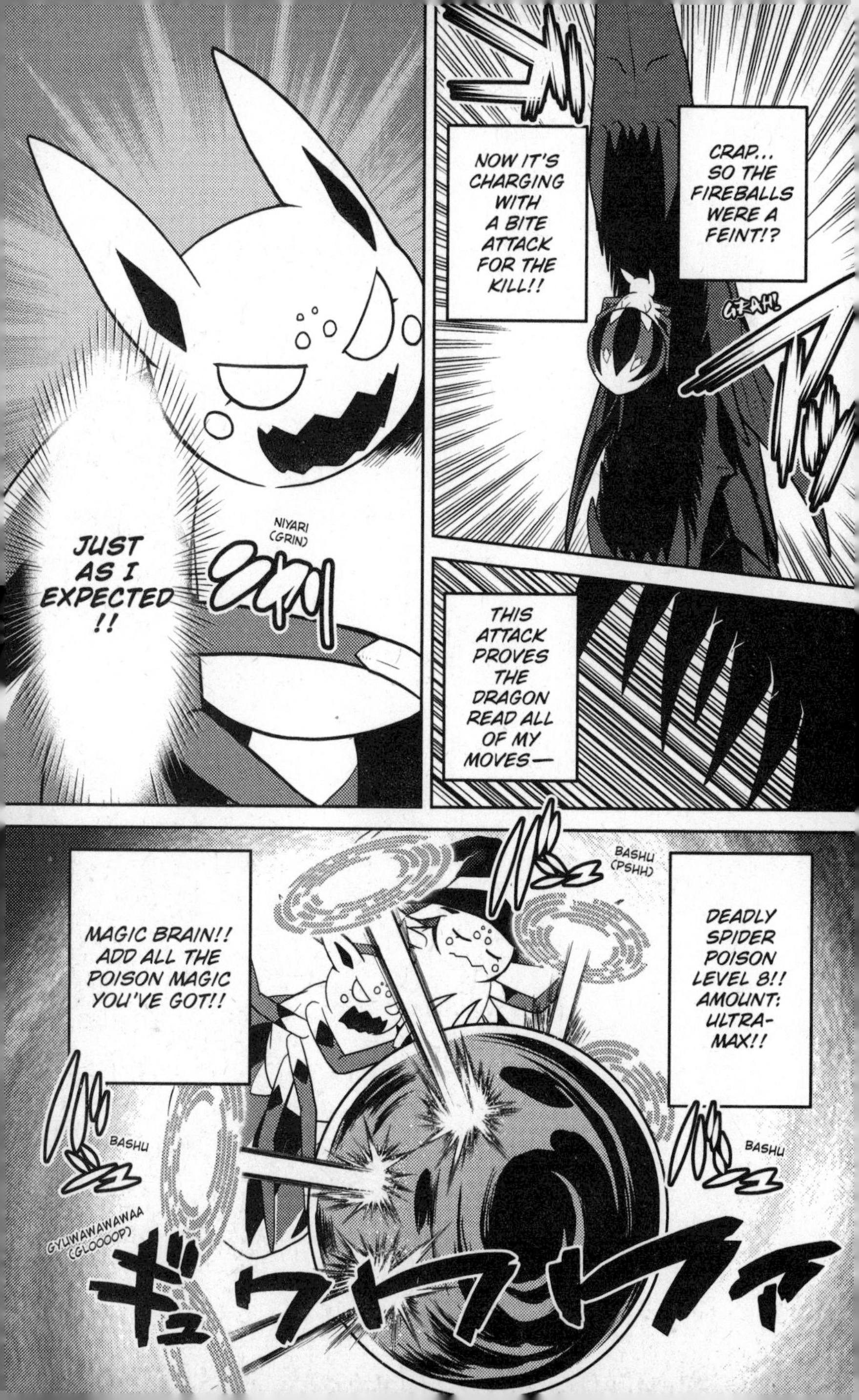

CRAP... SO THE FIREBALLS WERE A FEINT!?
NOW IT'S CHARGING WITH A BITE ATTACK FOR THE KILL!!
GRAH!
THIS ATTACK PROVES THE DRAGON READ ALL OF MY MOVES—
NIYARI (GRIN)
JUST AS I EXPECTED!!
BASHU (PSHH)
DEADLY SPIDER POISON LEVEL 8!! AMOUNT: ULTRA-MAX!!
MAGIC BRAIN!! ADD ALL THE POISON MAGIC YOU'VE GOT!!
BASHU
BASHU
GYUWAWAWAWAA (GLOOOOP)

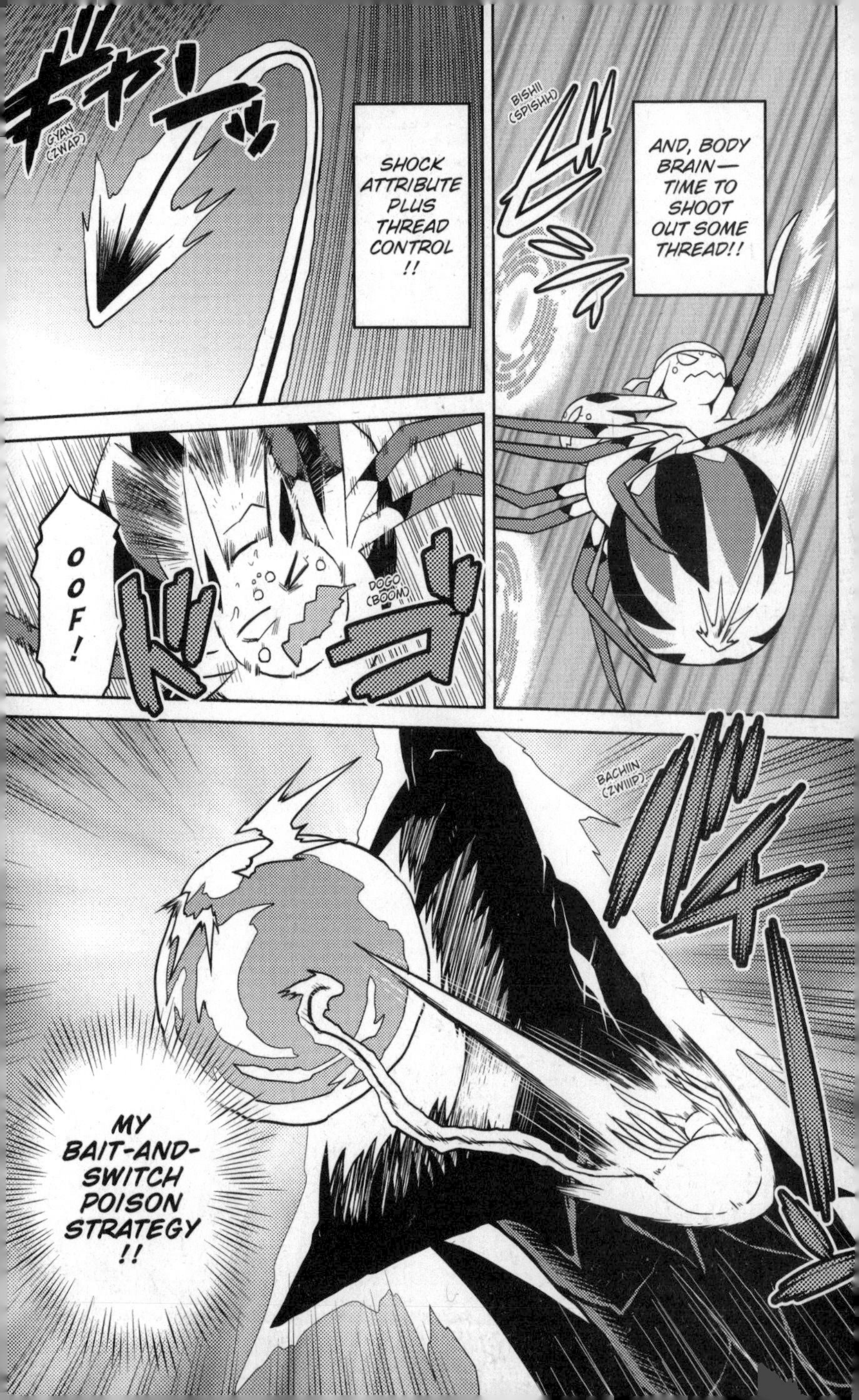
AND, BODY BRAIN—TIME TO SHOOT OUT SOME THREAD!!
BISHII (SPISHH)
SHOCK ATTRIBUTE PLUS THREAD CONTROL!!
GYAN (ZWAP)
DOGO (BOOM)
OOF!
BACHIN (ZWIIIP)
MY BAIT-AND-SWITCH POISON STRATEGY!!

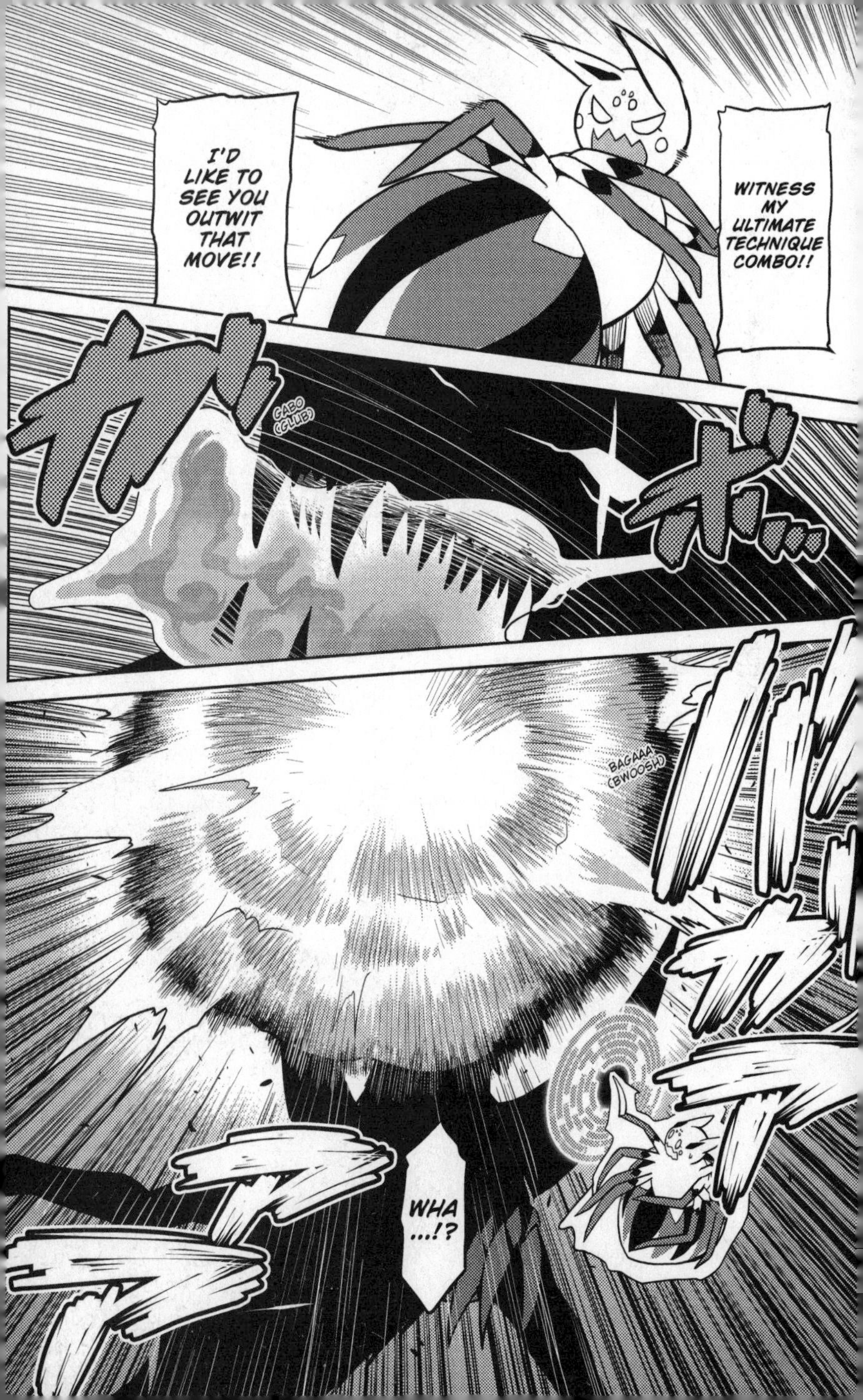
WITNESS MY ULTIMATE TECHNIQUE COMBO!!
I'D LIKE TO SEE YOU OUTWIT THAT MOVE!!
GABO (GLUB)
BAGAAA (BWOOSH)
WHA ...!?

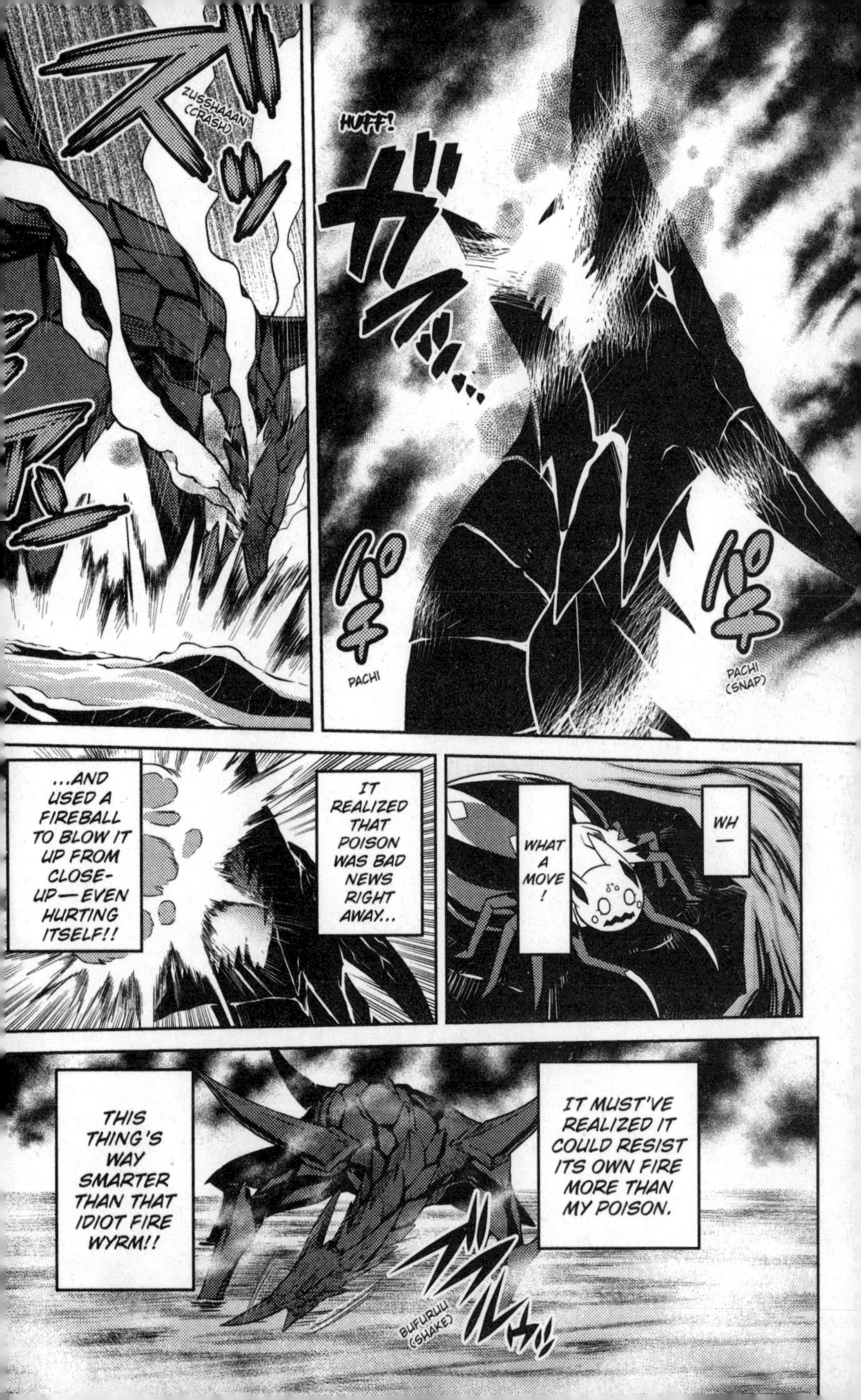
HUFF!
PACHI (SNAP)
PACHI
ZUSSHAAAN (CRASH)
WH—
WHAT A MOVE!
IT REALIZED THAT POISON WAS BAD NEWS RIGHT AWAY...
...AND USED A FIREBALL TO BLOW IT UP FROM CLOSE-UP—EVEN HURTING ITSELF!!
IT MUST'VE REALIZED IT COULD RESIST ITS OWN FIRE MORE THAN MY POISON.
BUFURUU (SHAKE)
THIS THING'S WAY SMARTER THAN THAT IDIOT FIRE WYRM!!

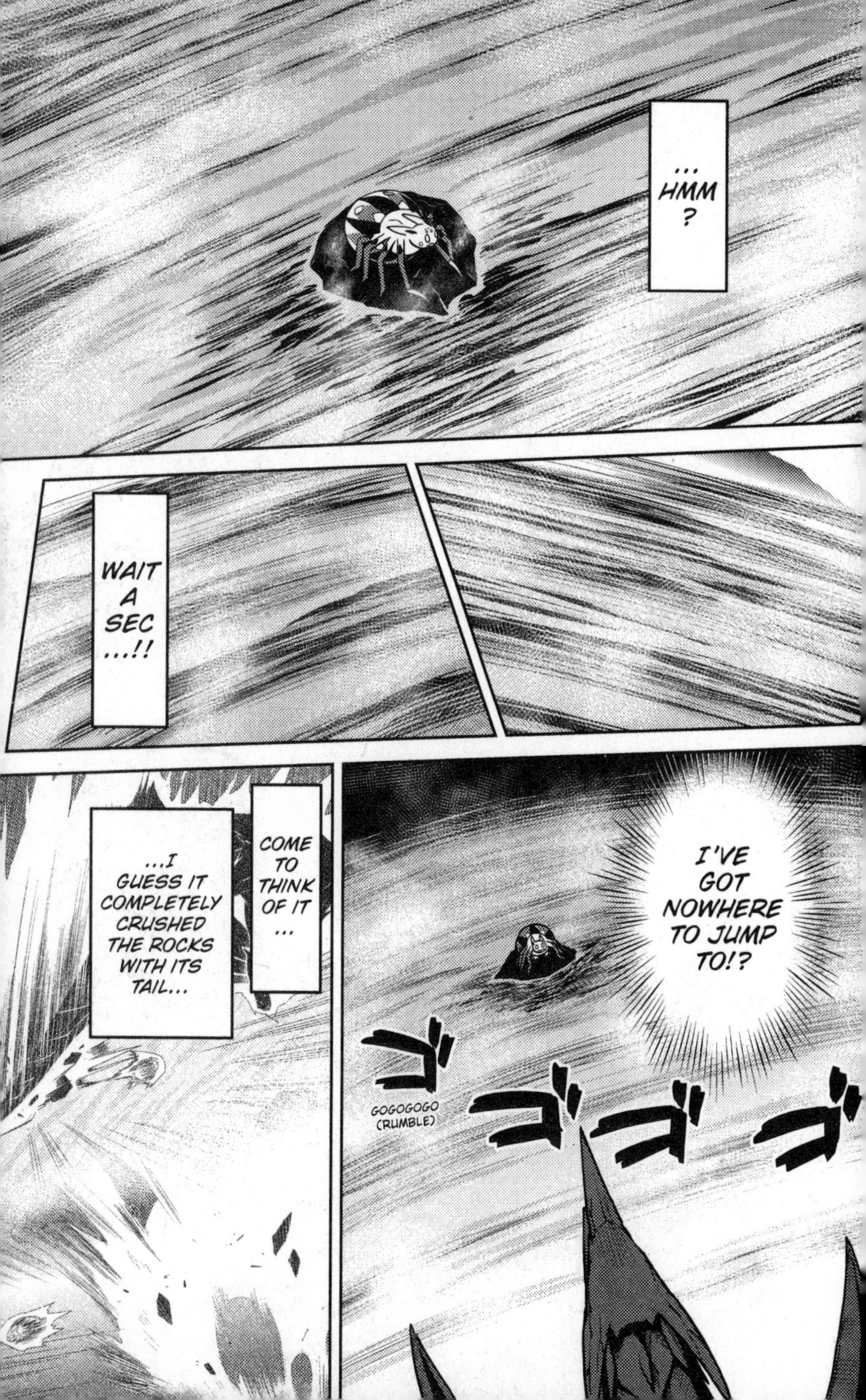
...HMM?
WAIT A SEC...!!
I'VE GOT NOWHERE TO JUMP TO!?
ゴゴゴゴ
GOGOGOGO (RUMBLE)
COME TO THINK OF IT...
...I GUESS IT COMPLETELY CRUSHED THE ROCKS WITH ITS TAIL...

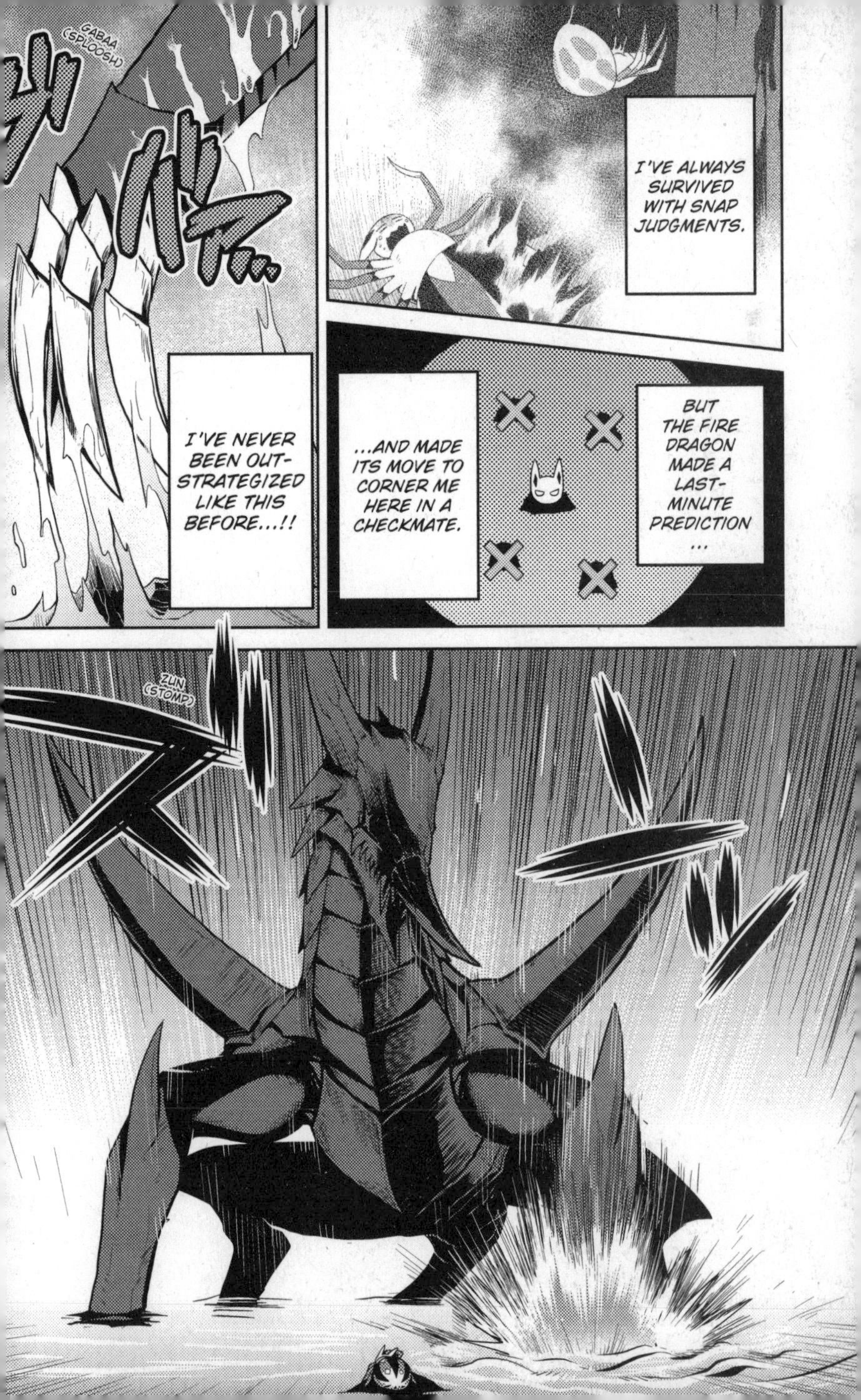
I'VE ALWAYS SURVIVED WITH SNAP JUDGMENTS.
BUT THE FIRE DRAGON MADE A LAST-MINUTE PREDICTION...
...AND MADE ITS MOVE TO CORNER ME HERE IN A CHECKMATE.
GABAA (SPLOOSH)
I'VE NEVER BEEN OUT-STRATEGIZED LIKE THIS BEFORE...!!
ZUN (STOMP)

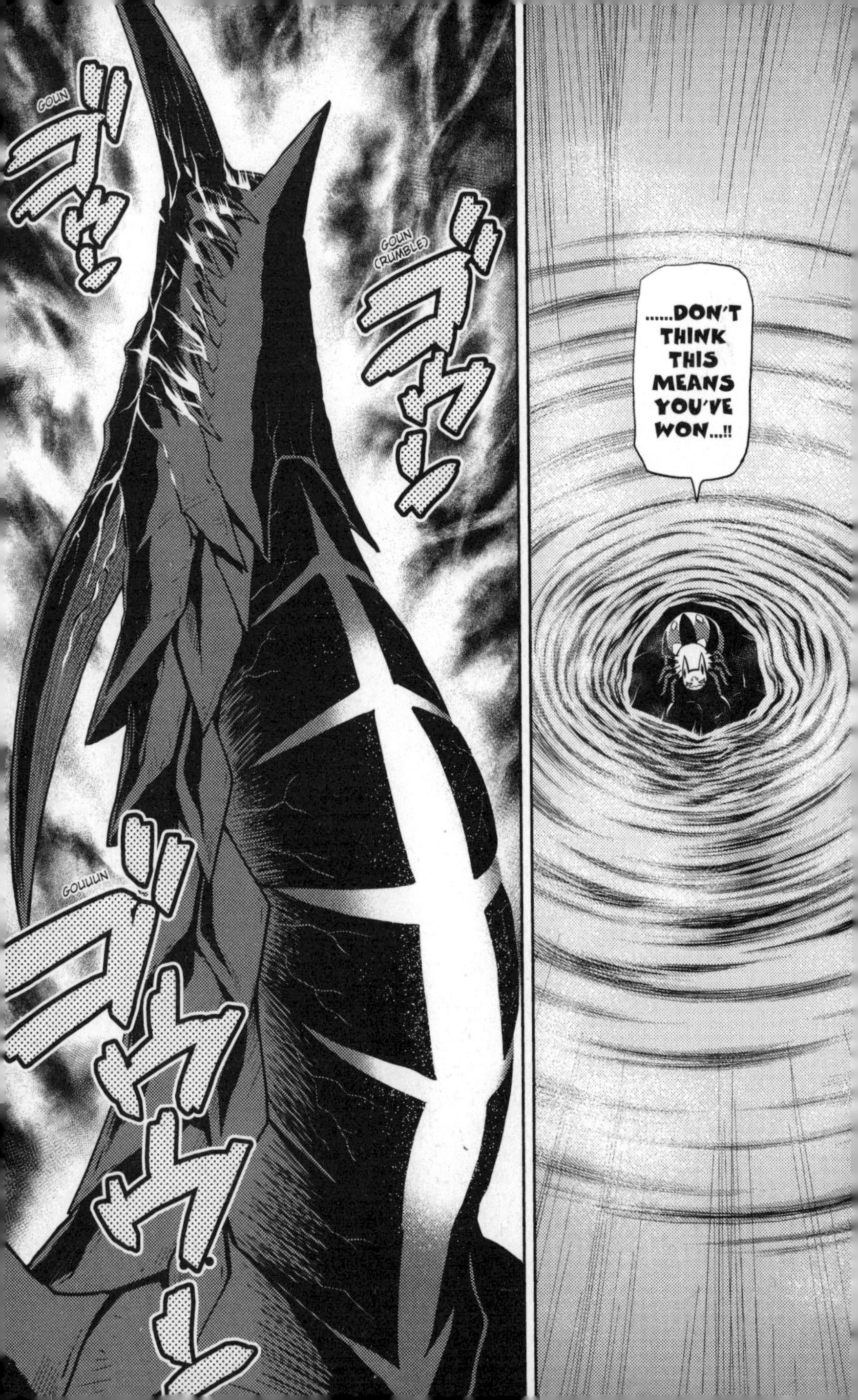
......DON'T THINK THIS MEANS YOU'VE WON...!!
GOUN (RUMBLE)
GOUN
GOUUUN

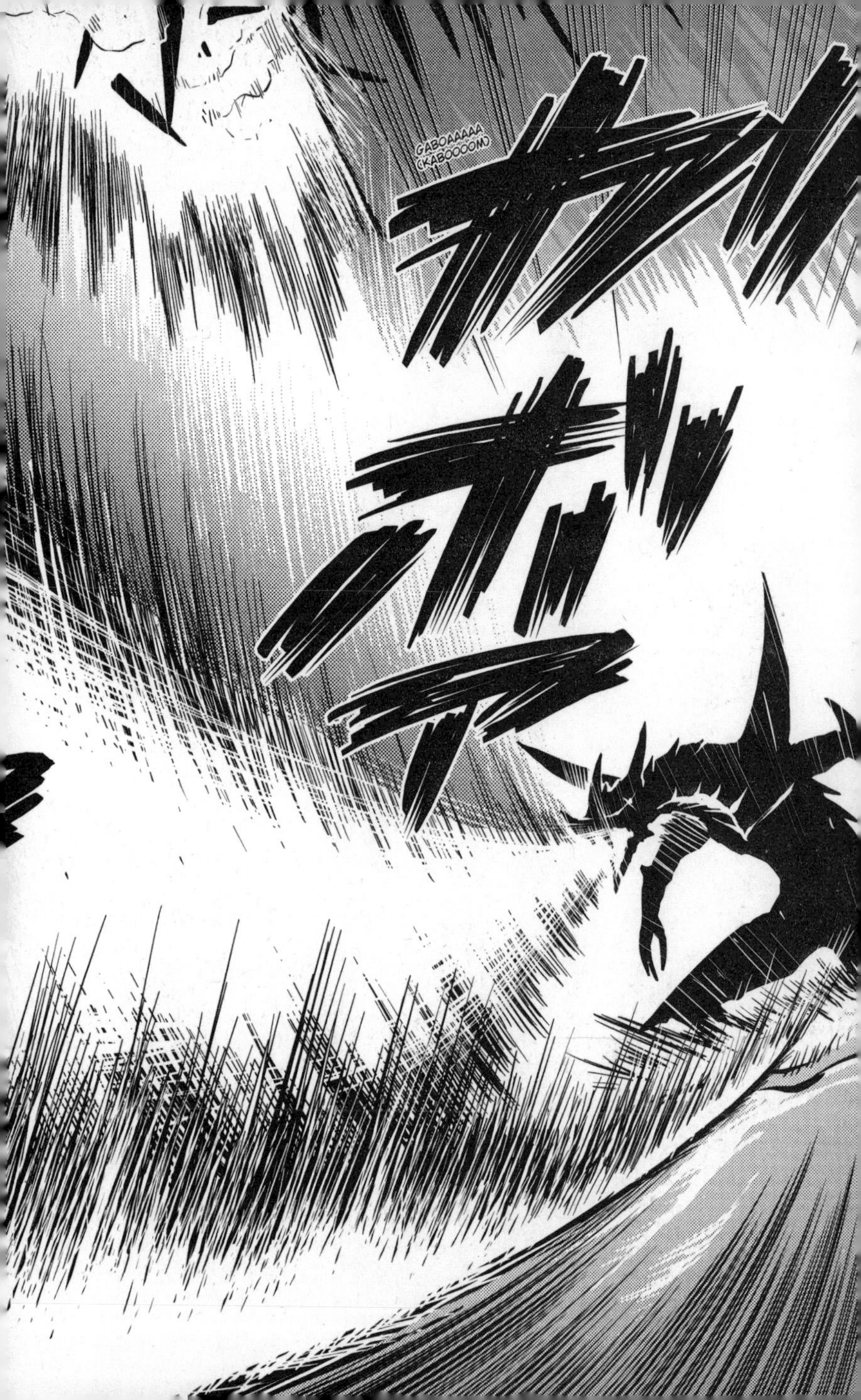
GABOAAAAA
(KABOOOOM)

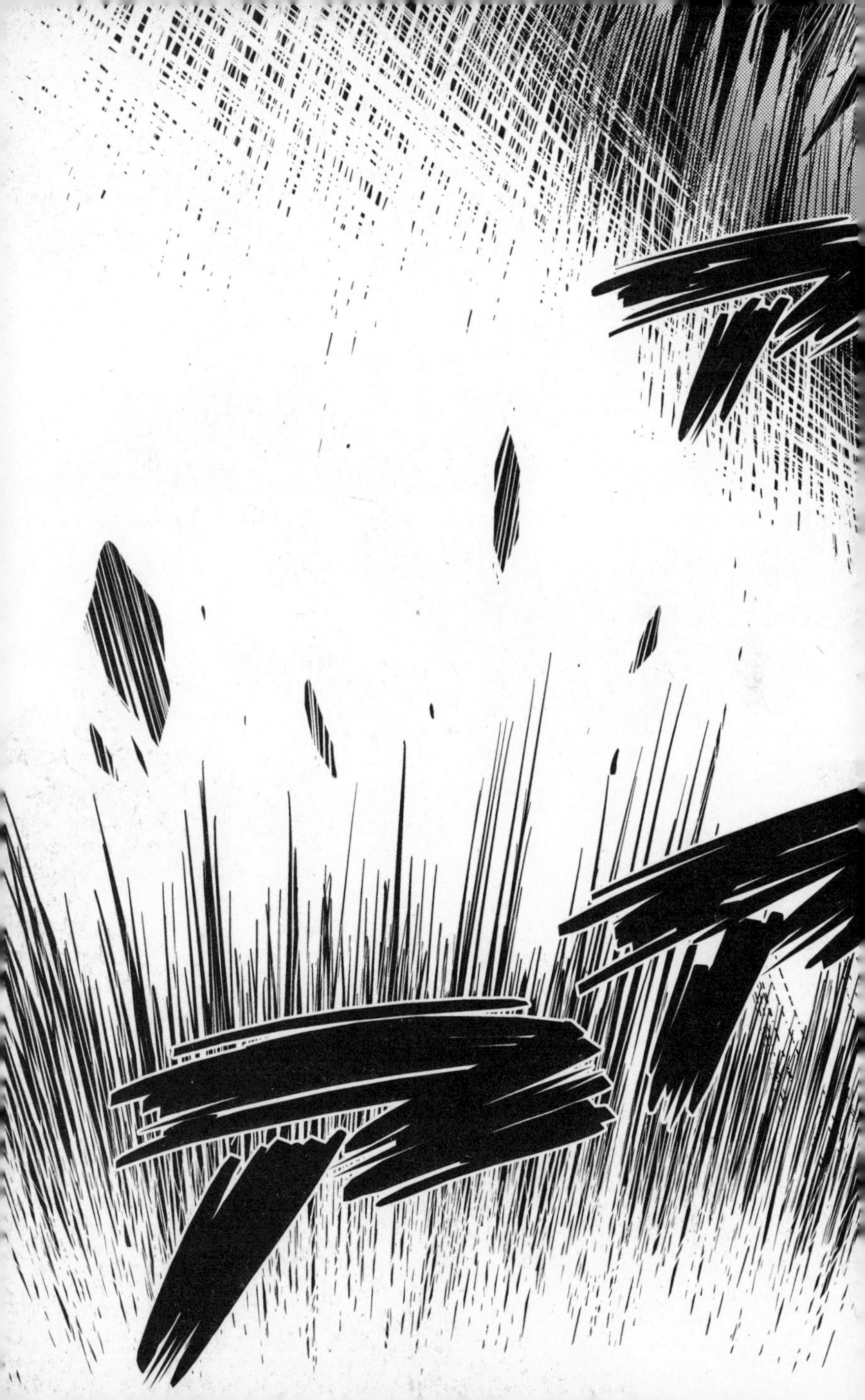

DOOOOO
(BWOOOOSH)

OOO
(WHOOSH)

PACHI
(SIZZLE)

PACHI

END

So I'm a Spider, So What?

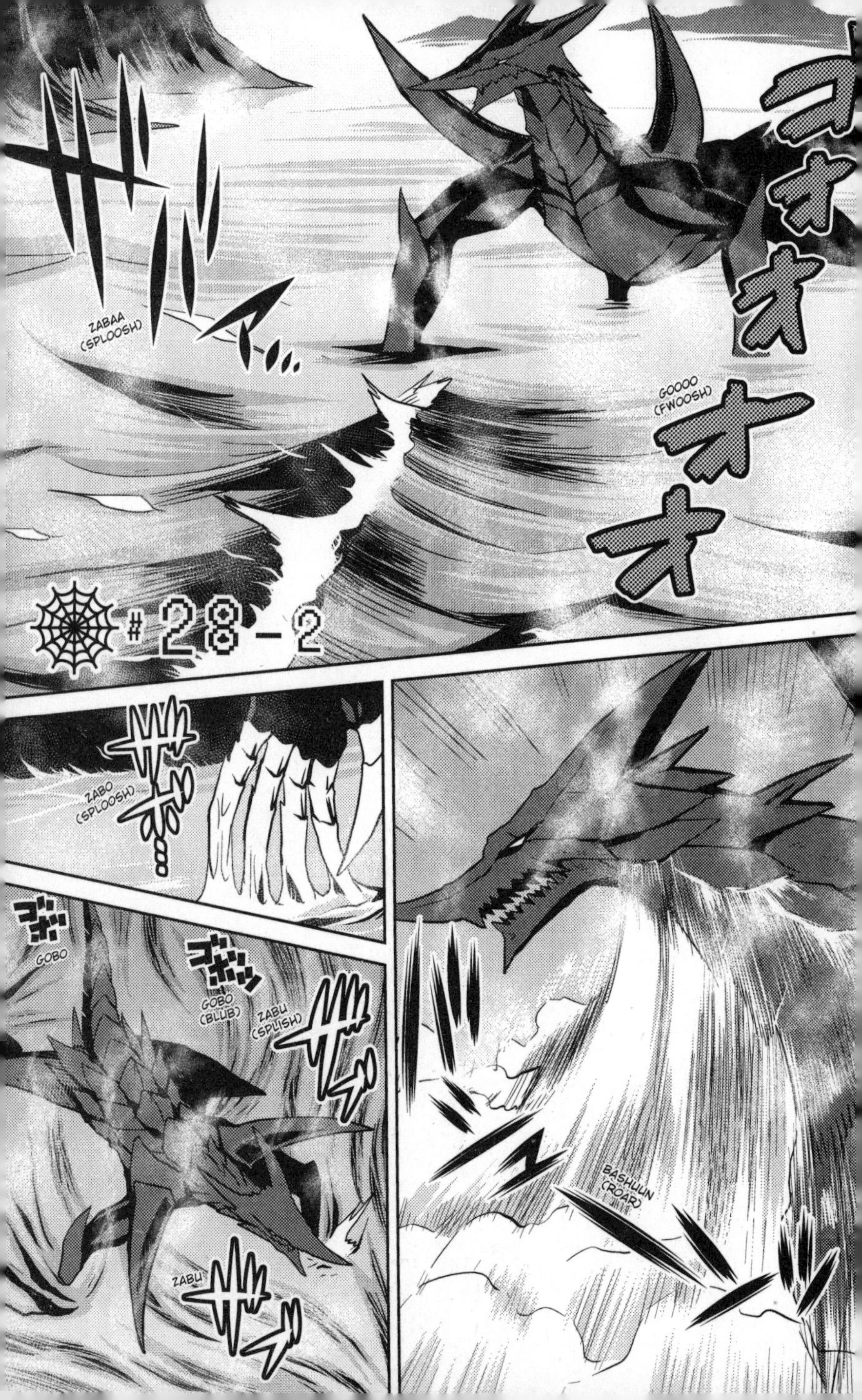
GOOOO (FWOOSH)
ZABAA (SPLOOSH)
#28-2
BASHUUN (ROAR)
ZABO (SPLOOSH)
ZABU (SPLISH)
GOBO (BLUB)
GOBO
ZABU

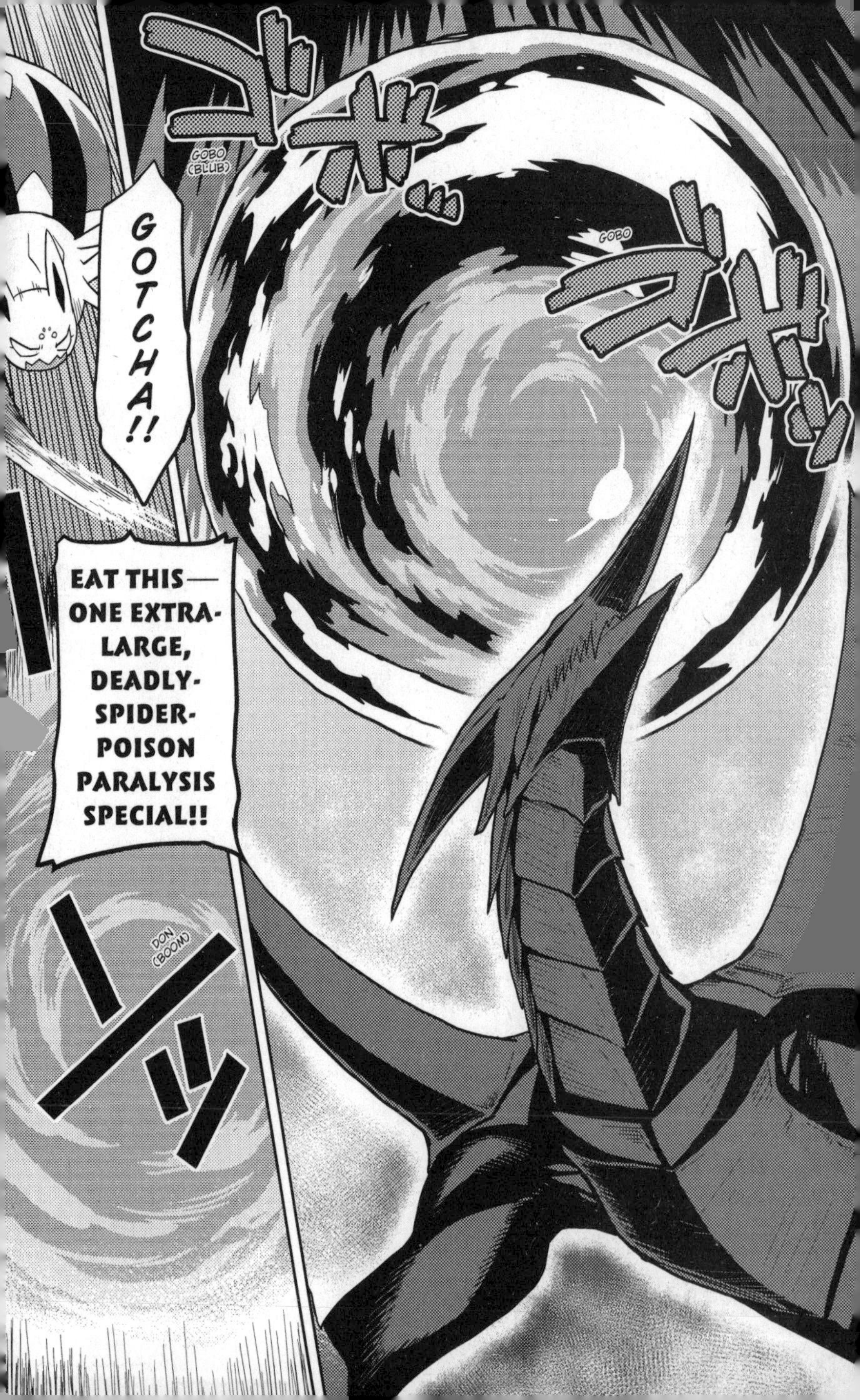
GOBO
GOBO (BLUB)
GOTCHA!!
EAT THIS— ONE EXTRA-LARGE, DEADLY-SPIDER-POISON PARALYSIS SPECIAL!!
DON (BOOM)

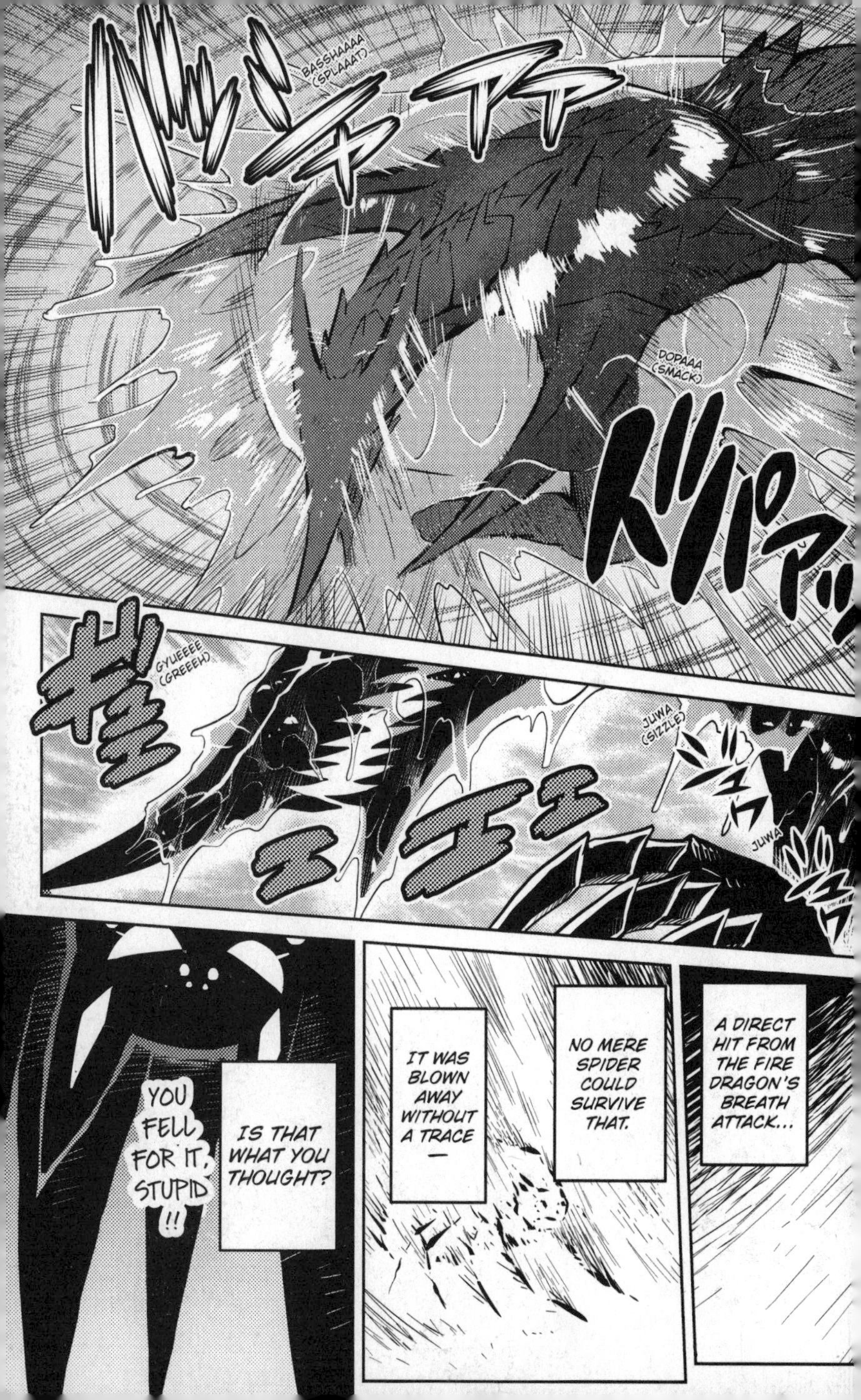
BASSHAAAA (SPLAAAT)
DOPAAA (SMACK)
JUWA (SIZZLE)
JUWA
GYUEEEE (GREEEH)
A DIRECT HIT FROM THE FIRE DRAGON'S BREATH ATTACK...
NO MERE SPIDER COULD SURVIVE THAT.
IT WAS BLOWN AWAY WITHOUT A TRACE —
IS THAT WHAT YOU THOUGHT?
YOU FELL FOR IT, STUPID!!

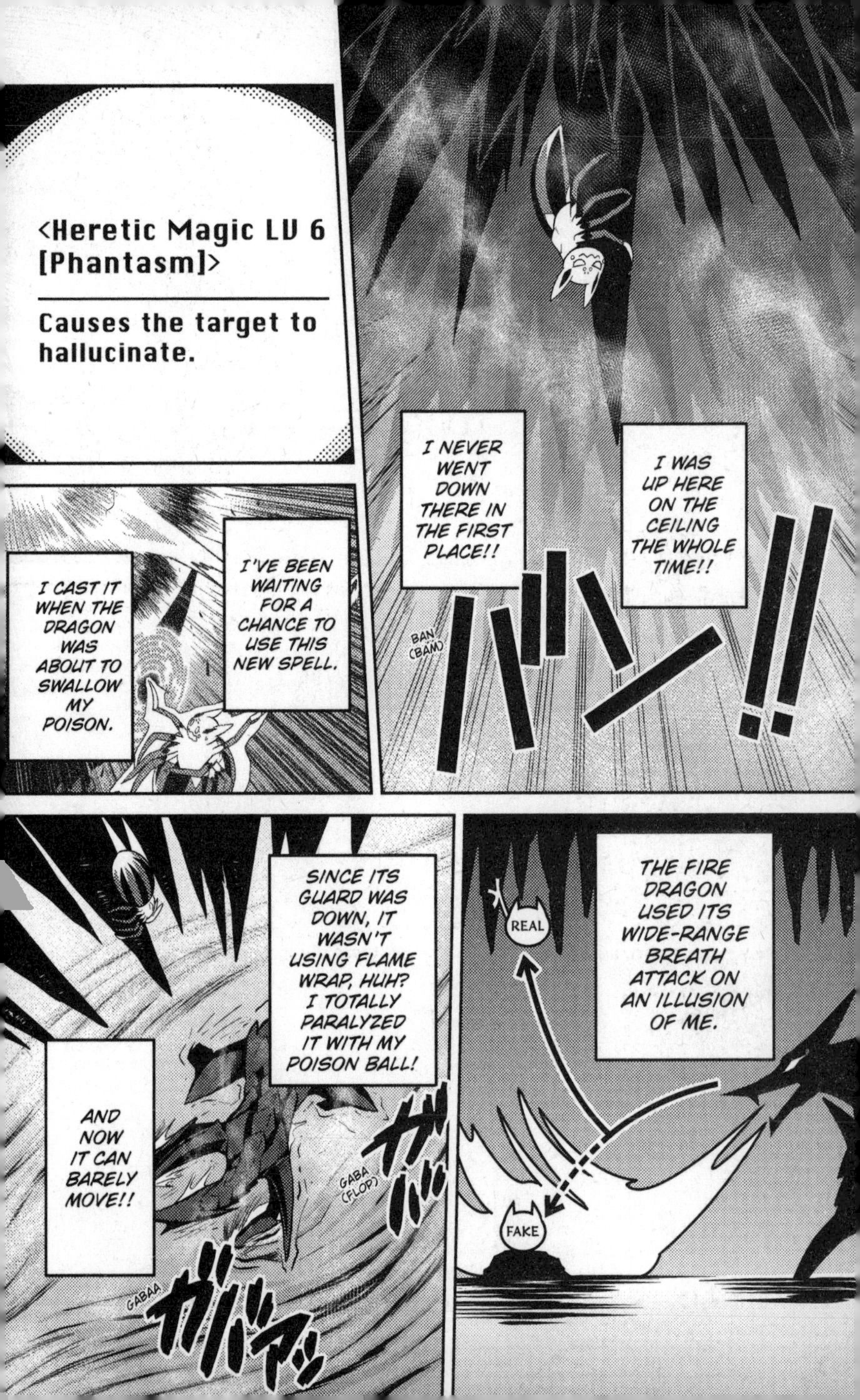
I WAS UP HERE ON THE CEILING THE WHOLE TIME!!
I NEVER WENT DOWN THERE IN THE FIRST PLACE!!
BAN (BAM)
<Heretic Magic LV 6 [Phantasm]>
Causes the target to hallucinate.
I'VE BEEN WAITING FOR A CHANCE TO USE THIS NEW SPELL.
I CAST IT WHEN THE DRAGON WAS ABOUT TO SWALLOW MY POISON.
THE FIRE DRAGON USED ITS WIDE-RANGE BREATH ATTACK ON AN ILLUSION OF ME.
REAL
FAKE
SINCE ITS GUARD WAS DOWN, IT WASN'T USING FLAME WRAP, HUH? I TOTALLY PARALYZED IT WITH MY POISON BALL!
GABA (FLOP)
AND NOW IT CAN BARELY MOVE!!
GABAA

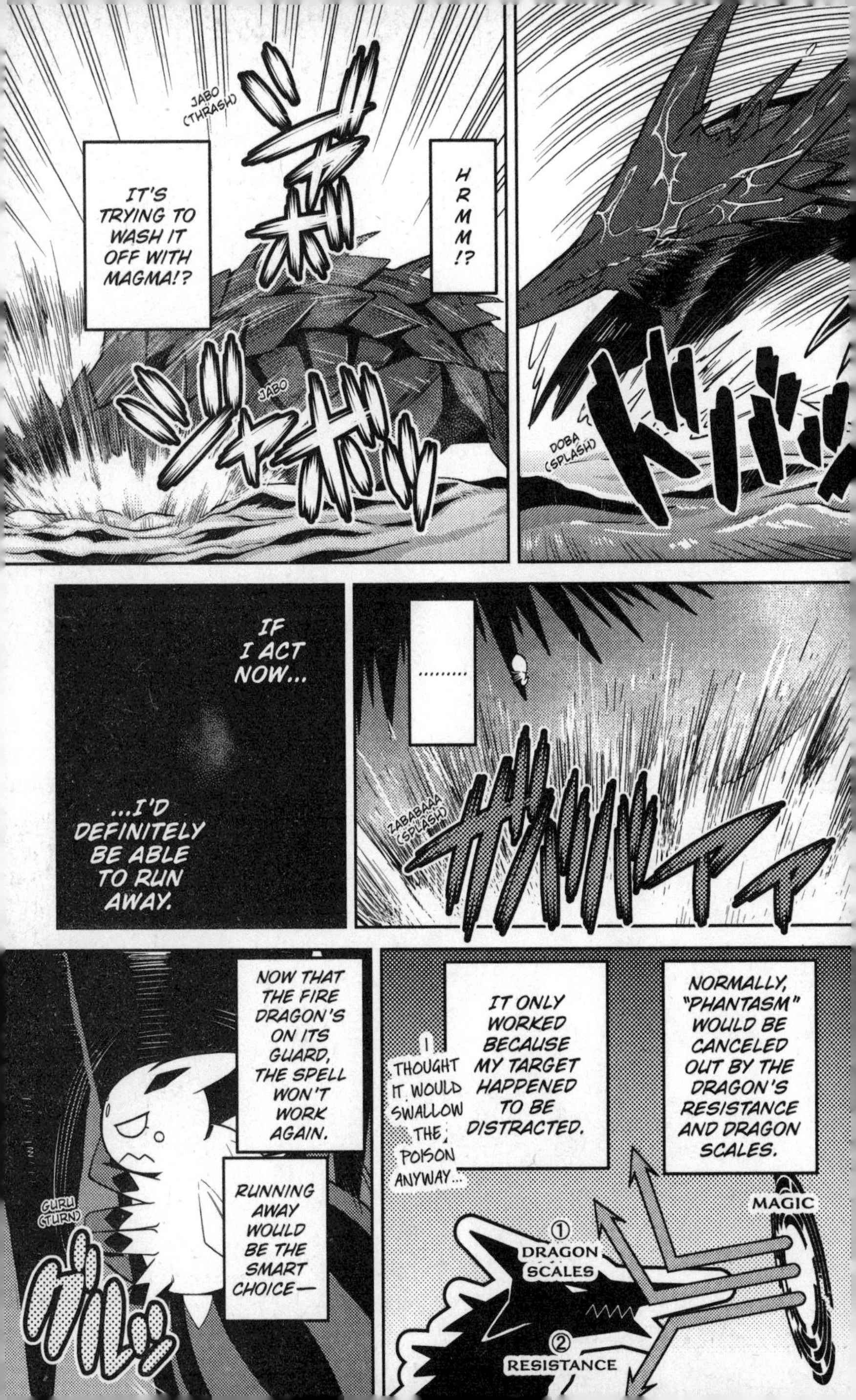
DOBA (SPLASH)
HRMM!?
JABO (THRASH)
IT'S TRYING TO WASH IT OFF WITH MAGMA!?
JABO
....
ZABABAAA (SPLASH)
IF I ACT NOW...
...I'D DEFINITELY BE ABLE TO RUN AWAY.
NORMALLY, "PHANTASM" WOULD BE CANCELED OUT BY THE DRAGON'S RESISTANCE AND DRAGON SCALES.
IT ONLY WORKED BECAUSE MY TARGET HAPPENED TO BE DISTRACTED.
I THOUGHT IT WOULD SWALLOW THE POISON ANYWAY...
MAGIC
① DRAGON SCALES
② RESISTANCE
NOW THAT THE FIRE DRAGON'S ON ITS GUARD, THE SPELL WON'T WORK AGAIN.
RUNNING AWAY WOULD BE THE SMART CHOICE—
GURU (TURN)

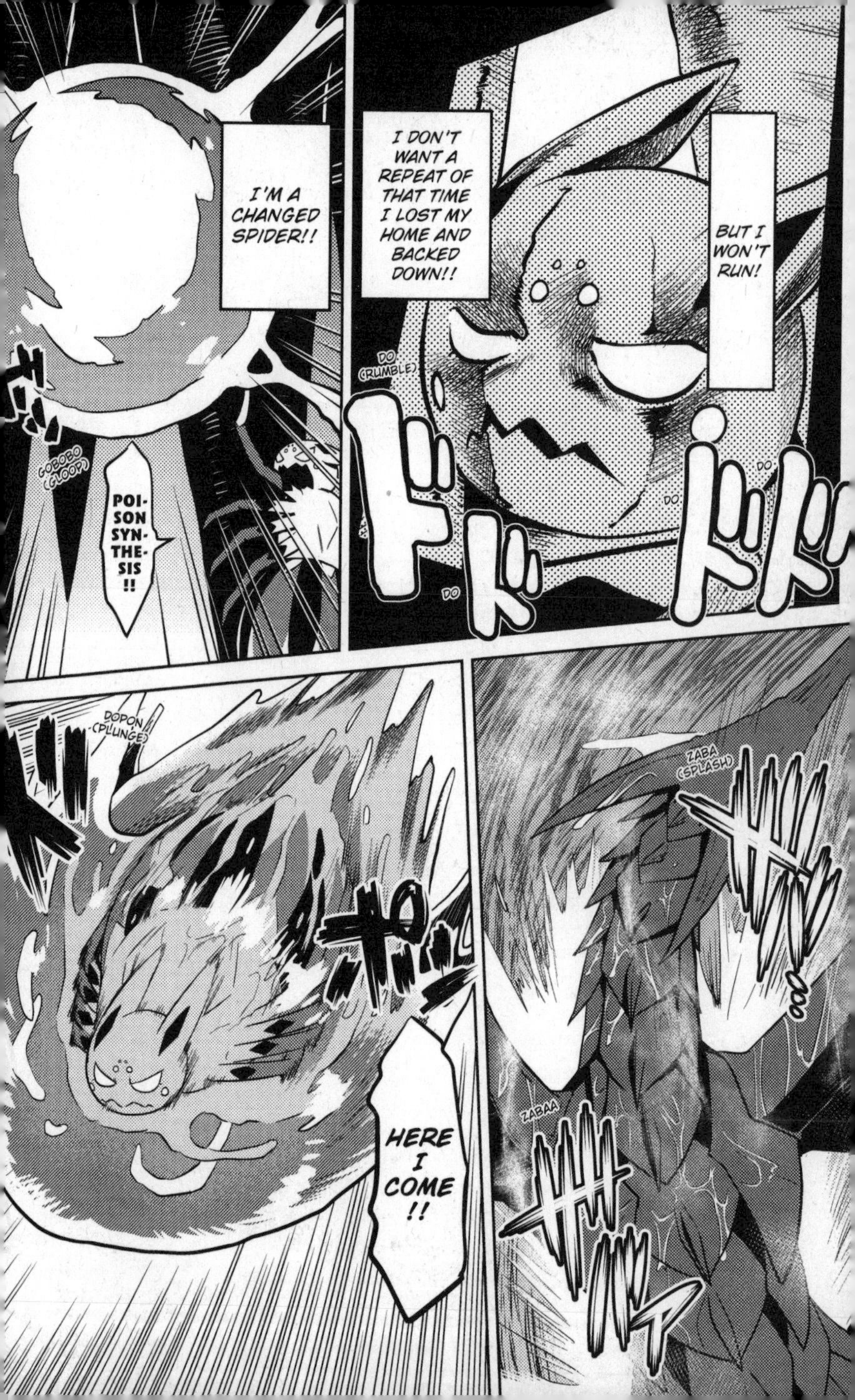

BUT I WON'T RUN!
I DON'T WANT A REPEAT OF THAT TIME I LOST MY HOME AND BACKED DOWN!!
DO (RUMBLE)
DO
DO
DO
I'M A CHANGED SPIDER!!
GOBOBO (GLOOP)
POI-SON SYN-THE-SIS!!
ZABA (SPLASH)
ZABAA
DOPON (PLUNGE)
HERE I COME!!

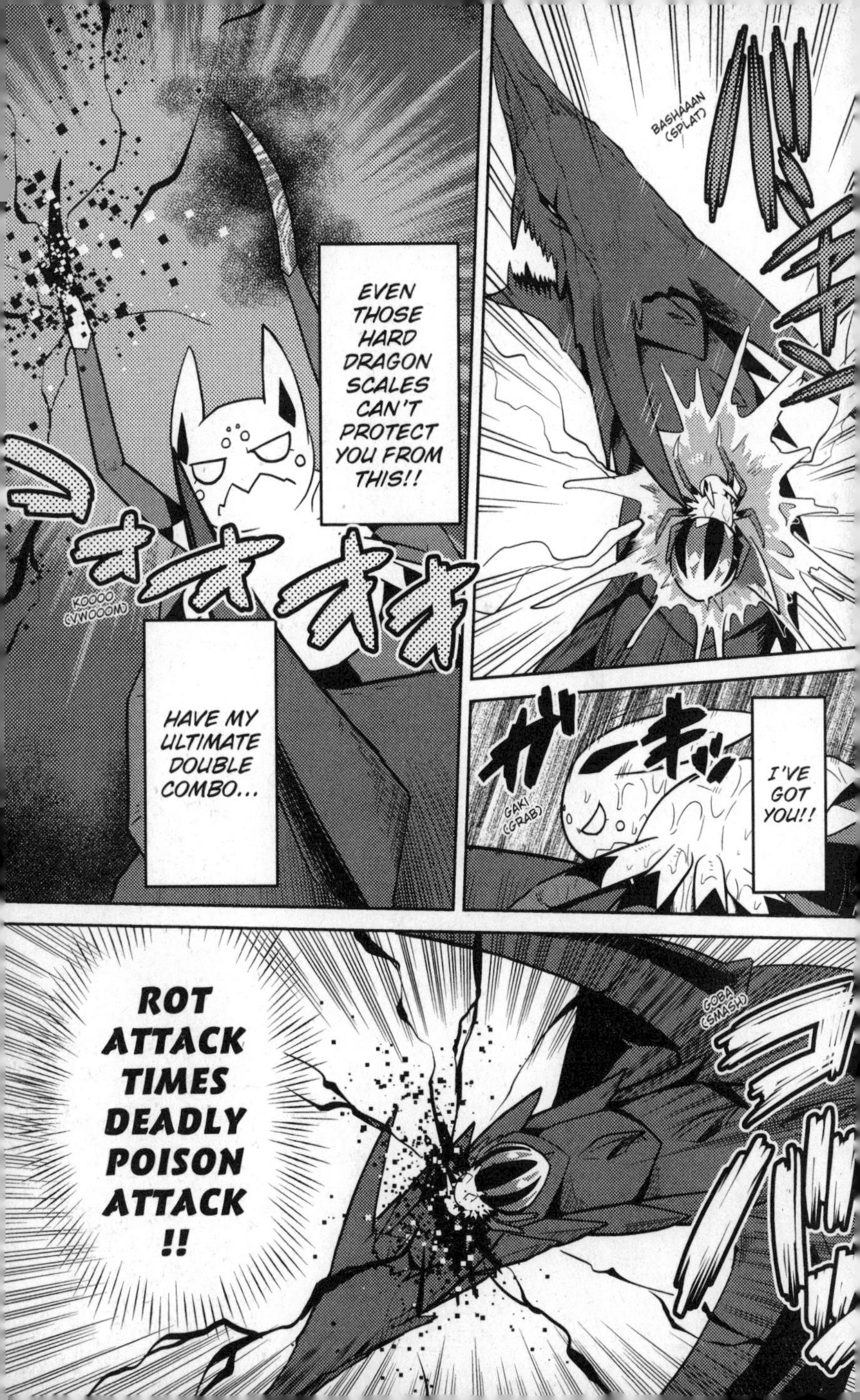
BASHAAAN (SPLAT)
I'VE GOT YOU!!
GAKI (GRAB)
EVEN THOSE HARD DRAGON SCALES CAN'T PROTECT YOU FROM THIS!!
KOOOO (VWOOOM)
HAVE MY ULTIMATE DOUBLE COMBO...
GOBA (SMASH)
ROT ATTACK TIMES DEADLY POISON ATTACK!!

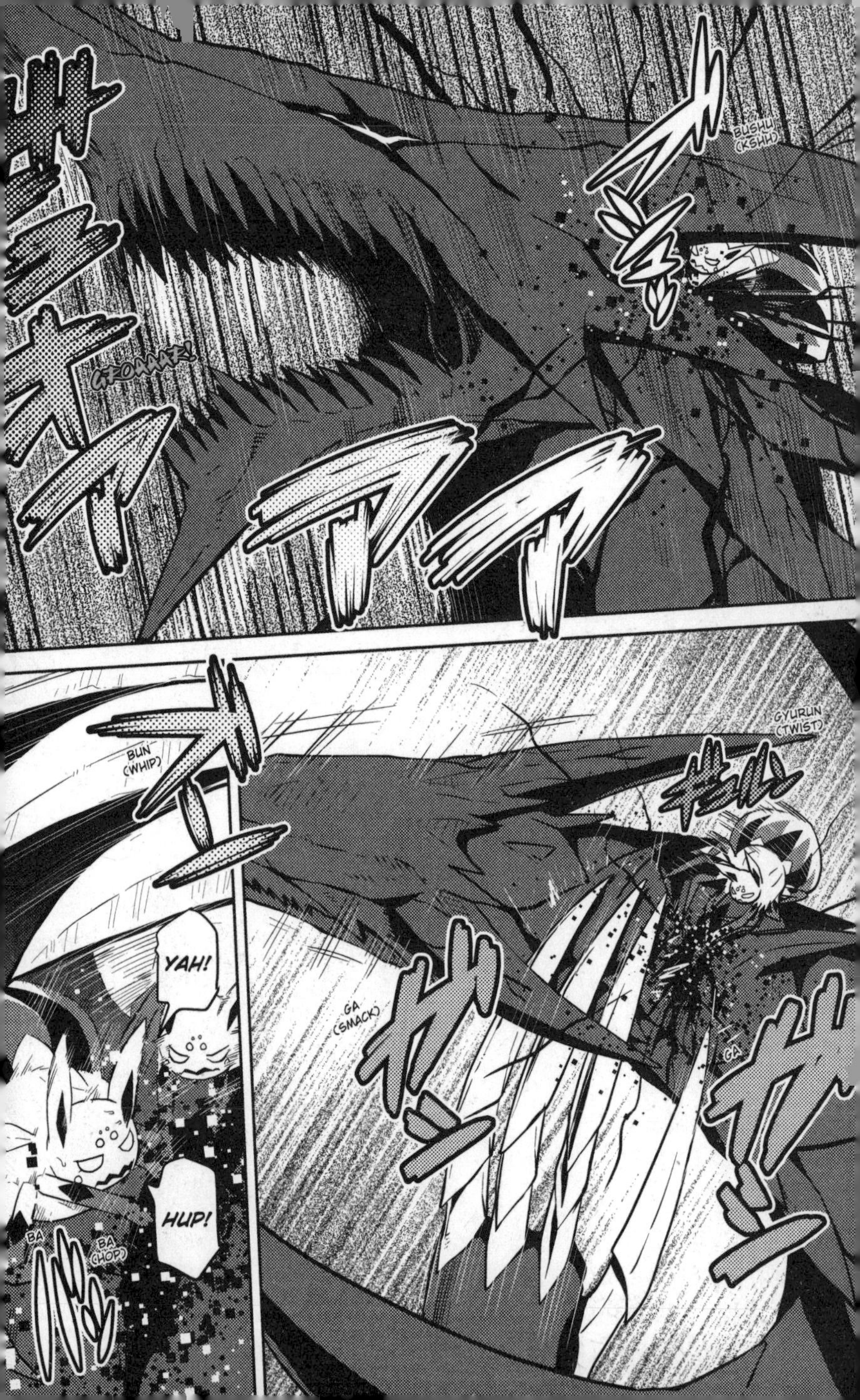
BUSHU (KSHH)
GROAAAR!
GYURUN (TWIST)
GA
GA (SMACK)
BUN (WHIP)
YAH!
HUP!
BA
BA (CHOP)

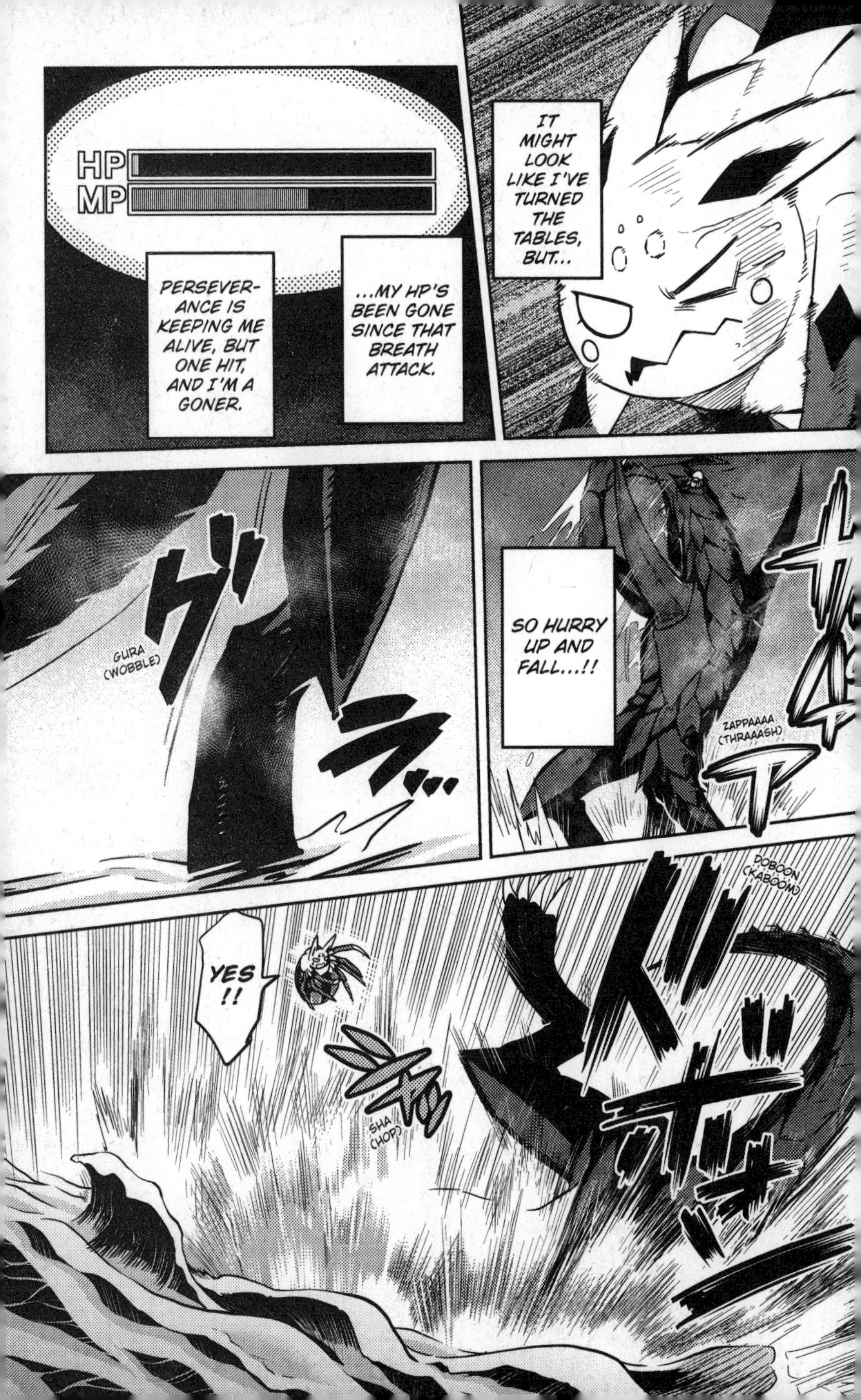
IT MIGHT LOOK LIKE I'VE TURNED THE TABLES, BUT...
HP
MP
...MY HP'S BEEN GONE SINCE THAT BREATH ATTACK.
PERSEVERANCE IS KEEPING ME ALIVE, BUT ONE HIT, AND I'M A GONER.
SO HURRY UP AND FALL...!!
ZAPPAAAA (THRAAASH)
GURA (WOBBLE)
DOBOON (KABOOM)
YES!!
SHA (HOP)

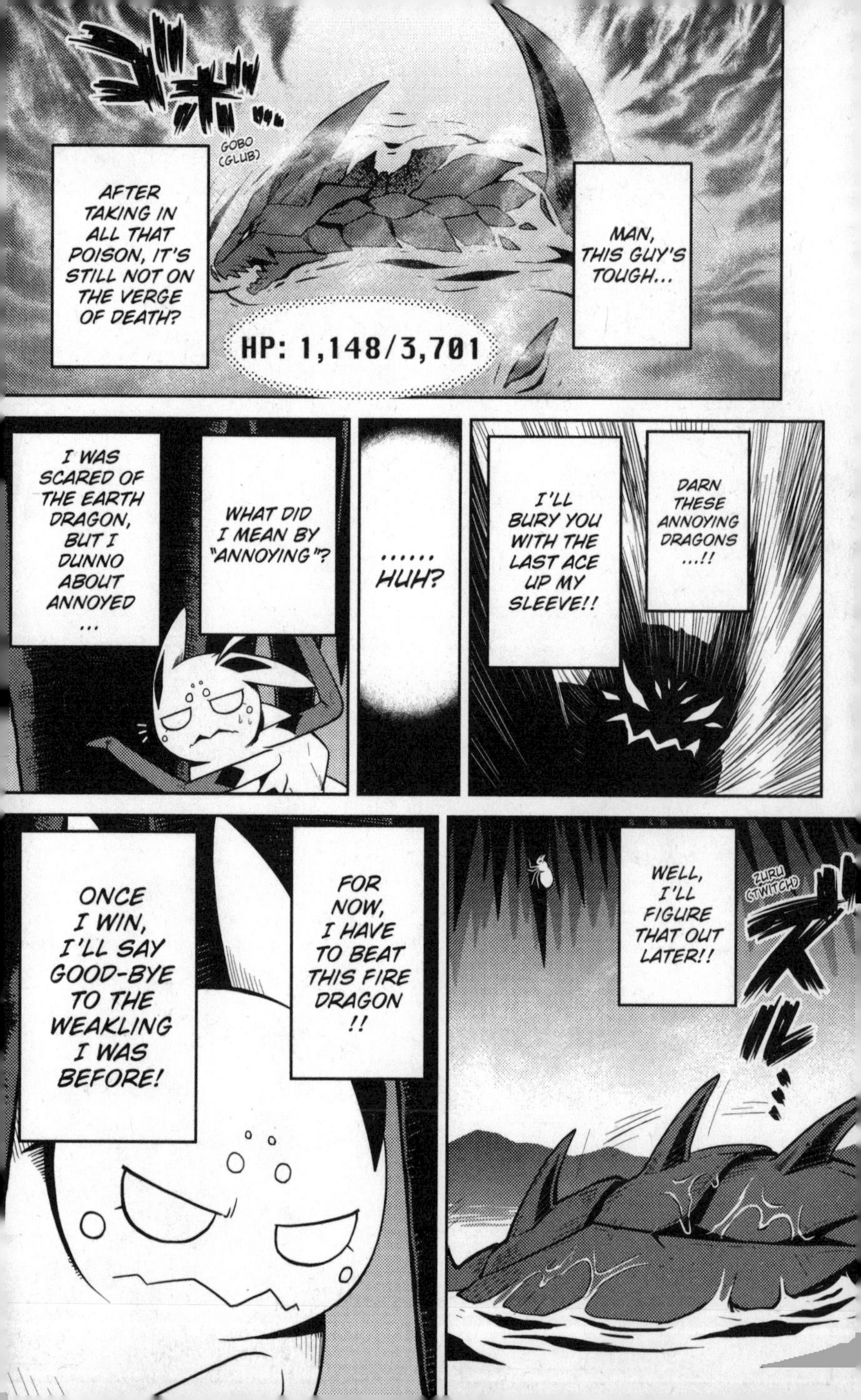
GOBO (GLUB)
AFTER TAKING IN ALL THAT POISON, IT'S STILL NOT ON THE VERGE OF DEATH?
MAN, THIS GUY'S TOUGH...
HP: 1,148/3,701
DARN THESE ANNOYING DRAGONS...!!
I'LL BURY YOU WITH THE LAST ACE UP MY SLEEVE!!
......HUH?
WHAT DID I MEAN BY "ANNOYING"?
I WAS SCARED OF THE EARTH DRAGON, BUT I DUNNO ABOUT ANNOYED...
WELL, I'LL FIGURE THAT OUT LATER!!
ZURU (TWITCH)
FOR NOW, I HAVE TO BEAT THIS FIRE DRAGON!!
ONCE I WIN, I'LL SAY GOOD-BYE TO THE WEAKLING I WAS BEFORE!

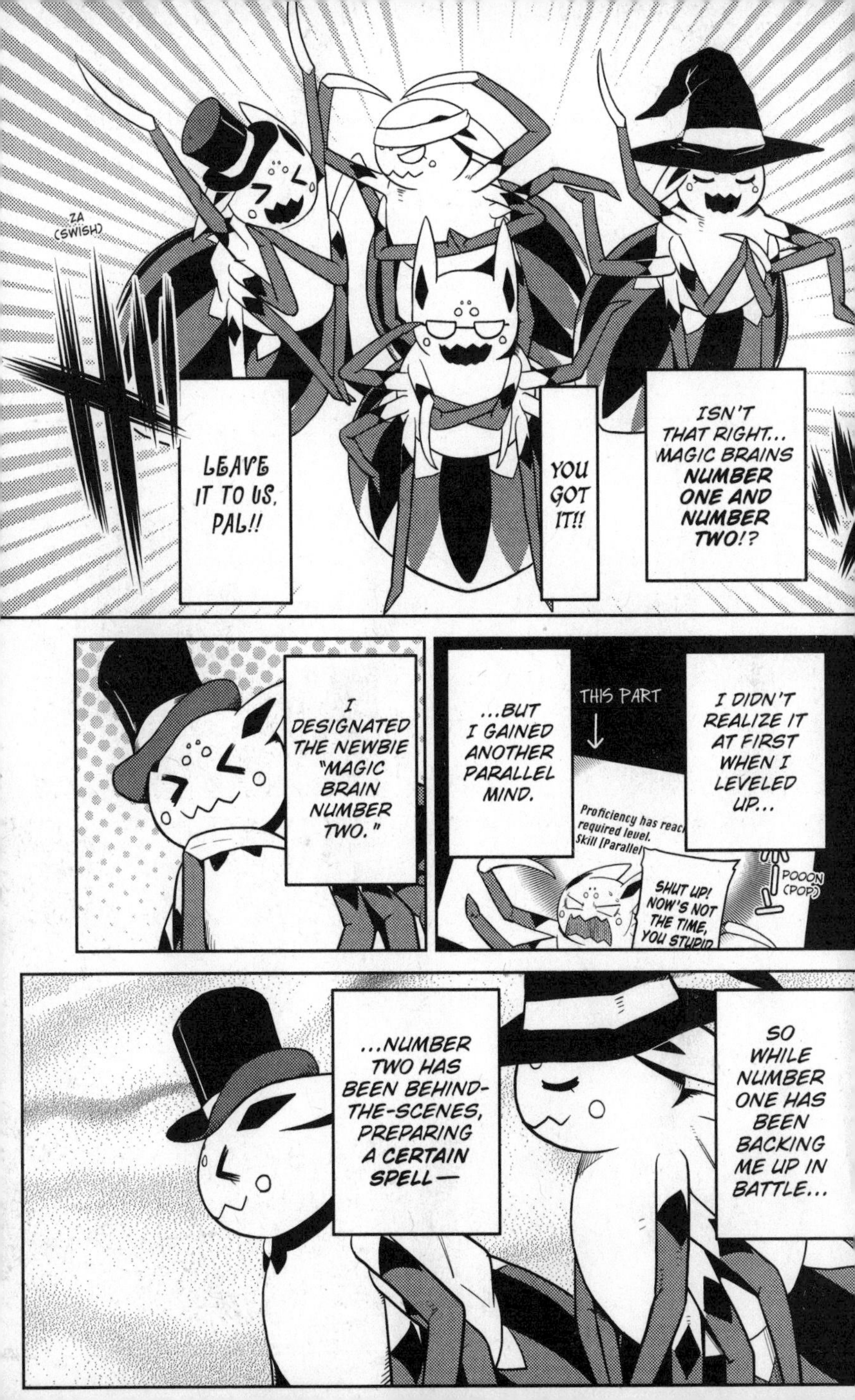
ISN'T THAT RIGHT... MAGIC BRAINS NUMBER ONE AND NUMBER TWO!?
YOU GOT IT!!
LEAVE IT TO US, PAL!!
ZA (SWISH)
I DIDN'T REALIZE IT AT FIRST WHEN I LEVELED UP...
THIS PART
...BUT I GAINED ANOTHER PARALLEL MIND.
Proficiency has reac
required level.
Skill [Parallel
POOON (POP)
SHUT UP! NOW'S NOT THE TIME, YOU STUPID
I DESIGNATED THE NEWBIE "MAGIC BRAIN NUMBER TWO."
SO WHILE NUMBER ONE HAS BEEN BACKING ME UP IN BATTLE...
...NUMBER TWO HAS BEEN BEHIND-THE-SCENES, PREPARING A CERTAIN SPELL—

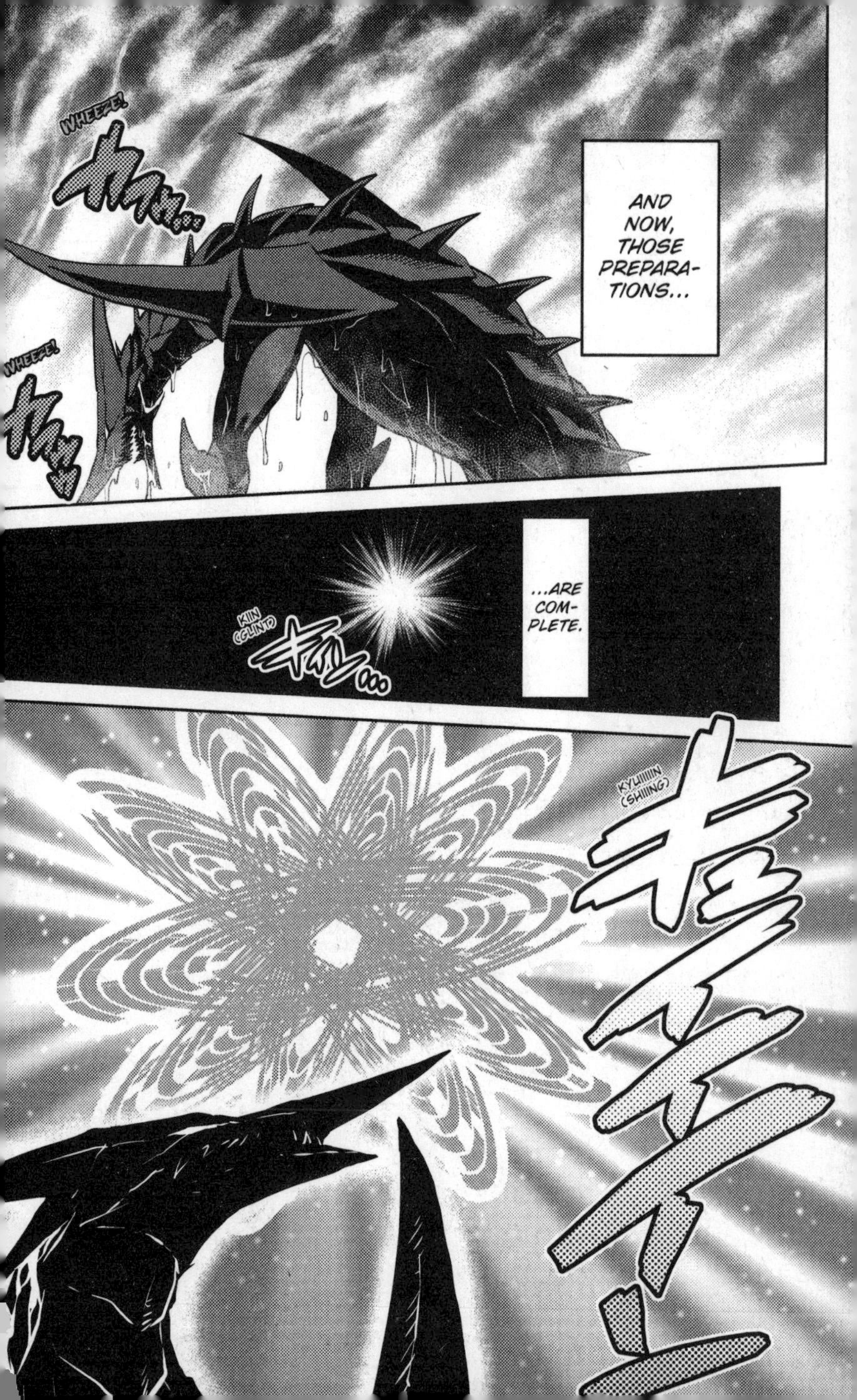
AND NOW, THOSE PREPARATIONS...
WHEEZE!
WHEEZE!
...ARE COMPLETE.
KIN (GLINT)
KYUIIIIIN (SHIIING)

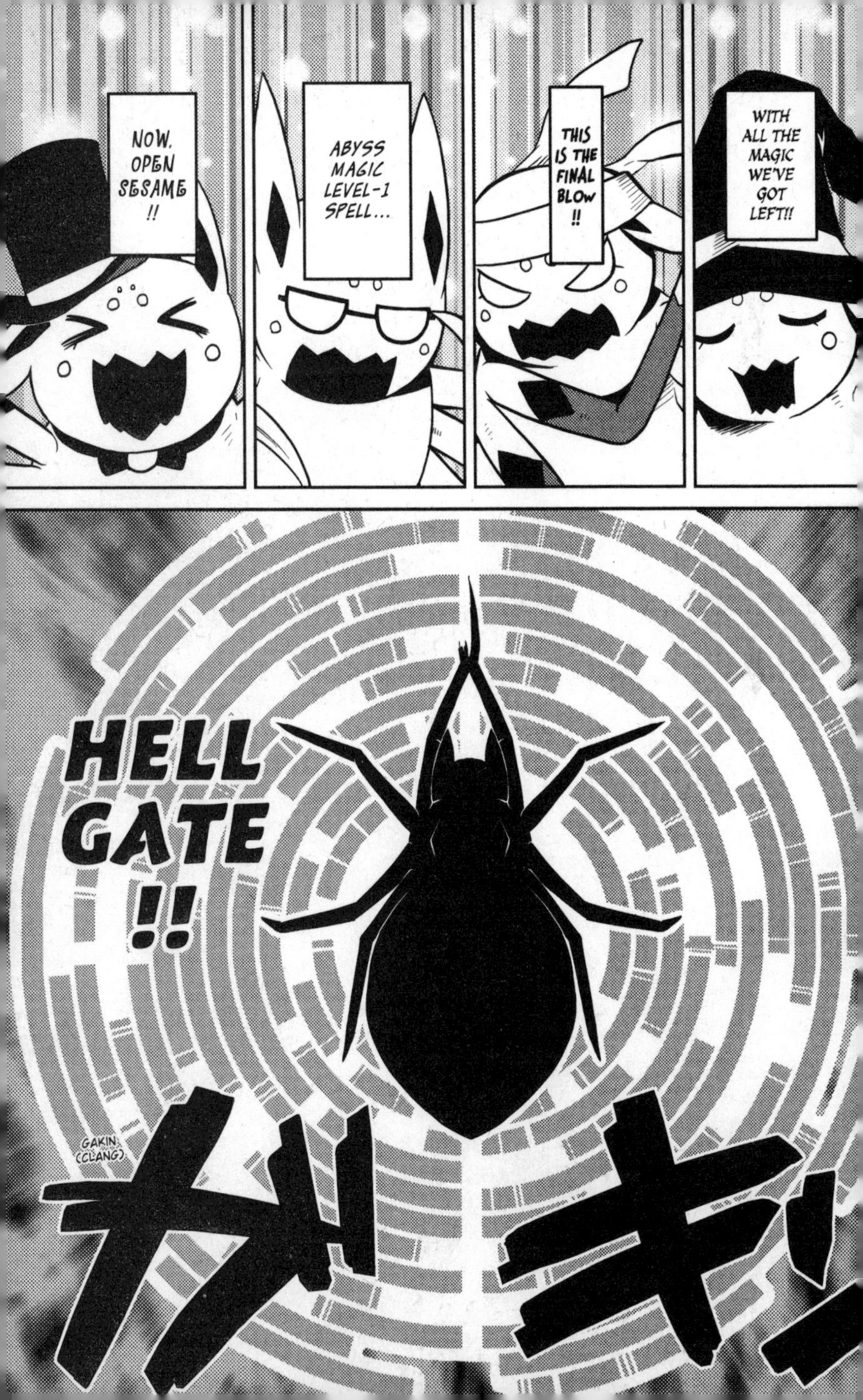
WITH ALL THE MAGIC WE'VE GOT LEFT!!
THIS IS THE FINAL BLOW!!
ABYSS MAGIC LEVEL-1 SPELL...
NOW, OPEN SESAME!!
HELL GATE!!
GAKIN (CLANG)

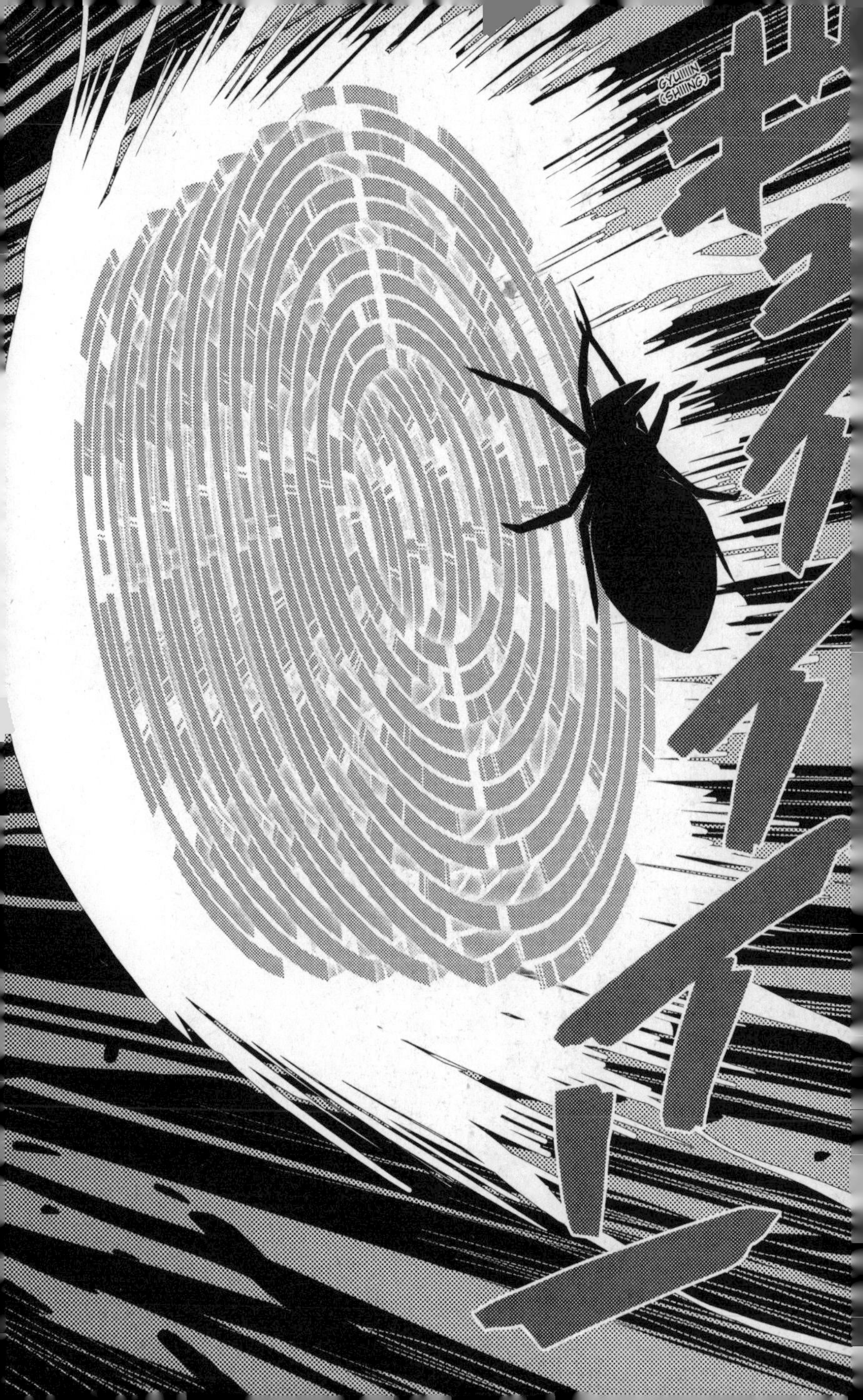
GYUIIIIN
(SHIIING)

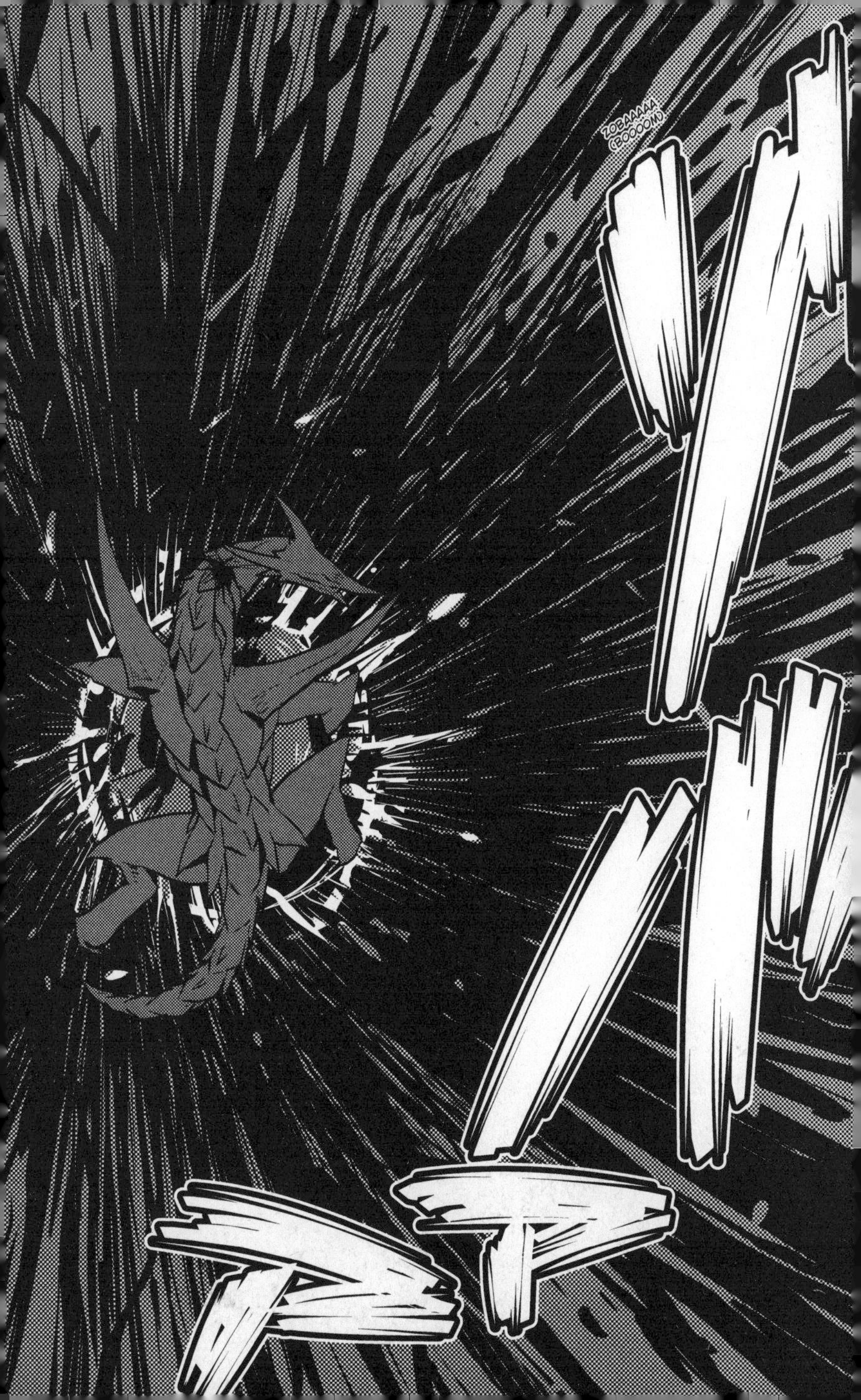
ZOBAAAAA
(BOOOOM)

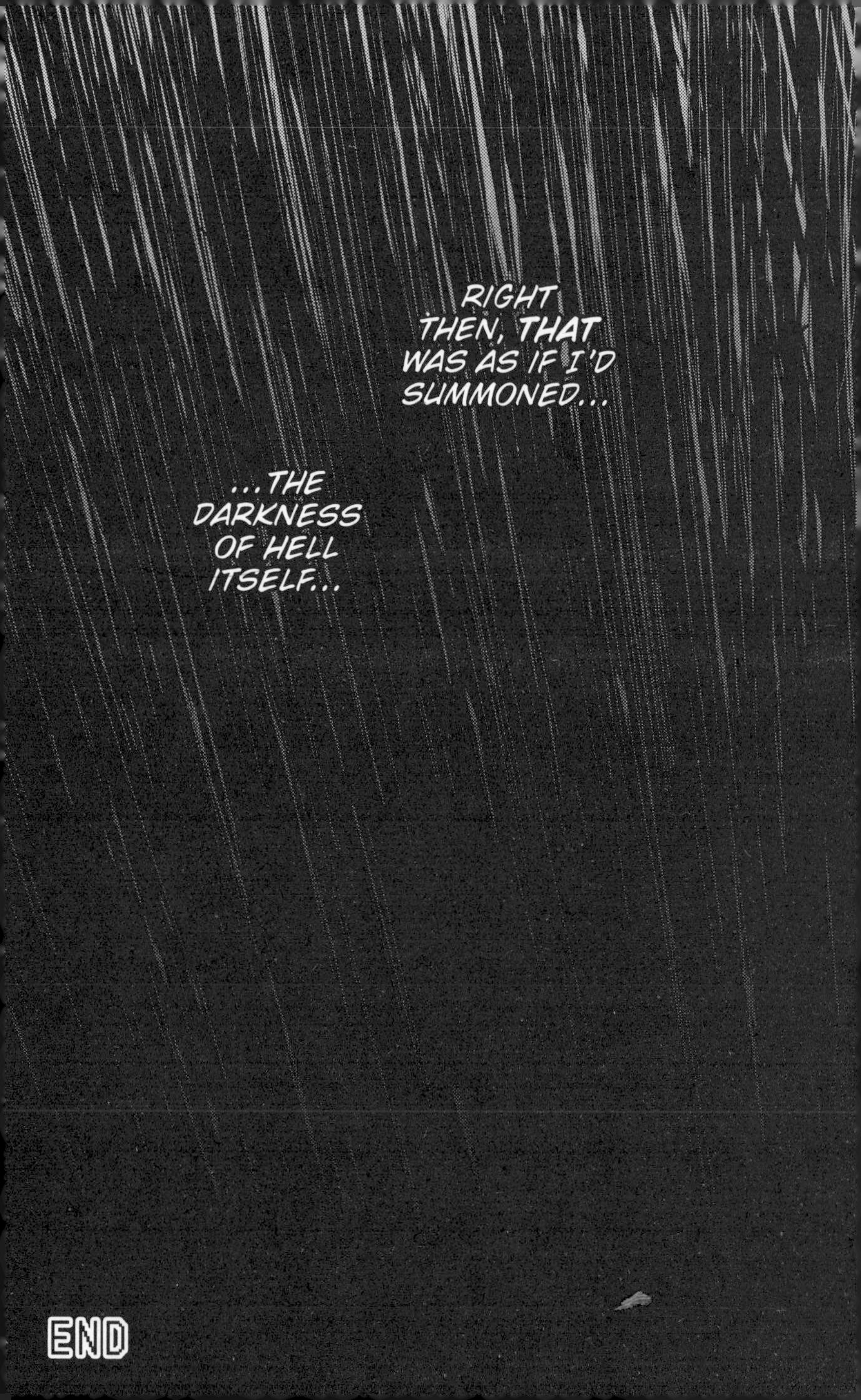
RIGHT THEN, THAT WAS AS IF I'D SUMMONED...
...THE DARKNESS OF HELL ITSELF...
END

So I'm a Spider, So What?

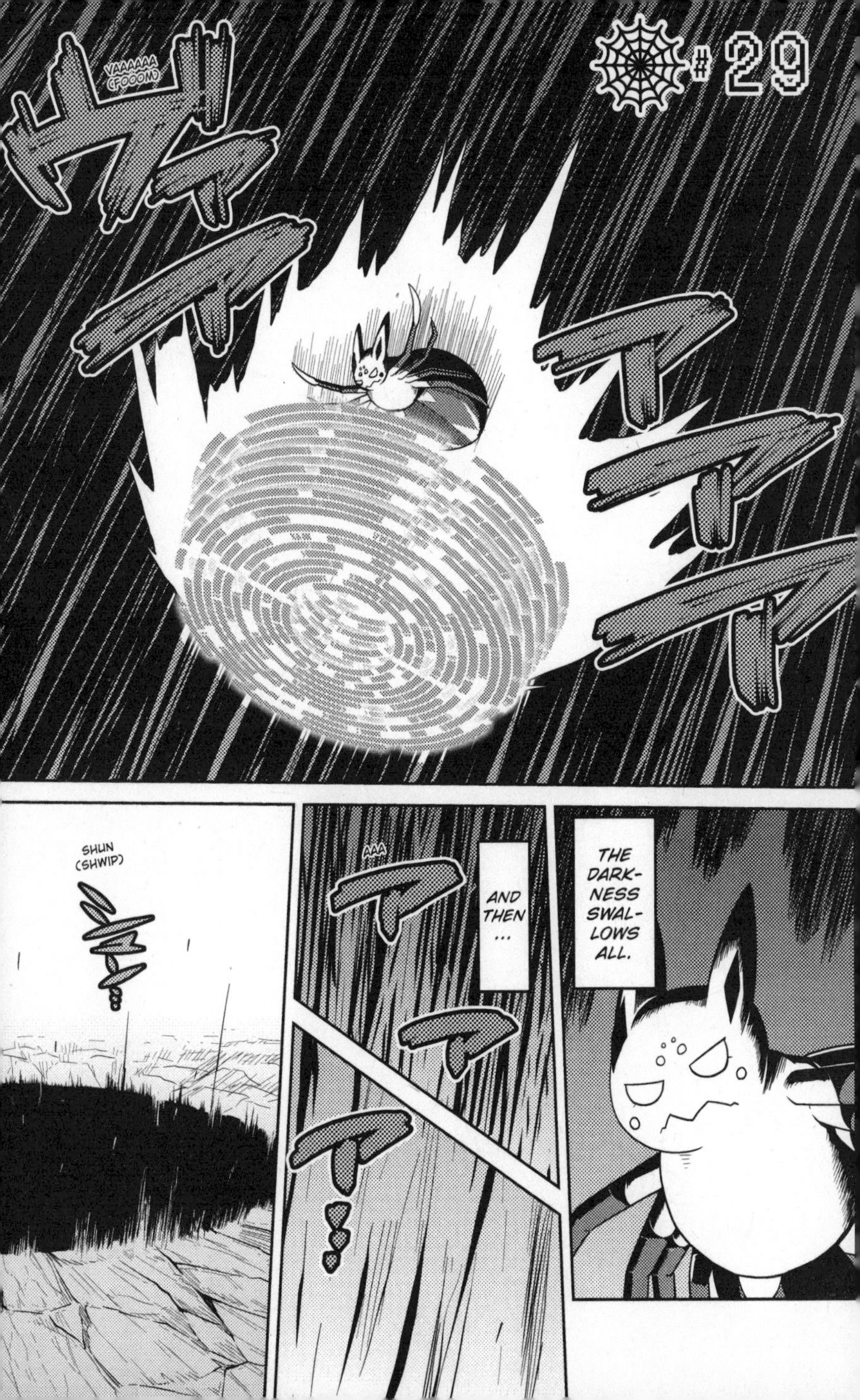
#29
VAAAAAA
(FOOOM)
THE DARK-
NESS
SWAL-
LOWS
ALL.
AND
THEN
...
AAA
SHUN
(SHWIP)

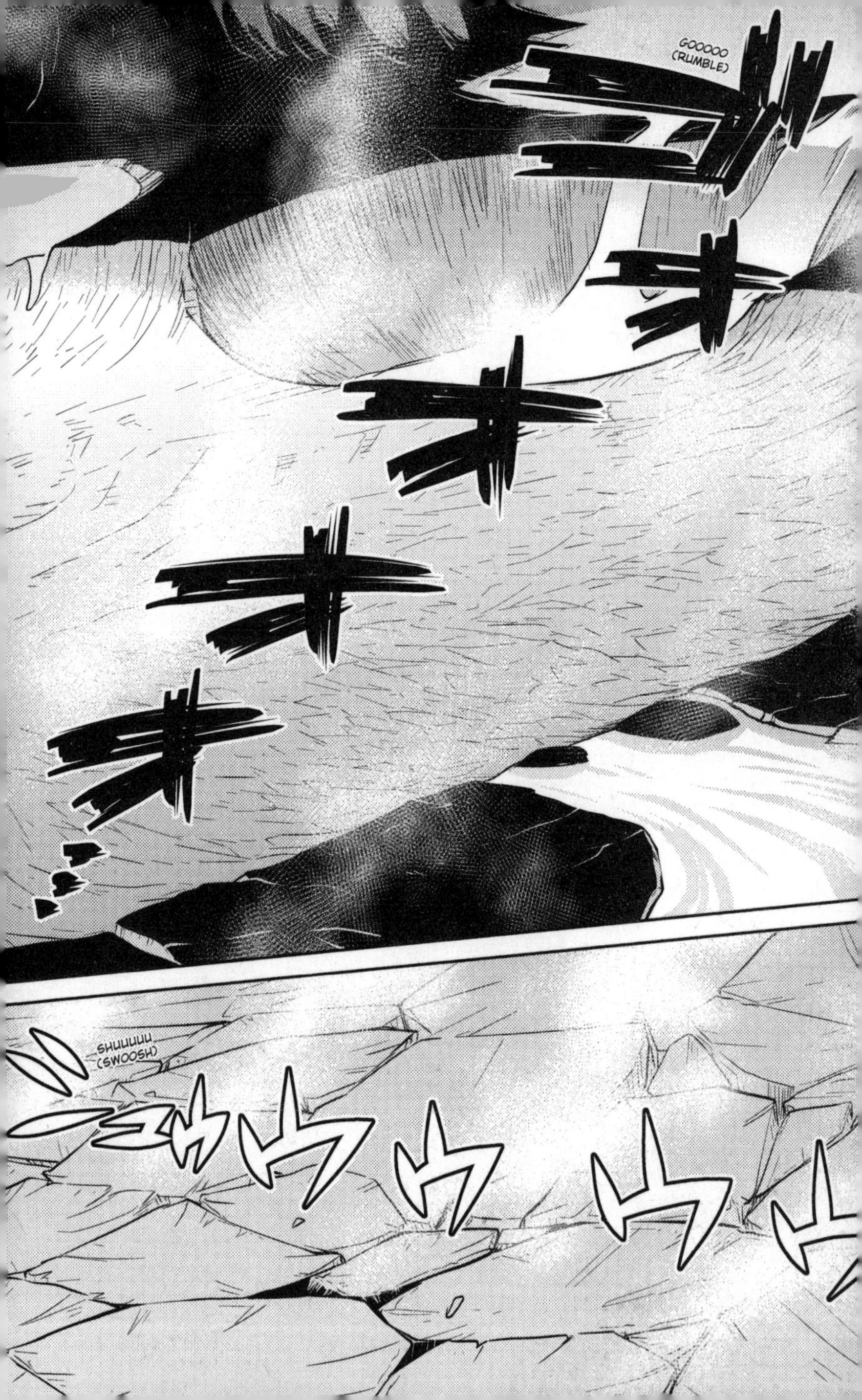
GOOOOO
(RUMBLE)
SHUUUUU
(SWOOSH)

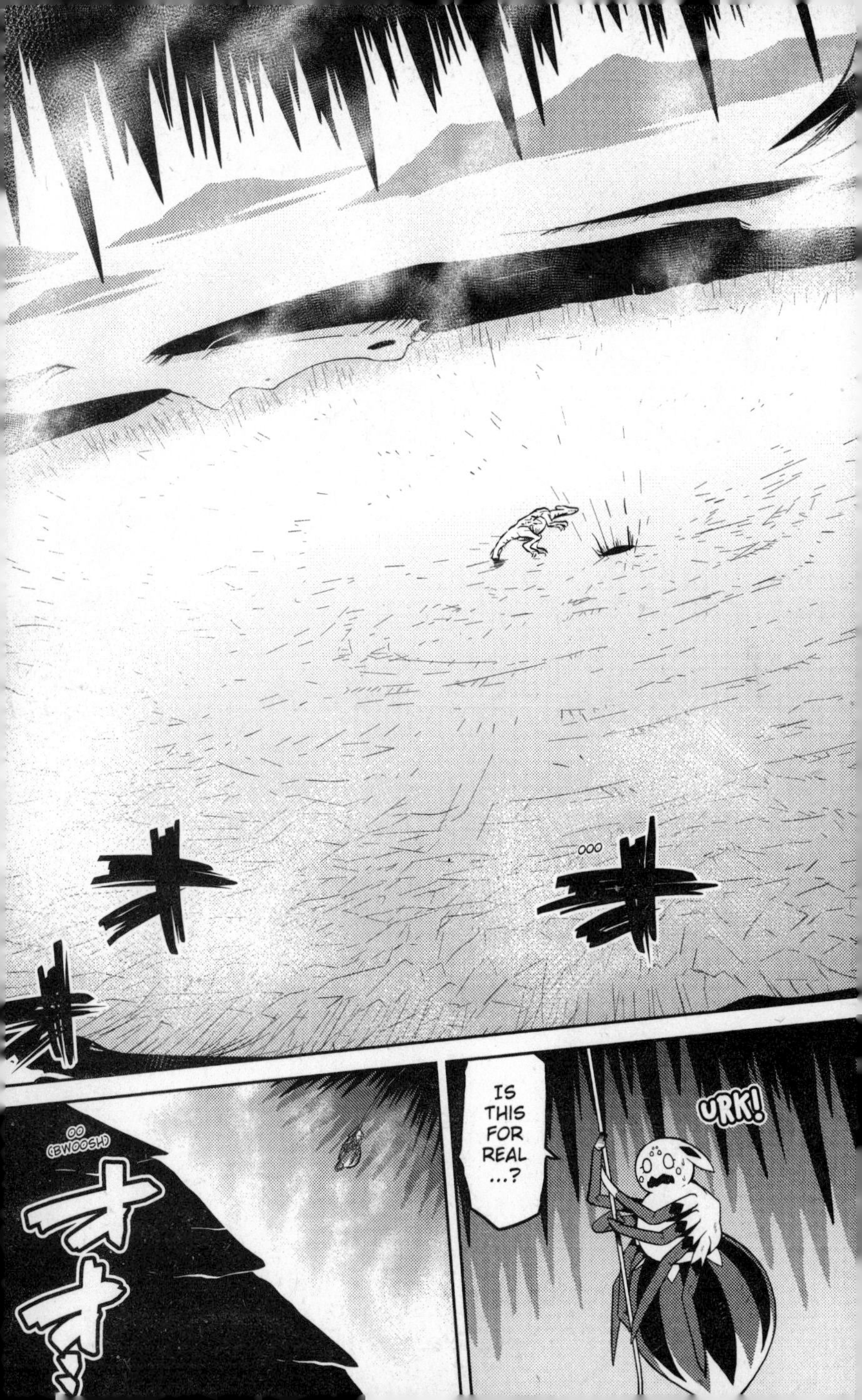
ooo
URK!
IS THIS FOR REAL ...?
OO (BWOOSH)

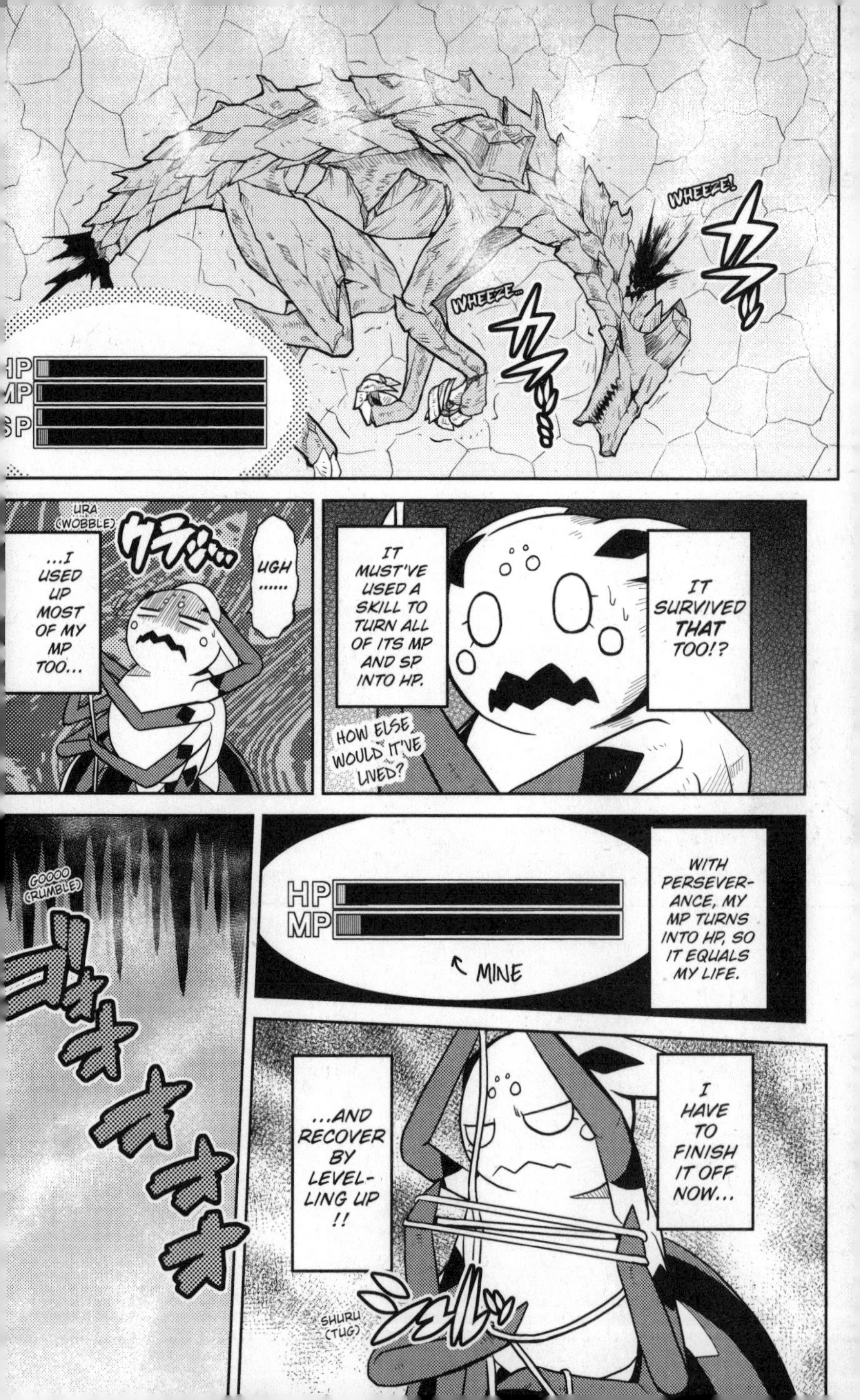
WHEEZE!
WHEEZE...
HP
MP
SP
IT SURVIVED THAT TOO!?
IT MUST'VE USED A SKILL TO TURN ALL OF ITS MP AND SP INTO HP.
HOW ELSE WOULD IT'VE LIVED?
UGH ......
URA (WOBBLE)
...I USED UP MOST OF MY MP TOO...
WITH PERSEVERANCE, MY MP TURNS INTO HP, SO IT EQUALS MY LIFE.
HP
MP
↖ MINE
I HAVE TO FINISH IT OFF NOW...
...AND RECOVER BY LEVELLING UP !!
SHURU (TUG)
GOOOO (RUMBLE)

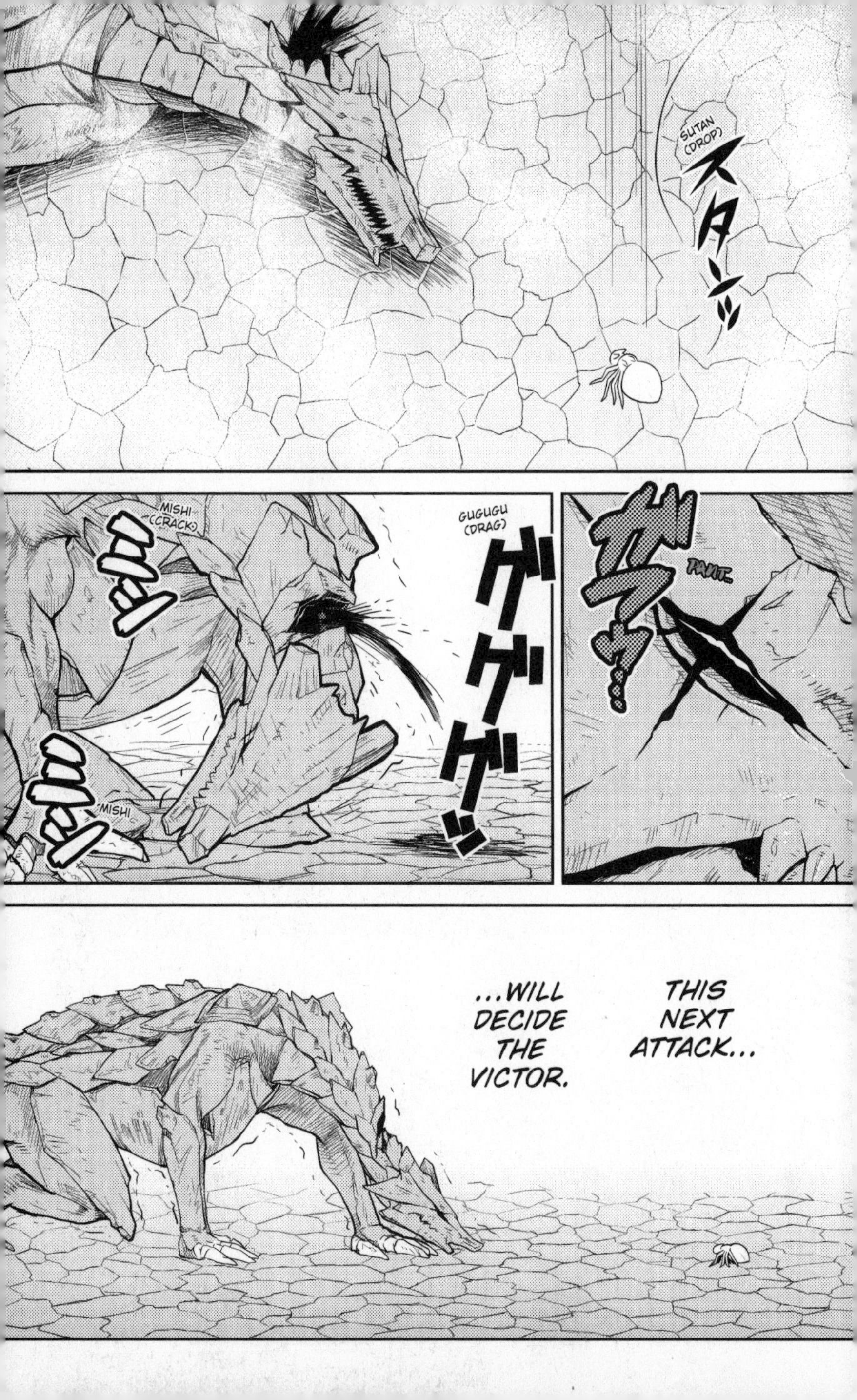
SUTAN (DROP)
スタンッ
PANT...
GUGUGU (DRAG)
ググググッ
MISHI (CRACK)
MISHI
THIS NEXT ATTACK...
...WILL DECIDE THE VICTOR.

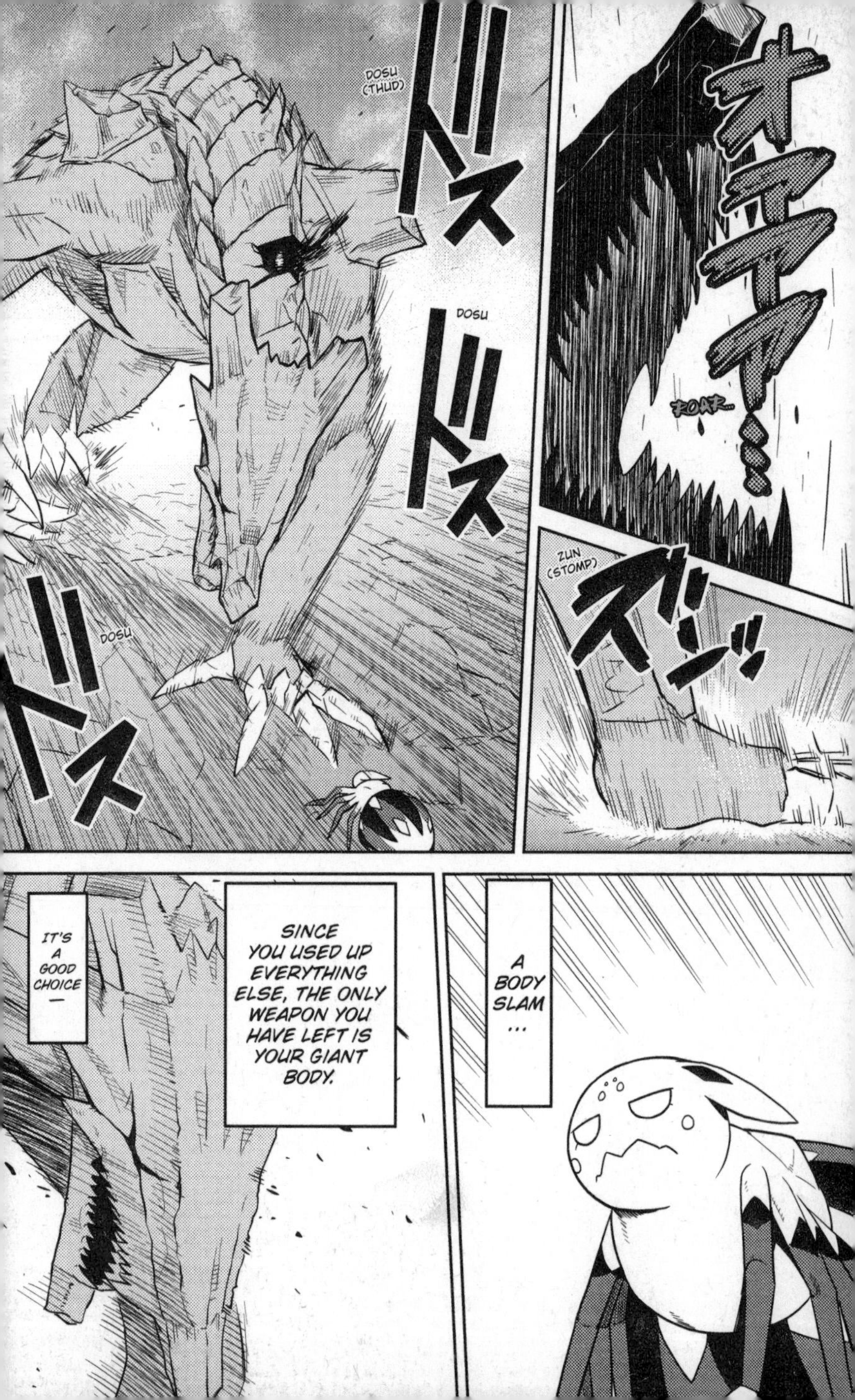
ROAR...
ZUN (STOMP)
DOSU (THUD)
DOSU
DOSU
A BODY SLAM ...
SINCE YOU USED UP EVERYTHING ELSE, THE ONLY WEAPON YOU HAVE LEFT IS YOUR GIANT BODY.
IT'S A GOOD CHOICE—

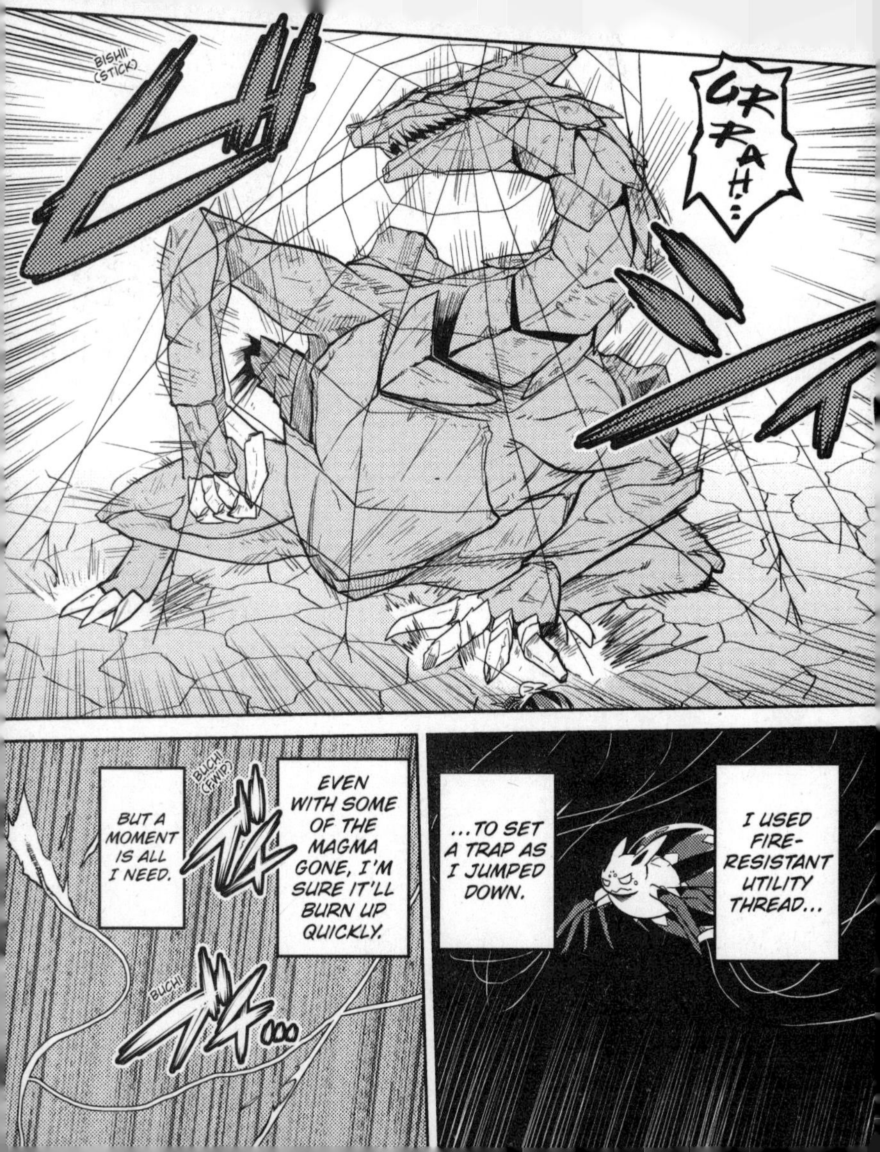
GRRAH!!
BISHII (STICK)
I USED FIRE-RESISTANT UTILITY THREAD...
...TO SET A TRAP AS I JUMPED DOWN.
EVEN WITH SOME OF THE MAGMA GONE, I'M SURE IT'LL BURN UP QUICKLY.
BUCHI (FWIP)
BUT A MOMENT IS ALL I NEED.
BUCHI

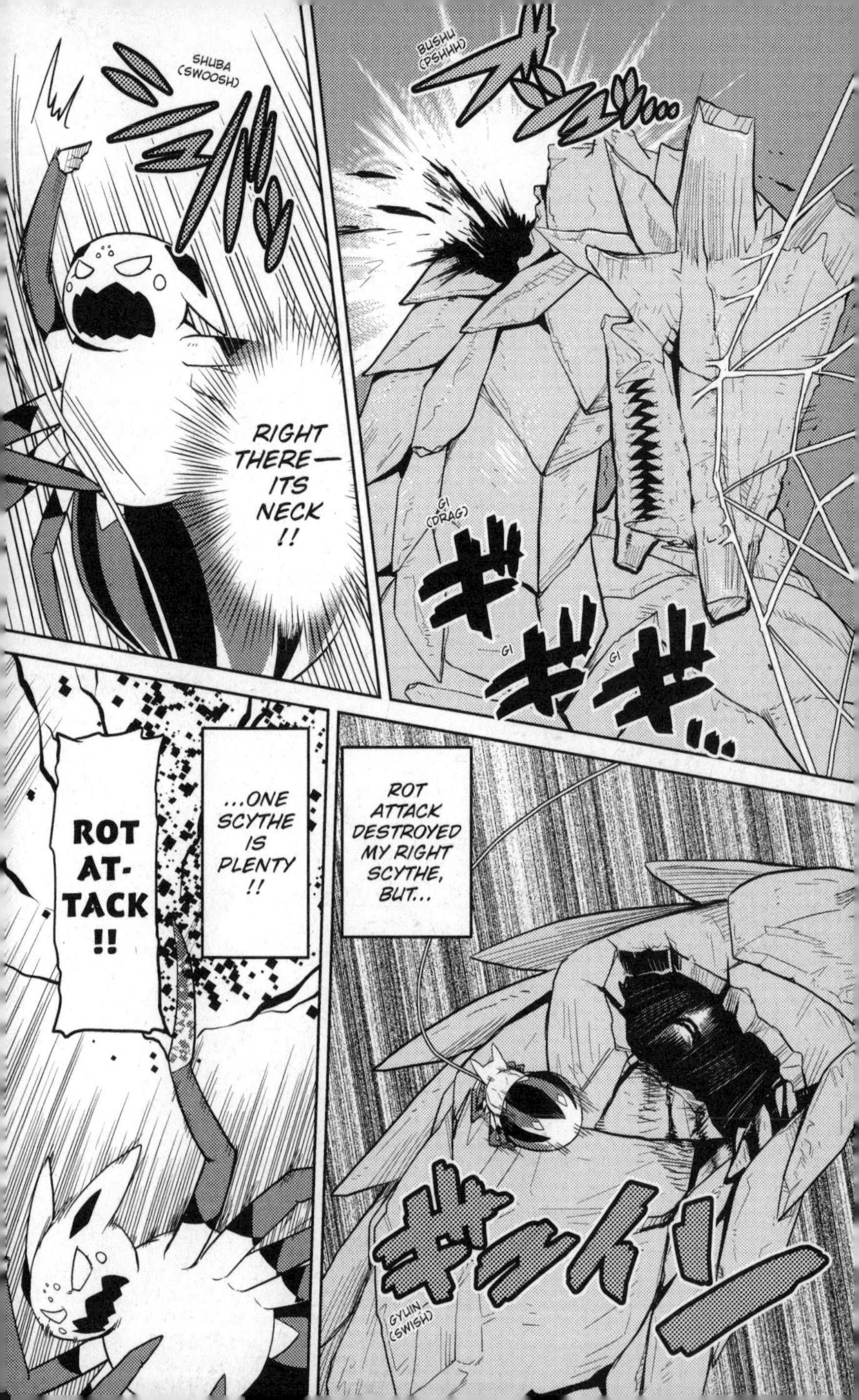
BUSHU (PSHHH)
GI (DRAG)
GI
GI
SHUBA (SWOOSH)
RIGHT THERE—ITS NECK!!
ROT ATTACK DESTROYED MY RIGHT SCYTHE, BUT...
GYUIN (SWISH)
...ONE SCYTHE IS PLENTY!!
ROT AT-TACK!!

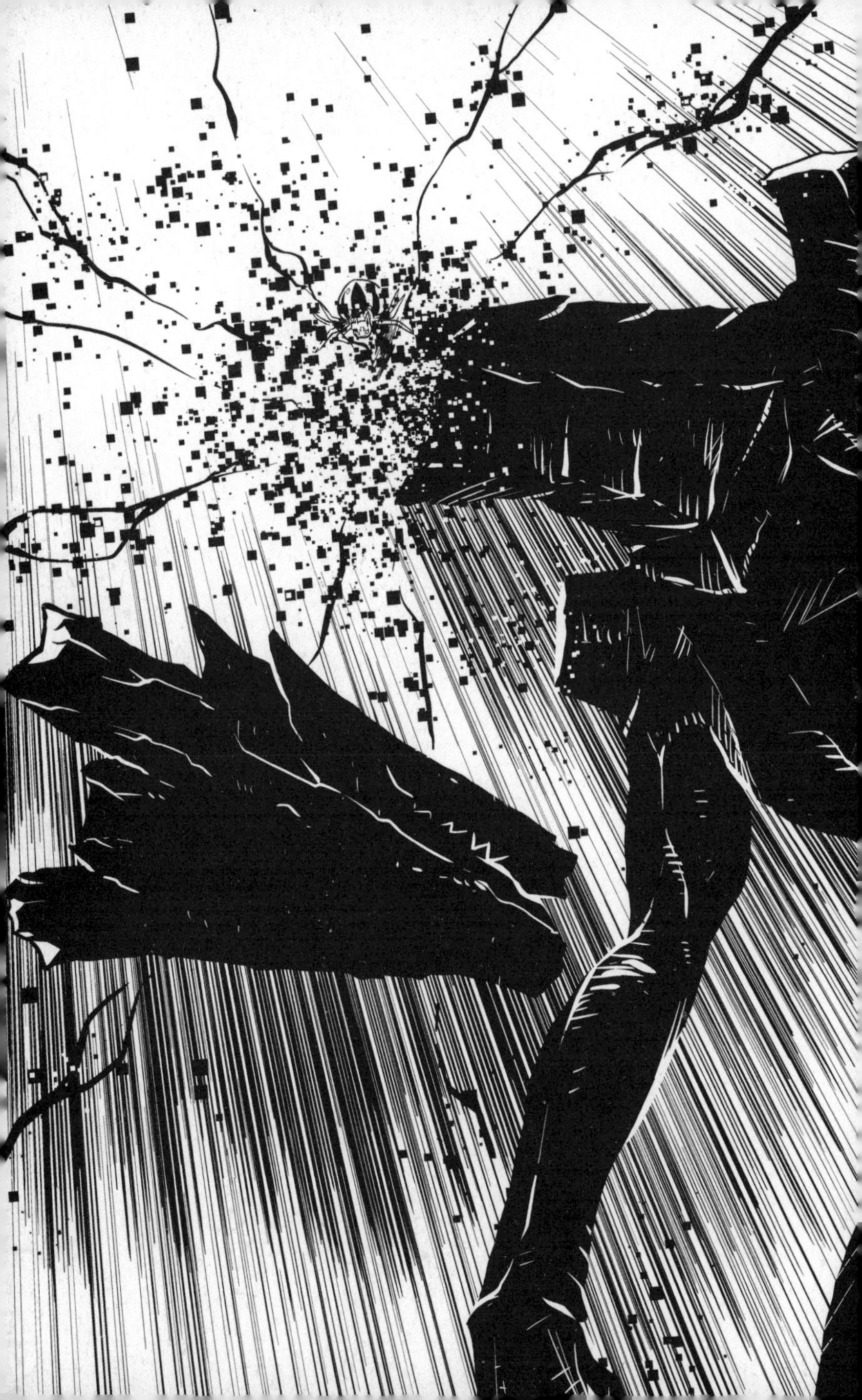

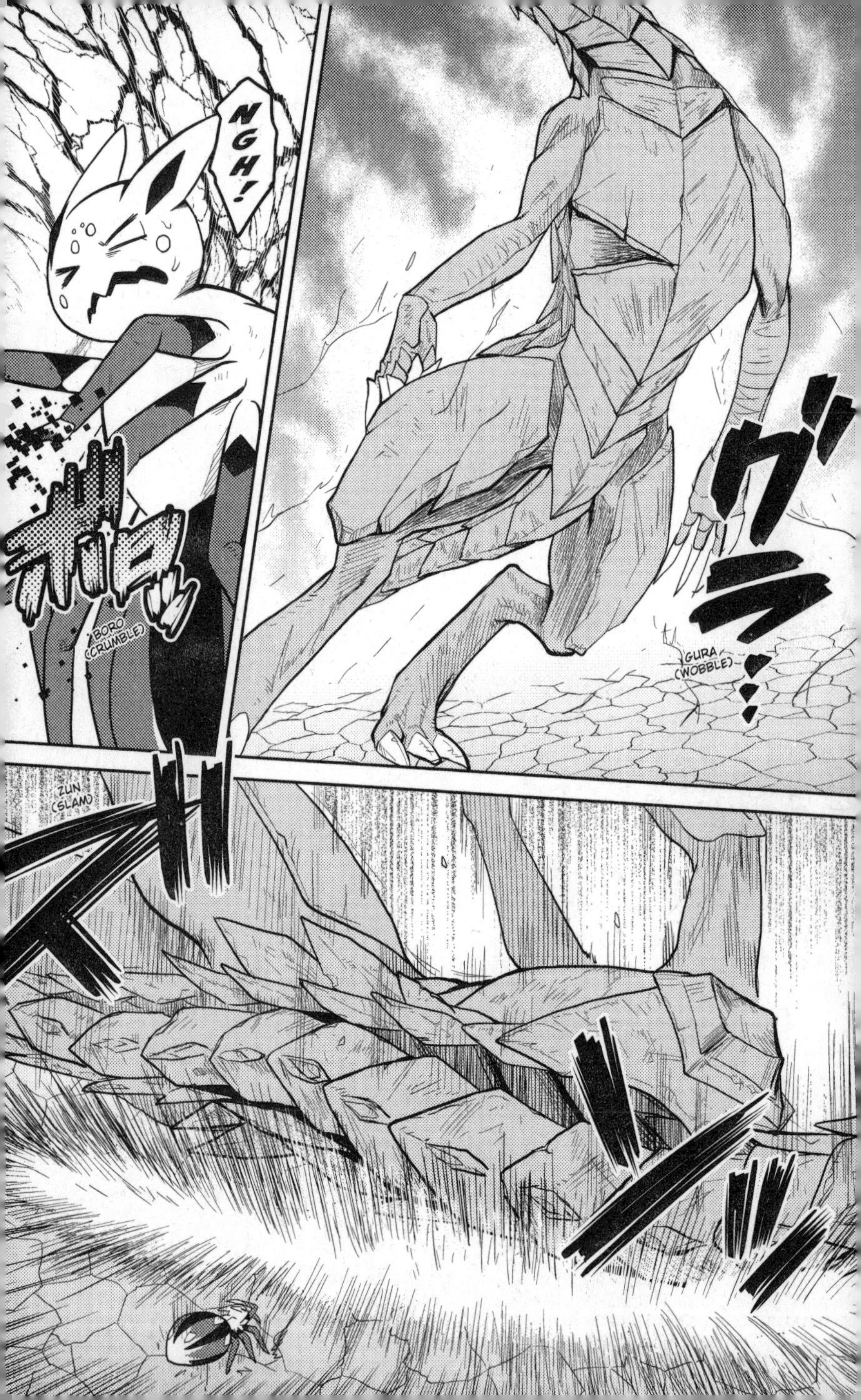
GURA
(WOBBLE)
NGH!
BORO
(CRUMBLE)
ZUN
(SLAM)

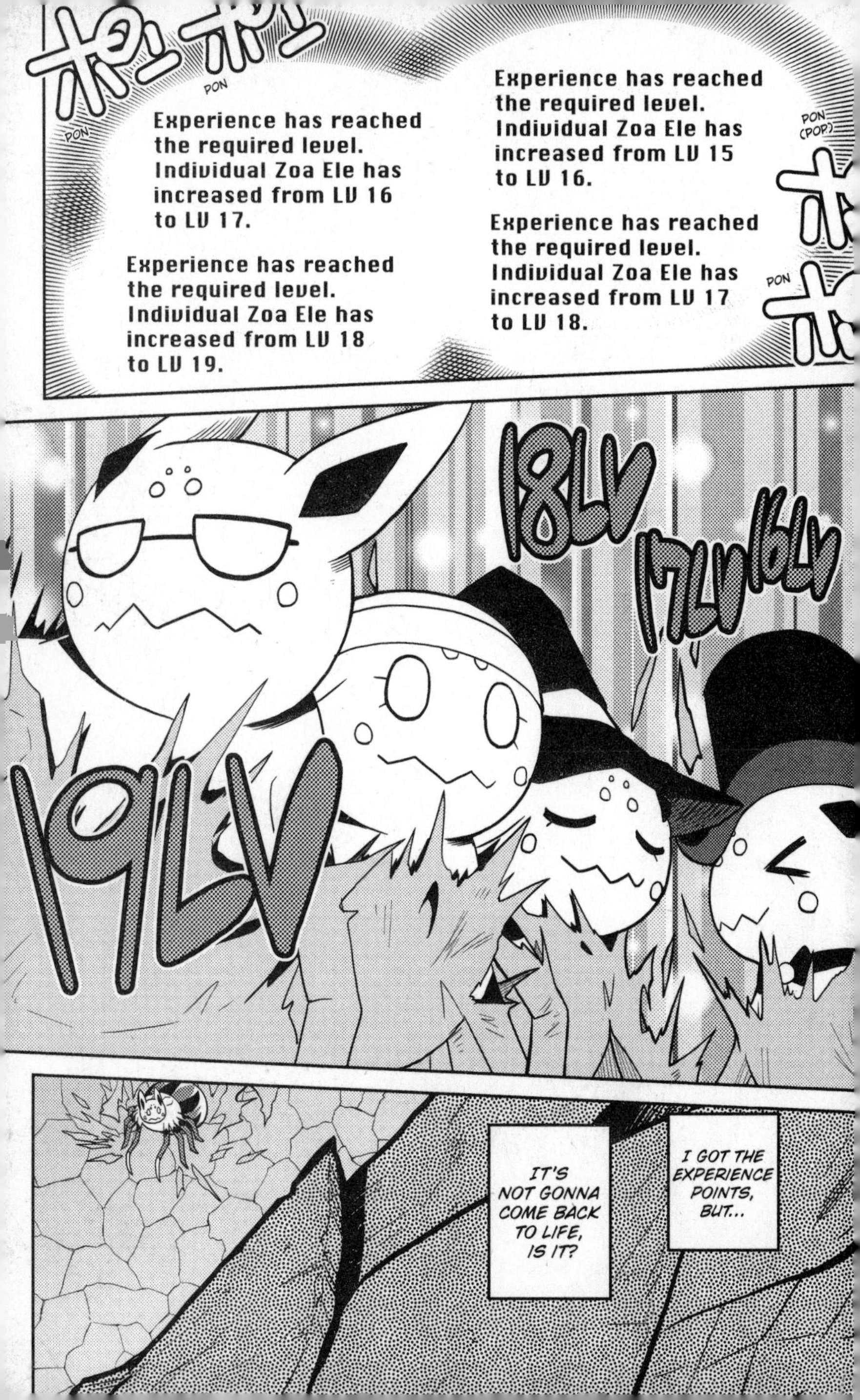
PON (POP)
Experience has reached the required level. Individual Zoa Ele has increased from LV 15 to LV 16.
PON
Experience has reached the required level. Individual Zoa Ele has increased from LV 17 to LV 18.
PON
PON
Experience has reached the required level. Individual Zoa Ele has increased from LV 16 to LV 17.
Experience has reached the required level. Individual Zoa Ele has increased from LV 18 to LV 19.
17LV 16LV
18LV
19LV
I GOT THE EXPERIENCE POINTS, BUT...
IT'S NOT GONNA COME BACK TO LIFE, IS IT?

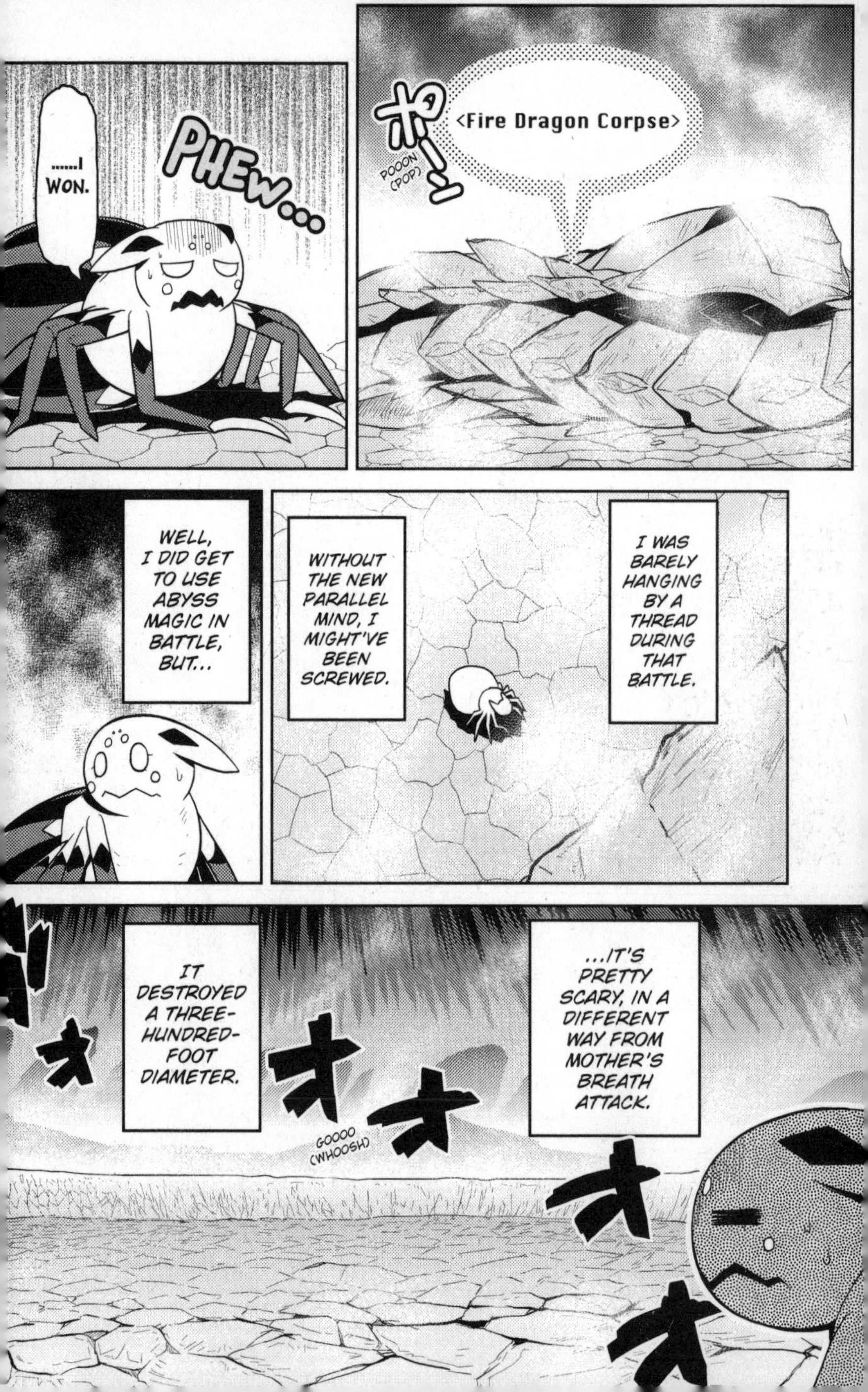
POOON (POP)
<Fire Dragon Corpse>
......I WON.
PHEW...
I WAS BARELY HANGING BY A THREAD DURING THAT BATTLE.
WITHOUT THE NEW PARALLEL MIND, I MIGHT'VE BEEN SCREWED.
WELL, I DID GET TO USE ABYSS MAGIC IN BATTLE, BUT...
...IT'S PRETTY SCARY, IN A DIFFERENT WAY FROM MOTHER'S BREATH ATTACK.
IT DESTROYED A THREE-HUNDRED-FOOT DIAMETER.
GOOOO (WHOOSH)

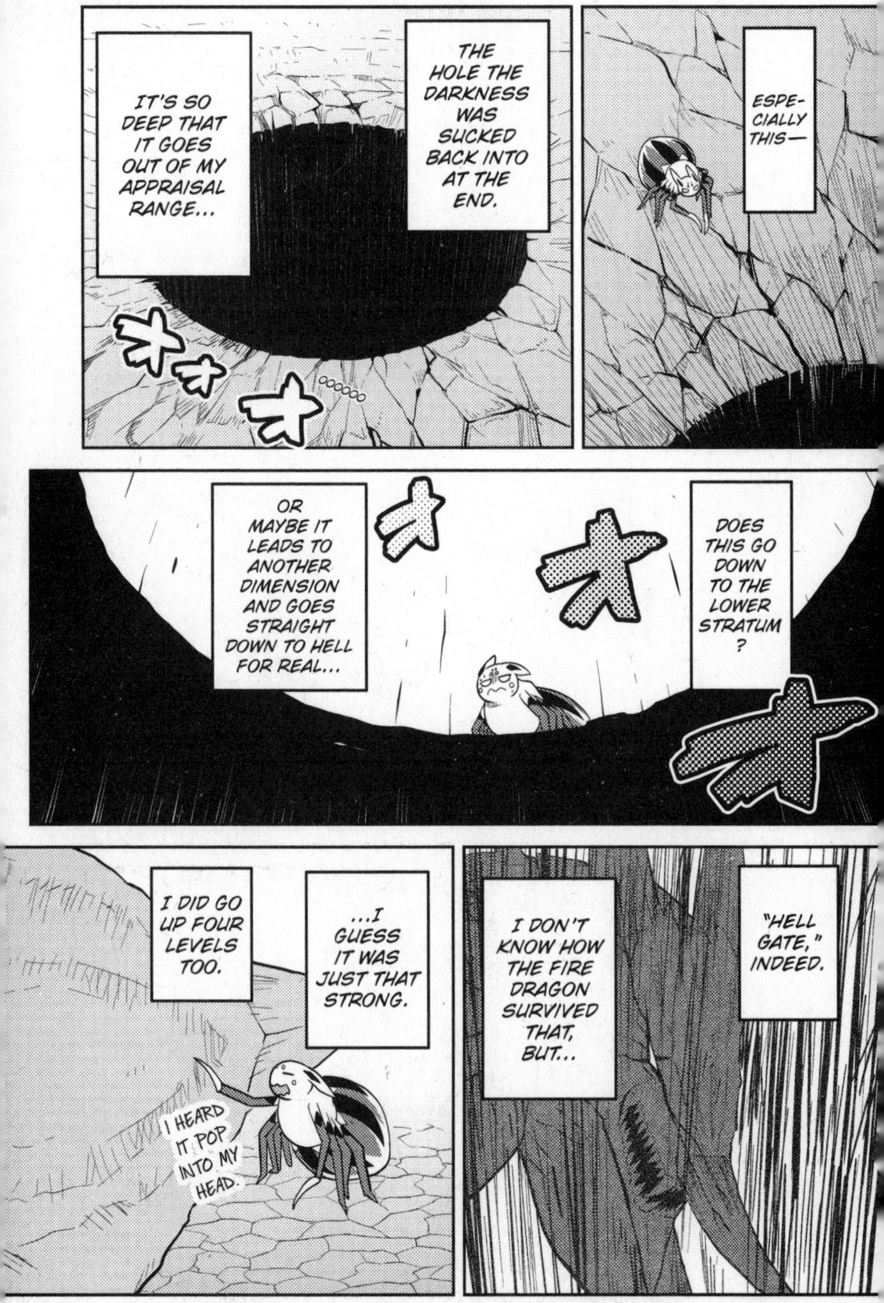
ESPECIALLY THIS—
THE HOLE THE DARKNESS WAS SUCKED BACK INTO AT THE END.
IT'S SO DEEP THAT IT GOES OUT OF MY APPRAISAL RANGE…
oooooo
DOES THIS GO DOWN TO THE LOWER STRATUM?
OR MAYBE IT LEADS TO ANOTHER DIMENSION AND GOES STRAIGHT DOWN TO HELL FOR REAL…
"HELL GATE," INDEED.
I DON'T KNOW HOW THE FIRE DRAGON SURVIVED THAT, BUT…
…I GUESS IT WAS JUST THAT STRONG.
I DID GO UP FOUR LEVELS TOO.
I HEARD IT POP INTO MY HEAD.

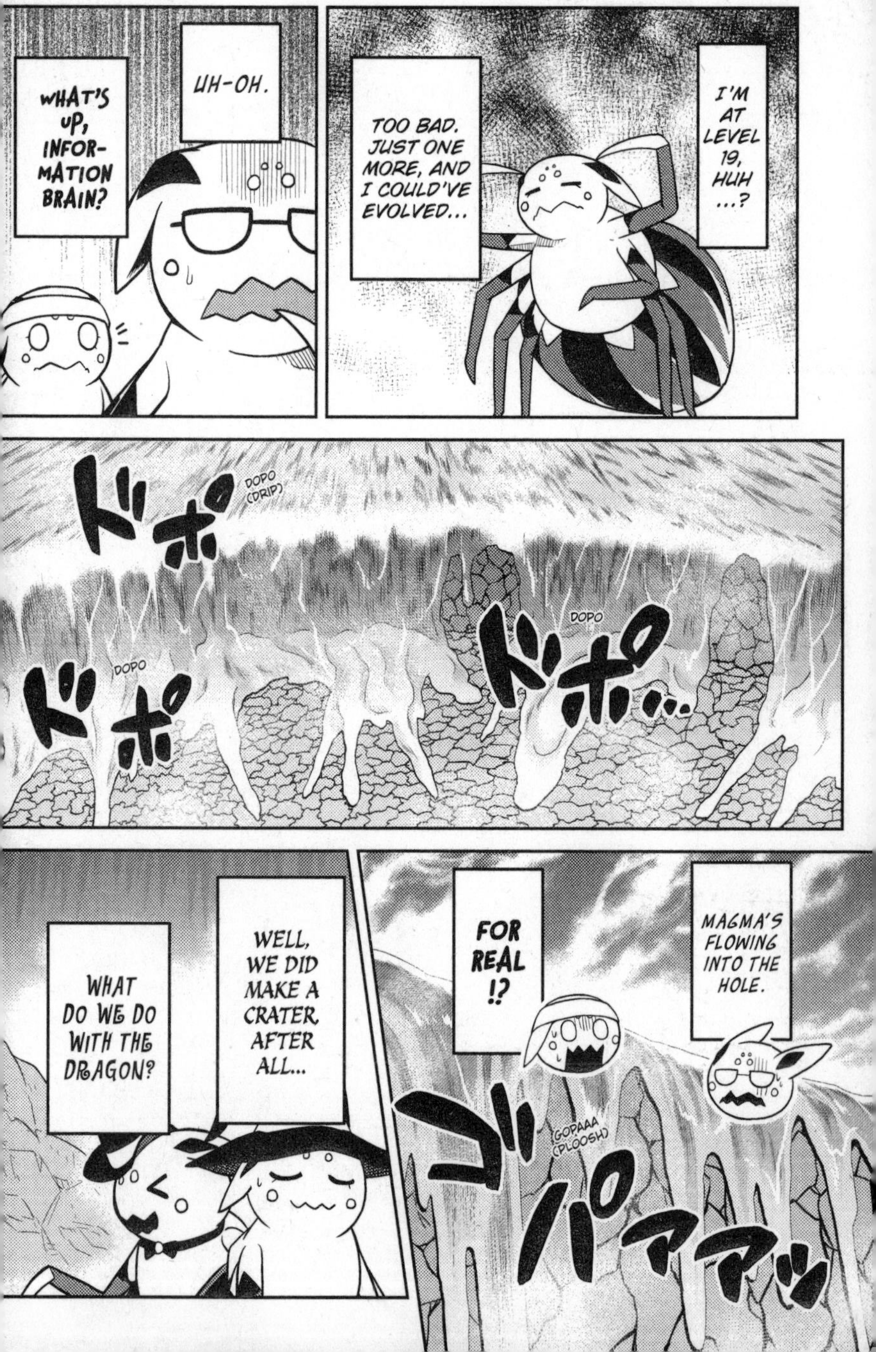
I'M AT LEVEL 19, HUH...?
TOO BAD. JUST ONE MORE, AND I COULD'VE EVOLVED...
UH-OH.
WHAT'S UP, INFORMATION BRAIN?
ドポ…
DOPO
ドポ
DOPO (DRIP)
ドポ
DOPO
MAGMA'S FLOWING INTO THE HOLE.
FOR REAL!?
ゴパァアッ
GOPAAA (PLOOSH)
WELL, WE DID MAKE A CRATER AFTER ALL...
WHAT DO WE DO WITH THE DRAGON?

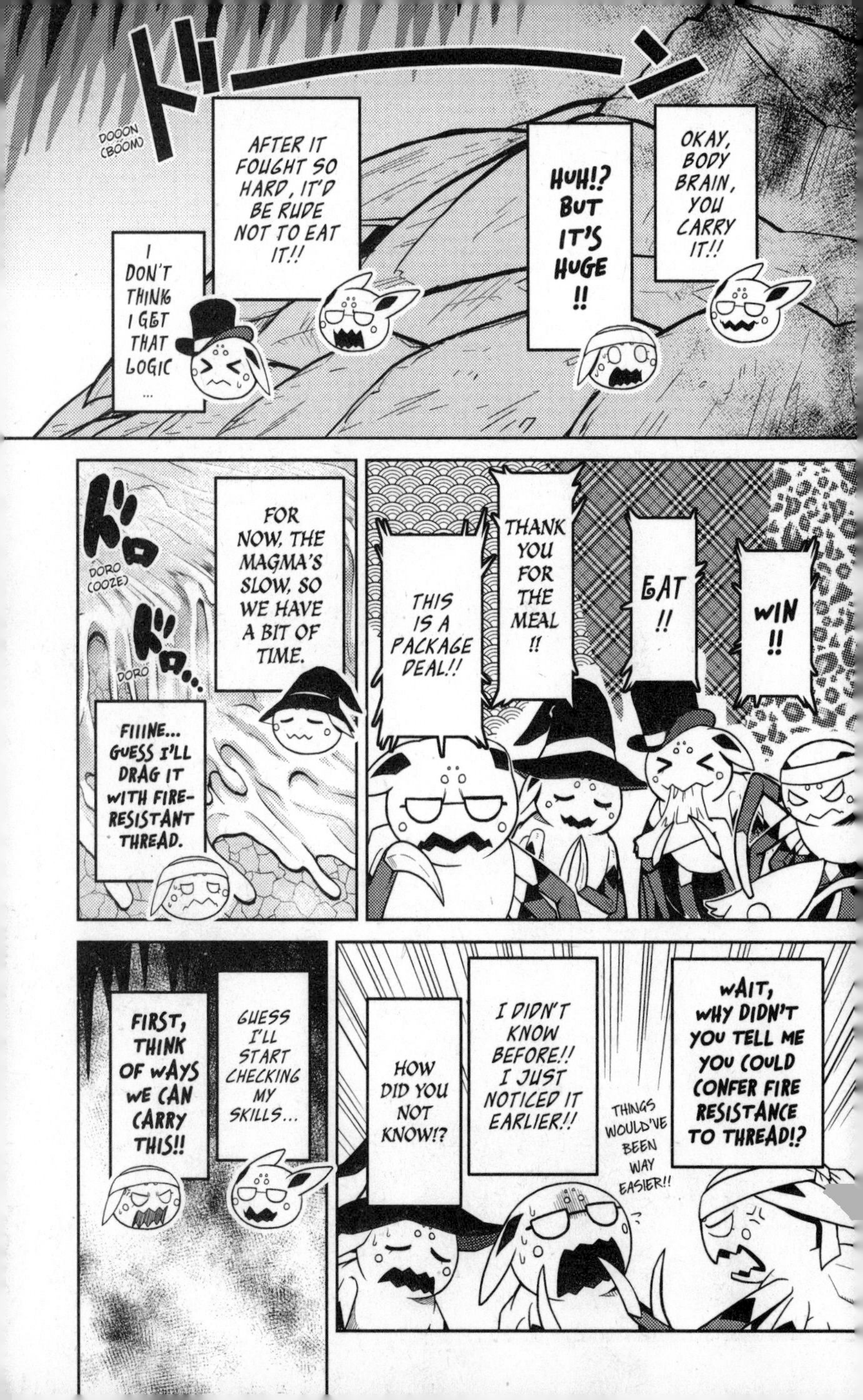
DOOON (BOOM)
OKAY, BODY BRAIN, YOU CARRY IT!!
HUH!? BUT IT'S HUGE!!
AFTER IT FOUGHT SO HARD, IT'D BE RUDE NOT TO EAT IT!!
I DON'T THINK I GET THAT LOGIC...
WIN!!
EAT!!
THANK YOU FOR THE MEAL!!
THIS IS A PACKAGE DEAL!!
DORO (OOZE)
FOR NOW, THE MAGMA'S SLOW, SO WE HAVE A BIT OF TIME.
DORO
FIIINE... GUESS I'LL DRAG IT WITH FIRE-RESISTANT THREAD.
WAIT, WHY DIDN'T YOU TELL ME YOU COULD CONFER FIRE RESISTANCE TO THREAD!?
THINGS WOULD'VE BEEN WAY EASIER!!
I DIDN'T KNOW BEFORE!! I JUST NOTICED IT EARLIER!!
HOW DID YOU NOT KNOW!?
GUESS I'LL START CHECKING MY SKILLS...
FIRST, THINK OF WAYS WE CAN CARRY THIS!!

OSSE
(HEAVEHO)

OSSEI

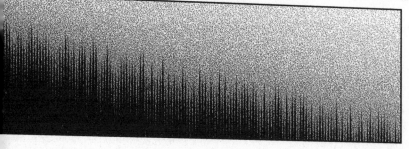

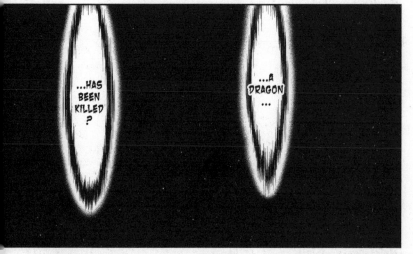

...HAS BEEN KILLED?

...A DRAGON...

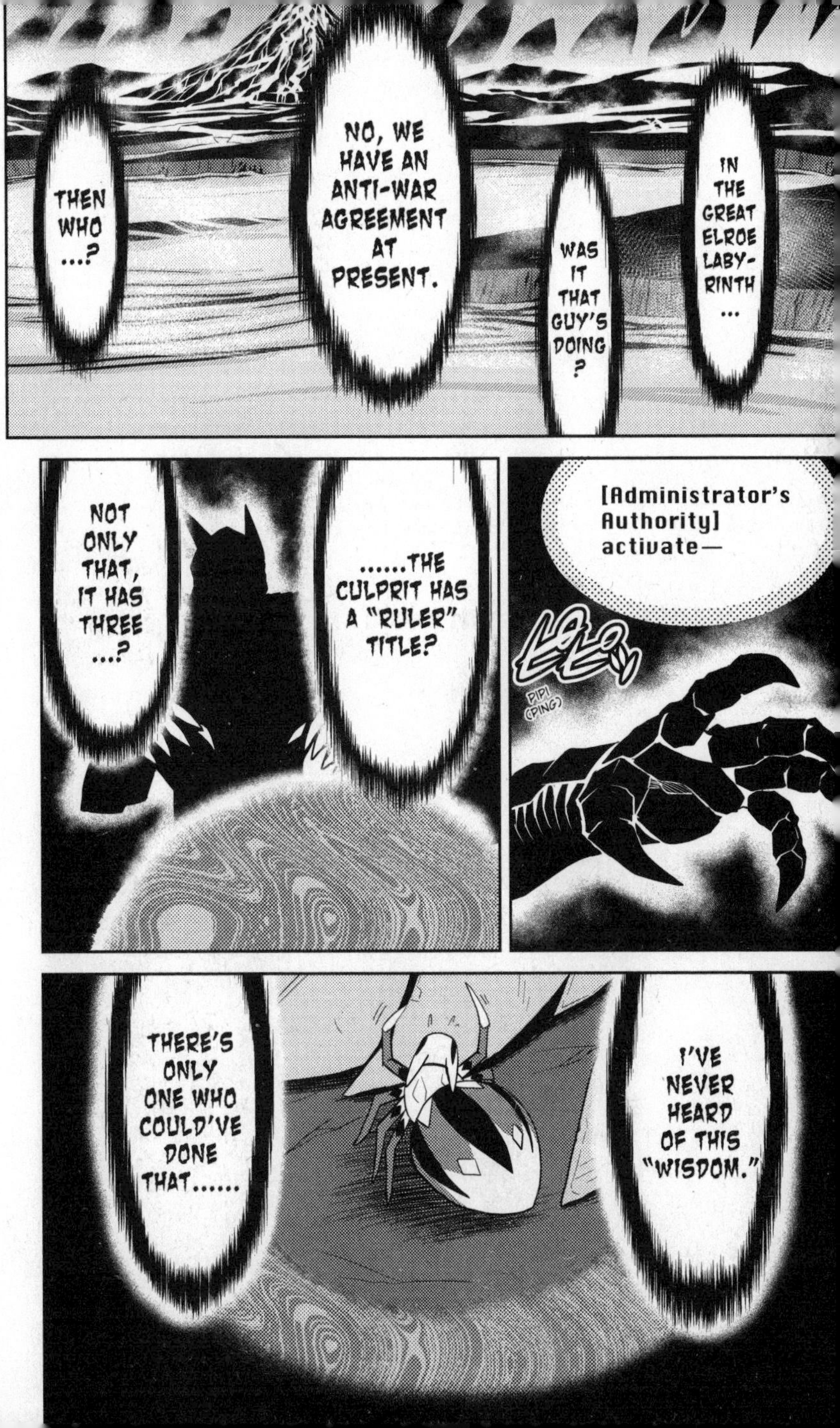
IN THE GREAT ELROE LABYRINTH…
WAS IT THAT GUY'S DOING?
NO, WE HAVE AN ANTI-WAR AGREEMENT AT PRESENT.
THEN WHO…?
[Administrator's Authority] activate—
PIPI (PING)
……THE CULPRIT HAS A "RULER" TITLE?
NOT ONLY THAT, IT HAS THREE…?
I'VE NEVER HEARD OF THIS "WISDOM."
THERE'S ONLY ONE WHO COULD'VE DONE THAT……

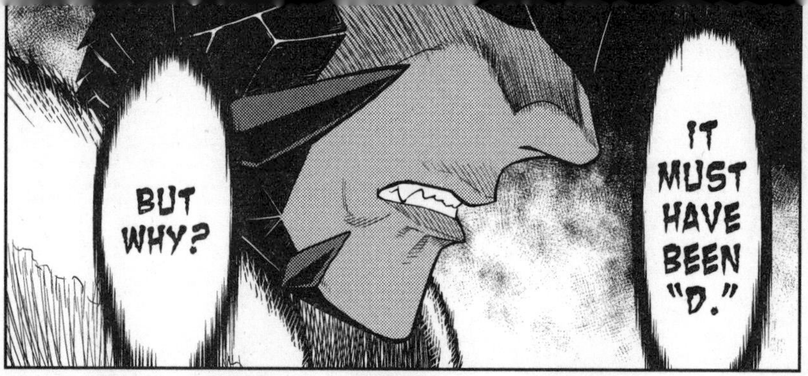
IT MUST HAVE BEEN "D."
BUT WHY?
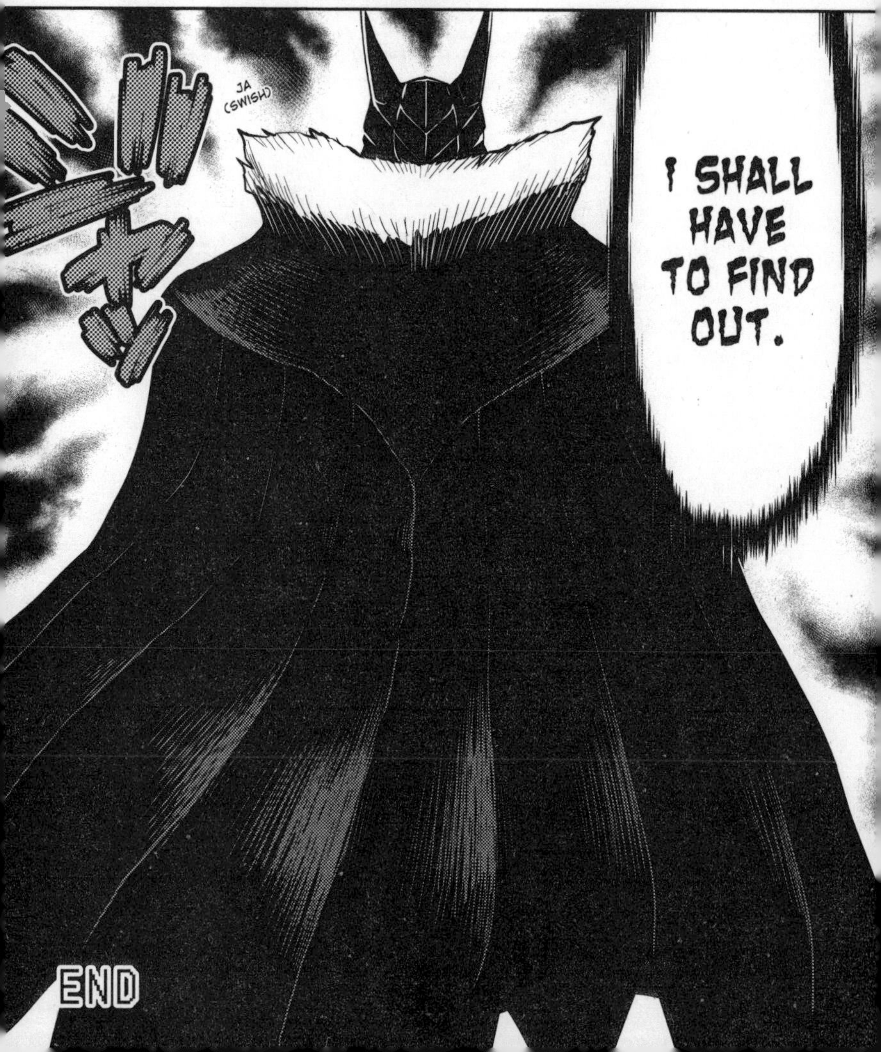
I SHALL HAVE TO FIND OUT.
JA (SWISH)
END

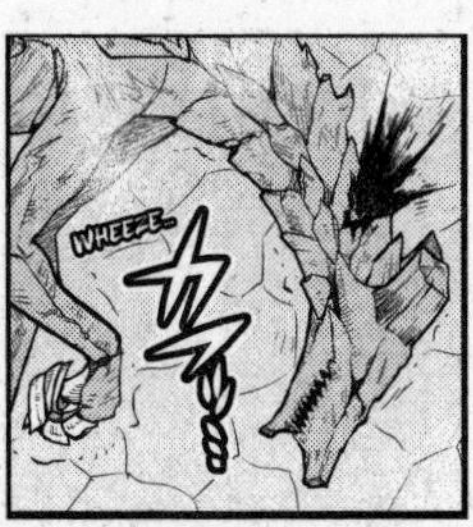
WHEEZE...

AFTERWORD

ORIGINAL CREATOR: OKINA BABA

IT MIGHT NOT BE AS BAD AS THE MIDDLE STRATUM, BUT SUMMER IN JAPAN STILL GETS PRETTY HOT... HELLO, I'M OKINA BABA, THE CREATOR OF THE ORIGINAL WORK, AND THAT IS WHAT'S ON MY MIND!

THE MANGA VERSION HAS ALREADY REACHED FIVE VOLUMES!

I GUESS WE'LL AIM FOR TEN VOLUMES NEXT?

THAT MIGHT SEEM PREMATURE, BUT AS OF MANGA VOLUME 5, WE'RE STILL ON NOVEL VOLUME 3.

SO THE GENERAL PACE IS TWO MANGA VOLUMES PER ONE NOVEL VOLUME.

IN OTHER WORDS, SINCE WE'RE ALREADY UP TO FIVE VOLUMES OF THE NOVEL, THE MANGA WILL DEFINITELY BE AT LEAST TEN VOLUMES!

BY THE WAY, WHEN THIS VOLUME COMES OUT, NOVEL VOLUME 9 WILL ALSO BE RELEASED [IN JAPAN]!

IT WOULD TAKE EIGHTEEN VOLUMES OF MANGA TO CATCH UP TO THAT...

IF YOU LOOK AT IT THAT WAY, IT SEEMS LIKE THE STORY'S STILL GOT A LONG WAY TO GO.

KAKASHI-SENSEI'S ADVENTURE IS ONLY JUST BEGINNING!

I SWEAR THIS ISN'T FORESHADOWING A SUDDEN END OR ANYTHING, SO PLEASE CONTINUE TO SUPPORT KAKASHI-SENSEI.

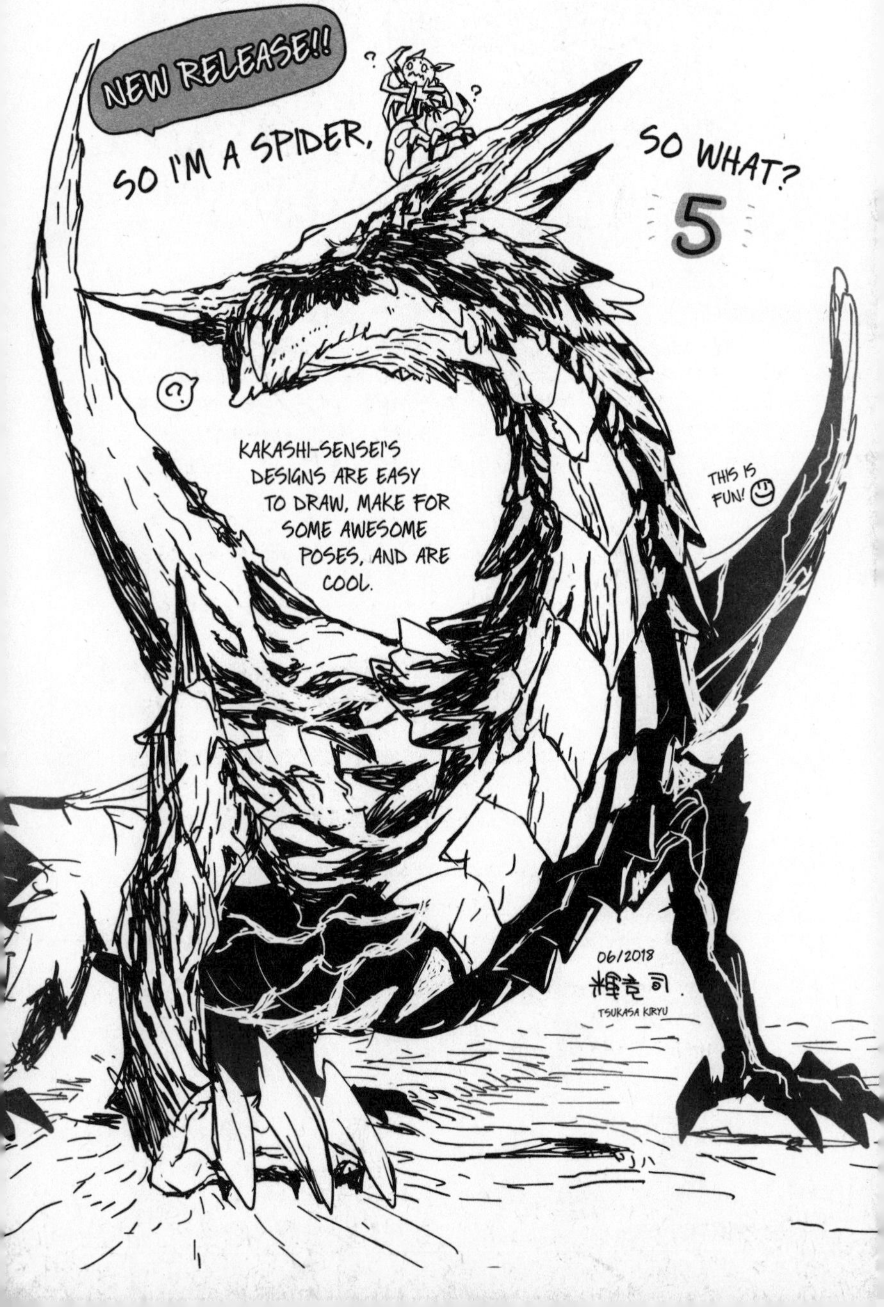
NEW RELEASE!!
SO I'M A SPIDER, SO WHAT?
5
?
?
?
KAKASHI-SENSEI'S DESIGNS ARE EASY TO DRAW, MAKE FOR SOME AWESOME POSES, AND ARE COOL.
THIS IS FUN!
06/2018
輝竜司
TSUKASA KIRYU

THE MAKING OF MANGA KUMOKO

(CREATOR)
ASAHIRO
KAKASHI

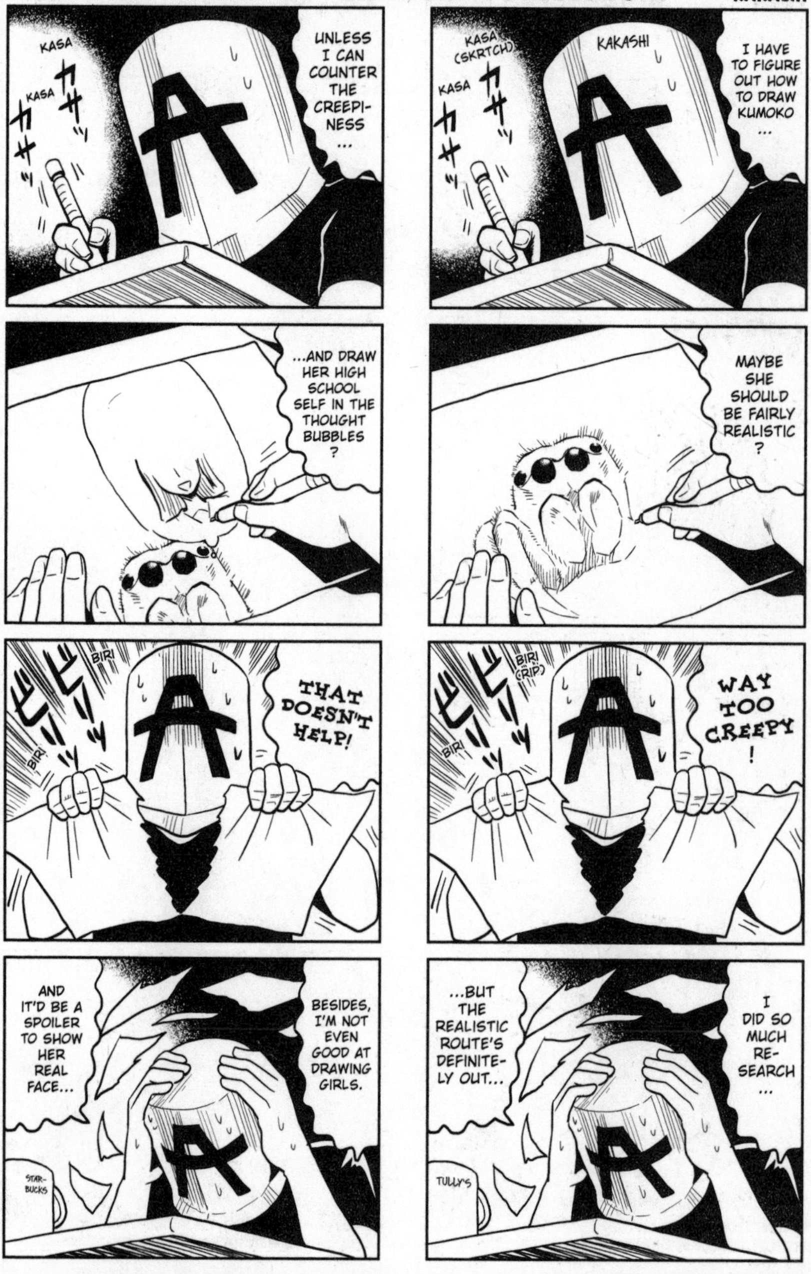
I HAVE TO FIGURE OUT HOW TO DRAW KUMOKO ...
KAKASHI
KASA (SKRTCH)
KASA
MAYBE SHE SHOULD BE FAIRLY REALISTIC ?
WAY TOO CREEPY !
BIRI (RIP)
BIRI
I DID SO MUCH RE-SEARCH ...
...BUT THE REALISTIC ROUTE'S DEFINITE-LY OUT...
TULLY'S
UNLESS I CAN COUNTER THE CREEPI-NESS ...
KASA
KASA
...AND DRAW HER HIGH SCHOOL SELF IN THE THOUGHT BUBBLES ?
THAT DOESN'T HELP!
BIRI
BIRI
BESIDES, I'M NOT EVEN GOOD AT DRAWING GIRLS.
AND IT'D BE A SPOILER TO SHOW HER REAL FACE...
STAR-BUCKS

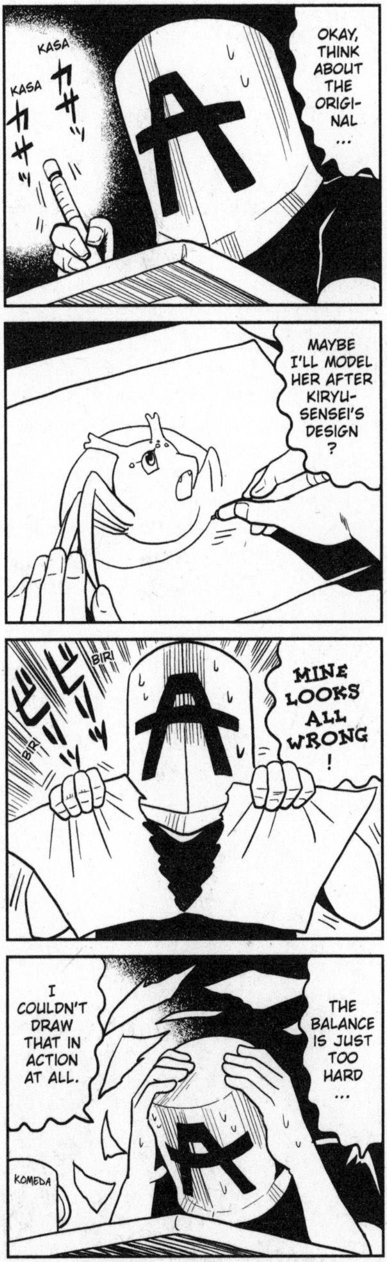
OKAY, THINK ABOUT THE ORIGINAL...
KASA
KASA
MAYBE I'LL MODEL HER AFTER KIRYU-SENSEI'S DESIGN?
MINE LOOKS ALL WRONG!
BIRI
BIRI
THE BALANCE IS JUST TOO HARD...
I COULDN'T DRAW THAT IN ACTION AT ALL.
KOMEDA

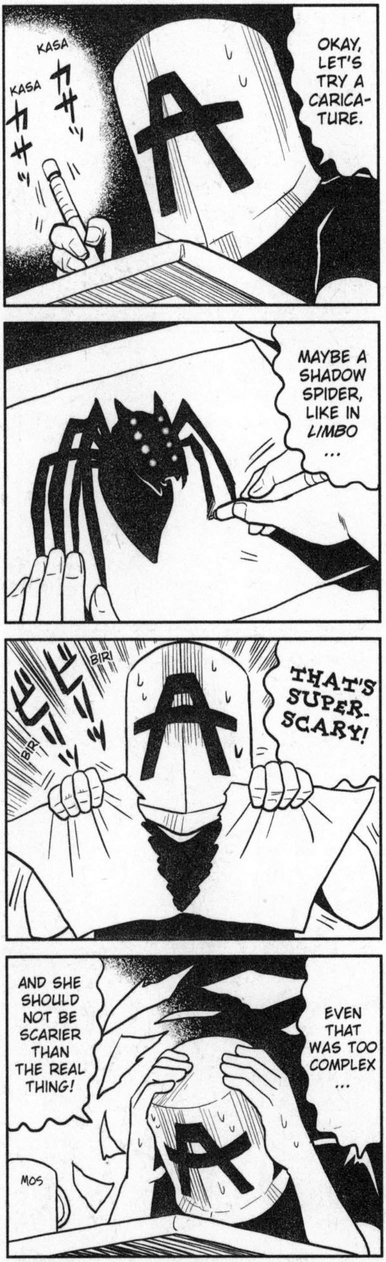
OKAY, LET'S TRY A CARICATURE.
KASA
KASA
MAYBE A SHADOW SPIDER, LIKE IN *LIMBO*...
THAT'S SUPER-SCARY!
BIRI
BIRI
EVEN THAT WAS TOO COMPLEX...
AND SHE SHOULD NOT BE SCARIER THAN THE REAL THING!
MOS

[END]

AFTERWORD

ASAHIRO KAKASHI

HELLO, I'M ASAHIRO KAKASHI. THANK YOU FOR READING ALL THE WAY TO THE END.

THE *SO I'M A SPIDER, SO WHAT?* MANGA LAUNCHED ALONG WITH THE *YOUNG ACE UP* MANGA WEBSITE, AND NOW IT'S ALREADY REACHED FIVE VOLUMES IN THE BLINK OF AN EYE.

I'VE TRIED MY HAND AT A FAIR AMOUNT OF GENRES BEFORE, BUT THIS WAS MY FIRST REAL ATTEMPT AT FANTASY (AS WELL AS MY FIRST MANGA ADAPTATION), SO I'M THRILLED THAT I'VE BEEN ABLE TO COME THIS FAR.

I OWE A LOT TO BABA-SENSEI, WHO HAS APPROVED ALMOST ALL OF THE MANGA VERSION'S CHANGES, KIRYU-SENSEI, MY EDITOR, UTSUMI-SHI, THE EDITORIAL STAFF, WHO HAVE GIVEN ME SO MUCH SUPPORT, AND THE FANS OF THE ORIGINAL WORK, AS WELL AS NEW FANS OF THE MANGA.
I WANTED TO USE THIS SPACE TO SAY THANK YOU.

THE MANGA HAS NOW REACHED ONE OF THE MAJOR TURNING POINTS IN THE STORY.
ALL KINDS OF EXCITING TWISTS AND TURNS ARE ON THE HORIZON.

WILL WE UNRAVEL THIS SPIDERWEB OF MYSTERIES IN THE END?
I DON'T KNOW JUST YET, BUT I REALLY PLAN TO TRY TO THE BEST OF MY ABILITIES.

I HOPE YOU'LL CONTINUE TO FOLLOW THE MANGA VERSION OF KUMOKO ON HER JOURNEY.

ASAHIRO KAKASHI

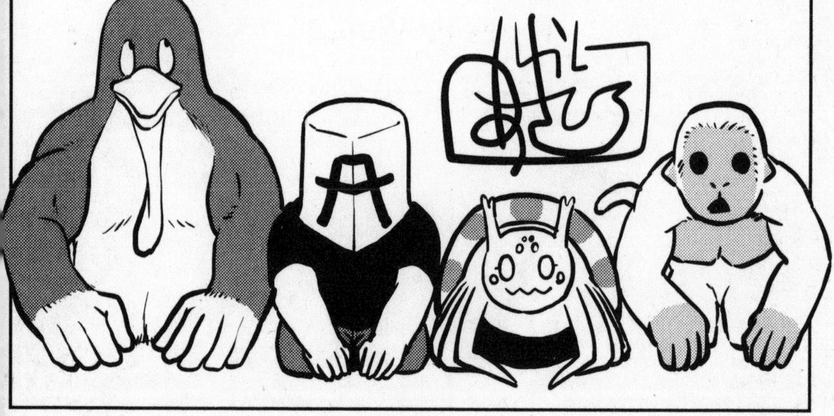

STAFF LIST

The author

ASAHIRO KAKASHI

Assistant

TERUO HATANAKA

Design
R design studio

(Shinji Yamaguchi)

You're reading
the wrong way!
Turn the page to read
a bonus short story by
So I'm a Spider, So What?
original creator
Okina Baba!

Shut up, you!

I mean, come on! From the second I was born into this world, I've had no choice but to fight for survival alone. I've never had a chance to team up with anyone!

Huh? My old life? Let's not talk about it.

Hmph. Whatever.

I don't mind being an outcast anyway. I'm not lonely at all.

【Yeah, you've got us!】

Thanks, body brain!

…Although, if you think about it, that was really just me comforting myself.

Let's forget this ever happened.

[The end]

And that weird effect would cost me a total of five thousand skill points!

What the hell?

Why is it ten times more expensive than a crazy-powerful skill like Perseverance? Hmm?

I don't get it.

On top of that, Leadership, which helps you direct other people, is ten thousand points!

And Creature Training, which is for controlling monsters, is also ten thousand points!

If you act now, you can get the worst bargain ever!

What kind of rip-off is this?!

If this were a store, you better believe I'd be storming in to speak with the manager!

Awful. Just awful.

I can get most other skills for a pretty normal price, but when it comes to skills that involve social interaction, the amount of skill points required suddenly skyrockets.

What could the reason be?

I thought long and hard to discover the truth.

And then it came to me.

Like a punch in the face.

Hang on, though. Is that even possible?

I don't want to believe it. But I can't think of any other reason.

【Information brain, I know you're trying to be serious, but you do realize it's obviously because you're a social outcast, right?】

Don't say it, body brain!

I don't want to hear it!

And yet, I can't deny that it's the only explanation!

In this life and in my old life, I've always been an outcast.

Fine, I'll admit it!

I have a terrible aptitude for social skills because I'm an outcaaast!

Outcaaast! Outcaaast! Outcaaast! That's an echo.

【Yeah, we know.】

So I'm a Spider, So What?
You're a Total Outcast!
Okina Baba

When it comes to skills, there's something called "aptitude."

See, depending on your nature, some skills will be easier to get than others.

For example, it takes me a long time to acquire fire-related skills.

This is probably because fire is my race's natural weak point; my spider body's very vulnerable to fire.

Which is why, even though I've been in the magma hell that is the Middle Stratum for ages now, my Fire Resistance skill level has barely gone up at all.

So yeah, aptitude.

Now, with Appraisal, I can see what skills I'm able to acquire and how many points they cost.

Basically, the more skill points it takes to acquire a skill, the less naturally inclined I am toward that skill. Right?

By that logic, it looks like I have another weakness besides fire.

And that would be all skills related to interacting with others!

Let me say it again.

All skills! Related to social interaction!

Take Cooperation, for instance.

As the name implies, it makes it easier to cooperate with others. That's all it does.

If you wanted to, you'd be able to sync your moves up perfectly with someone you just met, probably.

That could be useful, I guess, but it's kind of a weird effect overall, right?

So I'm a Spider, So What?

5

Art: **Asahiro Kakashi**

Original Story: **Okina Baba**

Character Design: **Tsukasa Kiryu**

Translation: Jenny McKeon Lettering: Bianca Pistillo

Kumo desuga, nanika? Volume 5
© Asahiro KAKASHI 2018
© Okina Baba, Tsukasa Kiryu 2018
First published in Japan in 2018 by KADOKAWA CORPORATION, Tokyo.
English translation rights arranged with KADOKAWA CORPORATION, Tokyo, through TUTTLE-MORI AGENCY, INC.

English translation © 2019 by Yen Press, LLC

Yen Press
1290 Avenue of the Americas
New York, NY 10104

Visit us at yenpress.com
facebook.com/yenpress
twitter.com/yenpress
yenpress.tumblr.com
instagram.com/yenpress

First Yen Press Edition: March 2019

Yen Press is an imprint of Yen Press, LLC.
The Yen Press name and logo are trademarks of Yen Press, LLC.

Library of Congress Control Number: 2017954138

ISBNs: 978-1-9753-0350-1 (paperback)
978-1-9753-0465-2 (ebook)

10 9 8 7 6 5 4 3 2 1

WOR

Printed in the United States of America

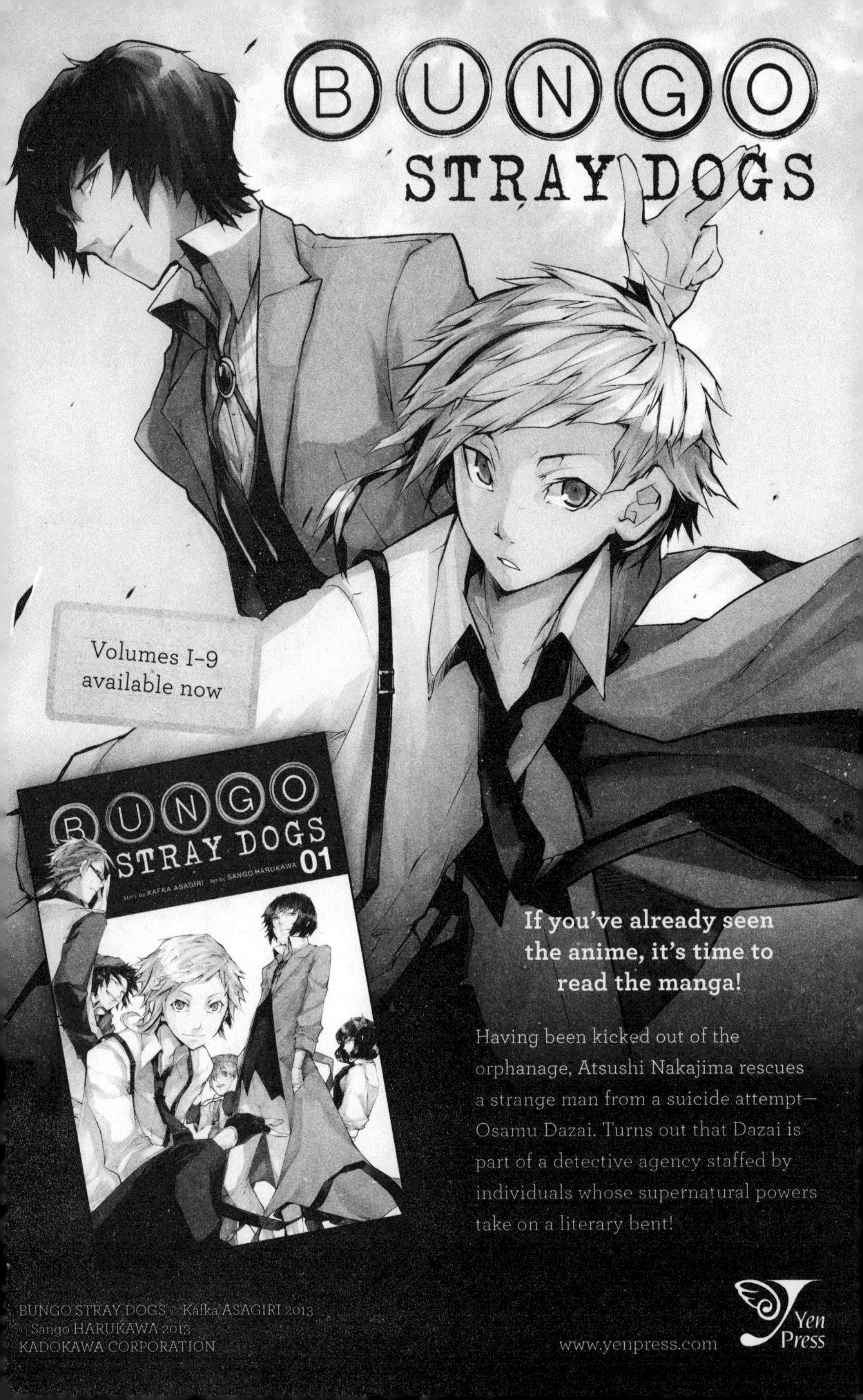
BUNGO STRAY DOGS
Volumes 1–9 available now
BUNGO STRAY DOGS 01
Story by KAFKA ASAGIRI Art by SANGO HARUKAWA
If you've already seen the anime, it's time to read the manga!
Having been kicked out of the orphanage, Atsushi Nakajima rescues a strange man from a suicide attempt—Osamu Dazai. Turns out that Dazai is part of a detective agency staffed by individuals whose supernatural powers take on a literary bent!
BUNGO STRAY DOGS © Kafka ASAGIRI 2013
© Sango HARUKAWA 2013
KADOKAWA CORPORATION
www.yenpress.com
Yen Press

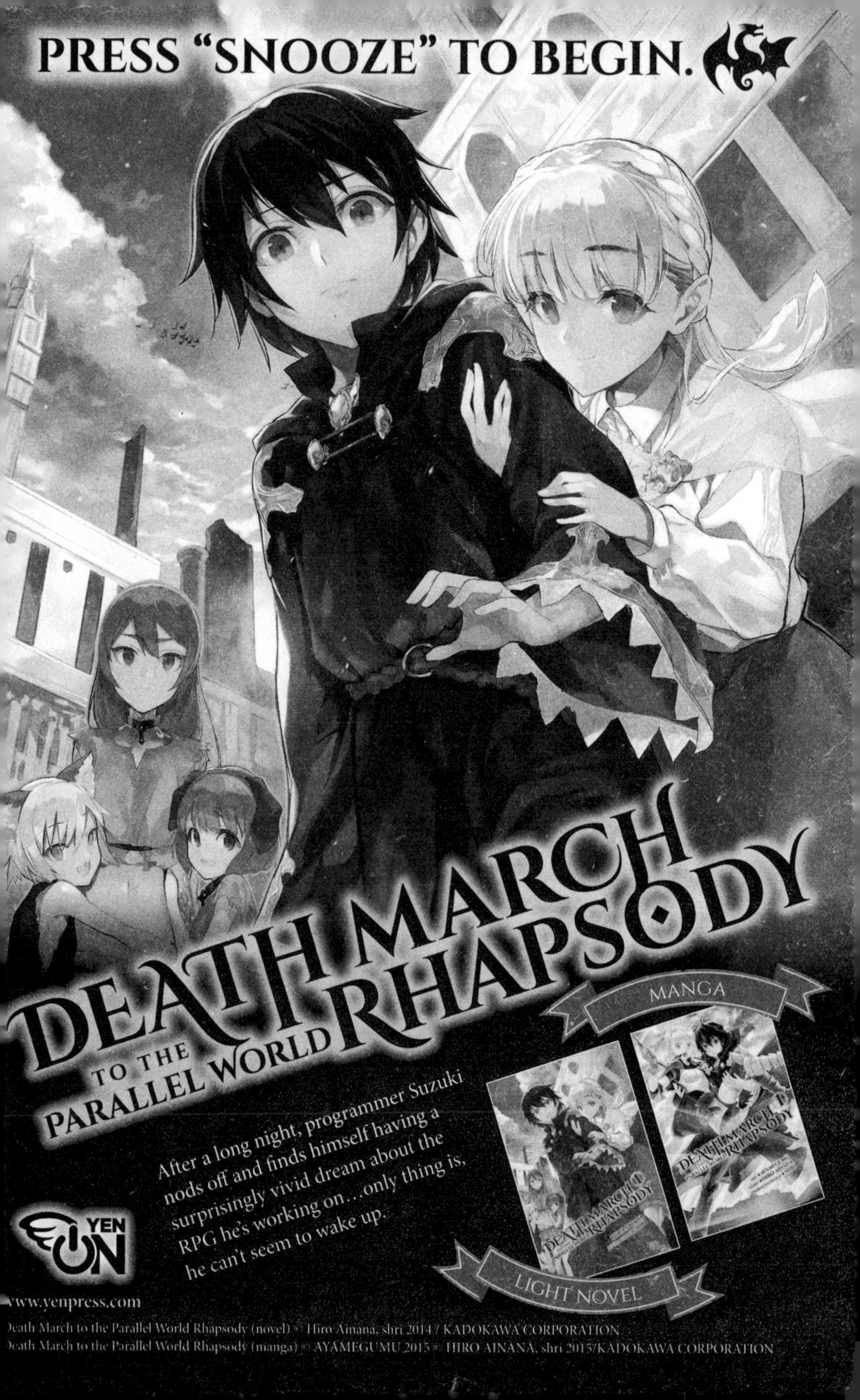
PRESS "SNOOZE" TO BEGIN.
DEATH MARCH TO THE PARALLEL WORLD RHAPSODY
MANGA
After a long night, programmer Suzuki nods off and finds himself having a surprisingly vivid dream about the RPG he's working on…only thing is, he can't seem to wake up.
LIGHT NOVEL
YEN ON
www.yenpress.com
Death March to the Parallel World Rhapsody (novel) © Hiro Ainana, shri 2014 / KADOKAWA CORPORATION
Death March to the Parallel World Rhapsody (manga) © AYAMEGUMU 2015 © HIRO AINANA, shri 2015/KADOKAWA CORPORATION